Rainbow's End

By Bob Adamov

This book is a work of fiction. Names, characters, places and incidents are either products of the author's imagination or are used fictitiously. Any resemblance to actual events or locales or persons, living or dead, is entirely coincidental.

The following publications provided reference material:

Put-in-Bay by Charles E. Frohman, Copyright 1971 by The Ohio State Historical Society

Rebels on Lake Erie by Charles E. Frohman, Copyright 1965 by The Ohio State Historical Society

The Caves of Put-in-Bay by Amy L. Newell, Copyright 1995 by Lake Erie Originals

Isolated Splendor – Put-in-Bay and South Bass Island by Robert J. Dodge, Copyright 1975 by Exposition Press

"Archaelaeological dig to use lasers, robots" by Anne Eisenberg, New York Times, November 22, 2001

ISBN: 1-929774-16-8

Library of Congress Control Number: 2002110844

Cover Art by John Joyce, red inc

Layout by Francine Smith

Submit all requests for reprinting to:
Greenleaf Book Group LLC
8227 Washington St. #2
Chagrin Falls, OH 44023

Published in the United States by
Greenleaf Book Group LLC, Cleveland, Ohio
and
Packard Island Publishing, Cuyahoga Falls, Ohio

www.greenleafbookgroup.com
www.packardislandpublishing.com

First Printing – September 2002
Second Printing – January 2003

Acknowledgements

My gratitude for the support and encouragement provided by George Ketvertis, Joe Weinstein, Tom Garrett, Jack Moore, Doreen Chester, Claudine Melich, Tony Decello, Greg Hite, Roger Emerson and John Emerson – one of my role models. And my gratitude to the public library staff in Put-in-Bay and Port Clinton for their assistance.

A special thank you to Sam Adamov for his coaching throughout the process and his fine artwork.

And a note of appreciation to my family – Kristie, Bobby and Jill – for their understanding and support when Dad was working in the cave on this book.

The National Multiple Sclerosis Society will receive a portion of the proceeds from the sale of this book.

They that wait upon the Lord shall renew their strength; they shall mount up with wings as eagles; they shall run, and not be weary; and they shall walk, and not faint. – Isaiah 40:31

This book is based on a number of historical facts.

Did you know?

- There was an international conspiracy to influence the outcome of the Civil War as the world's major nations sought to stem the growing strength of the United States which threatened the world's balance of power.

- Abraham Lincoln was at odds with his cabinet as to how the Civil War should end and contemplated firing them.

- A group of Confederate raiders in September 1863 attempted to free Confederate officers held prisoner on Johnson's Island in Sandusky Bay.

- John Brown Jr., the son of the abolitionist hanged at Harper's Ferry, resided on South Bass Island and grew grapes.

- It was common for islanders to row between the islands and the mainland before the advent of outboard motors.

- Rattlesnake Island was actually inhabited by a massive rattlesnake population.

- South Bass Island is honeycombed with numerous caves.

- The bow section of a Lake Erie freighter was hoisted onto a cliff on the western side of South Bass' Island and is used as a residence.

- Dairy Air is the name of an airline service headquartered on South Bass Island.

- Gibraltar Island is a six-acre island lying at the entrance to Put-in-Bay and was once owned by Jay Cooke – Civil War financier, banker and railroad baron who spent his childhood in nearby Sandusky. Ohio State University currently owns the island and calls it the North Coast Campus.

- South Bass Island's Victory Hotel, the largest summer hotel in the United States, burnt to the ground in 1919.

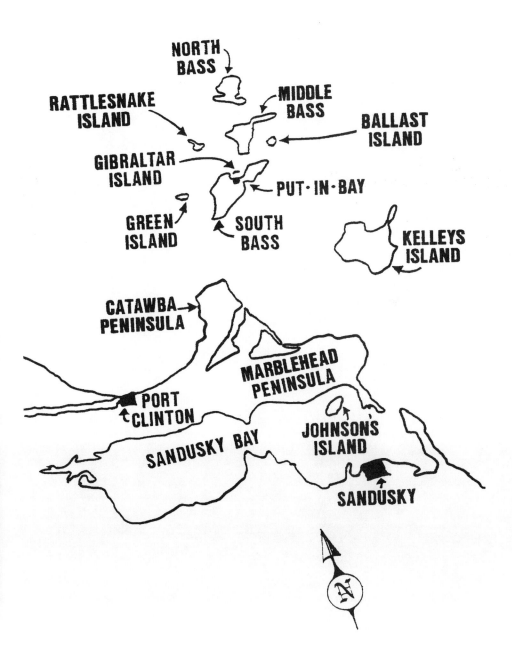

NORTH
BASS

MIDDLE
BASS

RATTLESNAKE
ISLAND

BALLAST
ISLAND

GIBRALTAR
ISLAND

PUT·IN·BAY

GREEN
ISLAND

SOUTH
BASS

KELLEYS
ISLAND

CATAWBA
PENINSULA

MARBLEHEAD
PENINSULA

PORT
CLINTON

JOHNSON'S
ISLAND

SANDUSKY BAY

SANDUSKY

N

~~~~~~~~~~~~~~~~~~

BOOK ONE

~~~~~~~~~~~~~~~~~~

The cry from a sea gull soaring overhead brought Colonel Shelby Harrington out of his daydreaming. He noticed that the Lake Erie waters were calming now that the storm, which had quickly swept out of the northwest, had subsided. His gaze focused toward Rattlesnake Island as the clearing skies revealed a rainbow, appearing to end on the island. It wouldn't be much longer before they would arrive at their third port of call, Put-in-Bay, to take on wood for the steamer. Then, it would be time for action.

They had boarded the *Philo Parsons* that crisp July morning as it prepared to disembark from Windsor, Canada. The other passengers and crewmembers had watched with interest as several of Harrington's men struggled to unload a large, padlocked trunk from the wagon and carry it aboard. The struggle was drawing too much attention to them Harrington thought to himself.

McCormick and his group of 16 men, disguised as workmen, had boarded in groups of two at the ferry's second stop in Malden, Canada. Four of the raiders had carried aboard a smaller padlocked trunk, the type that workmen used to store their tools. But this trunk contained revolvers, hand axes, knives and ammunition for the raiders.

All thirty of the raiders and LeBec were mingling with the crowd on the steamer as it had fought its way through the stormy water. Harrington had overheard one of the passengers commenting that storms had a way of blowing in quickly from the west, and because of the Lake Erie's shallowness, caused the lake to become rough within a few minutes. They were right. Harrington had seen several of his fellow raiders hanging their heads over the rail and retching. They were more comfortable on cavalry mounts and charging into Yankee lines.

It seems that it was just yesterday rather than 6 months ago that he had been summoned by James Mallory, head of the Confederate Secret Service, into President Jefferson Davis' office in Richmond.

≈ ≈ ≈

Mallory ushered Harrington into the dark walnut trimmed office early in the morning on January 5, 1864. A brightly burning fire in the stone fireplace provided the only warmth in the room as a cold wind blustered outside. The dancing flames cast ominous shadows in the room. Mallory had been hesitant to discuss with Harrington the reason for the meeting.

Mallory introduced Harrington to the President and to another guest in the room, Jacob Thompson, Secretary of the Interior for the Confederacy.

The President stood from his chair near the fire and extended his hand to greet Harrington.

"Colonel Harrington, Mr. Mallory speaks highly of your accomplishments with your cavalry on the battlefield and your displays of bravery," said the tired-looking President.

"Thank you sir, but I have a good group of men to lead," responded Harrington as he reflected momentarily on how many of those good men he had also seen buried.

"Humility! And yet a strong sense of confidence! I like that in my officers. James, I am even more impressed by this young man."

"I thought you would see what I was talking about when you met him personally, Mr. President," Mallory stated proudly.

"Well Colonel – James and I have been strategizing about a number of issues that we are faced with in order to win this war of secession. We have problems with providing arms and ammunition for our men and we are continuing to run our treasury dry. But, Colonel, we have a pressing problem to wrestle with – one that you can help us resolve!"

"Sir?" queried Harrington.

"Officers, son. The flower of southern manhood. We have plenty of soldiers, but are short on officers to lead them as you so ably do. We must have leadership on the field! The men are willing to fight, but we don't have enough officers to execute our strategies and lead our men successfully into battle. And do you know why we don't have enough officers Harrington?" The President paused as he asked the question.

"Sir?"

"Too many of our officers have been captured. Just too many have been captured," he repeated. "Mr. Thompson thinks he has the answer to our problems and he has convinced Mr. Mallory and me that his plan could be successful if we have the right person executing it. We believe you are the right person."

Turning to Thompson, the President said with a hint of mystery, "Jacob, tell Colonel Harrington about the trip to Johnson's Island that you have planned for him."

Moving to a table at the side of the room, Thompson said, "Colonel, please step over here so I can show you our map."

As Harrington followed Thompson and Mallory to the table, he glanced at the President and saw him staring sadly into the fire.

"Colonel, many Canadians are sympathetic to our cause and are participating in what is known quietly as the Northwest Conspiracy. They are supporting our efforts with material and money and will be supporting your mission.

"Lying before us is a map of Western Lake Erie. It shows a number of the islands and the southern shore of the Lake in Ohio. In particular, I'd like to draw your attention to this area on the southern shore, Sandusky Bay. On the east side of the bay is the town of Sandusky with a population of about 25,000.

"Two miles across the bay and on the bay's west side is a 300-acre island called Johnson's Island. This island is also one mile east of the Marblehead Peninsula. Johnson's Island is of significant and strategic importance to us. It contains an 18 acre stockaded Union prison camp with about 2,400 of our captured officers from second lieutenants to major generals. That's enough officers to lead 80,000 Confederate soldiers."

The President interrupted, "Many of them were captured at Gettysburg and Port Huron and after last year's suspension of the agreement for exchanging prisoners with the North."

The President added, "Harrington, you may know several of the captured officers imprisoned there. Men like General Archer of Maryland, General Edward Johnson of Virginia, Col. Thomas Kearns of North Carolina, Col. Scales of Mississippi, Col. Lock of Alabama, Col. "Ham" Jones of North Carolina and several of Pickett's divisional officers. They even have Col. Henry Kyd Douglas of Stonewall Jackson's staff."

Harrington nodded as he recalled meeting and fighting with several of them.

Thompson continued, "Working with agents in Canada, you and 30 of your men will board the lake steamer *Philo Parsons* from two points: Windsor, Canada – across from Detroit and in a Malden, Canada, its second stop. The *Philo Parsons* will steam to Put-in-Bay on South Bass Island to take on wood for fuel.

"Once the ship departs from Put-in-Bay, you and your men will overpower the crew and take control of the ship and then steam to Johnson's Island where you will free our officers. You will use the passengers initially as hostages and deposit them at the prison camp once you have freed the prisoners.

"You will ferry a group of about 1,000 officers to Marblehead Peninsula where they will be able to secure horses and weapons which one of our agents will have waiting for them. This group will raid south, free our imprisoned forces at Camp Morton in Indianapolis, cause interruptions to commerce and force the Yankees to divert soldiers from the front to try to capture them. This will ease pressure on our lines and enable us to implement plans we have for attacking northward.

"The larger group which we would like you to lead will be ferried across the bay to Sandusky where horses and weapons from the Sandusky ammunition warehouse will be available for you. Your group will conduct raids as it travels south to Columbus, Ohio where it will expand the size of its force by freeing our troops held prisoner at the Fort Chase prison camp. Both groups will then continue raiding and causing destruction along the way as they move south to rejoin our lines.

"By doing this, you will divert Federal troops from the East and the West who will have to respond to your sweeping path of destruction. This diversion of federal troops will aid us in our battle plans for the late summer months and coming fall months."

The President raised his head. "It's a big job, son. Think you can do it?"

Harrington thought for a moment before answering. People had been telling him for years that he had a particular knack for accomplishing anything that he set his mind to. He rarely failed in attaining his objectives.

"Sir, it's an honor to be considered for this mission and I believe that I can accomplish it. I know it's important to the Confederacy that I succeed."

Harrington added in a steady voice, "We're lacking officers in the field. Not only are officers being captured, but they're being picked off by Yankee sharpshooters during battles."

Mallory expounded with a hint of mystery, "We also know that there's an additional linkage in your past to this area of Lake Erie."

Harrington guessed that they had done their homework regarding his uncle. He was right.

"Your Uncle Michael captained one of the ships during the second war with England in the battle of Lake Erie near Put-in-Bay in 1813."

Harrington thought back to the many times that he had sat on the verandah as Uncle Michael recounted his role in defeating the British off the shores of Rattlesnake Island. And now, he would be playing a role on that same battleground.

"You're very thorough," Harrington commented.

"You can count on that," Mallory responded with an all-knowing air.

"Colonel," commented Thompson, "There's one more thing that you need to be aware of. It's a 16-gun federal gunboat, the *USS Michigan*. It patrols Lake Erie and typically anchors off of Johnson's Island. We will have an agent in place in the town of Sandusky who will prevent the gunboat from interfering with your task."

"He will schedule a social ball in Sandusky the night before you take control of the ferry. He'll invite the prison camp officers and their wives and the gunboat's officers to attend the ball. He will then drug the attendees that evening. He will also lure the gunboat into docking in Sandusky on the pretense of providing an artillery show at the ball's conclusion. Once it is docked, our agent will arrange to plant a mine on the gunboat and sink it. The next morning, you won't have to be concerned about the gunboat interfering with your plans and will be able to capture the prison camp by threatening to kill your hostages."

"Think you can do this, son?" the President asked from his chair.

"I will do my best sir." Turning to Mallory and Thompson, Harrington asked, "I assume that I can pick my own men?"

"Yes, but they should all be volunteers," Mallory responded as he glanced at Thompson and the President. "Colonel, could you excuse us. We need to talk about some other urgent matters. Why don't you plan on meeting me in my office in about an hour to go over more details of your assignment."

"Yes, sir."

President Davis stood and shook Harrington's hand.

"God bless you and Godspeed."

Harrington shook hands with Mallory and Thompson as the President returned to his rocking chair and stared sadly into the fire.

Harrington walked out of the office and closed the door.

"Do you think we should have told him the second phase of the mission?" the President asked.

"No, he will find out soon enough. We've told him a lot this morning," Mallory commented.

"He and his family have a strong reputation for their accomplishments. And it seems to run in the boy's blood too. I am absolutely confident of his ability to complete both phases of the mission. I would rather trust him and his ability than take the risk of using one of the blockade-runners. If the blockade-runner was sunk, which seems to be occurring rather regularly as of late, it would be lying at the bottom of the sea. We just can't take that risk! He is our best bet for getting it through enemy lines safely," Thompson added.

"Well, I hope you both are right. The viability of the Confederacy rests on that young man's shoulders and he isn't even aware of it."

"Jefferson, you will have to draft the orders for the mission's second phase so that we can have them delivered to him in Canada before he starts the mission," Thompson reminded the President as he handed him stationary and his pen.

"Yes, yes. I will draft them today," he said as he settled back in his chair as Thompson and Mallory left his office.

The President sighed deeply and looked sadly into the fire. A piece of wood fell from the grate and sent a shower of sparks upward. The President didn't notice it. He was concerned about the number of good men that had been killed so far in their efforts to secure the Confederacy's independence – and Harrington seemed to be a good man. The President stared again into the flames. Flames of Hell he thought to himself as he picked up his pen and began to draft his orders to Harrington.

~ ~ ~

Barely an hour had passed before Harrington arrived at Mallory's office. He was quickly ushered into the office of the head of the Confederate Secret Service.

Mallory raised his head from scanning several documents on his paper-strewn desk and looked through a cloud of smoke created by the cigar he puffed. There were boxes of papers and files throughout the office and stacked on any available desk or credenza surface.

"Colonel, I have someone here who I'd like you to meet. He is French-Canadian and will serve as your primary contact in Canada. Working with Confederate sympathizers in Montreal, he will supply you with disguises and weapons and coordinate your transportation through Canada to where you will catch the ferry."

Harrington had not noticed the man seated in the far corner of the room hidden by the shadows. As the man moved forward into the light, Harrington saw a sullen-faced, rather disheveled and seedy looking figure wearing a red hat which sat jauntily on his head.

"Meet Monsieur LeBec."

"Bonjour Monsieur," Harrington said as he extended his hand to the figure emerging from the shadows.

Not reciprocating with his hand, LeBec nodded curtly.

"Bonjour, comment ca va?"

"Bien, et toi?"

"So, you speak my native language?"

"Un pue. I have picked up a few words here and there."

Harrington had decided it would be wiser not to display his fluency in the event he may need to use it to his advantage in the near future. His first impression of this LeBec was not comforting. He had an uneasy feeling about the man.

"Good, now that you two have been formally introduced, let's discuss the next steps in your mission, Colonel. You depart for Canada in one week with Monsieur LeBec, so you will need to pick 30 of your men to accompany you. You will board the blockade-runner, *Southern Wind*, for the island of Bermuda. Assuming that you successfully make it through the blockade, you will be transported to Nova Scotia."

Shaking his head in frustration, Mallory explained, "Those damn Yankees have just been sinking too many of our blockade runners!"

Mallory went on.

"There, you will travel to Montreal where LeBec will arrange for your weapons and supplies. You and thirteen of your men will then move to Windsor to prepare for boarding the *Philo Parsons*. The remaining seventeen raiders will travel to Malden to board the ferry when it stops there. Monsieur LeBec will arrange for weapons to be placed in a trunk and delivered to the men in Malden which they will carry on board.

"Between LeBec, his agents and our agent in Sandusky, we are arranging for horses, ammunition and weapons to be available for the freed prisoners so that you can raid south."

LeBec interrupted haughtily, "And let me assure you Colonel that my agents will not let me down. I only hope that holds true for your men and your agent in Sandusky."

Arrogant little twit Harrington thought to himself. Smiling assuredly, Harrington responded, "I can speak only for my men and they have never let me down, sir."

LeBec's eyebrows rose at Harrington's sarcastic tone.

"Just see, Colonel, that they do not let me down," LeBec retorted coldly.

Watching the exchange, Mallory sensed that LeBec and Harrington could potentially be at odds during the mission. For the mission to succeed, they would have to work together.

"Gentlemen. Gentlemen. I fully trust that each of you will do your best to work cooperatively together and accomplish this mission. Colonel, I will tell you that Monsieur LeBec has been a very reliable ally and has sacrificed personally in order to help our cause," Mallory pronounced strongly as he puffed even more heartily on his cigar – causing more clouds in the smoke-filled room and additional ashes to drop onto his already ash covered vest.

LeBec smirked disdainfully as he looked at Harrington.

Harrington felt more uncomfortable with the idea of working with LeBec.

~ ~ ~

"Now, Henry, don't you go and be sampling my baked goods! If you eat them all, I won't have any to sell to the passengers when the ferry arrives."

Henry Warner looked at his pretty wife and smiled as he said, "Honey, it's just that you make these all the time for those passengers and we never have any left for us."

"Mr. Henry Warner, don't you look at me with those big soulful eyes like that! It won't get you another muffin in your hands. You know that we need to earn every penny that we can so we can save up and buy our own place!"

Just one year earlier, twenty-two year old Henry and his eighteen-year-old wife had completed their escape to freedom along the underground railroad to Sandusky. They and three other slaves had fled from a Georgia plantation.

Henry knew that he had to flee in order to protect Melissa from the planter's son. The son had begun casting an eye toward Melissa and making crude comments to her. It wouldn't have been long before he would be sending for her – just like he had sent for the other young female slaves on the plantation.

Henry recalled the incident when the planter's son

stroked Melissa's face and made a suggestive comment. Feisty Melissa threw caution to the wind and bit his hand. She paid and she paid dearly.

She received 5 lashes from a whip on her back. Several of the other slaves had to restrain Henry when they were gathered to observe her punishment.

Melissa had recovered and swore vengeance. She said that one day she would make Master Wylan pay.

When Henry and Melissa arrived in Sandusky, they heard a speech at the town square given by John Brown, Jr., the son of the John Brown who was hanged for his raid on Harper's Ferry. Following the speech, Henry and Melissa waited until the crowd had died down and approached him.

Henry thanked Mr. Brown for his speech and support in freeing the slaves. Upon learning that Henry and Melissa had escaped slavery via the underground railroad, Brown invited them to work for him at his Put-in-Bay farm and vineyard. He had purchased ten acres on the south shore of the island when ill health had forced him to resign as a captain in the Union army.

Working for Mr. Brown had been good for Henry and Melissa. They had housing and food and were saving up to purchase land for themselves. Life was getting better for them.

But Henry still had thoughts about Master Wylan and he shuddered as he saw Melissa waken from her nightmares about Master Wylan.

$$\sim \sim \sim$$

As the morning sun rose above Johnson's Island, Colonel Wellman stepped out of his office onto the covered porch and surveyed the prison enclosure in front of him.

He was pleased with his assignment. He and his officers along with their families were provided with adequate housing and were able to enjoy the warm waters of Sandusky Bay during the summer months. From time to time they would ferry to Sandusky to take part in its social gatherings and purchase ancillary goods. He was held in high regard by the townspeople since his prison contributed significantly to Sandusky's economic growth.

He allowed his eyes to sweep across the prison compound again.

The prison compound was located on 18 acres surrounded by a 12-foot high fence on three sides with two blockhouses. A high picket fence secured the fourth side which faced the water and the town of Sandusky across the bay. This wall was guarded by the gunboat, *USS Michigan*. Sentries on strategically-positioned elevated platforms to overlook the prison compound provided additional security.

Every prisoner understood that there was a deadline within thirty feet of the stockade walls. Any prisoner entering the deadline area would be shot.

The compound included thirteen two-storied buildings which housed the prisoners. They contained bunks in tiers of three and a large stove for cooking and heating.

For the most part, Wellman thought to himself, the prisoners were not troublesome. And that was due to the fact that escape was difficult to accomplish.

If someone was successful in crossing the deadline without being shot and scaling the stockade, they faced another major obstacle – the island's location in Sandusky Bay. It made escape attempts daunting.

In good weather, the long swims to the mainland were hazardous due to the dangerous currents and the *USS Michigan*'s constant patrol. In the winter, the lake froze over and there was always the risk of falling through thin ice. In addition, the lake's freezing winds drove temperatures to fifteen or twenty below zero, taking a toll on any escapee. These Southern prisoners were not used to the cold temperature extremes of the area.

Wellman recalled that there had been only three or four successful escapes. During this past cold January, Colonel Winston of Daniel's North Carolina Brigade scaled the stockade wall on one particularly dark night and headed north to Canada across the ice. He showed up nearly dead from exhaustion and cold temperatures in a farmer's house in Canada – and after recovering was able to return to the South by blockade-runner from the Bahamas.

After daily roll call, many prisoners engaged in hobbies such as building furniture from wood or making charms, pins and rings from shells. Many would be involved in plays or minstrel shows while others would read the northern newspapers which the guards supplied to them.

Wellman's thoughts were distracted by the booming of the guns from the *USS Michigan*, at anchor off of the compound's picket wall. Probably practicing for the salute to Sandusky following the end of tonight's ball which he and his officers and their wives had been invited to attend along with the *USS Michigan*'s officers.

Wellman turned and went back into his office as the *Michigan's* crew resumed practicing. Life is good he thought to himself.

~ ~ ~

The 60-pound cannon's final boom echoed over the quiet waters of Sandusky Bay.

"Captain, we've finished our firing practice," reported the officer standing in front of Captain Guadian.

"Secure quarters and stand down," commanded Guadian.

Guadian had ordered the firing practice in preparation for the evening's gala ball. He would be docking at the prison camp so the camp's officers and wives could board and be ferried to Sandusky for the ball which would be held near the water's edge.

Guadian looked over the *Michigan* with a critical eye. He had pushed the crew a bit harder than usual to make sure the ship was clean, polished and orderly for the evening's festivities.

The *Michigan* was the North's first iron hull ship and responsible for maintaining control of Lake Erie from Buffalo to Detroit. She was a sidewheel steamer with three sailing masts, a length of 163 feet and a 25-foot beam.

Guadian noted how well his armament shined. She had fourteen 12-pound cannons and the 60 pound cannon.

Guadian chuckled to himself as he recalled the rumors over the last few years that Confederate pirates would attempt to free the prisoners on Johnson Island. Just let them try and he'd show them 15 guns and a well-trained crew.

Guadian and the prison camp commander, Colonel Wellman, had talked occasionally about the rumors, especially since they were aware of a great number of Confederate sympathizers in the Sandusky area.

Neither of them had any serious concerns. No ship existed on Lake Erie that could come close to being a match for the *Michigan*. The *Michigan* could blow any ship out of the water.

Guadian was looking forward to the ball, especially the abundance of food and drink – and perhaps a few dances with the ladies of Sandusky.

∾ ∾ ∾

Sweating profusely under the hot July sun, Charles Mills eased his portly frame into the carriage seat and picked up the reins. As the rented carriage careened down the road toward Sandusky, he thought about how much he had accomplished since Mallory had given him this vital assignment several months ago during a meeting in Richmond. This assignment was going to pay handsomely – making Mills a very wealthy man.

While in Richmond, he had also met the vile Frenchman, LeBec – who had given Mills a chill up and down his spine. Mills had been a spy for a long time and was immediately leery of LeBec.

Mallory indicated that LeBec had several agents located in the Lake Erie area who would be providing support to Mills as needed.

Mills had arrived in Sandusky three months ago with a wad of cash that he made sure to flash around for others to see. He spread his money around freely and took the best room in the best hotel in Sandusky.

From all appearances, it seemed that Mills was exactly what he said he was – a very wealthy entrepreneur who marketed horses to the union army. He had told the townspeople and area horse breeders that he was in the market for two thousand horses to deliver to the Union supply depot in Philadelphia by July 15th.

Mills had purchased every available horse that he could in the immediate area and had to widen his search area eastward to Cleveland. He had hired local men to water and feed the horses that had been delivered on July 1st. He had rented two staging areas for holding the horses – one in Sandusky and the other, as LeBec had directed, across Sandusky Bay on the Marblehead Peninsula.

Tonight, he would be hosting a pre-Fourth of July gala ball on the hotel's grounds overlooking Sandusky Bay. He had arranged for the *USS Michigan* to dock at the water's edge so that it could fire its cannons as a salute to Sandusky after the fireworks festivities.

Mopping his sweaty brow, Mills was proud of himself. Of the various missions he had carried out for the Confederacy, this was his most critical. He had been successful in purchasing the required number of horses, stabling them nearby and confirming that the arms storage dump in Sandusky was full of arms and ammunition.

He had established himself quickly as a man of influence to Sandusky society, flashed wads of cash and established bank accounts at the city's banks. He went out of his way to invite the prison camp commander and his officers and wives to dinner and musical shows at the Music Hall from time to time in order to build relationships.

He also was successful in establishing friendships with the *USS Michigan*'s captain and her officers. Many times they enjoyed dining with Mills and numerous rounds of after dinner drinks at Mills expense as they discussed the latest war news.

The gala was the talk of the town. Mills noted with glee that people were more excited about the gala than the normal Fourth of July festivities and long speeches planned for the next day.

Arriving at the livery, Mills stepped gingerly from the carriage and pulled his usual wad of cash from his pocket. He paid the livery owner as the scruffy-looking, red-shirted stable boy stopped momentarily from leading the carriage away. The recently-hired stable boy's eyes widened at the sight of the cash in Mills's hand. Mills grinned to himself at the stable boy's staring and turned to make his way to his hotel room.

He inserted his key into the door lock, and entered his second floor room. The room overlooked Sandusky

Bay and afforded Mills a view of the prison camp and the *USS Michigan*, its guns bristling as it anchored off the camp.

When the night's over, your guns will be bristling on the bottom of the bay Mills thought confidently to himself.

Smiling, he turned to unlock the first of two chests that had been smuggled across Lake Erie by LeBec's agents to him earlier in the week.

The smaller one held a number of French wine bottles and two smaller bottles which contained the drugs. Mills carefully uncorked the wine bottles and, after opening the smaller bottles, began to add the drugs to each wine bottle. He then carefully resealed each wine bottle.

The bottles would be reopened and served to the *USS Michigan*'s captain and officers as well as the prison camp's commander and its officers when he would have them join him for a special toast at the gala. A very special toast – one that would knock them out for close to 24 hours.

After placing the two empty small bottles in his valise, Mills closed the first chest and turned to the second chest. He very carefully inserted the key and turned it.

He recalled how cautiously he had tried to drive the carriage with the two chests to the hotel from the small inlet east of Sandusky where he had met LeBec's accomplices as was prearranged. The two had rowed ashore from a small schooner that was riding at anchor and awaiting their return.

The two advised Mills that one large jolt could cause the mine in the one chest to explode. Mills had noticed how relieved the smugglers had been when the chest was taken from their boat.

Carrying the chest with the mine up the flight of stairs to his hotel room had been nerve-wracking for Mills.

Mills cautiously opened the chest and peered inside.

Somewhat cushioned inside was the mine which Mills would that evening affix to the side of the *USS Michigan* where the ammunition and powder were stored as shown on the ship's diagram. Mills reached in and picked up the fuse. He went over again in his mind the procedures for setting the fuse as he had been trained in Richmond.

Sweating more copiously he thought about the final steps in his mission. He would briefly slip away from the gala to get the mine, row his previously rented skiff the short distance in the darkness to attach the mine and set the fuse. He'd then return to the gala, open the drugged wine and offer the special toast just before the *USS Michigan* exploded in a ball of flame.

He reveled as he thought how the drugged officers would see the explosion, but be so incapacitated as not to be able to react. The drug would take effect quickly.

Mills closed and locked the chest. He would have to be just as careful in carrying the mine in the chest down the stairs and out to the skiff as he was in transporting it to the hotel and carrying it up to his room.

He then began packing his valise. Once he completed his deeds tonight, he would need to leave town and coordinate the delivery of the horses to the dock at Sandusky the next morning.

After the freed prisoners were ferried to Sandusky and raided the warehouse with the arms and ammunition, they would need the horses for their trip South.

Mills would make his own way back and collect his fees upon arrival in Richmond.

Only a few hours to go Mills thought to himself as he lay on the bed to rest up for the night's activities.

~ ~ ~

Harrington recalled the trip across Canada and the rendezvous on a small farm outside of Windsor. As he leaned against the steamer's rail he remembered the events of the previous night.

There were 14 raiders in his group. They were good men, men he knew he could count on. They had been hard-nosed in battle and fiercely committed to achieving their objectives.

Each man was focused on getting ready for tomorrow. Some were checking their disguises. Some were reading. Some had their heads bowed in prayer. Some were writing to loved ones in preparation of exchanging letters with each other so that the letter could be forwarded in the event they were killed tomorrow.

Culbertson was busily studying the stolen charts of the waters around the islands and Sandusky Bay. Culbertson had been another surprise, but probably a good addition to the team of raiders.

Prior to leaving Richmond, Mallory had assigned Culbertson to the raiders on loan from the Confederate

Navy. Culbertson had operated steamers in Savannah and Charleston prior to the outbreak of war. He would be responsible for piloting the steamer after they took control of it and navigating it to the Johnson Island prison camp to free the prisoners.

Culbertson had a haughty attitude about him that made Harrington uncomfortable. It centered on the immense pride he took as a captain in the Confederate Navy. At times, he had a tendency to want to lord his position over the other raiders.

The two had a confrontation when Culbertson had defiantly told Harrington that he planned on changing into his Confederate Naval uniform just prior to taking over the steamer. Harrington had firmly given Culbertson direct orders that it was too risky to bring along his naval uniform and that he would be checking Culbertson's valise before boarding to make sure that the valise did not contain it.

Culbertson had stormed away after the meeting.

A shout from one of the raiders on sentry duty at the farm broke everyone's concentration.

"A wagon with two people turned off the road and is heading up the lane."

It must be LeBec returning. He had left the raiders to go into Windsor for a meeting and to make sure that there were no problems with the steamer's scheduled departure for the next day.

If it wasn't LeBec, they were at risk. They had no weapons so as not to raise suspicion as they traveled. Weapons were being delivered to McCormick and his team of raiders in Malden where they would inspect and clean them before stowing them in a trunk. The trunk would be carried aboard at the Malden stop and opened when the raid started.

As Harrington peered anxiously through the partly opened barn door, the heavily loaded wagon drew near.

"C'est moi," came a shout from a figure wearing a red hat in the wagon. The shout was followed by a sinister laugh. It was LeBec and he appeared to enjoy putting the raiders on edge.

Not a man to be trusted Harrington again thought to himself as he stepped back to allow the raiders to swing open the barn doors to allow the wagon to enter. Most of the wagon bed was taken up by something large that was covered by canvas and secured with rope. There were also small boxes of food and a cask in the rear of the wagon.

Harrington wondered what the next surprise would be. He did not like the way the surprises were materializing.

"Mes amis, I bring food and drink for everyone to enjoy!" shouted LeBec as he swung down from the wagon and walked to its rear. He set down boxes of food and began to open a cask of wine when Harrington stopped him.

"Just a moment LeBec."

"Oui?"

"One drink per man."

Turning to his men, Harrington continued, "I want you all to have clear heads tomorrow. There will be plenty of time for celebrating once we complete our mission."

Turning back to LeBec, Harrington questioned, "And just what do you have under the canvas?"

LeBec turned the manning of the cask over to the wagon's driver and motioned for Harrington to join him in a remote corner of the barn.

"When I arrived in Windsor, I made sure that the steamer was still scheduled to depart on time tomorrow. As you know, I also had previous instructions to attend a meeting in Windsor. I did not know who was going to be in attendance at this meeting, I just follow instructions like you, mon ami."

"Go on," Harrington commented impatiently.

"Apparently they are not ready for me and have me seated in a waiting area. I hear a carriage arrive and I am surprised to see a high-ranking member of my government, carrying a satchel, enter from outside, walk by me and enter the meeting room. They fail to close the door completely – so I am able to hear bits of the conversation.

"I hear them talking that this is the best for France, England, Canada, the North and the South. Then, someone noticed that the door was not closed, footsteps could be heard coming near to where I was listening on the other side of the door. I moved back just in time as one of them stuck his head out the door to check the waiting area. He then closed the door.

"In a few minutes, I am then asked to enter the meeting room. As I walk in, a door closes on the other side of the room and I am meeting with just one person. The others have left. It is then that I see this large trunk which now sits in that wagon."

LeBec tilted his head toward the wagon.

"The man tells me that our mission has been expanded and that you, mon ami, will tell me more when I see you."

LeBec looked quizzically at Harrington.

"I am not quite sure what they are talking about," he responded to LeBec's look.

LeBec continued, "The man said that the trunk must accompany us on our journey and he'd arranged for a wagon and driver to deliver it to us. The wagon driver then joined us. With the help of some servants, we carried the trunk to the wagon and he and I drove here. Mon Dieu, the trunk was heavy! The wagon driver will drive it to the steamer boarding area tomorrow and your men will have to carry it on board. The man in the meeting room also said that they had just locked the trunk and that one set of keys would stay with him in Windsor. What is going on mon ami?"

"You know more than I do at this point, LeBec."

LeBec reached into his waistcoat and produced an envelope.

"Mon ami, they instructed me to give you this letter tonight. It is from your President. Perhaps it will tell us what is inside the trunk," stated LeBec slyly as he handed an envelope embossed with President Jefferson Davis's seal.

Moving closer to a barn post where a lantern offered better light, Harrington sat down on a bale of hay and began reading.

Richmond, Virginia
January 5, 1864

Dear Colonel Harrington,

You are on the verge of commencing a major mission on behalf of the Confederacy.

The successful completion of your mission is of paramount significance to us in order to win our war of secession.

During our meetings, we had communicated to you the purpose of your mission as freeing the officers on Johnson's Island and raiding south in two groups to free prisoners in Indianapolis and Columbus before rejoining our lines.

In addition to this mission, there is a highly secret assignment which is of greater importance. It is of such importance that I was not able to disclose it to you during our meeting nor am I able to fully disclose it to you now in this letter.

What I can tell you on a limited basis is that the viability of our Confederacy lies in you completing this additional assignment. It will play a significant difference in our ability to win our independence.

The fact that you are now reading this letter means that you commence the first part of your mission tomorrow and that Monsieur LeBec has arrived at your meeting place with his cargo.

You are ordered not to ask any questions about the

contents of the trunk, but you are to make sure that it is well-guarded and that no one unlocks or attempts to unlock the trunk to view the contents.

Your additional assignment is for you and LeBec to deliver the trunk to me in Richmond.

Once you and your men free the prisoners and your group lands in Sandusky, you must transport the trunk with you. Monsieur LeBec will accompany you and the trunk.

Colonel, I hope you will understand the need for the utmost in secrecy. I will reveal to you the contents of the trunk in my office when you deliver it and you will then understand why it is vital to the Confederacy.

We had considered alternative methods for delivering the trunk including blockade runners – but we just could not take the chance of our hopes for success lying at the ocean's bottom. The North has been too successful in sinking our ships.

You will note that there are two envelopes enclosed with this letter – one with your name and one with LeBec's. Each envelope contains a key to unlock the trunk. Please give LeBec his envelope and the following instructions apply to both of you.

In the event you see your assignment failing and the trunk falling into the hands of the enemy, you should open the trunk – it takes both of your keys to unlock it. Remove the contents so that you can access the bottom of the trunk.

There is a hidden compartment which you should open.

Inside the compartment is a document folded in oil-skin. Bury the document and then surrender.

I know it is difficult for you to surrender. But it is extremely important that you surrender and are able to be in a position to write to us from a prison camp to tell us where the document is buried. I will expect you to identify the location by using the code which Mr. Mallory has provided you.

It is absolutely critical that we are able to recover the document.

Once you have completed reading this letter, you should destroy it.

I trust that you will understand the importance of this mission when we see each other again in my office and I share the contents of the oilskin with you.

Godspeed.

Jefferson Davis
President
Confederate States of America

Harrington looked up from the letter with a look of puzzlement. What was this all really about? Why all the secrecy? Didn't they trust him? Didn't they expect him to succeed? But then again, they had selected him for this critical mission. They had to have confidence in his ability to accomplish his mission.

Putting his doubts aside and trying to exude his usual confidence, Harrington looked directly at LeBec and handed him the envelope addressed to him.

"LeBec, President Davis has just provided orders for you and me to transport the trunk to him in Richmond. There, he will reveal the trunk's contents to us and we will understand why the contents are vital to the Confederacy's independence."

Harrington added, "Two keys are required to unlock this trunk in case of an emergency. You will have control over one key in this envelope and I will have the other. I do not anticipate that we will have a reason to use the keys."

LeBec looked with disdain as he received the key and watched as Harrington tucked his envelope containing his key in his pocket. With his eyes gleaming, LeBec wondered how he could get his hands on Harrington's key for a quick look inside the trunk to see what it contained. It must contain something very valuable he thought to himself.

Looking at LeBec, Harrington sternly said, "LeBec, one more thing. I want you to understand that we will only use these keys in an emergency. Is that clear?"

"Of course, of course. I understand my friend," LeBec responded unconvincingly.

Harrington walked out the back of the barn and over to a small fire where the men had been making coffee. He bent over the fire and dropped the letter into its flames.

Stepping back to watch it burn, he thought to himself, "What other surprises am I going to encounter?"

Grabbing a nearby stick, he scattered the charred remains of the letter and strode back to the barn.

Mills woke from a deep sleep and anxiously looked at his watch. There was no need for concern. He had not been asleep that long.

Mills dressed for the gala and finished his packing.

Mills took one last look around the room as he paused in the doorway to leave. Everything was in order. He locked the door and descended the stairs to go to the ballroom.

Mills wanted to be sure to be early to greet his guests, especially some of the pretty ladies from Sandusky's society. He would especially enjoy the conversation with them before he turned to mixing with the officers and the more serious business at hand.

All was going according to plan.

≈ ≈ ≈

Music from the gala drifted across Sandusky Bay to the prison camp that evening.

Many of the prisoners gathered in the darkness along the bayside stockade wall to listen to the music and recall memories from home. Many of the guards tilted their heads toward the music and tapped along with the tunes.

Word had filtered through the prison camp that there was a pre-Fourth of July gala in Sandusky that evening with fireworks followed by the firing of the *USS Michigan's* cannons. The attention of almost everyone on Johnson's Island was directed toward Sandusky as the evening progressed.

Suddenly, a huge explosion echoed across the bay and the sky was filled with light. The music stopped abruptly and screams could be heard coming across the bay from Sandusky.

Off duty guards ushered the prisoners into their housing units and, not knowing what to expect next, quickly manned the stockade walls.

～ ～ ～

Harrington moved away from the rail and began to make his rounds of the steamer's three decks. He noted that most of the 300 passengers had congregated on the second deck where the lunchroom and private parlors were.

He observed his raiders lounging at various places on board. They appeared to be blending in well with the crowd and not bringing attention to themselves. He had warned them about talking to fellow passengers as he was convinced that some of their southern drawls would give them away.

The strains of piano playing and the sounds of singing carried from the open door of the steamer's main salon which also housed the bar. Harrington was concerned that some of the raiders may have disobeyed orders to refrain from drinking and headed for the salon.

He anxiously stepped into the elegantly paneled salon and looked toward the piano. Leaning over the piano, surrounded by a number of ladies and directing the passengers in a loud rendition of *The Battle Hymn of the Republic*, was Mac – using his rich Scottish bass voice. Not quite what Harrington had in mind as far as keeping a low profile and not attracting attention.

Waiting until the final chords were complete, Harrington motioned to Mac to join him.

"Mac, what are you trying to do to by bringing attention to yourself? This is not what I would expect from one of my top officers!" a frustrated Harrington fumed.

"Well, it was the pretty ladies that begged me to sing for them. I had been humming a few bars of one of me favorite Scottish tunes when they overheard me and engaged me in conversation. I couldn't have turned them down when they learned that I loved to sing. You know how the pretty ladies have their way with me."

Harrington listened to the response from his trusted friend. They had been through many battles together and he knew that there was no one else that he preferred to have next to him than Mac. And Mac had an eye for the ladies. His handsome features coupled with his easygoing personality seemed to always attract them. But Harrington couldn't afford to have their cover blown inadvertently. He needed Mac to help him make sure that the rest of the raiders stayed out of trouble.

"Mac, why don't you accompany me in my rounds as I check on the rest of the team," he suggested softly.

"I'm with ye."

A loud roar of voices arose from the other end of the salon, interrupting their conversation. Harrington and Mac hurried to where the other passengers were gathering.

When they looked into the middle of the melee, they saw a shoving match between a passenger and one of the raiders, Mulberry – a 25 year old cavalryman. They quickly moved through the crowd to the front of the fracas.

Mac lunged forward and with his long arms restrained Mulberry just as Mulberry began to swing again at the passenger.

Harrington turned to the passenger who had just as quickly pulled out a derringer from his coat and was in process of aiming it at Mulberry.

"Sir! Sir! There is no need for this. May I assist in resolving this altercation between you two gentlemen?"

The passenger, looking around Harrington at Mulberry who was now ashen at seeing the derringer, replied indignantly, "It seems that this young man took extreme offense during our conversation about the origin of various songs. In fact, he seemed especially perturbed when I told him that the Confederacy couldn't come up with their own national anthem. They had to steal *Dixie* from the North. It was written by a fine northern gentlemen from Mount Vernon, Ohio."

Looking for a way to extricate Mulberry from the situation and the center of attention, Harrington suggested as he turned to Mulberry, "Young man, I believe that this gentlemen is correct and this is surely not a matter to end in fisticuffs or more. I'd suggest that you apologize for your actions and pay for this gentleman's next drink."

Mac released Mulberry who then looked at Harrington.

Harrington nodded his head to signal Mulberry to apologize.

Mulberry reached in his pocket for a coin and casually threw the coin on the bar.

"I certainly do apologize for my error, sir."

Mulberry turned and began to walk to one of the salon's doors – followed by Harrington and Mac.

"Just one minute young man," a voice boomed from behind the bar.

The three of them turned to see the bartender holding the coin up to the light, as he looked it over.

Harrington's heart sank. It appeared that Mulberry had given him a Confederate coin. This would really cause problems. Harrington did not like the way things were developing.

Mulberry, still enraged, questioned, "What is it now?"

"Where have you been, boy? Can't you read the sign about the cost of drinks here? You owe me another one of these."

Harrington breathed a sigh of relief as Mulberry strode to the bartender and gave him another coin. All three of the raiders then left the salon.

As they gathered at the rail, Mac turned to Mulberry and angrily grabbed him behind the neck with his massive grip.

"Son, what are ye trying to do to us? Ye know better than to pick a fight with a passenger! And what if he had fired that derringer? Ye would have jeopardized the entire raid! Ye wouldn't want that burden on yer shoulders, would ye?"

Before Mulberry could reply, Harrington asserted, "Mac, let him go! I believe Mulberry's learned a very important lesson."

Looking sheepishly, Mulberry responded, "Sir, I know I let you down. That guy just got me riled up about the South stealing the *Dixie* song. He was pompous and uppity – and I wanted to set him straight. I'll make this up to you. I promise."

Putting his arm around Mulberry's shoulder, Harrington commented, "Let's just put this behind us and be careful going forward. Now, you just go and find a couple of the boys and stay with them."

Mulberry saw two of the raiders standing at the stern of the steamer and went to join them.

Harrington made his rounds of the steamer's deck to make sure that all was well with the rest of his raiders.

Harrington observed Culbertson near the pilothouse watching the operations of the captain and his first mate as they navigated the steamer. Culbertson had struck up a conversation with the captain, as planned, to show his interest in steamer operations. It appeared that they were having a very deep conversation and the captain had invited

Culbertson into the pilothouse for a first hand look at the steamer's navigational gear.

As Harrington turned a corner on the lower deck, he noticed that LeBec continued to stay near the trunk that was boarded in Windsor. LeBec appeared to know a lot more than he was letting on.

Harrington had instructed Mac to assign one of Mac's men to keep an eye on LeBec and the trunk – and he saw that Mac had stationed Lieutenant Somers nearby.

Somers was a good man but there had been rumors about how he treated people. He could be very aggressive. In battle that was good, but in everyday relations, it could be a problem.

LeBec glared at Harrington and said, "All is well mon ami. You were checking on me, nes pas?"

Harrington, leaning closer to LeBec, said, "There is something about you LeBec that just does not sit right in my gut. I don't know what it is. But you have a job to do and so do I. Let's just get it done."

LeBec breathed a sigh of relief. Harrington had just missed seeing LeBec trying his key in the trunk's lock when Somers' attention was momentarily diverted. He wanted to see if what he had been told was true – and it was. His key would only unlock the one lock.

The steamer left Rattlesnake Island with its high cliffs on the north side astern as it bore down on Put-in-Bay. Remembering the maps and charts that he had studied, Harrington saw Middle Bass Island off to his left and Gibraltar Island to the right. Gibraltar Island rose high with its cliffs from the water. The charts had indicated that, when the lake's water level was low, one could almost walk from Gibraltar Island across the sand bar and Alligator Reef to Put-in-Bay.

The steamer had made a turn to its right and headed to the dock at Put-in-Bay. Once the steamer took on wood and left the bay, it would be time for Harrington and his men to take command of the ship and steam to Johnson's Island. Momentarily, Harrington wondered to himself what his Uncle Michael would think about his act of piracy on Lake Erie.

≈ ≈ ≈

Captain Joshua Denton had captained steamers for more than 20 years and took special pride in his ability to stay on schedule for the Detroit to Sandusky run. On occasion, his schedule was disrupted by Lake Erie's storms. But today, he was on schedule.

As the *Philo Parsons* turned to head to Put-in-Bay's dock, Denton looked to his left to see his wife and children waving from the dock on Middle Bass Island where his home was, less than a mile across the bay from Put-in-Bay. He wouldn't be returning home until the week-end. He gave a short pull of the steamer's horn to acknowledge his family.

He figured that his wife had also brought the children to the Middle Bass dock so that they could look westward and see the rainbow ending at Rattlesnake Island now that the storm had passed.

Rattlesnakes infested that island which was so aptly

named. For some reasons, the attempts to rid that island of rattlesnakes were not as successful as the attempt to clear them off of South Bass Island. The rattlesnakes were so bad there that no local would venture on the island. The non-islanders who visited usually showed up at Put-in-Bay for medical treatment from numerous rattlesnake bites.

He looked out of the wheelhouse and over the passengers that he could see lined at the rails and eagerly watching as they approached Put-in-Bay's dock. This would be the only stop where passengers could step off the steamer for two hours and stretch their legs. The crew would be busy as they unloaded cargo and livestock destined for the small village here and loaded wine from the island's vineyards and wood for the steamer's hungry boilers.

He was proud of his ship. The *Philo Parsons* was a wood hulled, sidewheel steamer. He carefully nudged her 135-foot length and 22-foot width against the dock.

Two of his crewmembers quickly secured the steamer to the dock and lowered the gangplank. Denton was looking forward to making his way down the stairs and crossing the ramp to report in with John Cassidy, his old friend, who had been harbormaster for years. They would enjoy their usual cup of coffee together and argue good-naturedly about politics, the weather, and the year's expected wine output from the island's grape crop.

≈ ≈ ≈

John Cassidy had heard *Philo Parsons'* horn and got up from his desk. He checked his watch and saw that Denton had her fairly well on schedule considering the storm that had just blown through.

He stepped over to the potbelly stove and added a few more pieces of wood to make the coffee hotter. He returned to his desk and brought out his ledger so that he would be ready when Denton came by to first take care of his business and dockage fees – and then to sit back for their usual round of coffee and friendly chat.

$$\approx \quad \approx \quad \approx$$

Passengers who planned to stay at Put-in-Bay for the Fourth of July festivities disembarked to check in at their hotels while new passengers boarded and cargo was unloaded and loaded.

Some of the other passengers stepped ashore to buy baked goods, wine or lemonade from the street vendors who crowded the dock. Some stepped ashore just to stretch their legs on tierra firma.

Melissa Warner made her way through the crowd on the dock as she sold her fresh, hot baked goods to the passengers. Business was good, especially on this Fourth of July holiday.

As she completed her sale to a passenger, she recoiled in horror at what she thought she saw out of the corner of her eye and turned her back to the steamer.

No, it's impossible she thought. It just can't be. We are too far north. We are free. Get a hold of yourself girl! she lectured herself.

She faced the steamer and looked toward its lower deck.

It was him. Looking over the crowd on the dock from the lower deck. She didn't believe that he saw her by the casual way he continued to gaze about the dock and the park.

It was Master Wylan. What was he doing all the way up here? So far away from the Somers plantation? She had heard that he was considering signing up for the cavalry before she and Henry had escaped.

She shuddered with revulsion as she recalled the way he treated her and wanted her.

Keeping her head bowed and hidden by her bonnet she began to run from the dock area. She ignored the passengers' cries for her to stop as they sought to buy more baked goods from her.

She saw one of Mr. Brown's neighbors beginning to pull away from the general store and flagged him down. She explained that she had to head home quickly and asked if he could drive her to Mr. Brown's place on the southeast side of the island where Henry was working. They set off at a fast trot in his carriage.

Henry and Mr. Brown were weeding the grapes when they saw the carriage moving quickly up the long drive and leaving a trail of dust. They looked at each other apprehensively and walked briskly to meet the carriage.

Melissa jumped off the carriage and ran to them as the neighbor waved goodbye and drove off.

"It's Master Wylan, Henry!" she shouted as she neared them.

"What? Where? Slow down girl. What are you talking about?"

"On the *Philo Parsons* just now. I was selling baked goods when I saw him." She shuddered again at the thought of him.

Henry placed his arm around her to comfort her and to help her gain her composure.

"Are you sure it was him? It could just be someone that resembles him."

"Yes, Henry. It's him! I will always remember him. He didn't see me. I turned around and then took another look at him. He was on the lower deck of the steamer where they load and unload cargo. It was definitely him."

Turning to Mr. Brown, Henry asked, "Do you think he's looking for us, Mr. Brown? I thought we would be safe here."

"As I've listened to you two talk, I've been trying to figure that out myself. It just doesn't make sense that he would come this far north just to hunt down the two of you. I've heard you two talk about this Wylan on several occasions. One thing that's for sure – he's not here today to celebrate the Fourth of July."

Furrows deepened on his brow as he pondered the sighting of Wylan.

"There's got to be more to this," added Brown. "Let's go down to the house. I have an idea."

Upon reaching the farmhouse, Brown swiftly penned a letter and turned to Henry.

"Henry, I want you to take this letter and my row boat down below and row to Marblehead Peninsula by the light-house. Then I want you to make your way as fast as you can to the prison camp on Johnson's Island and deliver this to Colonel Wellman, or if you can deliver this directly to Captain Guadian on the *USS Michigan*, that would be better."

"Yes sir Mr. Brown. What do you think is happening?" asked Henry.

"There have been a rumors over the last two years that the Confederacy might launch an attempt to free the prisoners on Johnson's Island. The fact that your Mr. Wylan is here is very unusual – and we don't need to take any unnecessary risks. We need to get to the bottom of this!

"While you're rowing, I'll ride into town to advise the mayor and talk to the others who are gathered here for the Fourth of July speeches. If I recall correctly what I read in the Gazette, I also believe that there are members of the 130th Ohio Infantry here to participate in today's celebration – and they should be armed."

Turning to Melissa, Brown instructed her, "You stay put on this farm until I get back. Let's go Henry – and let's hope this is a false alarm."

"Henry, be careful," called an upset Melissa as Henry ran to the rowboat and pushed off.

Henry began pulling at the oars with his strong muscles. A brisk wind was beginning to blow in from the west. It would help him today as he headed east toward the Marblehead Lighthouse.

Brown headed to town on his hastily saddled horse.

Denton exited the *Philo Parsons* pilothouse and inadvertently knocked down the man who had introduced himself as Culbertson. He had exhibited an unusual amount of interest in the steamer's operations with his constant questioning of Denton and any of the crew who had come near him. While he asked intelligent questions and appeared to be familiar with good seamanship, it would be a relief to be free of his pestering questions and sense of superiority once he was landed at his final destination – which he said was Sandusky.

As Culbertson fell, a portion of his waistcoat snagged on the rail and ripped open a long gash in his jacket.

Denton was stunned by what he saw – a Confederate naval jacket under the waistcoat.

"Now, just what in the world is going on here?" shouted an aroused Denton to Culbertson.

"One moment. Please help me up and I'll explain."

Momentarily forgetting his disbelief, Denton bent over and offered an arm to assist Culbertson.

Culbertson grabbed Denton's arm with one hand and with the other, which had been partially concealed, swung a small baton which Culbertson had retrieved from his boot.

Denton fell back against the rail as blood gushed from a wound to his brow. He lost consciousness and tumbled over the rail into the water.

"Man overboard! Man overboard!" rang the cry from two crewman on the cargo deck when they saw the body hit the water.

One jumped in and swam to the body and upon turning it over yelled, "It's Captain Denton!"

Seeing that Denton was alive, but unconscious, the crewman began to drag him through the water to the *Philo Parsons.*

≈ ≈ ≈

When he heard the cry, Harrington hurried to the rail on the bay side of the steamer. As he looked down at the activity in the water, the crewman in the water suddenly yelled, "Repel boarders! There's a rebel at the pilothouse!"

Harrington's head swung around with a snap and looked up. There was Culbertson discarding his waistcoat and standing defiantly in his Confederate Naval jacket. He was brandishing his baton and a small revolver which he had pulled from concealment under his jacket.

Culbertson shouted to Harrington and, for that matter, any other person within hearing distance, "To arms. It's time to take the ship!" He then began swinging his baton at several of the nearby passengers.

The passengers began to fall back as Culbertson threatened them by waving his revolver at them. Some ladies screamed, adding to the commotion.

Harrington raced down a flight of stairs to the cargo area where he met several out of breath raiders. Mac and

Mulberry had been the first to arrive and were busily unlocking the second chest that had been brought on board.

Upon opening the chest, Mulberry began distributing the revolvers, ammunition, axes and knives to the raiders.

Turning to Mac, Harrington grimaced as he shouted, "We're a bit ahead of schedule Mac."

"Aye Colonel, but we can still pull it off!"

Harrington caught his friend's eye and noticed that he had a look of concern.

"Mac, assign some men to support that idiot Culbertson and secure the pilot house."

More of the raiders arrived to grab weapons and ammunition.

"Mac, we need to clear the decks. Take some of the men and herd the passengers into the salons and station marksmen at strategic positions on each deck. I saw infantry with rifles resting in the park. We're no match for the rifles!"

"Consider it handled," Mac responded affirmatively and briskly began barking out assignments to the other raiders.

Seeing Mulberry, Harrington directed, "Mulberry, have 5 men take control of the engine room and get up steam. We're going to have to depart early for Johnson's Island and get out of rifle range!"

"Yes sir."

Mulberry ran off to carry out the orders.

Harrington grabbed extra revolvers and ammunition for LeBec and Somers, who were guarding the first chest, and ran to their area in the cargo deck.

"LeBec! Somers! Here are two revolvers for you," Harrington yelled as he approached them.

LeBec replied with a wicked grin, "But my friend, I am already prepared" and opened his waistcoat to show two hidden revolvers.

Somers took both weapons and crouched behind the cargo in a defensive posture.

"So my friend, we are premature in our actions today. What caused this?"

Harrington quickly explained and then moved to support the rest of the raiders as gunshots began to emit from the park.

LeBec could not hold back and yelled to Harrington, "You incompetent fools! It's no wonder that you are losing your war!"

Harrington ignored his remark to run to the dock side of the boat to survey the town and what forces might become a threat to them. He would take care of LeBec later. LeBec would pay for his remarks.

≈ ≈ ≈

Brown had just dismounted from his horse near the infantry who were resting in the shaded park across from the dock when the cries "Man overboard and repel boarders" echoed across the dock toward the park.

Brown ran to the Major in charge of the infantry and told him about the sighting of Wylan Somers and his suspicions. The major agreed that it appeared raiders may be attempting to take over the steamer.

Looking to the steamer, they saw passengers taking cover. The dock, which just a few minutes earlier had been crowded with passengers and street vendors was now virtually deserted as everyone fled the immediate area to seek cover.

A gunshot rang out from the pilothouse on the upper deck and they could see the wheelsman slump over the wheel. A tall, commanding figure in what appeared to be a Confederate uniform, cast the slumped body aside and stepped to the wheel.

The 50 infantrymen moved forward through the park and took up positions from which they could commence firing.

The steamer's horn began sounding, adding to the confusion of the early afternoon and drawing attention to the pilothouse.

Amidst the noise of the horn and screams of the people, the Major was barking orders to his troops.

"Fire at will at the pilot house! Kill that man and anyone else who you see on board with a pistol or who's firing at us. We'll make sure that the steamer doesn't leave the dock."

The infantry now opened fire on the pilothouse. Shattering glass could be heard between the gunshots.

Smoke began billowing out of the steamer's stack as the *Philo Parsons* built up steam. The smoke blew to the East as the wind became more brisk and the sky began to darken.

The major was concerned that they maintain steady fire on the pilothouse. If the *Philo Parsons* was able to pull away from the dock, there would be nothing that anyone could do to catch them.

$$\approx \quad \approx \quad \approx$$

Culbertson strode into the pilothouse and, aiming his revolver, shot the crewman standing at the wheel. The crewman slumped over the wheel.

Culbertson shoved his body aside and called down to the engine room for steam. He was proud of his role. He'd show everyone what a Confederate naval officer was capable of doing.

He pulled the steamer's horn to announce that the Confederate Navy was in command.

Breaking glass and bullets whizzing by him brought him back to reality. He ducked down and moved away from the horn.

Where was that steam? he wondered to himself.

Culbertson crawled to the bay side of the steamer, stood up and went to the rail where he saw Harrington below.

"I need more steam!" he bellowed to Harrington. "Cast off or cut the lines and pull away the gangway. Time is..."

Culbertson's bellowing was cut short as a rifle bullet struck him in the head and killed him instantly. His body tumbled over the rail and into the water, dropping like a weighted sack.

John Cassidy, the harbormaster, put down his smoking rifle. "That's for what you did to my friend, Denton," he said under his breath. Cassidy had seen the struggle between Denton and Culbertson from his vantage point. Cassidy looked toward the steamer and sighted for more targets.

Harrington saw Culbertson's body hit the water. This meant sure disaster for the mission he thought. Culbertson was the only one who knew how to operate the steamer and was the only one who had studied the charts of the waters in this area.

Watching Culbertson's body hit the water, LeBec could see that the entire plan was falling apart in front of them. He had Somers slip over the side and swim to a rowboat near the harbormaster's office. Once he was in the water,

Somers was below the sightline of anyone on the dock or on the island so that he could maneuver freely.

~ ~ ~

A large explosion rent the air, stopping everyone in their tracks. All attention, all firing stopped as everyone turned their heads to the east where the explosion originated.

With black smoke billowing from her stack and waves breaking on the bow as she surged forward under full power, the *USS Michigan* fired a second warning shot from her 60-pound cannon.

She could be seen across the marshland as she steamed to round the island's peninsula and then enter its harbor.

~ ~ ~

"Fire another warning shot! I want those bloody Rebel pirates to know that we are coming. We'll put a swift end to their shenanigans," shouted Guadian to his 60-pound cannon gunner.

The events of the past 24 hours had been very strange he recalled to himself. Everyone at the gala had been feasting on the food and enjoying the good music and conversations – even the conversations with that chubby horse trader and host, Mills, had been delightful.

Then, in the early evening darkness, the air was rent by an explosion behind the hotel. As he and the other officers raced to the rear of the hotel, they discovered bits and pieces from a horse, carriage, chests and a man.

When someone mentioned that Mills was nowhere to be seen, Guadian, Wellman and several officers went with the hotel's manager to Mill's room.

When the door was opened, they discovered Mills' body lying in a pool of blood.

The blood still oozed from what appeared to be a fatal blow to the head. Mills' pockets had been turned inside out as if someone had been searching for something of value. It must have been a robbery.

As they looked around the room, they noticed that there was no luggage. Every personal item of Mills had been taken away.

They made their way down the stairs and to the site of the explosion where they encountered a distressed livery owner.

Guadian asked, "Sir, may I be of assistance?"

"It's gone. Blown up. My stable boy is missing and it looks like this was one of my carriages. I assume my horse was blown up too."

Holding a piece of a red shirt, Colonel Wellman from the prison camp asked, "Do you recognize this material?"

"Yes, Yes. It looks like my nephew's shirt. I had just hired him two days ago as a stable boy to help out his mother. He had always been getting in trouble – and now this." He lowered his head and began sobbing.

Wellman asked, "Did your nephew know Mr. Mills?"

"No, No. Well, not really. Mr. Mills had just returned a rented carriage today and my nephew saw him display a large amount of cash when he paid me. I didn't think anything about it when he asked me where Mr. Mills was staying in town," he sobbed.

Wellman and Guadian looked at each other as Wellman spoke, "Well, that seems to explain what happened to Mills in his room. The boy apparently killed and robbed him. But what caused an explosion and blew up the boy?"

Looking at the crowd of partygoers that had gathered around the site of the explosion and seeing that several of the ladies had fainted, Wellman and Guadian decided that the gala should be cancelled at this point. It would be too difficult to continue following the murder of the host and the death of the stable boy.

Guadian ferried Wellman, his officers and wives to the prison camp and the *Michigan* took up station in the Bay next to the camp.

Guadian had decided to take the *Michigan* on patrol out of Sandusky Bay the next day.

As they rounded the Marblehead Peninsula, a black man in a rowboat hailed them,

The *Michigan* slowed as it cautiously approached the man.

Guadian ordered, "Battle stations for all hands!"

This could be a trap he thought.

"I have a letter for the Captain from Mr. John Brown," yelled the man in the rowboat as he frantically waved what appeared to be a letter in his hands. "It's an emergency, sir. There may be Confederate raiders on a steamer in Put-in-Bay. Mr. Brown thinks they are going to try to free the prisoners on Johnson's Island."

Recognizing Brown's name, Guadian had the man quickly hauled aboard and brought before him.

"Mr. Brown wrote this letter to you sir. He wanted me to find you and give it to you," the man continued as he leaned against the rail. Sweat from his rowing cascaded down his face and chest.

Quickly reading the letter, Guadian began to see how the events of the past 24 hours tied together. Mills had probably been a Confederate agent and the notion of him buying horses for the union was a front. He would have needed the horses for the freed prisoners. He had enticed the officers to attend a pre-Fourth of July gala so that he could damage the *Michigan* and do, Lord knows what, to the officers.

It appeared that Mills' plans were thwarted by the unexpected robbery. Mills must have returned to his room to get an explosive when he was robbed. And the stable boy's escape was ended when whatever explosive Mills had intended to use on the *Michigan* exploded in the carriage.

Guadian looked up from the letter and cleared his mind for action.

"Thank you for delivering this to me young man. I'd

like you to stay aboard with us. You deserve experiencing what we are going to do to those Johnny Rebs."

"Thank you sir," responded Henry.

Turning to the helmsman, Guadian said, "Steer for Put-in-Bay. Full speed ahead."

As the *Michigan* changed course and headed in a northeasterly direction, Guadian noticed that the waves were beginning to build and the sky was darkening.

Guadian turned to his officers and briefed them on his interpretation of what had transpired in the last 24 hours. He also told them that Rebel raiders might be taking over the *Philo Parsons*.

The *Michigan* plunged through the growing waves and darkening sky. It looked like another storm was brewing.

As the *Michigan* drew abreast of the low swampy area which separated Put-in-Bay's harbor on the east from Lake Erie, Guadian could see the Philo Parson moored at the dock and gunfire being exchanged between the steamer and Union troops in the park.

He ordered the 60-pound cannon fired as a warning to the rebels. He wished that the *Michigan* could cut across the swampy area. Time was short. But it was just too shallow. They would lose sight of the harbor as they continued to steam around the island's peninsula and then enter the harbor from the north side.

Guadian was relishing his anticipated victory. He knew that he would be able to end this attempted piracy on Lake Erie.

The booming of the cannon caused Harrington to look up quickly toward the eastern horizon. His heart dropped as he saw the clouds of black smoke billowing from the gunboat. It looked like the mission was a disaster.

Harrington sensed someone near him and turned to see LeBec standing next to him at the rail and staring in disbelief at the gunboat.

"Your agent apparently did not destroy the gunboat last night!" he sullenly commented.

"C'est magnifique!" he added sarcastically.

They ducked as gunshots continued to pepper the steamer from the infantry along the shore.

LeBec gazed across the deck toward the chest he had been guarding so carefully.

"The trunk! What is in it? We need to see what is in the trunk that is so important for your Confederacy, mon ami. Let's use our keys and unlock is so we know what to do with the contents."

Remembering his instructions from the President, Harrington quickly agreed. "You're right. We need to see the contents and to save them from falling into Yankee hands."

Keeping a low profile, LeBec and Harrington raced across the deck to the trunk. Both withdrew their keys, inserted them in the trunk's locks and unlocked it.

Opening the top of the trunk, LeBec and Harrington gazed in amazement at its contents.

Harrington was in awe. No wonder Jefferson Davis placed so much secrecy on this aspect of the mission. Now they would have to empty the trunk so that he could get to the secret compartment which LeBec did not know about.

Hearing oars splashing in the water, Harrington saw that Somers was rowing a boat to the steamer. Harrington could use it to row to land and bury the contents of the hidden compartment before surrendering as he had been instructed. He looked into the trunk again.

A brilliant flash of light ended Harrington's thoughts.

"Adieu, mon colonel!" LeBec said with an evil smile.

LeBec lowered the revolver which he had placed next to Harrington's head and fired.

No one but he needed to be aware of the contents of this trunk he thought as he quickly locked it with both keys and put them in his pocket.

Seeing Somers return with the rowboat, he shouted for his assistance in lowering the chest into the rowboat.

Somers scampered up the side on the rope ladder that LeBec had dropped and over the rail. He saw Harrington's body and questioningly looked at LeBec.

"He was hit by one of the rifleman on shore," he offered as a hurried explanation. "Now help me transfer this to the rowboat. We must hide this trunk."

Somers helped him with the boom and in winching it from the deck. They swung the boom over the water and carefully set the chest in the boat. The boat settled deeper in the water which was beginning to stir up in the harbor as the wind increased.

"I'll need your help now Somers," commanded LeBec.

Somers looked up to see the revolver in LeBec's hand pointed at him.

"Into the boat and to the oars."

Somers climbed down the ladder and sat at the oars under the watchful eye of LeBec. LeBec then descended the ladder and sat in the stern of the boat where he could watch Somers.

"Quickly now, mon ami. Take us to the channel between this island and Gibraltar Island. The water there should be deep enough for a rowboat but too shallow for that gunboat."

Somers pulled hard at the oars.

They were more than halfway there when the gunboat rounded the peninsula and began to move toward the *Philo Parsons*. It ignored the two figures in the rowboat.

"Once we are through the channel, where will we go?" asked Somers.

LeBec had to shout his response to be heard over another warning shot from the *Michigan*'s cannon which had been directed to the steamer.

LeBec turned to look at the action behind him.

Seeing him momentarily distracted, Somers stood up and dove into the harbor. He didn't trust the Frenchman.

Hearing the splash and feeling the boat rock, LeBec turned back around.

"Sacre Bleu!" he said to himself as he fired several times into the water trying to hit Somers. LeBec looked around but didn't see Somers. He angrily moved to the oars and began pulling for the channel.

~ ~ ~

Somers had dove deep and swam hard toward a dock that he had seen on the west side of the village. He had been fortunate in avoiding LeBec's gunshots.

Somers surfaced, took a deep breath and began taking powerful strokes to the dock. Reaching the dock, Somers climbed up the ladder.

As his head came over the top of the dock, his mouth opened in fear as he recognized the figure holding a pistol aimed at his head.

"Master Wylan, you ain't my master no more."

Melissa pulled the Colt's trigger and heard the empty click of the hammer on the round. She looked down at the pistol in fear and astonishment.

Somers face relaxed and broke into a contemptuous grin. He continued his climb up the ladder and, smiling thinly, said, "Well, well, well. It's that pretty little Melissa.

The only one who ever got away from me."

Seeing the woods on the horizon, Somers quickly thought he would take her with him and escape to the woods. He certainly could use her as a hostage and could settle an old score with her.

Turning back to her, he heard her say with firm resolve, "I said, Master Wylan, you ain't my master no more!"

She confidently pulled the trigger again and this time it fired.

Somers' eyes stared in disbelief at her and then down at the blood gushing from the gunshot hole in his chest. As his life left him, he fell back off the dock and into the harbor.

Melissa collapsed on the dock, emotionally drained and began to sob. She had been too anxious about remaining at the farmhouse. She had hitched the wagon, grabbed one of the Mr. Brown's pistols and driven to the village.

She had gone to the hotel's third floor to have a better view of the fight and saw Master Wylan and another man in a red hat lower something into a rowboat. When she saw them rowing away, she ran down the stairs and along the shore so that she could watch where they were going.

When the cannon fired, she heard the man in the red hat yell. Must be where they were going, she thought to herself.

Seeing Master Wylan dive into the water, she guessed that he might be swimming to the Village's western dock and ran to it. She might have a chance to repay Master Wylan.

And she did.

∾ ∾ ∾

LeBec entered the channel. Several times he worried as the bottom of the rowboat grazed the top of the sand bar in the channel. He tried to recall where Alligator Reef was so that he could avoid the sharp rocks just below the water's surface. The gunboat would not be able to follow him.

He pulled at the oars harder as he moved through the channel.

∾ ∾ ∾

The *Michigan* rounded the island's northeast peninsula and entered the harbor.

Guadian realized that there would be a danger in firing its cannons at the steamer as it appeared to still have passengers on board.

"Lieutenant Smithson, distribute arms to the men and order them to fire on anyone on the steamer who has a weapon in their hand."

Turning to his gun crew on the 60 pounder, Guadian continued, "Take aim on the steamer's sidewheel. If they attempt to escape, we'll put a shot into her to disable her sidewheel. But, don't fire until I issue the command!"

"Aye Captain," came the gun crew's response as they positioned the cannon.

The *Michigan* took position abreast of the steamer in order to lay down cannon fire if it became necessary. Guadian was trying to cover all options.

Shots now began to ring out from his crewmembers as they opened fire on selected targets.

≈ ≈ ≈

Mac gently laid Harrington's head down and wiped tears from his own eyes.

He looked around the steamer. About 10 of the raiders had been killed and an equal number were wounded. Mac had ordered the raiders up from the engine room to help in returning fire.

Revolvers against rifles – not quite a fair match Mac thought to himself.

The *Michigan* had taken station abreast of the steamer and her crew was firing on the steamer. Shots were also striking the boat from the island as the Yankees were relentless with their deadly fire.

Mac had seen LeBec and Somers in the rowboat, making their way across the harbor in what appeared to be an attempt to save that first trunk from the Yankees.

Mac remorsefully looked around and then shouted the one command that he dreaded giving.

"Lay down your arms boys! We're outnumbered and outgunned! The jig is up!"

His fellow raiders also realized the hopelessness of the situation and dropped their weapons and raised their hands in surrender.

The firing ceased and the infantry began to board the steamer.

~ ~ ~

From the deck of the *Michigan* which had now tied up to the steamer, one of the crewman focused his attention to the western harbor and the figure in a red hat pulling vigorously at the oars of a rowboat.

The crewman shouted, "One's getting away!"

Guadian looked and saw the rowboat crossing the shallow channel with the sand bar between the western edge of Put-in-Bay and Gibraltar Island. He knew that the water was too shallow for his gunboat to go in direct pursuit.

"We'll steam around Gibraltar and catch him on the open lake water," Guadian shouted back.

Just then the skies opened and a torrential downfall started. The figure in the rowboat disappeared through a wall of rain that quickly swept through the harbor. The waves now began to reach heights of 1 to 2 feet.

"We will find him when the storm abates," yelled Guadian over the thunder.

$\sim$ $\sim$ $\sim$

Once the raiders surrendered, Henry Warner jumped across from the *Michigan* to the deck of the *Philo Parsons* and hurriedly made his way to the dock and toward the western end of the village.

From the deck of the *Michigan,* he had spied Melissa running to the dock. He saw her aim a pistol and shoot someone before falling on the dock's surface.

As Henry ran along the edge of the park and through the sheets of rain, he encountered Mr. Brown and rapidly explained what he had seen. Brown joined Henry and they raced to Melissa's side.

Holding her in his arms, Henry tried to console his sobbing wife, the tears on her face mingling with the pouring rain. Brown picked up his pistol from the dock.

"It was Master Wylan, Henry! It was Master Wylan!" she sobbed.

"The man you shot? That was Master Wylan?" asked Henry incredulously.

"Yes. I saw him from the hotel. He and the man in the red hat were in the rowboat and rowing to the channel. I followed them along the shore and heard them yelling at each other. Then, I saw Master Wylan dive into the water and start swimming away.

"I ran to the dock when I saw that's where he was headed and waited for him. When I saw his head come up over the edge of the dock as he climbed the ladder. I, oh Henry, it just all came back to me. How he treated the girls. What he planned to do to me. The whipping he had them give me."

Sobbing, she drew closer to Henry and shuddered as he held her tighter.

"I told him he wasn't my master anymore and pulled the trigger. It didn't fire and I had to pull it again."

She sobbed harder.

"Honey, everything's going to be ok. Isn't that right Mr. Brown?"

Brown, who had been listening intently as he examined his .44 caliber Colt, responded, "Things will work out just fine now Melissa. Did you see where the fellow in the red hat went?"

"Just through the channel, Mr. Brown. But I thought I heard him holler to Master Wylan while they were rowing. They were going to where rainbows end. It was hard to hear with all the guns being fired."

"Good, good, and that would be Rattlesnake Island. I'll tell Captain Guadian." Turning to Henry, Brown instructed, "You take Melissa home. I'll be along later."

Brown stood up and took long strides through the rain back to the *Philo Parsons* and the *Michigan*. This was important information that needed to be passed on.

$\approx \approx \approx$

After the storm passed and the waves subsided, the *Philo Parsons*, accompanied by the *Michigan*, steamed from Put-in-Bay to Johnson's Island with the captured raiders who were guarded by the infantrymen.

Once the ships docked at the camp, the prisoners carrying their wounded and dead disembarked from the steamer.

Mac stepped off the steamer and entered the prison camp. This was not what they had planned he thought as he helped transport Harrington's body. It would be a long visit for Mac and his fellow raiders.

The next day, the dead raiders would be buried in the cemetery near the prison camp.

~ ~ ~

Once the raiders were transported to the prison camp, the *Michigan* set course for Rattlesnake Island. Their search plans were based on the information provided by Mr. Brown wherein he conveyed Melissa hearing them shout in the rowboat that they were headed to where rainbows end. Everyone on the island would know it meant but one place – Rattlesnake Island.

Guadian would commence a search for the missing raider in the red hat, the harbormaster's rowboat and a trunk with two locks that had been closely guarded by the raider in the red hat according to statements taken from the passengers.

It would be interesting to find the trunk and see what was so valuable. Rumors had already begun to circulate about what was in the locked trunk.

The *Michigan* steamed northwest of Put-in-Bay to Rattlesnake Island. They circled the eleven-acre island but could not find any evidence that a boat had been pulled ashore there.

Guadian was reluctant to anchor and put a boat ashore to investigate further because of the rattlesnake infestation. Even the islanders were leery of going ashore because the island was so thick with rattlesnakes.

Guadian then suggested that they steam around Green Island, just south of Rattlesnake Island. With the squall that blew in from the west earlier, Green Island may have been a more preferable destination.

The *Michigan* steamed around Green Island and they did not see any evidence of a recent boat landing. Regardless, Guadian ordered a boat launched and 10 men to thoroughly search Green Island.

After a two-hour search, the men returned empty-handed.

Guadian wanted to return again to Rattlesnake Island, but seeing more storm clouds on the horizon, ordered his gunboat to return to station off of Johnson Island.

Guadian planned to make sure that the prison camp on Johnson's Island was secure and then to resume his search for the missing raider the next day.

Guadian thought to himself that the boat could have swamped and sunk in the heavy sea. They may not find any remains.

The *Michigan* turned and headed toward the Marblehead lighthouse which guarded the entrance to Sandusky Bay and its Johnson Island.

~ ~ ~

The next day, they returned to Rattlesnake Island. As they approached the south side of the island, they spied the body of a man in a red hat lying next to the stolen rowboat which had been pulled up on its stony beach.

Guadian joined the crew as a boat was launched from the *Michigan* and headed to the island. Guadian wanted to be directly involved in his capture.

The boat grated on the stones as it landed.

Guadian and the men took several steps onto the beach and froze at the sound of the rattles. Cautiously looking to the right, they saw two rattlesnakes – one on the body and the other next to the stolen rowboat.

After a few minutes, the two rattlesnakes uncoiled and slithered into the brush.

Guadian turned the body over and LeBec's eyes stared lifelessly at him from under the brim of his red hat. Guadian pulled the hat up and off his forehead and just as quickly pulled it back down to cover most of his face.

"He's dead," he said emotionlessly.

Guadian quickly searched the body and its clothing.

Finding nothing, Guadian stepped away from the body and approached the rowboat.

Peering over the side, Guadian saw that the boat was empty.

Guadian muttered to himself, "Now, just where is that trunk? Did he drop it overboard before he beached the rowboat or hide it on the island?"

Guadian and his men decided to search the island. As they approached the brush at the edge of the beach, they heard numerous rattles. Knowing the reputation of the island, they withdrew, taking with them LeBec's body and the stolen rowboat to return to its owner.

Guadian wanted to put this whole incident to rest.

≈ ≈ ≈

LeBec's body was taken to Johnson's Island where one of the captured raiders, Mac, confirmed its identification.

Mac made sure that LeBec was buried in a far corner of the prison camp's cemetery, away from Harrington and his men.

≈ ≈ ≈

For years there were rumors about the missing trunk. Some said it was full of gold coins. Others said it held jewels.

As time passed, the islanders became more aggressive in their tactics to clear Rattlesnake Island of its rattlesnakes. They finally achieved the goal in ridding all rattlesnakes from the island.

Some said the islanders were motivated to kill off the rattlesnake population by their desire to find the missing trunk. Many scoured the island looking for the trunk. To no avail many dug around the island looking for buried treasure. Interest never completely died down.

For Rattlesnake Island, where so many rainbows ended, the treasure at the rainbow's end took on a more significant meaning. The mystery remained unsolved.

Book Two

The late morning sun glistened on the bits of paradise in Lake Erie's western basin. From three miles off the Catawba Peninsula, the islands were scattered like broken pieces of crystal, shining on the blue water.

The island names added to the allure of the area: South Bass with its Put-in-Bay resort village, Middle Bass, North Bass, Gibraltar, Green, Rattlesnake, Ballast, Sugar, Starve, East Sister, and Hens & Chickens. Sandusky Bay had its Johnson's Island and north from the Marblehead Peninsula with its historic Marblehead lighthouse was Kelley's Island. North of Kelley's and in Canadian waters was Pelee Island.

The area is a true island paradise for vacationers. Many visit the islands during the warm summer months and stay in the various hotels, inns, summer vacation homes or the state run campgrounds. Some made the islands their permanent, year round home.

Visitors would arrive by one of several ferry services, private watercraft or flying aircraft to one of the several landing strips on the larger islands. In the cold winter months, the Lake would freeze over and vehicles could be driven across the ice as they dodged a multitude of fishing shanties scattered across the ice.

It was a typical hot day in late June. Boaters were at play – skiing, fishing and just plain relaxing around the islands.

To the southwest of South Bass Island, a boat was speeding through Lake Erie's still waters from Port Clinton on the mainland to the island's resort town of Put-in-Bay.

The boat was the Jet Express, one of the fastest jet powered catamaran ferries in the world. It could make the 10-mile trip in an unbelievably fast 22 minutes.

As the three level Jet Express drew near the southwestern shore of South Bass Island, a tall, athletic, deeply-tanned man with dark hair looked up from reading the island guide which he had acquired at the ferry ticketing office.

Emerson Moore thought to himself how long it had been since he had visited Put-in-Bay. The last time had been when he was fifteen, and he was forty-two now. As a teen, he had traveled on the old, slower ferry service which had seemed to take forever to reach the island when he spent his fun-filled summers there.

It was difficult returning to the island now. Over the years he had provided a number of excuses to his Aunt Anne and Uncle Frank as to why he couldn't return for a visit.

He knew that they had forgiven him for any part that he had in the incident – in fact, they had told him over and over that they didn't hold him responsible or feel that he in any way had contributed to the death of his sixteen year old cousin, Jack.

But he still felt guilty and occasionally had nightmares about the incident.

$$\approx \ \approx \ \approx$$

Jack and he had enjoyed their summers together on the island. Jack and his parents were year round residents in their green Victorian style home with white gingerbread trim on East Point Boulevard, overlooking the harbor on its eastern side. From the front porch of the house, they looked out over their dock to Gibraltar Island and to the right and farther out, they would see rainbows occasionally ending on Rattlesnake Island.

While Uncle Frank worked for one of the ferry services and Aunt Anne worked at one of the restaurants in Put-in-Bay, Jack and he were able to wander the island and its surrounding waters as they wished. They biked the island, hiked, swam at its beaches, sailed and flirted with the pretty girls vacationing on the island. Sometimes, they would have opportunities to sample small quantities of wine for which the island was known.

On Sundays, Uncle Frank would start up his 1929 Model A Ford truck and the boys would ride with him in the weekly parade of old cars through town. They would wave wildly at the crowds of vacationers lining the streets as they threw them candy from the back of the truck.

They'd bike out Langram Road to the landing strip to watch the old Ford Trimotor plane, the tin lizzie of the air, land as it transported residents and visitors to the island. The plane with its corrugated-metal skin would slowly descend as the pilot throttled back on the three 7 cylinder, 235 horsepower Wright Whirlwind engines. Even with the engines throttled back, they were noisy and the boys would playfully cover their ears.

The plane would taxi near the metal hangar where the pilot would turn off one engine and idle the other two so that he could make a fast take off to Middle Bass Island, the next stop, once the new passengers boarded and cargo was loaded.

After strong storms during the day, they would bike to Peach Point to see if a rainbow would appear and end as it usually would on Rattlesnake Island.

At night, they'd stroll Bay View Avenue along the waterfront to watch the antics of the boaters who had tied up for the night in the harbor and were partying. From watching people stumble to falling in the harbor to vomiting – it was fun for the two teenagers.

They would cut across the park to Delaware Avenue and peek inside the Beer Barrel Saloon with the world's longest bar, Frosty's Bar, Roundhouse Bar and the other establishments on the strip to observe the wild goings on of the vacationers.

When they got tired of exploring South Bass Island they'd pack lunches in their backpacks and sail to the neighboring islands. The boys received strong lectures from time to time from Jack's parents if they didn't pay attention to the weather and were caught on the Lake by a sudden storm. They had some real scary moments together, but would

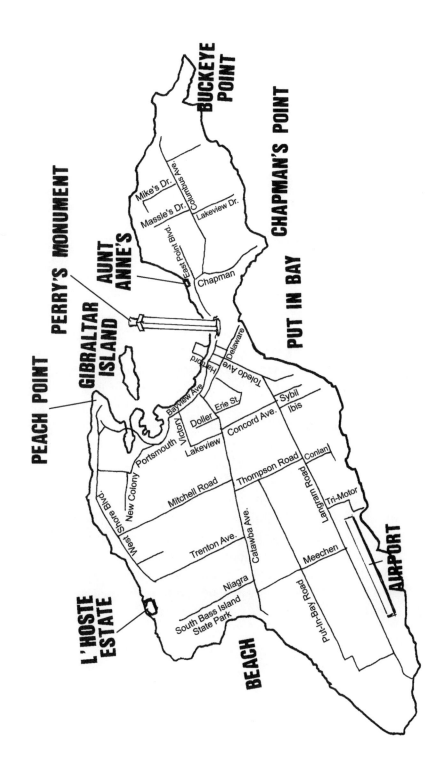

BUCKEYE POINT

CHAPMAN'S POINT

Mike's Dr.

Columbus Ave.

Massle's Dr.

Lakeview Dr.

East Point Blvd.

Chapman

PERRY'S MONUMENT

AUNT ANNE'S

PUT IN BAY

PEACH POINT

GIBRALTAR ISLAND

Delaware

Hanford

Toledo Ave.

Bayview Ave.

Victory Ave.

Sybil

Doller

Erie St.

Ibis

Portsmouth

Concord Ave.

Lakeview

New Colony

Thompson Road

Conlan

Langram Road

Mitchell Road

Tri-Motor

West Shore Blvd.

Catawba Ave.

Trenton Ave.

Meechen

AIRPORT

Niagra

Put-In-Bay Road

South Bass Island State Park

L'HOSTE ESTATE

BEACH

never tell Jack's parents how scared they had been at times in those storms.

On several occasions during those summer vacation visits, Jack and he had to beach the sailboat on a nearby island and wait out a violent southwester overnight. Oh, the wrath they incurred from Uncle Frank and Aunt Anne when they returned the next morning. It didn't matter that they were unharmed.

Emerson fondly recalled when the two of them attached a sign for island tours to Uncle Frank's four seater golf cart and positioned themselves at the ferry boat dock to greet the arriving ferry and Uncle Frank.

Uncle Frank with a twinkle in his eye would tell disembarking passengers, especially the pretty teenaged girls, that the boys gave some of the best tours of the island, including the Perry Monument. It towered over the harbor in recognition of Commodore Perry's victory over the British in the battle of Lake Erie. Uncle Frank was a good promoter for the boys and he enjoyed helping them earn extra spending money for pizzas and ice cream – and in meeting girls.

Emerson also recalled how they would sneak over to Mr. Cassidy's farm and steal watermelons each summer. Mr. Cassisdy, who was the harbormaster, would run out of his farmhouse and fire a shotgun blast of buckshot. But he never hit the boys and they would laugh as they ran home carrying watermelons. In all of those summers, Mr. Cassidy had never caught them.

The good memories couldn't suppress the memory of the accident. Emerson had tried to erase it from his memory, but it just would not go away. Well, he thought to himself, I won't think about it now.

≈ ≈ ≈

The cry of a sea gull brought Emerson back from his thoughts and he looked up in amazement at what appeared before him on a high promontory on South Bass Island's western side.

Looming majestically over the Lake Erie waters was the ominously, huge bow section of a Lake Erie freighter. Lettered on its bow was the name, *SAUVIGNON*.

Behind the bow section was what appeared to be a stone French chateau style house.

Emerson's eyes trailed below the ship's bow and to the edge of the promontory where an iron stairwell clung tightly to the side of the rocky cliff. At the base of the stairs was a small guardhouse which sat on a large, u-shaped dock protruding from the base of the cliff into the lake.

Tied to the dock, he saw a bright yellow high performance boat. It resembled an ocean racing superboat.

Emerson's attention was diverted by the noise of a loud thumping filling the air. A Bell 206 JetRanger helicopter appeared on the horizon and made its way toward the promontory.

The helicopter with the name "L'Hoste" lettered on its side began its descent. It landed on the promontory in an area next to the freighter's bow.

Someone's got a lot of money Emerson thought to himself.

Seeing a member of the Jet Express crew walking

nearby, Emerson stopped him and, nodding toward the promontory, asked, "Who's got the big bucks?"

The crewman responded, "Oh, that's the L'Hoste Estate. They run the biggest fleet of freighters on the Great Lakes out of Cleveland. They just cut off the bow of the *SAUVIGNON*, their fleet's pride and joy. Put it on a barge and had it hauled from the Port of Cleveland to the island about 20 years ago. Caused quite a commotion when the cranes were set up and she was lifted from the barge to the top of the cliff. Then they went and attached the ship to that mansion. They've got a lot of money."

Emerson then remembered that his aunt had written him about some wealthy family attaching the bow of a freighter to a French chateau on the western side of the island. He had no idea that the freighter would be so large.

A great place from which to watch sunsets and rainbows Emerson mused.

"You'll see them flying in and out on that helicopter and running around in that cigarette boat. And if you're doing any boating, keep an eye out for the cigarette boat. They don't seem to care about their wake or running over people."

Looking at his watch, the crewman glanced to the northwest and said, "About any time now, you'll see the *Aragon* on her way to Cleveland's steel plants. She's the biggest and fastest freighter on the Great Lakes."

Looking to the northwest, Emerson didn't see the *Aragon*. He would have to keep his eyes open for her. He thanked the crewman who went on his way.

High in the pilothouse of the *Aragon*, Captain Neuhouser fretted about making up their delayed departure from Duluth. There had been an equipment failure with one of the ore loaders on the dock, causing the delay.

He didn't like to be late. He had a reputation for making his port of calls on schedule and took any delay personally.

Neuhouser's pride had swollen when the L'Hoste family christened the *Aragon* and gave command of the queen of their fleet to him. He would never let them down.

As he saw the Lake Erie islands on the horizon, he ordered more speed.

The *Aragon*'s bow knifed cleanly through the blue waters with the extra surge of power.

~ ~ ~

Running late today my dear Captain Neuhouser? he thought as he stepped away from the telescope which had been aimed at the horizon on the northwest and was mounted near one of the salon's windows in the *SAUVIGNON*.

Movement below and to his left caught his eye and he looked down at the Jet Express bringing another load of passengers to his island Mecca. He unconsciously pulled on his right ear lobe as he watched the Jet Express progress across the lake.

He had heard the copter landing as it returned from Cleveland and their corporate offices. He knew that his son would be joining him momentarily.

Moving to his swivel chair in his elegant study, Jacques L'Hoste slowly eased his weary body into it. He worked out every day in his fully equipped exercise facility to try to fight the aging effect. His 68 years were catching up to his body a bit, but he felt that his mind was crystal clear.

He looked around his study and smiled. He was quite pleased with the remodeling of what had formerly been the *SAUVIGNON*'s foyer and observation lounge. He had expanded the area by incorporating the dunnage area and the captain's quarters into the study. The final touches included black walnut paneling, leather furniture, a marble fireplace, oil paintings, tapestries, fine assorted tables and chairs, and a massive desk and the chair which he now occupied.

He savored the attention he created amongst the islanders and the national media when he had the bow lifted onto the promontory and had it attached to the rear of the chateau which his father built. He enjoyed the solitude that his new study offered and the planning he could accomplish by sitting quietly in the pilothouse on the upper deck.

Life had been fairly good for him mostly due to his tough dealings with people and questionable business interests. He knew how to manipulate and push people. If they didn't cooperate, he had used other methods, including threats and violence, to convince them that it would be in their best interests to align with him.

Some would call his methods despicable or vile. He just called them practical. After all, his methods delivered results and kept in line with the L'Hoste tradition. The underhanded secrets of the trade had been passed down from generation to generation. But unfortunately, it appeared that it would not be passed to his son.

The door opened and his son entered the room.

"Bonjour Papa."

"Bonjour. Where in the hell have you been? I've been waiting for your phone call about the Millington acquisition all morning," Jacques roared contemptuously at his son as he pulled at his right ear lobe.

The Millington Trucking Company with $5.3 billion in revenues would dovetail nicely with the shipping business and Jacques did not want to risk losing it to the other suitors. He should have known better than to have given his son responsibility for the transaction.

Every time that Jacques tried to give his son more responsibility, his son struggled to accept it and deliver results. He wanted his father's title as Chairman & CEO of the L'Hoste Groupe given as a gift. Jacques preferred that he earn it, but his thirty-eight year old son, he realized, was more interested in spending money frivolously than making money for the family.

Francois thought to himself as he watched his father's countenance change into a more imposing style that it was amazing how quickly his father could steal his joie de vivre. Sometimes, he wished that he didn't visit with his father in his study.

Over the years as he watched his father's business style, he observed that his father could use his voice in an interesting and inviting way to make people very comfortable.

So comfortable that he could extract confidential information. His father could also use his deep voice as an effective tool and actually thrived on using it to create a pressure-filled atmosphere.

He did not think that it would be wise to disclose to his father that he had decided not to go into the office. Instead, he played tennis most of the morning with the new secretary in the freight department. But then again, his father probably was already aware of it. His father had a way of knowing things about him that surprised him.

"There must have been a miscommunication Papa. I didn't understand that you meant for me to be involved in the discussions today. Besides, our finance and legal folks are working through the numbers and have not updated me," Francois tried to explain.

Besides, Francois thought quietly, I'm not really interested in the aspects of daily business operations. I would rather travel, race my boats and chase women.

"This is unconscionable that you did not call me as I instructed you! Furthermore, it is presumptive of you not to be fully involved in the negotiations. How do you ever expect to run this massive organization when I retire? How are you going to expand your business acumen?" Jacques lashed out angrily.

He began to flick his right ear lobe as he talked. Francois recognized the sign. When his father began flicking his ear lobe, it meant that he was ready to explode in anger. Francois, the staff at the residence and the senior management team recognized the sign that they were about to incur Jacques' wrath.

"I'll be ready when it's time for me to take over," he replied. What he would never tell his father was that he planned to sell off the business and live off the proceeds while he enjoyed life in Miami where two of his ocean racing boats were docked.

Flicking his ear lobe, Jacques looked down at his desktop for a moment and then exploded.

"You have no savoir-faire! I'm not sure that you will ever be ready! I'll call in to the office and I'll handle this acquisition, just like I usually end up doing."

Reaching for the phone, Jacques hotly continued, "You're just like your good-for-nothing mother."

Francois felt his own anger begin to well up from within.

"Don't talk about her in that manner!"

Enraged himself, Francois turned on his heels and walked quickly out of the study, slamming the door behind him.

When Francois reached his quarters in the chateau, he picked up the phone and dialed the guardhouse on the dock.

"As soon as I change, I'll be down to take the *Mon Ami* for a run. Make sure it's ready for me."

He hung up the phone and began to change, throwing his clothes angrily across the room.

He would take out his frustrations on the lake by opening the throttle on his Merccruiser 425 horsepower engine. He was glad that he had purchased the powerful Carrera 310 Elan.

≈ ≈ ≈

Following the unexpected death of Emerson's wife and three-year old son in a tragic auto accident in Washington six months earlier, Emerson had been drifting. He had been going downhill as he retreated and found solace in drinking in Washington's numerous bars.

He knew that the drinking was not the answer. It wouldn't chase away the ghosts haunting him.

His co-workers at the *Washington Post* had been supportive during his grieving process. John Sedler, his managing editor, had urged his top investigative reporter to take some extra time off to recover.

Emerson had been deeply in love with his wife, Julie, and their son, Matthew, was the apple of his father's eye. He missed both of them intensely.

He knew that they would have wanted him to pick up and go on. Julie had always told him during their 12 years of marriage that he could always do anything that he set his mind to do. She was such a supporter and raving fan. She had called him, her champion.

He didn't feel like anyone's champion.

When he received the news that his Uncle Frank had died, Emerson couldn't bring himself to attend another funeral of a loved one just a month after Julie's and Matthew's – and especially in Put-in-Bay.

He read the last letter from Aunt Anne about how she was struggling emotionally with the loss of Uncle Frank. Over the years, she was prolific in writing him. She continued to encourage him to visit them and would comment on the success Emerson was having in his journalistic adventures around the world.

She had never given up on him – and it was time for Emerson to encourage her and visit her at Put-in-Bay.

~ ~ ~

As the Jet Express rounded Peach Point and moved swiftly past Gibraltar Island, it approached the entrance to Put-in-Bay's harbor. Emerson could see Rattlesnake Island to the northwest and wondered if the rainbows still ended there. The catamaran's jet powered engines began to throttle back as they entered the harbor's no wake zone.

What a panoramic vista presented itself to Emerson as the catamaran moved toward the dock. To the left Emerson could see his aunt's house on East Point Boulevard with the dock stretching into the harbor, then Perry's Monument to the right of his aunt's house, and the waterfront park laid in front of him with its strip of hotels and bars behind it. As his eyes continued their sweep he saw the large number of boats tied up to the docks and sailboats moored in the harbor. He saw a new wharf called The Boardwalk at one end. His gaze continued to the yacht club and Peach Point, across the narrow, shallow channel and finally rested on Gibraltar Island, guarding the entrance to Put-in-Bay's harbor.

It was good to be back. There just was something calming and inviting about the island he thought to himself as he slung his duffel bag strap over his right shoulder and grabbed his lap top computer case in his left hand.

He moved with the disembarking passengers who were chatting happily. The long dock was crowded with taxis, the tour tram and bicycle and golf cart vendors trying to attract clientele.

In order to avoid the people massing near the small general store on the dock next to the harbormaster's office, Emerson began walking on the right side of the dock near the water where a number of boats had been tied or were in process of being tied.

He had just been walking on this side for a few seconds when he heard a grunt and felt someone fall against him. He awkwardly tried to stop the person's fall and steady them when he caught the whiff of perfume.

It was Giorgio – the same kind that his wife, Julie, had worn. Sensing the fragrance brought a sudden rush to Emerson.

He noticed the striking auburn hair and heard a voice saying, "Oh silly me. I am so sorry. I was securing the launch's lines and tripped over my own two feet."

Her head turned and Emerson was looking into a pair of deep green eyes, the color of emeralds. Her face framed a cute nose and the nicest, prettiest smile that Emerson had ever seen – it was just perfect! Her smile widened as she looked at Emerson.

The smile caused Emerson to break into a big grin. Then he felt a sense of warmth spreading over his face as he realized that she was talking to him, and he was so focused on how beautiful she was that he wasn't paying attention to what she was saying. He was drinking in her beauty.

She was about five foot seven, suntanned and looked breathtaking in her white Ohio State tee shirt and denim short shorts.

He was embarrassed that he hadn't been listening. This was a first for him.

"I said I am so sorry. Are you ok?" he heard her ask as his mind returned to earth.

Somewhat sheepishly he replied, "Oh, sure. No problem. Glad I was here to catch you!"

"Sometimes, I am so clumsy ...," her comment was interrupted by a scream from the launch that she had just tied up.

"Mommy!"

The scream was followed by a splash on the far side of the launch.

"Austin? Where are you?" she called. "It's my son!"

Setting down his lap top and dropping his duffel bag, Emerson leaped from the dock to the launch and quickly reached the far side. The boy's mother followed on his heels.

Seeing the boy's head disappearing beneath the harbor's surface, Emerson pulled off his shoes and dove into the harbor.

His strong strokes took him immediately to where the boy had sunk. Taking a deep breath, Emerson dove beneath the water's surface.

Feeling around, he quickly found the boy, gripped him tightly and returned to the surface.

"You OK son?" He asked as the boy began coughing water out of his mouth and gasping for air.

"I think so," replied the boy between gasps.

"Let's get back to the boat. You're safe with me." Emerson pulled the boy in close and swam him to the launch's side.

Looking up from the water, Emerson saw that a crowd had gathered and several hands were extended to pull both the boy and Emerson on board.

Seeing that all was under control, the people who had gathered began to leave.

Emerson turned to the boy, now being comforted by his mother.

"Are ya doing better now bud?" he asked the boy.

"Yes sir," he replied nervously.

"Austin, what were you doing? I told you to sit still while I tied the lines," his mother lectured.

"Mommy, I was just looking over the side and I saw the baby ducks swimming by with their mommy and I tried to touch them."

They looked toward the water and saw the mother duck and her ducklings swimming close to the shore.

"Kids!" his mother commented feeling somewhat frazzled by the incident.

"Kids, they're great aren't they? You just don't know what they will get into," said a grinning Emerson as he slipped his shoes on.

"Especially four year olds like this one. Oh, how can I thank you for what you did?" Then realizing that he was wet, she said, "And you're wet. Do you have dry clothes? Do you need a place to change?"

"I'm fine. I'm fine." Seeing that someone had set his bags in the boat, Emerson bent to pick them up and continued, "I can change when I check in at the hotel across the park."

As the three of them stepped onto the dock, Emerson decided to do something that he hadn't done in years. He took a deep breath and cast a quick glance at her left hand. He saw the wedding ring.

Of course she would have to be married he mused disappointedly.

"Mommy, can I give him a hug? I like him," said Austin as he looked from his mother to Emerson.

"Well, you're both wet so that won't create a problem. Go ahead," she responded and looked up with an inviting smile at Emerson.

Kids always liked him. No matter where he went. For some reason, they wanted to be with him. Emerson bent down and gave Austin a big hug.

"OK, Austin. Now you listen to your mom and do what she says, OK?"

"Yes sir." Turning to his mother, Austin asked, "What's his name Mommy?"

Looking down at her son, she replied, "Well, we'll just have to find out!" Turning to Emerson, "With everything that's just happened, I didn't introduce myself. I'm Martine Tobin and, as you can gather, this is my son, Austin."

Gazing into those deep green eyes, Emerson offered, "I'm Emerson Moore, rescuer extraordinaire."

Laughing, Martine said, "You certainly did come to our rescue today."

He beamed. "And are you vacationing here?"

"We're visiting my father here for a month."

Pointing to Gibraltar Island across the bay, she explained, "He's a geology professor at Ohio State and is working the whole summer at their research facility on Gibraltar Island. Something to do with studying the caves on South Bass Island."

The cave comment sent a shiver up Emerson's spine.

As Martine looked at his duffel bag, she observed, "And I take it that you are here for the week-end."

"Maybe a week." Pointing to his aunt's house on East Point, he continued, "I'm actually going to spend some time with my aunt since my uncle died earlier this year. It's been years since I've visited the island and I'm looking forward to getting reacquainted with it again. I may be doing some biking and sailing while I'm here."

"Perhaps I'll see you around then," she smiled as she spoke. Taking Austin's hand, she said, "OK young man, let's pick up some groceries for grandpa."

"Wait, I forgot my recorder." Austin jumped back into the launch and retrieved a recorder. Smiling, he held it up for Emerson to see and pushed the play button.

"This is my favorite movie." And the soundtrack from Disney's *The Littlest Mermaid* began to play.

"And one of my favorites, too," responded Emerson with a touch of melancholy as he recalled watching it with his family.

"Bye-bye Mr. Moore," said Austin.

"Be good," Emerson called. "Hope to see you around too!"

Martine smiled as she realized the comment was directed at her.

"Thank you again," called Martine as they began to walk away with the music playing from the recorder.

He paused for a moment to watch her as she walked away and then turned. My but she is so gorgeous – and so nice and so married he lamented to himself.

What a sweetheart! Wait a second he thought to himself. It's only been six months since the death of his wife and son. What was he doing even thinking about someone else already? Life is funny he mused. You never knew what it would present you with. He did know one thing for certain – he missed his wife and son!

He dodged a speeding golf cart driven by some weekend visitors on Bayview as he started his trek across De-Rivera's waterfront park to the Park Hotel.

$$\sim\ \sim\ \sim$$

Gripping Austin's hand tightly, Martine thought to herself – what a nice gentleman Emerson Moore was. And nice looking too!

She cleared her mind of her thoughts. After all, she was married – even if her husband was becoming more of a jerk lately. She was resolved to being his wife and staying committed to him.

She opened the door and they entered the store to make their purchases

$$\sim\ \sim\ \sim$$

The Park Hotel's clerk looked up from her work momentarily and out to the sun-drenched street to the park across the street from the hotel. She observed a man carrying a duffel bag and a smaller bag set the bags down and begin to look from one end of the street to the other as if he was trying to find someone or a particular business. From the looks of him, she was hoping that he would check in there. She went back to her work.

As the Park Hotel's door opened, the clerk looked up and saw the somewhat ruggedly, good-looking man enter the hotel's Victorian style lobby.

"Good morning, sir. And how may I help you?" the twenty year old clerk inquired cheerily as she now realized that his clothes were wet. She decided not to ask why.

"Reservations for Emerson Moore."

Emerson's aunt had invited him to stay at the house, but he just wasn't sure that he could handle it. He thought there would be too many memories of Jack.

His aunt also wanted to greet him at the ferry dock, but he had told her that he wasn't sure which ferry he would catch and that he would just show up sometime that day.

Emerson set his duffel bag and lap top computer on the floor and leaned against the counter. He cast a look around the lobby and took in the Victorian furniture arranged in the spacious lobby area. The walls of the lobby were covered with a blue Victorian wallpaper – something his wife would have enjoyed.

"I've got it right here. One non-smoking room for one occupant for seven nights."

"Right and I had requested a room which overlooked the harbor."

"Yes sir. We've got you on the third floor waterfront view.

You'll be able to see the whole harbor from your window. Check in isn't really until three, but the room is available now, so we can get you checked in now. If you'll just sign here, please and let me have a credit card to swipe through."

Emerson produced his credit card from his wet wallet and then picked up the pen that the attractive desk clerk slid across the counter. He smiled at a couple walking through the lobby.

Completing the registration form, Emerson commented, "That should do it." And retrieved his returned credit card and the key that she had extended.

Picking up his bags, he walked up two flights of stairs to his room.

Unlocking the door, he entered the high ceilinged room complete with Victorian style furnishings. It reminded him of his aunt's home.

He approached the three narrow windows which gave him a view of the harbor. To the east, he could barely see his aunt's home over the park's trees. He saw the harbor and Middle Bass Island across the harbor. To the north he could see Gibraltar Island, and he thought momentarily of Martine and her fragrance. He thought that he could make out her launch moving toward the Gibraltar Island dock.

It had been a long time! A long time since he had visited here and a long time since he had looked at a woman and felt that he would like to get to know her.

Changing into dry clothes, he sat in a rocker that was conveniently positioned near the windows and resumed gazing at the surrounding area and allowing fond memories to cloud his mind. He soon fell asleep.

~ ~ ~

A gnawing feeling in his stomach, which was probably triggered by the aroma of roasted chicken floating into his room, awoke Emerson from his nap. He realized he forgot to have lunch and decided to grab some chicken at the Chicken Patio in front of the hotel.

The Chicken Patio was famous for its tasty chicken from its open-air charcoal grills. Placing his order, Emerson sat at one of the picnic tables and watched people stream by on the sidewalk which fronted the eating area.

When the order was delivered, he savored his first bite. Just like he remembered. At least some things hadn't changed.

Once he completed the meal and paid his bill, he began the walk to his aunt's home.

~ ~ ~

Emerson walked across the park, and past the towering Perry Monument. It was the second highest monument in the United States, topped only by his hometown's Washington Monument.

As he walked past the Islumate house, he looked at the detailed workmanship on the steamboat style, white home across the street from his aunt's. It had been designated as a national historical landmark.

He opened his aunt's gate and heard a small squeaking noise as it swung shut. He thought to himself that it needed some oiling. He looked around the yard. It wasn't quite as well kept as it used to be, probably due to his uncle's death. He could busy himself and help out a bit. He mounted the steps and knocked on the white door of the green Victorian house.

"Coming," came the feminine reply from within.

He looked around the old familiar screened-in porch as he waited. The porch where they had sat and visited or played Monopoly and cards until late at night under its solitary light. The dock appeared to be in good repair and there was a small, motorized dinghy tied to the dock.

It was good to be back in these familiar surroundings he decided.

The white gingerbread screen door swung open and his sixty-five year old aunt appeared. Her blonde hair had grayed but she still seemed to have that high energy level that would drive Uncle Frank wild. She didn't know how to sit and completely relax he would often say.

"Emerson, Emerson. My, my. Just look at what a handsome man you have become!" she cooed incessantly as she reached to draw him into a giant hug.

"Aunt Anne, you're just the same," Emerson said as he wrapped his arms around her.

"I've missed you tremendously." And she began to sob as she held him tighter. He was all the family that she had left.

Emerson held her tighter and tears welled up in his

eyes. He realized that he had been wrong in all of these years. He should have visited her and Uncle Frank.

"Now enough of this feeling sorry for each other. Let's go in the house. I've got a fresh apple pie that's due out of the oven right about now. Come on." With a burst of energy, she turned to go into the house. "I don't want it to burn. I hope you do recall that your aunt makes the best apple pies – that's what you used to tell me!"

"Yes ma'am," he replied. He followed her into the house fresh with the pleasant odor of a baking apple pie.

They walked through her antique filled front room to the kitchen in the rear of the house. She opened the oven door and a fresh burst of apple pie aroma filled the air.

"Hmmmmmmmm," Emerson moaned as he recalled how tasty her pies were.

She turned to him as she set the pie on the stovetop.

"I bet this brings back fond memories!" she said proudly. She was the best cook in his mother's family.

"It sure does."

"While it's cooling a bit, I'll show you the house so you can see the changes that have been made since you were last here."

She pointed out the renovated downstairs bath and led him up to the second floor. She opened the door to her bedroom and Emerson saw that she still had the carved mahogany queen size bed with the step stool stored neatly underneath it.

She had redecorated the room with yellow floral wallpaper and sheer Victorian curtains with draped valances. Her fainting couch had been recovered and the room was completed by two nightstands, two lamps, a dresser and her rocker which was located next to the window overlooking the harbor.

"I like the wallpaper. It brightens the room," Emerson offered to make sure that his aunt realized that he recognized some of the changes.

"I needed to bring something to this floor to cheer it up."

Emerson understood her comment. His uncle had died in bed of a massive heart attack.

She walked by the closed door to his cousin Jack's bedroom without making a comment.

"I've still got two guest bedrooms up here," she said as she opened a door to reveal the room that Emerson used to stay in.

The bedroom was furnished by a queen size oak sleigh bed with a step stool and nightstand. It had pale gold and rose floral wallpaper and gold draw draperies on triple windows making it a bright room.

Emerson had always felt that the room was gaudy, but he would never hurt his aunt's feelings.

The room was completed by an armoire and a wicker chair and desk. And what he had called during his summer visits the "Gone with the Wind" lamp was still there.

They walked past the bathroom with its claw foot tub to the last bedroom and Emerson saw that it had been completely redecorated. Gone was the lavender wallpaper. In its place was a blue and green floral wallcovering. The brass queen sized bed was covered with a green floral bedcover

"You've been busy. When do you rest?"

"Rest. Don't have time for rest. I've got too many things to do," she retorted.

"This year, I was elected President of the Put-in-Bay Library Women's Association," she proudly explained.

He wasn't surprised. She had always been civic minded and supportive of the community. So had been his uncle.

They returned to the kitchen where he took the seat that she offered to him. He couldn't get over her high energy level. It certainly had not diminished over the years.

They spent the rest of the afternoon enjoying her hot apple pie and catching up on the past twenty years. They talked about Uncle Frank's death, her grieving process and his loss of his wife and son. They both avoided any conversation about Jack.

≈ ≈ ≈

They had been so engrossed in catching up that they failed to notice the time.

Aunt Anne looked up at the kitchen clock.

"Land sakes. Look at that time. You're probably hungry for some dinner and I haven't started cooking yet."

"Aunt Anne, tonight's on me. Let's go to one of your favorite restaurants and I'll treat."

"We don't need to do that. I can make something real quick."

"No, no. You could use some relaxing. Where would you like to go?"

She thought quickly and responded, "The Boardwalk has lobster bisque that is out of this world. And they have fresh Lake Erie walleye and perch at the Fish Shack which is also located on the Boardwalk. They've got an upper deck where you can eat and enjoy the sunset."

Rising from his chair, Emerson said, "Let's do it then!"

Grabbing a sweater from the back of her chair, Aunt Anne stood and led the way to the detached garage. Opening the garage door, Emerson saw the golf cart and the 1929 Model A Ford truck that had been his uncle's pride and joy.

"We kept that truck all of these years. You recall riding in it, don't you?"

"Oh yes," Emerson remembered the Sunday parades and throwing candy at the onlookers from the back of the cream colored truck with its deep green fenders. He had never been permitted to drive it. Maybe he would have a chance now.

"Looks like I might be spending some time in giving it a good cleaning," Emerson commented as he saw the truck in need of a good wash and waxing.

"Have at it. I do windows. I do floors. I do dishes. I do laundry. I don't do washing and waxing trucks or oil changes," his aunt responded.

"I'll take care of all of that while I'm here."

"Maybe you can drive it in the Fourth of July parade while you're here," she suggested.

"I'd like that."

Parked next to the truck was a 4-seater golf cart with a roof and cargo baskets in the rear. It had a windshield with wipers, headlights, taillights and a rear view mirror. Quite an upgrade from the basic cart that his aunt and uncle owned previously.

They walked to the cart and Aunt Anne settled into the passenger side. Emerson started its gas-powered engine and drove out of the garage to town.

≈ ≈ ≈

Business was picking up as more people began to gather on the Boardwalk on the old Doller Dock which extended into Put-in-Bay's harbor. People were jostling for good tables on the upper deck in anticipation of the coming sunset at 9:30.

Loud music was being played by the band in the Marvin's Garden bar area and dance floor on the first level. Even though it was early, some partyers were already showing the signs of too many drinks and were dancing energetically.

Emerson, carrying an order of lobster bisque and

perch, wove his way through the boisterous crowd and made his way up the steps to the more sedate crowd seated on the upper deck.

Setting the food on the table that his aunt had secured, he sat down and they both began to devour the delicious meal.

As they looked westerly, they could see the sun in its final stages of setting. The bright blue sky came alive with streaks of orange as the massive, fiery sun began to sink below the horizon.

What a beautiful sight thought Emerson. He realized how much he had missed the island.

A round of applause broke out from the watchers as the last vestiges of the sun disappeared from sight, announcing the official start of the nightly festivities in Put-in-Bay.

Emerson excused himself to briefly visit the men's room on the first level.

As he was returning from the men's room and approaching the bar area he noticed a well attired man brazenly putting his arm around a red-headed lady who was seated with her back to Emerson and with an older, white-haired gentleman. It appeared that he wanted her to dance with him.

For some reason, the lady appeared familiar to Emerson. He paused to watch in hopes that he might get a glimpse of her face.

The lady seemed to be uncomfortable with the man's attempts to put his arm around her as she continued to push his arm away from her. He looked like a lounge lizard to Emerson.

The lady's body language indicated that she was visibly distraught.

When the older gentleman arose to face the brazen man, he was shoved back into his chair.

Emerson did not like what he saw.

Just then, the redheaded woman turned her head to the side and Emerson realized that it was Martine.

He immediately stepped into the bar area and approached the man from behind.

As the man took a step backwards, Emerson stuck out his leg and the man tripped, falling on his back.

The band stopped playing and a hush grew over the crowd. All eyes were focused on Emerson and the man lying on his back on the dance floor whose narrow eyes were sinisterly glaring up at Emerson.

A second man with a slight build and shifty eyes pushed his way through the crowd and quickly bent to assist the first man in getting back on his feet.

"What do you think you're doing?" asked the second man as he tried to act in an intimidating manner to Emerson.

Before Emerson could respond, Martine stood and addressed the second man, "Tim, he wouldn't take no for an answer. He wanted to dance with me and I didn't care to dance with him. Dad and I are trying to have dinner."

Glaring back at her, Tim screeched, "I told Francois that it was all right to have a dance with my wife. He had admired you from the bar and I said to go ahead and take you to the dance floor for a dance."

So this wimpish looking fellow was her husband Emerson thought. What a mismatch!

"I do have a say in who I dance with and don't dance with. I don't need to take orders from you!" she snapped angrily.

"And I agree with her," chipped in the older gentleman.

Ignoring her comments, Tim turned to Emerson and angrily stated, "And who do you think you are getting involved in our family matters?"

Smelling the alcohol on Tim's breath, Emerson quipped, "A knight in shining armor who slays dragons for pretty damsels in distress."

"You should mind you own business." Looking at Francois, the first man, he smiled and said, "And Francois is not a dragon. In fact, he's the only prince in this bar."

Oh boy, a real suck up too Emerson thought.

"Thank you my friend," responded Francois. Turning to Emerson and seeing that a crowd had gathered around them, Francois continued haughtily, "Perhaps I was a little out of line in my persistence to dance with this beautiful lady. Perhaps it was the wine that we have consumed. Who knows?"

Growing more sullen and ominous, Francois moved closer to Emerson and lowered his voice, "But you my unwise friend have entered dangerous waters by causing embarrassment to me. This I will not forget. You'll regret the day you met me. Remember that."

"I'm shaking in my shoes," retorted Emerson as he brushed aside the comment.

A voice shouted from the steps.

"Emerson, there you are. You were gone so long I thought someone had kidnapped you."

Aunt Anne descended the steps from the upper deck.

Tim placed his arm around Francois and said, "Let's go to the Beer Barrel and the drinks will be on me. Besides, there's more room to dance there."

As Tim and Francois began to leave the bar, Tim shouted back to Martine in a threatening manner, "And you! When I get back tonight, we'll have a talk and it won't be pretty!"

They left the Boardwalk and headed across the park toward the Beer Barrel. As the band began to play, Martine turned to Emerson as his aunt joined them.

"Well, you're becoming my rescuer extraordinaire, my knight in shining armor."

"Sometimes, I just happen to be in the right place at the right time."

"That's twice today, Emerson – and I do appreciate it," she said sincerely as she looked up at him.

Those eyes are so green and so alluring Emerson thought to himself.

"Oh, I'm forgetting my manners. Let me introduce you

to my father, Professor Anderson. Dad, Emerson is the man who rescued Austin today."

Extending his hand in a warm handshake, Professor Anderson commented, "A pleasure. A real pleasure. I also appreciate what you did for Austin today and your help this evening. If it hadn't been for my bad back slowing me down, I would have put L'Hoste in his place tonight, even though Tim works for him. His actions were entirely inappropriate."

Two interesting facts tonight Emerson mused to himself. Martine's husband works for Francois L'Hoste and Francois seems like a real piece of work. He'd have to be careful of him if he encountered him in the future.

"Now Dad, you're going to raise that blood pressure of yours," Martine said soothingly as she tried to get him to settle down.

"It's my pleasure sir. Say where's my buddy Austin?" Emerson asked.

"He's spending the night with one of Dad's research assistants on Gibraltar."

"And just when do I get included in this conversation? Or am I just chopped liver?"

Realizing that his aunt had been standing next to him without being introduced, Emerson made the introductions and they chatted briefly about life on the islands.

As the noise on the boardwalk grew and the evening waned, they decided it was time to return to their respective homes.

As they reached the entrance to the dock and to the

shuttle for Gibraltar Island, they paused to say goodnight.

"One of these days, I'm going to make it out to Gibraltar Island for a tour. When I summered here, the island was officially off limits to visitors," Emerson commented wistfully.

"How about a tour tomorrow? That's the least that I can do for everything you've done today for Austin, Dad and me. And Aunt Anne, you're welcome to come too," Martine offered warmly.

"Oh my no. I've been on the island. No need for me to go. Emerson, you go along and take the tour." Turning to Martine, Aunt Anne with a mischievous look on her face said, "Lord knows that Emerson was chased off that island for trespassing enough times when he was a teen."

"You knew?" Emerson was flabbergasted.

"Of course. The security guards would tell me about it when they came into the restaurant for meals," she grinned.

"Let's make it 10:00 sharp. I'll meet you at the island's dock," Martine suggested.

"See you then. Good night Professor."

Martine and her father made their way to the shuttle while Emerson and Aunt Anne stepped into the parked golf cart for the short drive home.

Emerson planned to use his aunt's dinghy which was tied to her dock next to the small sailboat which belonged to one of the neighbors.

~ ~ ~

The morning sun cast a reflection off the harbor water which seemed as smooth as glass that morning. Emerson turned the bow of the dinghy toward the dock at Gibraltar Island.

As he grew nearer the dock, he could see Martine on the dock waiting to greet him. She waved as he neared and he returned her wave.

"Welcome to Ohio State country," she cheerily called as he tossed her the mooring line and shut off the small outboard motor.

"I've never had a tour of the island and am looking forward to it."

As they began to walk from the dock, Martine pointed to a three story, limestone building.

"That's the Stone Laboratory Building. There're labs on the first floor where they study birds, fish and environmental issues. They're doing some work on the zebra mussel infestation of the Great Lakes and trying to resolve some of the problems they create. Dad says that they can clog up the intake pipes at water processing plants."

"Yeah, I've read about some of the issues in the *Post* and in *USA Today* articles," responded Emerson. "Where's your husband today?"

"Oh, he was out late last night partying with Francois. He's up at Dad's cottage sleeping it off."

As they continued up the path past the student dining hall and Gibraltar House, she paused momentarily at the edge of a cliff which provided a view of the harbor and downtown Put-in-Bay. She pointed to an area at the base of the cliff which had a small beach. It was an area for bonfires surrounded by benches.

"The summer students often have bonfires there," she offered as an explanation. "Dad, Austin and I have roasted marshmallows around a fire down there. And to the left is the old boathouse which now houses bats. They actually call it the Bat House now."

Climbing farther up the hill, they approached a gazebo which provided a view of Lake Erie on two sides of the island.

Seeing a group of Adirondack chairs painted red and gray clustered in front of the gazebo, Emerson commented with a grin, "You sure can tell that you're in Ohio State country."

They could hear the shouts of a lively sand volleyball game underway on the other side of the gazebo as some of the summer students played an energetic game.

Seeing that one of the teams was short a player, Emerson shouted, "Need another player?"

"Yes. Come and join us!" several shouted.

"Do you mind if I play one game? I love volleyball, and it's hard for me to pass up a game."

"No, no. Go ahead. I'll just enjoy the breeze and sit here and watch."

Martine positioned one of the red and gray painted chairs

in the shade of a maple so that she could watch the game.

Playing hard and furious, Emerson's team began to edge ahead of the other team. Bodies were flying and landing in the sand. The setting and spiking were challenging. Twenty minutes passed and the game was over with Emerson's team's come from behind victory.

"Good game. Good game. Just one more game," came the congratulations and pleadings from Emerson's teammates.

Mopping his brow with his already wet tee shirt sleeve, Emerson smiled, "Thanks guys. But I promised the pretty lady that I'd play just one game."

Martine felt her face flush. "Don't mind me. Go ahead and play another."

"No, no. I said just one and I need to keep my promise." Leaning closer to her so that the players could not over-hear, he continued, "Besides, I'm having a more difficult time than I expected in keeping up with those twenty-year olds! I need a break!"

Laughing mischievously Martine countered, "Too much for you old timer? Maybe you need to borrow some of Dad's vitamins. Come on. I'll show you the rest of the island."

They walked past the main residence hall and neared Cooke's Castle which was constructed from limestone and offered a panoramic view of the water surrounding three sides of the island.

"Dad said that the castle was built by Jay Cooke who financed the civil war by selling war bonds in support of the Union. He used the castle as a retreat from the summer

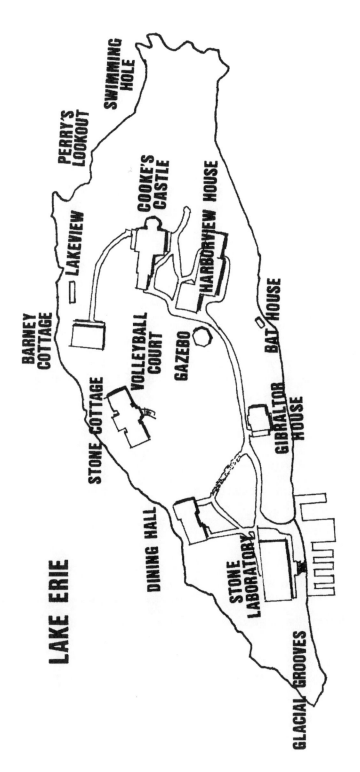

LAKE ERIE

BARNEY COTTAGE

PERRY'S LOOKOUT

SWIMMING HOLE

LAKEVIEW

COOKE'S CASTLE

HARBORVIEW HOUSE

STONE COTTAGE

VOLLEYBALL COURT

GAZEBO

BAT HOUSE

GIBRALTOR HOUSE

DINING HALL

STONE LABORATORY

GLACIAL GROOVES

GIBRALTAR ISLAND

heat in Philadelphia and often had important visitors here including Presidents and Union Generals. Ohio State University is in process of restoring the castle," she said as they climbed the steps to the first floor.

Entering the 15-room house, Emerson was amazed by the workmanship. He peered into Cooke's study and admired the built-in wood bookcases and the view from its numerous windows. Pointing to a monument in the front yard, he asked, "Do you know what that's about?"

"Yes, Dad said that Cooke was an admirer of Commodore Perry who won the Battle of Lake Erie and had that monument erected to honor his victory. Cooke wanted to build a larger monument here but a decision was made to build the monument on South Bass."

They both looked above the treetops and could see Perry's Peace Monument on South Bass, towering over both islands.

Still sweating from playing volleyball, Emerson suggested, "Let's find the swimming beach on the island. During those wild summer visits of my youth, my cousin and I used to boat over to the island and sneak onto it. We'd swim there as long as we could before we would be run off for trespassing."

"Sure, it's over the rise."

They followed a winding path to the top of an iron stairwell which lead down the side of the cliff to a limestone rock precipice and a stony beach. They descended the stairwell and carefully made their way down the slippery rock to the beach.

Shucking his shoes and shirt and emptying his pockets of his wallet and keys, Emerson said, "I need just a quick dip to cool off. Want to join me?" He carefully walked onto the rocky lake bottom and enjoyed its crystal clear water.

"Oh my gosh, no! I don't have my suit. But you go ahead and cool off!"

The water felt good and quickly cooled Emerson. He emerged from the water, slipped on his shoes and picked up his other belongings.

"I'll just carry these until the air dries me, and with this heat and breeze, it shouldn't take too long."

Martine glanced at his muscular chest and quickly averted her eyes. He is a well-built man she thought to herself as they climbed up the iron staircase and headed back toward the Cooke Castle.

"OK. Let's go past the Castle and I'll take you to the Barney Cottage. That's where Dad is staying while he is on the island and we are staying with him."

"Great. I'm looking forward to seeing your dad and hearing about his work in the caves."

As they crested a hill the Lakeview shelter house came into view and they saw her dad and Austin sitting together and reading a book. *The Littlest Mermaid* soundtrack music was playing from Austin's recorder.

As they approached, Austin saw Martine and Emerson. He jumped down and ran to greet them.

"Mr. Moore!" he cried excitedly. "My hero!"

And he wrapped his arms around Emerson's legs in a big hug.

"I thought I was your hero!" came a surly voice from the doorway of the cottage. Everyone's head turned and they saw Tim sullenly standing in the doorway and rubbing his forehead. "Does anyone around here know where you keep the damn aspirin?"

Austin saw his father in the doorway and hid behind Emerson's leg so that he could peer around it.

"I'll get it for you. You couldn't see it if you tried," stated Martine stonily and she began to stride to the cottage.

"Hey Bub, where's your shirt? You always walk around like that to show off?"

Quickly slipping his shirt over his head, Emerson did his best to maintain his composure, especially in front of Austin. "Thanks for reminding me. I took a swim to cool off after a quick volleyball game here and it looks like I'm dry enough now to put the shirt back on."

"Volleyball. All that shouting woke me up. I need to get my rest. Go play your volleyball somewhere else. You don't belong on this island!"

Biting his tongue, Emerson began to reply when Professor Anderson interrupted him.

"Now that will be just about enough Timothy. I should remind you that you are a guest on this island and I expect you to be cordial to all visitors – as difficult as that may be for you. And if the students here want to play volleyball during the day, that is their right!" he said perfunctorily.

"Whatever!" Tim retorted sarcastically and reentered the cottage as Martine handed him his aspirin.

Turning toward Emerson, Professor Anderson said, "I apologize for the display of poor manners by my son-in-law. I would trust that you will understand."

"No problem Professor."

The professor motioned for him to take a chair as Austin began to play with a toy truck in the dirt nearby.

"This used to be a more peaceful place until Tim joined us two days ago. We could sit here and actually enjoy the view of the lake and Rattlesnake Island."

Martine rejoined them and took a seat next to her father.

"Dad, did Tim say anything to you about his newest business venture?"

"You mean newest business failure!" Turning to Emerson, the professor added, "One of the biggest mistakes that I made in my life was allowing her to marry that idiot!"

"Now Dad!" Martine began.

"No. I will not have anymore 'Now Dad's'! Everything that wonder boy does backfires. He continually gets you into financial problems with his harebrained idea of the month attempts to get rich quick. If it wasn't for you and Austin, I'd kill him myself." The professor's face began to get red as his anger grew.

"Emerson, Tim means well. It's just that he has run into some problems from time to time that cause his endeavors to fail!" Martine tried to explain. It seemed that part of her role in life was in becoming a peacemaker between her husband and father.

"The problem is called too much alcohol. And that will be the downfall of his marriage!"

A cool breeze drifted from the lake but did very little to reduce the climbing temperature in the Professor.

"Emerson, the L'Hoste son who accosted me last night at the Boardwalk is Tim's boss. Tim has a position in the L'Hoste marketing department and is working on a developmental project for a L'Hoste resort on South Bass Island. It's hush hush now until they make the public announcement. We would have to move from Columbus to the Cleveland area initially, which is the reason that Dad is so upset. If the project moves forward, then we would move to South Bass Island. "

"Sounds like a great opportunity, and the island is an idyllic setting to raise Austin," Emerson offered encouragingly.

"Can you imagine being frozen in here on the island during the winters with that idiot? She wouldn't suffer from cabin fever during those long winter months, she would suffer from cabin plague. Both of them – Martine and Austin, living with that creep! He stole my wife away from me and now he wants the rest of my family."

An edge of bitterness had crept into the professor's voice.

Emerson looked questioning at Martine and she mouthed silently, "Later."

"Dad, we're getting distracted and forgetting why we

invited Emerson to visit the island today. I finished giving him a tour and thought you'd enjoy telling him about your work here."

"Yes, yes. You're quite right." Turning to Emerson, the professor continued, "South Bass Island is honeycombed with more than 26 caves. You have to be careful if you step in a depression on the island. It may be over an undiscovered cave and signal that the cave's roof is weakening. I'd advise you to be wary of them if you're out and about the island."

Emerson felt a shudder run through him as he again recalled his cave experience.

"I can assure you that cave exploration is not on my list of island activities. I saw enough caves when I summered here."

"So then, you are probably familiar with some of the findings such as human bones from the Erie Indian tribe and their cooking utensils, stone axes and flints?"

"Yes, I am."

Martine saw that her dad was becoming oblivious to their earlier conversation as he moved forward with the discussion about his passion – geology. She looked at Emerson and saw how intently he was listening.

"What you are probably not familiar with are the geophysical properties that caused the creations of the caves. In 1904, Edward H. Kraus advanced a theory about the cave's formations as a result of his studies. While there had been no volcanic activity in the area, there was evidence of some sort of disturbance which caused the caves to form. He advanced that the cave formation was the result of anhydrite hydration which formed gypsum. The hydration process increases volume by thirty-three to sixty-two per cent and, at the same time, creates great pressure. After the expansion process and the gypsum is formed, water absorbs the gypsum over time – resulting in the creation of the caverns."

The professor, now fully enjoying his lecture, continued, "My efforts this summer are to substantiate Kraus' theories, take samples and observe the horizontally stratified rock formations within the caves. I have been provided with two student assistants to further my research and to accompany me on my explorations of the caves.

"In addition, I will be taking samples of the glittering white crystals of strontium from Crystal Cave which is located below the Heineman Winery. You may not have known that strontium has been used in the manufacture of fireworks, dyes and sugar refining. I will also be running some tests on several of the Crystal Cave's stalactites and stalagmites.

"I'll spend time exploring Paradise, Mammoth, Dunn, Victory and Perry caves to confirm several of our initial findings and to correlate the daily variance in the level of the caves' water to the rise and fall of the water in Lake Erie. There may be evidence of subterranean channels."

With a smug look of pride on his face, the professor expectantly looked at Emerson.

"Impressive sir. You do have your hands full."

Martine looked at her watch and said, "It's about lunchtime. Could we invite you to stay for lunch, Emerson?"

"No. I should be going back to my aunt's house." Standing he reached to shake the professor's hand. "Thank you sir for enlightening me about the cave formations. I found it most intriguing and may want to do a story on this for *The Washington Post* at some point in the future."

"Quite a story it would make!" the professor responded with a raised eyebrow in a display of interest.

Feeling his legs being hugged, Emerson looked down and saw Austin. "I've got to go little buddy."

"Please stay. You're so nice!" he begged.

"Maybe some other time." He patted Austin on the head as he turned to leave. He didn't want to take a chance of running into Martine's husband, especially with the mood that he was in.

"I'll walk you down to the dock," stated Martine as she matched her stride to Emerson's.

As they descended the path, she explained her father's earlier comment.

"Emerson, what my father meant when he said that Tim stole his wife away was in regards to an accident 6 years ago. My folks and Tim and I all had too much to drink at a New Year's Eve party in Columbus.

"As best as I can recall, Dad and Tim got into an argument about who was going to drive us home. Tim said he would because it was his car. My mother sat up front because she gets carsick if she rides in the back.

"I sat behind her and Dad sat behind Tim. Long story

short. We ran a red light and a truck crashed into us. It was Tim's fault. The other driver, Tim, Dad and I had minor injuries. Mom was in bad shape with brain damage.

"It didn't appear that she was going to come out of this very well and Dad had to make a decision concerning her quality of life. It had been something that he and she had talked about in the past. If one of them should become incapacitated, the other was expected to make the hard decision.

"Dad had them turn off the life support system and just medicate her to make her feel comfortable. She lasted for five days and he was there the whole time. He never has forgiven Tim for what he did that night. And he has never truly forgiven himself for allowing Tim to drive when he knew it was the wrong thing to do."

Emerson could see the tears in Martine's eyes.

"I am so sorry," he consoled her.

"Ever since then, Tim has struggled with his drinking and business ventures. He has failed at just about everything he has tried. And I struggle to support him. Dad has never forgiven him for taking his wife away. He holds him responsible," she added.

"That's a tough one," was all Emerson could say.

Emerson thought to himself as they neared the moored dinghy that Tim has no idea what he had with his wife. Her outside beauty was surpassed by the beauty within. What a saint she was for tolerating and supporting her husband! She had a heart of gold.

Emerson felt the stirrings in his heart. Why did she have to be married? He'd have to remind himself constantly that she was married, and he needed to respect that marriage vow.

They reached the boat in an awkward silence.

"Well, thank you again for inviting me to tour Gibraltar Island. I've always wanted to tour it, and I enjoyed the time here."

Affectionately, she placed her hand on his arm. "It was a pleasure. After all, you're my knight in shining armor!"

He smiled up at her as he caught whiffs of Giorgio and stepped into the dinghy. He untied the line and started the motor. As he pulled away, he looked back at the dock and Martine. She waved to him and then walked toward the Stone Laboratory Building.

On the hill overlooking the docks, a figure partially concealed in the shadows took another swig from his beer bottle and turned to go back to the cottage. He had noticed Martine placing her hand on Emerson's arm, but could not make out what they were saying.

≈ ≈ ≈

Emerson was making his way through the moored sailboats and power craft in the Put-in-Bay harbor on his course back to his aunt's dock. As he cleared the "No Wake" buoy, he heard the thundering jet engines of a boat approaching at a fast pace.

Looking up, Emerson saw the yellow bow of a cigarette boat bearing down on him. He swerved and throttled the motor to full power in an effort to move out of the yellow monster's path.

The boat lettered *Mon Ami* narrowly missed Emerson – and only due to Emerson's quick reaction. He heard laughter as the boat went by and recognized Francois L'Hoste at the wheel. He was accompanied by several other people – all of whom were looking in Emerson's direction and laughing.

Emerson's dinghy bobbed in the boat's wake – almost capsizing.

Was this attempted payback for last night?

The *Mon Ami* slowed as it eased further into the harbor and moored next to the Boardwalk where its occupants disembarked.

Emerson returned to his original course setting and continued to his aunt's dock.

≈ ≈ ≈

Emerson secured the dinghy to Aunt Anne's dock and walked toward the house. As he drew nearer to the porch, he could hear voices.

"I see you had an encounter of the third kind," a voice bellowed from the porch.

"That's one way you might put it," Emerson called back as he began to climb the steps to the porch.

"That's the trouble with the world today! Everybody in a hurry. No courtesy any more – and the L'Hostes think this is

L'Hoste Island, not South Bass Island!" the voice continued.

As Emerson opened the screen door to the screened porch, he could see his aunt and another gentleman seated together with iced teas next to them. The white haired, bearded man seemed to be around his aunt's age and looked vaguely familiar.

"Emerson, do you recall meeting Mr. Cassidy? He was the harbormaster and a good friend of Uncle Frank's," his aunt offered as an introduction.

"Why yes, I do recall you sir. It's been a long time," Emerson said as they shook hands.

"Yeah boy! It's been ages. You should have come back for visits after Jack's death. Your aunt and uncle sure thought highly of you. They were always trying to find articles that you wrote for that newspaper you worked for."

Emerson noticed Mr. Cassidy's large eyes and the way his tongue seemed to constantly extend from his mouth and lick his lips. He seemed somewhat bent over due to an apparent back problem and there was a cane next to where he was seated.

"Emerson, Mr. Cassidy is retired now and is spending a lot of time on his small farm on the island. He comes by here from time to time to see if I need any help with keeping up this place of mine."

"Yeah boy, I may be seventy two and have curvature of the spine, but I still get around fairly well. I can't help your aunt as much as I'd like to, but I have my boy, Jimmy, come over from time to time to help her. He took over as harbormaster when I retired. It's been sort of an island tradition that a Cassidy will always be a harbormaster here. Goes back to the 1860's."

"I didn't realize it went back that far," Emerson responded.

"It started with the old Fox's dock which is now Duggan's Dock. A lot of history has gone through our family. We've seen a lot of change here on the island."

"Mr. Cassidy still runs a small island tour service, taking people around the island for rides in his boat," Emerson's aunt supplied.

"Got to stay busy son. I work when I want and it keeps me in pocket change."

"Mr. Cassidy, do you still raise watermelons on that farm of yours?" queried Emerson.

Breaking out in laughter, Cassidy responded, "Nope, not anymore with this spine of mine. If I did, were you planning to sneak over and steal some like you and Jack used to?"

"You knew?" said Emerson aghast.

"Of course. Why do you think I planted the watermelons? It's an old family tradition that we plant watermelons for the boys on the island to steal. We would sit on the porch and watch the island boys sneak over to the watermelon patch. They'd get their arms full – then we would switch on the spotlight and fire a couple rounds of birdshot from the 12 gauge shot gun. Made a big bang!

"You boys would piss yourselves when we fired the shotgun!" he chuckled. "You'd drop your watermelons and skedaddle. We'd sit on the porch and laugh about it. The next morning, we'd go in the patch and check the wire fence to see if anyone left pieces of material on the fence as they tore their clothing. And we'd laugh some more!"

Emerson shook his head in amazement. He had no idea that this was a set up.

They all had a good chuckle over the attempted theft.

"Emerson, would you like an iced tea? And it looks like John's tea could be freshened," commented Emerson's aunt as she rose and entered the house, leaving the two men to talk amongst themselves.

Emerson leaned toward Mr. Cassidy and asked, "Mr. Cassidy, can you tell me a little bit about the L'Hoste family? The only thing I recall is that they had a walled estate on the western side of the island when I visited as a teenager. We didn't go in there because it had a guarded gate – and there was a house there, not the bow of a freighter which I see has been added."

"Well it goes back a long time," Mr. Cassidy began as he settled more comfortably in the green cushions of his white wicker chair.

"According to what has been handed down through the Cassidy family, the first L'Hoste to settle on the island was Jacques L'Hoste. He was French-Canadian and built an inn in Put-in-Bay about 1855. Well boy, he didn't have a good reputation and ran with a rough crowd. Some said he had been a pirate on the high seas and, some would say later, that he changed his name to L'Hoste to escape from the Spanish and British governments who were tracking him.

"There were problems with counterfeit money and inn guests being robbed after they left the inn. Some thought that there was a connection between staying at the inn and the robberies, but nobody could prove it. L'Hoste was crafty. Finally, the folks in the village got tired of his crowd and ran him and his gang out of town.

"He built a new inn on the west side of the island where the estate is now. His inn drew the rough crowd out to that side of the island. He pretty much minded his own business and the village folks minded theirs as long as he stayed on that side of the island. It was said that he never forgave the Put-in-Bay folks for running him out of town and he swore that one day the L'Hoste's would get their revenge on the islanders. It's been seething in that family over the years.

"About 1865, there was a fire at the inn and it burned to the ground. Shortly after the fire, L'Hoste left his wife and a ten-year-old son living in a small log cabin that he had built and disappeared for a while. Around 1870, L'Hoste returned to the island and was a different man – he had become very wealthy and prosperous. People learned that he and his crowd had moved on to the port of Cleveland where he started a successful steamer business. He sent his son to Ohio State to study business and they have been businessmen ever since.

"Did you know that President Abraham Lincoln himself signed the Land-Grant Act in 1862 which established Ohio State University? Just a bit of trivia I thought I'd pass on to you."

Mr. Cassidy smiled at his display of knowledge. He was quite proud of himself.

Emerson's aunt returned with the iced teas and served

them without interrupting Mr. Cassidy's story. She settled into a chair to listen.

"Thanks for the refill Anne," Cassidy continued with his story.

"In the 1800's, there was a growing demand in the building industry for the limestone that is so common in the islands and on the mainland. L'Hoste saw an opportunity to take control of the local market. He began buying up the local limestone quarries including a 2,500-acre quarry on Kelley's Island and a 3,000-acre quarry on Marblehead Peninsula."

"L'Hoste saw another opportunity. Since he was already in the shipping business per se. He was shipping people and freight on his steamers. He expanded his business by buying freighters and starting the L'Hoste Freight Line. He quarried the limestone and shipped it around the Great Lakes. He became even more wealthy."

"Absolutely intriguing," admired Emerson.

"Well boy, L'Hoste was getting old and he turned the reins of the business to his son, Jules – the one who had gone to Ohio State University. Jules looked for more business opportunities and split his time between their corporate headquarters in Cleveland and South Bass Island. Oh, I forgot to mention that his father built a new home in 1871 on the grounds near the site of his inn.

"Jacques died in 1875 on the island at the age of 70. His wife died two years later. The business grew and Jules eventually passed the reins to his son, Francois. Now, Francois was the real smart one. They had quarried the first 20 feet of limestone in their quarries. He found that the next level of limestone could be used in the production of concrete aggregate. And it started all over. He increased their wealth again, tore down the old home and built the French chateau style home. Francois died around 1963 and his son, another Jacques, took over.

"Jacques is the one who had the bow of the freighter placed on the cliff. Caused quite a stir here on the island with all the logistics that had to be worked out. He put in a new dock with stairs down the side of the cliff and a helicopter landing pad so they can commute between here and Cleveland faster."

Emerson added, "I saw the helicopter landing from the Jet Express as we went by."

"And your aunt tells me that you met Jacques' son at the Boardwalk last night. Be careful of him. People say he's not all there, if you know what I mean. That was his cigarette boat that we saw try to run you down in the harbor. I'll have a talk with the Division of Watercraft officers and the Coast Guard about what he tried to do to you."

"No, that's all right. I can handle it myself," Emerson protested.

"OK, enough talk about the L'Hostes. You're going to bore the boy, James!" Emerson's aunt sternly admonished Mr. Cassidy.

"Oh no. Quite the contrary. I find this interesting. Could be the idea for a story for the *Post*," retorted Emerson.

"Well boy – you've got a great source for information in me. I'm the past President of the Lake Erie Island Historical Society! When you're island bound in the winter because of the ice, I read a lot of history – and I have a good memory, too!" exclaimed Cassidy proudly.

"I was curious about your wealth of knowledge," joked Emerson.

"Then there's the mystery," Cassidy grinned slyly.

"Where L'Hoste got the money to start with?" queried Emerson.

"That would be another mystery. We figured that he robbed someone in Cleveland or won it at cards. But the real mystery is: Who set the fire at the Victory Hotel and Resort?"

"I remember that the resort was at the southwest tip of the island and some of the ruins could be seen at the State Park when Jack and I biked there. Who did set the fire?" asked Emerson.

"Bear with me a moment. The Victory Hotel and Resort opened in 1892 with 625 rooms on 100 acres at Stone's Cove. It was the largest summer hotel in the United States at that time. It had a history of financial difficulties and was opened then shut down on several occasions. There were rumors that visitors were discouraged to spend time there by a group of rough characters. Some of this could trace back to the L'Hoste family.

"They were against the construction of the hotel from the very beginning. Remember that the first L'Hoste was run out of town by the townspeople to the west side of the island. And now the town, so to speak, was moving in next door. The L'Hostes valued their privacy and did not want visitors over-flowing from the hotel property to their property.

"When they couldn't get their way legally, there were rumors of bribes to shut down the building process. Supposedly, the L'Hostes put pressure on the banks financing the hotel's construction and operations. Then, in August 1919, the hotel was totally destroyed by fire.

"The official investigation's findings were inconclusive but suggested that defective wiring started the fire. I think that was due to L'Hoste bribes. Others suspect arson and would tell you that Jules L'Hoste arranged for the hotel to be torched. It remains unsolved today," Cassidy said with an air of finality.

"Sounds to me like the makings for a good article in the *Post*," Emerson stated.

"Ah, but there is more to add to the story."

"And that is?"

"Just who do you think is rumored to be trying to develop that corner of the island into a new resort and development?"

"L'Hoste?"

"You betcha boy! Francois and his father. They won't admit it publicly, but they have agents trying to buy up land and homes out there. Some of us believe he fronted a couple of shell companies to put pressure on the boys in state government in Columbus."

Emerson's aunt's voice broke further discussion as she interrupted, "Enough, enough for now. Let's tell Emerson about the regattas and some of the other exciting things that have been going on at the island. Did you know that Lily

Mae Smith gave me the best recipe for turtle soup?"

Emerson repositioned himself in his chair. It was now time to be courteous and listen to some of his aunt's ramblings about her favorite past time – cooking.

≈ ≈ ≈

Jacques L'Hoste stepped over to the handcarved, solid mahogany refectory table along one wall of his study. He had found the table with its intricate filigreed organic carvings in an Italian hunting villa. A richly carved roping motif framed the tabletop edge. The table was supported on two wide hand-crafted filagreed legs which also showcased the hand-carved roping motif.

Above the table hung Monet's "Giverny Garden" reproduced on a rich tapestry which had been woven at L'Hoste's instructions on a jacquard loom in France. The garden scene which had a tapestry border welcomed visitors with a sense of peace, elegance and dignity to his study.

Below the tapestry and on the refectory table was displayed a model of L'Hoste's Victory Resort and Development. The model had been completed in accordance with his instructions and met his expectations.

The only thing that was not meeting his expectations was the progress in meeting his deadlines. He was growing inpatient. Some said that he inherited that trait from his namesake, his great-grandfather who had founded the beginning of the L'Hoste business empire.

He felt that more pressure needed to be placed on the

state government in Columbus to assist him in his land acquisition plans.

A knock on the door interrupted his thoughts.

"Mr. L'Hoste?" came his aide William's voice from the other side of the door as the door opened.

"Yes, yes. What is it?"

"The governor and his aides have arrived at the heli-pad sir."

"Bon, show them into my study when they make their way to the house. Is Francois back from the harbor yet?"

"He radioed that he would be here within ten minutes, sir."

"William, please see to it that he joins us immediately in my study. He needs to be more focused on business issues and less on his cigarette boat."

"Yes, sir, I will be sure that he joins you right away, sir." William knew that he could get caught in the middle between the elder and younger L'Hoste and the disagreements that they had had. Their arguments were strong. They both were self righteous and extremely opinionated.

The L'Hostes had been good to William and his family. William oversaw the estate and lived there also. He had to sign a confidentiality agreement not to reveal anything that he overheard or saw while in their employ. And with some of the unsavory characters that he saw visiting from time to time, he knew that a violation of any type could warrant harmful repercussions.

Hearing a resonant knock from the doorknocker, William opened the massive door to the chateau's foyer.

"Welcome to the L'Hoste residence gentlemen. Mr. L'Hoste has asked me to escort you to his study. If you will follow me gentlemen." William began to lead the way to the third level where the study was located.

The visitors ooed and awed about the rich furnishings as they passed through the hallways and stairwells.

William knocked on the study door, opened it and stepped aside to allow the gentlemen to enter.

"Mr. L'Hoste, it's good to see you again. This is the first time I've been here. Saw pictures of the freighter's bow before on one of the state's vacation brochures for the islands – and I just love your doorknocker. Don't see many like that in Ohio," greeted Governor Jesse Hogan profusely as he extended his hand to L'Hoste.

"Good seeing you too, Governor. The doorknocker is a sculpture of a gargoyle with wings outstretched, a grimacing face and with a crown of gold. He's named Monsieur Attitude du Mauvais. In English, Mr. Bad Attitude. It dates back to a legend that this bad boy gargoyle would sit on a high perch on the Vitre Cathedral in France and poke fun at local royalty. But alas, there is no royalty here on the island to poke fun at, only the local peasants."

"You're right about that," quipped the Governor nervously. At least he wasn't being poked fun at. Not yet.

"Hey, is this really a Renoir?" called one of the other visitors who had spied a painting just inside the study doorway.

"Yes, it's 'La Danse a Bougival' which was painted in 1883 and had been on display in the Museum of Fine Arts in Boston until I made them an offer that they could not walk away from. To me, the dancing couple convey a sense of ardor and delicious abandonment. Wouldn't you agree?"

"Well, yes. I could agree with that." Extending his hand, the man continued, "I'm Martin Nelson."

"Welcome, and you must be Mark Antal," Jacques said as he turned to the third visitor. It was good to have the Secretary of State and the Director of the Department of Commerce for this meeting.

"Yes, I am," Antal replied as he shook the extended hand.

The door opened and Francois entered the study.

After making introductions, small talk and taking refreshments served by William, Jacques led the group to the refectory table and pulled off the white sheet to reveal the model of the new Victory Resort.

"Gentlemen, we are running into some resistance in our efforts to quietly acquire property between my estate and the state camp grounds where the former Victory Hotel existed."

The governor was the first to speak up, "Mr. L'Hoste, we are doing everything that we can do to be supportive of your efforts here. The creation of new jobs for the state of Ohio is paramount in my mind."

L'Hoste cut him off as he pulled at his right ear lobe, "You're not talking to a voter Governor, so cut the election speech. What I need to know is what you can do to help me!"

The governor was not used to being talked to in this manner and was taken aback. He knew that the L'Hoste Groupe provided a huge economic benefit to northern Ohio and he was also aware of rumors about they unsavory manner to which they could resort to complete business transactions. He looked at his Secretary of State to respond.

"Mr. L'Hoste," Mark Antal began nervously as Jacques glared at him, "we are looking at a number of options that we can pursue in order to expand the state park grounds to include the former site of the entire Victory Hotel. We expect to have our analysis complete by next week – and early indications are that we should be able to meet your requirements. Our hands are somewhat tied though with issues regarding the acquisition of the remaining property that you wish to obtain from private homeowners."

Jacques slammed his hand down hard on the refectory table shaking the model as a result.

"This is all you have to report since our last meeting two weeks ago? Let me make this perfectly clear to you. You find a way to resolve the issues!" Jacques' voice was rising as he began to flick the back of his ear with the backside of his fingers. "Governor, why is it that your people cannot be responsive to my requests? When you request donations from me, don't I respond quickly to you?"

The governor nodded as his fingers nervously tapped on the top of the refectory table.

"I was under the impression that we had a mutual understanding of my expectations for this meeting. I trust that your next contact with me will be productive. You all are dismissed. Francois will take you to the pilothouse for a brief tour and then show you to the door."

Jacques paused and then in a tone conveying that he meant business said, "A word of advice gentlemen. The next time you appear before me, I expect answers and not excuses. I do not want to hear that you are studying alternatives. You'll study things to death. Give me answers, do you understand?"

"You can count on it, Mr. L'Hoste," the governor said uneasily.

Jacques turned his back to them to signal the meeting's end and looked out the salon windows at the lake.

Francois quickly escorted them from the room.

~ ~ ~

The desk clerk at the Park Hotel looked at the guest standing in front of her. "Checking out so soon, Mr. Moore?"

"I've decided to accept my aunt's invitation to spend my time on the island in her house," Emerson offered as an explanation. "Will there be a problem in canceling my reservation for the rest of my stay?"

"Oh no. With the upcoming Fourth of July, we have people on a waiting list. It should be no problem at all."

Emerson was relieved that he wouldn't cause a problem. He didn't want to tell her that the real reason that he wanted to check out was the amount of noise that carried up to his room from the late night partying on the street the prior evening. But more than that, it would be better to spend some long overdue time with his aunt.

He finished checking out and stepped out the door, carrying his duffel bag and lap top computer. He walked to the curb's edge, threw his gear in the back of his aunt's golf cart and drove back to her house.

She'd have dinner ready when he returned and then, on the pretense of crashing early, he wanted to go on line with his lap top and search the internet about a number of the topics that had been discussed that afternoon with Mr. Cassidy.

He chuckled to himself as he recalled Mr. Cassidy's comments about the watermelon patch. He's such a rascal, that Mr. Cassidy!

≈ ≈ ≈

Emerson left his aunt's house with his lap top at ten o'clock the next morning to visit the Put-in-Bay Library. He wanted to leaf through the books and material there about the island's history.

The library was located in the rear of the Put-in-Bay school. Emerson parked the golf cart in one of the parking spaces and entered.

"Young man, may I help you?" asked a gray haired lady as she peered up at him over the rim of her glasses.

"Yes Ma'am. I'd like to do some research on the history of the island – especially about the L'Hoste business empire and take some notes on my lap top as I look through any material you have."

Rising from her seat, she beckoned him to follow her to one of the worktables.

"You just sit yourself right here and I'll bring you several books to review. I also have several newspaper clippings regarding the island's history that may interest you. Is there any particular period that you're interested in?"

"I like to start with the early history and follow that up to current history," responded Emerson.

She disappeared briefly and returned with about eight books for Emerson to start with. From time to time, she would check in to see how he was doing and drop off additional material.

"You going to be here all day?"

Emerson had not heard her walk up to him. He had been engrossed with several articles concerning an attempt by Confederate raiders to capture a steamer and free the Confederate prisoners on Johnson's Island prison camp.

He looked at his watch and saw that it was noon.

"I should be here another hour or two."

"Well, I have to go to the post office to pick up a small package. I'm going to put you in charge of the library while I'm gone. I'll just be gone about fifteen minutes. That OK with you?"

"Sure, that's fine."

She began to walk away and then hesitated. She turned to Emerson and asked, "Are you writing a book?"

In amazement, Emerson looked up and responded, "No, what would make you ask that kind of question?"

"Well you seem so serious and focused on what you're doing. I see that you are taking notes – and it just made me wonder."

Before she began walking away, Emerson added, "No, I'm not writing a book, but I may be doing a story on the island for my newspaper. You see, I'm visiting my Aunt Anne for a few days and..."

He didn't get a chance to finish his sentence.

"Oh, Lord have mercy. You're Anne's nephew. The one who was involved with the cave incident many years ago?"

"Yes, Ma'am."

"Well, it's about time you got yourself back up here to visit that poor woman," she began to lecture. "You're Emerson, the one who works for *The Washington Post*?"

"That's right."

"Well, I want you to know that the only reason this library has a subscription to *The Washington Post* is so your aunt could keep up with your writing. She sure is proud of you. I'm glad that you're here for her now with Frank dying here a while ago. Well, I'm jibber jabbering too much. I've got to get to that post office. Be right back," she called as she walked out of the library.

Emerson turned back to the details of the attempted piracy on Lake Erie. He was so engrossed in the data he was reviewing that he didn't hear the librarian return fifteen minutes later.

Emerson continued to be enthralled by the research and lost all track of time.

"Excuse me, Emerson. But the library closes in 10 minutes."

Emerson was startled. He had been so engrossed in the research data that he didn't realize that the librarian was standing next to him. He glanced at his watch. It was 1:50 PM.

He quickly shut down his lap top and stood to thank the librarian.

"I hope you found our material helpful," she commented.

"Definitely. Thank you very much."

"Emerson, just one more thing."

Emerson paused and looked back at her.

"If you publish a story, could you be sure to send us a copy?"

"Oh sure, no problem. It'll be in the *Post* or I'll send you a copy. Again, thank you very much."

Emerson walked out of the library and sat in the golf cart. He reached into his brief case and produced his cell phone. Hitting the AutoDial, he called his good friend, Slamming Sammy Duncan in Virginia.

The phone was answered on the third ring.

"Sam here," came the cheery answer to his call.

"Sam, it's Emerson."

"Hey E! Look who's back among the living. You sober now?"

"Now, I am."

Emerson paused for a moment to think about how caught up in his island visit he had become. He hadn't felt the need to get lost in drinking like he had over the prior few months. Maybe this is a step in the right direction he thought to himself.

"Listen Sam, it's a long story but I need your help."

"You name it, E."

"Can you access the national archives for data on the Northwest Conspiracy during the Civil War? And I need a run down on key leaders in the US and Confederate government and the governments of Britain, France, Spain and Canada at the time."

"Sure. Can do and will do. What you working on? I guess I can take it that you're back to work."

"No, not really. I'm on leave, but I'm running down some potential story ideas."

"How soon you need it? I can call a few friends to help secure the information."

"The sooner the better. It's not a matter of life or death, but I'm only here for a week."

"And where is here?"

"Put-in-Bay on South Bass Island. It's on Lake Erie."

"E, how do I get the data to you?"

"I'm staying at my aunt's house on East Point and she doesn't have a fax. So, just FedEx the information to my aunt's home. You have my e-mail address if you need to get in touch with me."

"And the address for sending the FedEx is?"

Emerson provided his aunt's address and phone number to Sam.

"Anything dangerous going on? You need me there?"

That would be like Sam. If there was going to be any action, Sam Duncan, former Navy SEAL, would want to be in the middle of it. Since their initial meeting during a story about the SEALs that Emerson had been researching, the two of them had become close friends.

"No, all's under control. I just need the data as soon as possible. I appreciate anything you can do to expedite the data, Sam."

"OK, E. You can count on your main man to deliver the data on time. Snow, rain nor fog will keep me from delivering the e-mail," Sam responded humorously.

"Thanks, I appreciate it."

Emerson ended the call and drove quickly to Tipper's Restaurant on Delaware. He devoured a quick salad and walked across the street and down the alley past the Put-in-Bay Police Department to the Lake Erie Islands Historical Society.

He wandered throughout the buildings to familiarize himself with additional background data on the history of the islands and island transportation. The data concerning steamers and rowboats was of particular interest to Emerson.

Concluding his tour of the museum, Emerson headed up the stairs to its research files. He spent the rest of the day going through photos of island history, newspaper articles and other historical documents as well as updating the file on his lap top.

When the research staff indicated that the museum and research center were closing, Emerson packed his notes and the copies that he made on the center's copier and his lap top.

Dinner tonight would be very interesting. He hoped that Mr. Cassidy would drop by so that they could continue yesterday's discussion.

As Emerson approached the door to leave, he saw the rain drizzling down. And here he was without an umbrella. He stuffed everything into his lap top case and bolted through the doorway and down the alley to Delaware where he had parked the golf cart.

As Emerson approached the cart, he noticed that the two tires on the curbside were flat. One flat he could understand. But two flats seemed to be more than a mere coincidence. As he bent closer to look at the tires, he could see that the sidewalls had been slashed by a sharp object, probably a knife.

Sheltering his lap top computer case as well as he could – he sure hoped it was waterproof – he peered through the warm July drizzle in both directions.

The street was fairly well deserted other than a few people walking by with their opened umbrellas. He didn't see any taxis at the stand. With the drizzle, they would surely be busy transporting the island's visitors.

He ran across the street and went into the Island Market next door to Tipper's Restaurant. As he entered the door, a booming voice bellowed, "Well, well. Look what the cat drug in, and it's all soppy wet!"

Emerson looked to his left and saw Mr. Cassidy standing in the check out line with a bunch of flowers. Emerson grinned as he observed Mr. Cassidy's nervous habit of constantly extending his tongue to lick his lips. Mr. Cassidy seemed quite unaware of his little quirk.

When Mr. Cassidy noticed Emerson staring at the flowers, he quickly commented, "They're for your aunt. Sort of a way to brighten her house on a dreary, rainy afternoon."

"Sure!" Emerson responded as he thought that Mr. Cassidy might be a bit sweet on his aunt.

Emerson explained what had happened to the golf cart's tires and his suspicions that someone had targeted the vehicle. Mr. Cassidy was surprised that someone would do such a thing – and right around the corner from the police department. He offered to give Emerson a ride home, especially since he was headed that way anyhow. Walking hunched over and with the aid of his cane, Mr. Cassidy led Emerson out to the parking lot.

As Emerson and Mr. Cassidy climbed into his old Jeep wagon and pulled out of the Island Market's parking lot, Emerson thought he saw a figure watching them from the window of Tipper's Restaurant. He couldn't recognize who it was because of the drizzle and the shadows.

The figure stepped away from the window and with-drew his hand from his trouser pocket where he had been fiddling with his knife.

≈ ≈ ≈

Unsuccessfully trying to dodge raindrops, Emerson and Cassidy made their way from the parked vehicle to the house where Aunt Anne was holding the door open for them.

"I heard you pull in," she began and stopped. "James C. Cassidy, what are you doing with those flowers?"

First looking sheepishly at Emerson, Mr. Cassidy with a growing redness in his face turned to Emerson's aunt and responded, "Well, it's no big thing."

He continued unconsciously to run his tongue over his lips.

He stammered, "Well Annie, they uh... had them on closeout at the Island Market. And no one else was going to buy them. So, I thought, I'd, well, I'd just go on and bring them over here for you."

He looked down at his feet and awaited her reply.

Emerson was chuckling silently to himself. He hadn't seen Mr. Cassidy at such a loss for words.

With a look of astonishment on her face, she replied, "Well, you're probably right. No sense in letting these pretty flowers go to waste. I'll just run and put them in water."

As she hurriedly left the room, she called back, "You boys need to get out of your wet shirts. Emerson, you run upstairs and change. James, I'll get one of Frank's old shirts that I still have and you can slip into it. And I'll make you a pot of hot tea to warm you up."

"That would be nice, Annie," Mr. Cassidy responded. He looked at Emerson who had reached the stairs to the second floor bedrooms and grinned.

Emerson grinned back and bounded up the stairs. It appeared that his aunt would not be lonely for long, he thought happily.

About twenty minutes later, Emerson and Mr. Cassidy were seated on the enclosed front porch and sipping hot tea to offset the chill that had settled in with the early evening rain. They could barely see across the harbor as the drizzle continued.

His aunt had served the tea and was bustling in the kitchen readying dinner for her two boys.

Emerson took another sip on his tea from his aunt's antique teacup and leaned towards Mr. Cassidy.

"Mr. Cassidy, I spent quite a bit of time today in the library and the museum researching the island's history and obtaining background information on the L'Hoste family and business. I also ran across some interesting articles about piracy on Lake Erie during the Civil War. Can you tell me what you know about it? I saw a Cassidy's name mentioned as harbormaster – any relation?"

"Yeah boy. That would be John Cassidy and he was my great grandfather. The Cassidys have a long history of being harbormasters here. I told you my son, Jimmy, is harbormaster here now," he stated proudly.

"What about the piracy?"

Emerson noticed that Mr. Cassidy made himself more comfortable in his chair which Emerson took as a sign that a long explanation would be forthcoming.

"Well, it all happened around the Fourth of July in 1864. A group of about 30 Confederate raiders tried to capture the *Philo Parsons* and free the Confederate prisoners on Johnson's Island."

For thirty minutes, Mr. Cassidy regaled in telling the story.

"Boys, dinner's on. Come on into the kitchen," came the call from Emerson's aunt as Mr. Cassidy was concluding the story with the capture and imprisonment of the raiders and the finding of LeBec's body on Rattlesnake Island.

"And nobody ever found the missing trunk?" Emerson asked.

"No, people searched Rattlesnake Island for years. There were two reasons why people focused on Rattlesnake Island. The first was that the girl who worked for John Brown heard LeBec yell that they were heading to the Rainbow's End – and that would be Rattlesnake Island. The second was that LeBec was found there.

"Once most of the rattlesnakes were cleared from Rattlesnake Island, people scoured the island trying to find the trunk. There were rumors that it was filled with gold coins to support the Confederacy. Today, people stay away from the island. Some millionaires bought it and have armed guards patrolling it. They even have their own private air strip."

They both rose from their chairs and began to head for the kitchen when Mr. Cassidy paused and softly commented with an air of mystery.

"One strange thing about LeBec's death."

"Yes?" quizzed Emerson anxiously.

"Most people were led to believe that he died as a result of rattlesnake bites. They even found one on his body when the captain of the *Michigan* located his body."

"Go on," Emerson urged.

"Well, the *Michigan*'s captain, who was a close friend of my great grandfather, wanted to calm everyone's fears about potential agents and other raiders on Lake Erie. He confided in my great grandfather that when he raised LeBec's red hat to look at his face, he quickly pulled it down. The reason he did that was so that no one else could see what he saw. And he stayed near the body to make sure that no one else could get as good a look as he had until the body was buried on Johnson's Island."

"What did he see?"

"If I tell you, you will be only one who has not been a harbormaster to know this secret. We have kept this one in the family all these years, and I will only tell you because of how highly I think of your aunt and the great things she says about you. Will you swear to keep the secret?"

"Yes, yes!" he affirmed impatiently.

"LeBec had been killed by a gunshot wound to the temple."

"What? Who shot him?"

"Who knows?"

"Didn't anyone with the *Michigan*'s captain see the blood on the beach? A head shot results in a dramatic loss of blood. There should have been blood all around LeBec."

"Maybe the waves washed it away. That's all I know. Enough for island history tonight. Dinner's waiting."

Emerson's mind raced with questions and possibilities. But respecting Mr. Cassidy's request, he tried to put it aside as they walked into the warm kitchen for dinner.

Following dinner, Emerson excused himself and secluded himself to his room to review his research work from the day and to set up his lap top so he could search the internet for additional information.

It was going to be a long evening, searching for answers and leads.

≈ ≈ ≈

After spending the morning replacing the cut tires on the golf cart, Emerson headed back to his aunt's by driving along the harborfront.

Emerson applied the brakes to bring the golf cart to a screeching halt by the Boardwalk's dock as he saw Martine, wearing oversized, dark sun glasses and Austin preparing to enter one of the island's taxis.

"We have better rates here, Miss," Emerson yelled jokingly.

Martine paused momentarily to look in his direction to identify who was doing the shouting. When she saw Emerson, her face broke into a warm smile and she told the cabbie that she had changed her mind.

What a smile Emerson thought to himself. She radiated an inner beauty and strength that he was having a very difficult time resisting. For some reason, she just seemed to emit such positive energy and recharge Emerson.

"Mr. Moore!" called Austin as he recognized Emerson who was stepping out of the golf cart.

"How's my special buddy?" he teased as he returned Austin's hug.

"I'm doing fine, Mr. Moore." And in the next breath, he said, "I have a secret."

"Austin, that's private," cautioned Martine nervously.

"You do?" queried Emerson. "I just heard one last night from someone else."

"Good, I'll tell you!"

"Austin!"

"Mommy's got a black eye!" he blurted quickly.

Feeling anger well up inside of himself, Emerson turned to look more closely at Martine. Martine put one hand up on her glasses to hold them securely and looked down.

"She walked into the bedroom door," Austin added proudly.

Moving closer to Martine, Emerson lowered his voice and asked, "Did your husband do this to you?"

"Please, I don't want to talk about it. Please. Don't make an issue here in front of Austin. I'm trying to make it into a fun day for him."

"I've written articles on spousal abuse and can suggest some counseling agencies if you like."

"Please, let's just drop it."

Turning to Austin, she tried to add excitement to her voice and said, "We have a big day planned, don't we, Austin?"

"Yep, we're going to go to Perry's Cave"

"Well, since you've lost your cabby, I guess that I am at your service to drive you there," Emerson offered.

"I get to ride up front with Mr. Moore." And Austin plopped himself into the passenger's seat while placing his tape recorder on the floor.

Emerson stepped into the cart as Martine settled into the back seat.

They dodged several tourists who stepped onto the street without looking and made their way through the village and the two miles to the cave site.

Austin's face lit up when Emerson asked him to help

steer the cart on the way to the cave and as they parked the cart at the cave's entrance

"I'll walk you up to the ticket counter," Emerson suggested.

"Mom, can Mr. Moore come with us into the cave?"

"If you like Austin. It's fine with me," Martine responded.

"Will you? Will you, Mr. Moore?" Austin asked eagerly.

Emerson felt a chill go through him. He had not been inside a cave since the incident and he wasn't sure that he could go inside one.

"Austin, I believe I'll pass this time," he responded uncomfortably.

"Austin, we need to honor Mr. Moore's decision."

Ignoring his mother's advice, Austin continued. "Please, Please!!!"

Bending down to Austin's level, Emerson said, "Austin, I'd love to go with you, but I haven't been in a cave in years – and the last time I was in one I had a very bad experience."

Martine looked at Emerson quizzically.

Austin's eyes widened. "Is it scary down there?"

Trying to calm Austin, Emerson answered, "No, caves can be very beautiful places to visit, but you must be very careful. I've been in a lot of the caves on the island when I was a boy – and, for the most part, had fun visiting them."

"Please come with us," Austin begged as he reached up to his mother's hand. "When I get scared, I hold Mommy's hand – and you can too. Can't he Mommy?"

Turning a bit red as she looked at Emerson, Martine replied hesitantly, "Well, sure. That would be fine if you'd like."

"Oh, no. I should leave now," Emerson's instincts cried out to him. But he just could not resist being with her longer, and the invitation was really harmless he tried to convince himself. Besides, I do get to hold her hand. How could I pass that up Emerson pondered.

"OK, I'll come along." He extended his hand to clasp Martine's hand. How comfortable her hand felt as it fit into his.

They marched into the building to purchase their tickets. Emerson had a sigh of relief when he saw that the tour would only be twenty minutes long.

When their group was called to descend the stone steps carved into the walls of the cave, Martine had to remove her sunglasses.

Emerson stole a glance at her blackened eye and commented, "Martine, I am so sorry about your eye."

She smiled and they entered the stairway.

The cool air from the cave greeted them as they began the steep descent to the cave floor 52 feet below.

Emerson shuddered as they descended the 44 steps, and the walls closed around him. Martine felt the shudder and looked at him with concern. She gave him a reassuring squeeze with her hand.

As they entered the calcium-encrusted cavern, Emerson had to crouch for the first twenty feet as the cavern roof was so low. It seemed claustrophobic to him. His breathing became shorter and more rapid.

Austin and Martine were enjoying the comments of the tour guide who explained that the cave had been discovered by Commodore Oliver Hazard Perry's men who had used its underground lake. They used it as a source of clean drinking water after the men had become ill from drinking from Lake Erie.

Emerson's face was bathed in sweat despite the coolness of the cave.

They made their way on the slippery floor past the rock formation resembling a lion, the stalactites, and the stalagmites to the underground lake where the tour guide explained that the water rose and fell with that of Lake Erie.

Austin's head swiveled around as he took in all of the interesting rock formations and colors.

Then, Emerson heard the best news of the tour. It was time to return to the top.

Martine had noticed Emerson's shortness of breath during the tour. She had squeezed his hand several times for emotional support. She thought on several occasions how much she enjoyed holding his hand. He appeared to be such a good man and had such a nice way of relating to Austin.

Emerson's breathing began to return to normal as they reached the bottom of the steps to ascend to the ground level.

As they emerged from the stairway, Martine turned to Emerson and asked, "Are you better now? I kept my eye on you while we were down there."

Taking a deep breath of fresh air, Emerson replied, "I'm fine now. It just brought back some unpleasant memories."

"Care to talk about it?" she asked.

"Not now, I..."

Austin interrupted, "Look, look!!! Putt putt golf. Can we play?"

Smiling down at Austin, Martine responded, "Sure, Honey." Turning to Emerson with a warm smile, she asked, "Emerson, do you have time to join us?"

"Sure, I wouldn't miss it for the world!"

Martine placed her sunglasses back on.

Following the golf game, they returned to the golf cart with Martine in the passenger seat this time and Austin riding in the back seat. He began playing the music on his tape recorder,

About halfway to the village, a cry came from Austin, "Mom, I gotta go!"

Emerson grinned as Martine turned to respond.

"Austin, number one or number two?"

"Number two, Mom."

"OK, Honey. Just squeeze your cheeks tightly and we'll stop at the first bathroom in the village."

Martine turned back around in her seat and Emerson looked up in the cart's rear view mirror. Emerson broke out in deep laughter.

When Martine looked at him questioningly, he nodded his head for her to look at Austin.

Austin had both hands on his face and was squeezing his cheeks tight.

Martine joined Emerson in laughing at Austin's innocence.

Emerson stopped at Tipper's Restaurant so that they could use the bathroom and take the short walk to the dock to return to Gibraltar Island.

"Martine, thank you for inviting me today. I enjoyed it."

"I'm glad you came with us. I enjoyed it too."

As he looked deep into her green eyes, Emerson said, "I owe you an outing in return for this one. I'll be in touch."

"I'd like that," she smiled.

They both looked up and saw Austin holding his tape recorder and jumping from one foot to another anxiously waiting to go inside to use the bathroom.

"Bye, Austin"

"Bye, Mr. Moore."

Emerson pulled away from the restaurant and returned to his aunt's house where he found a FedEx package from Sam Duncan waiting for him. He hurriedly wolfed down his dinner and excused himself to his room so that he could study what Sam had sent him.

~ ~ ~

Francois' face reflected the anger within him. He threw the contract across the room as Tim stepped aside to dodge the flung document.

"This is unacceptable. Absolutely, completely unacceptable. When I hired you to handle our marketing campaign, I expected you to deliver results. Not this drivel!"

Francois' anger continued to well up and explode at Tim.

"You're incompetent and I should fire you now! I should make you go deliver this bad news directly to my father. Do you think I want to go in there and feel the brunt of his wrath?"

Without realizing it, Francois' sounded exactly like his father. They were more alike than either one realized.

Looking up from his bowed head, Tim began to explain. "There were certain circumstances beyond my control."

Francois stopped him abruptly.

"I don't want excuses. I want results."

~ ~ ~

Emerson sat back wearily amidst the files that were now scattered around the bedroom and rubbed his eyes. Sam had done his usual exceptional job in pulling together a wealth of information and related website links.

Absolutely fascinating Emerson thought to himself as he recalled the information he had reviewed and tried to organize the more salient data in his mind.

It appeared that the attempted raid to free the Confederate prisoners on Johnson's Island was just one of several covert actions attempted by the Confederacy and supported by the Northwest Conspiracy.

There were plans to attack the prison camp, Camp Douglas, in Chicago, an attack by 30 Confederate raiders on St Albans, Vermont and a plan to burn New York City.

By late 1863, there was a widespread weariness in the North for how long the war was lasting and its high casualties. It was more apparent that the North would win the war, but at a high loss of life. People were questioning whether it was worth the price.

The copperheads' strength in the North had grown to more than 500,000 and they were trying to influence public thinking about ending the war with a negotiated peace.

Farmers in Ohio, Illinois, Indiana and Missouri were grousing about their inability to ship produce down the Mississippi to New Orleans for shipping to the East Coast markets. They were forced to ship directly to the East Coast markets by rail – and they felt the railroads were gouging them with higher rates.

Lincoln's own cabinet was alarmed by the high cost of

the war and heavy casualties as well as issues concerning an economic recovery and healing of a war torn nation.

They were pushing Lincoln to authorize secret peace negotiations in Canada with representatives of the Confederacy. Lincoln's resistance to discussing peace was worn down by the relentless efforts of his cabinet. He finally gave his approval to explore a negotiated surrender with the caveat that the Confederacy would be reunited with the North. Lincoln's preference was for a full and absolute surrender so that the southerners and the countries of the world did not underestimate the strength of the North.

There were many heated discussions and disagreements between Lincoln and his cabinet members over negotiations. Lincoln felt at times that he should replace them all – but realized an action of that nature would have dire consequences in the middle of a war.

The secret negotiations were applauded and encouraged by England, France and Spain. They were concerned about restoring a balance of power worldwide. Prior to the beginning of the Civil War, the United States was prospering and was perceived as a major threat to the old powers' dominance of world economic and political issues.

By supporting a Northwest Conspiracy, they felt they could divide the United States and lessen its impact on worldwide issues. The formation of a Northwest Confederacy of Illinois, Indiana, Ohio and Missouri would create a second front for the North to fight – easing pressure on the South's battlefronts and increasing its odds to win battles and emerge as a separate country.

Their goal was to carve the United States into three countries made up of the North, South and the Northwest

Confederacy.

Emerson didn't realize how late it was. His head began to nod and he fell asleep with intrigue swirling in his dreams.

≈ ≈ ≈

Emerson spent most of the morning doing exterior maintenance of the house for his aunt by using the chore list that she provided him.

Late morning found Emerson parking his aunt's golf cart at the Put-in-Bay airport. Emerson stepped through the doorway of the airport's small lobby and approached a grizzled looking man with a large smile, standing behind the counter and under a banner which read "Dairy Air Island Tours." The man was wearing a cap and vest patterned after the markings of a black and white Holstein cow.

"Hey bub, looking for an exciting tour of the islands?" Without waiting for a response, he continued, "I can squeeze one more on the next tour which departs in about 45 minutes."

"I'm not interested in a typical tourist tour," answered Emerson.

"Well, what then? How about our moonlight madness tour? We soar to the stars and dive to the beacon light of Perry's Monument and then fly low level straight over to Marblehead Lighthouse on the mainland. Is that more in line with your untypical tourist tour idea?" he prodded.

"No. It's really quite simple. I'd like a low attitude flight around Rattlesnake Island and then a low flyover the L'Hoste Estate. Is that viable?"

The man cocked his head at an angle and scratched his ear as he thought.

"I could do the Rattlesnake Island part but no low flyovers of the L'Hoste Estate. They wouldn't be liking that. I wouldn't fly over their property at any level. They are kind of particular about people nosing around there. Besides, there's another reason."

"And that is?" Emerson asked.

"I've been warned."

"Warned?"

"Yessiree! A couple of years ago, I flew one of my island tours too close and too low to their estate. Within two hours of landing, one of their goons stopped by and warned me in a roundabout way not to do that again."

"How's that?"

"Let's just say when he was done talking to me, he and his buddy, who I didn't see with him, got into the car and drove away. Later, when I went out to refill my plane's fuel, I saw that someone had opened the engine hatch, pulled out wires and threw them on the ground. Good thing that I'm a mechanic because I could put everything together. Yessiree, I didn't lose any business that day because of what they did."

"Did you go to the police?" asked Emerson.

"Nah," he answered as he shook his head. "You see, in these parts, it don't pay to go up against someone like the L'Hoste family. Wait a minute here, why am I telling you my life story? Who are you and why are you so interested in the L'Hostes?"

Extending his hand, Emerson offered, "I'm Emerson Moore, and I'm researching a story about the islands. The L'Hostes seem intriguing and I was interested in getting a better view of their place plus the hull of the ship that they are living in."

"That ship's hull is right beautiful, yes she is." Taking the extended hand, he responded, "I'm Denny Watson, and I wish I could help you, but I can't take the risk."

"I understand. If you change your mind after thinking it over, maybe you could give me a call at my aunt's house where I'm staying."

"Who's your aunt?"

"Anne Gates."

"Well, why didn't you say so sooner? Frank and Anne are good people. Uh, well I should say I'm sorry about your uncle's passing."

"Thanks. I'd better be going."

"Now just a minute here, Boy. Maybe there is one way I can help you."

Emerson paused and turned, "Yes?"

"Come on out back with me."

They walked out the back door and toward the hangar. As they walked past two aircraft, Emerson noticed that the planes had the same black and white Holstein cow pattern along the plane's fuselage.

"Cute," he commented.

Watson turned and saw Emerson looking at the markings on the plane.

"Yessiree. We are known as Dairy Air," he commented proudly.

"Well at least it's not derriere, which I bet the L'Hostes would call it," Emerson quipped.

Chuckling, Watson responded, "Sometimes we do fly by the seat of our pants! Here we are!" And Watson pointed to an ultralight aircraft tucked into a corner of the hanger next to one of his other Dairy Air planes.

"Since you're Anne's nephew, I'd be willing to let you rent this if you know how to fly one. Then, you're on your own as to where you fly, and I'm out of it." He continued, "I took this in trade from a guy who leased a parking space from me for a few summers."

It had been two years since he had last flown one, but Emerson welcomed the opportunity. He approached the craft as Watson continued.

"Yessiree. She has a top speed of 55 knots and you'll need to be careful with her as she stalls at 24 knots. She carries 5 gallons of fuel so you should be good for about 1 1/2 hours depending on all the crosswinds and headwinds you encounter. She's also equipped with floats for water landings."

They agreed on a rental fee, wheeled the craft out to the runway and positioned it for takeoff directly into the wind. They filled the fuel tanks and spread the chute on the ground behind the craft.

Emerson walked around the craft inspecting it and the chute. Everything seemed to be in excellent condition including the chute. Emerson had seen some chutes damaged by wear and tear caused by being dragged through brambles and bounced landings.

Emerson settled into the seat and looked up as Watson pointed out the hand deployed emergency parachute which was attached to the aircraft instead of to the pilot. This eliminated the need for the pilot to bail out. The craft and the pilot would descend together provided the pilot threw the hand-deployed 10-pound package containing the chute out into the airsteam in enough time for it to deploy properly.

After a few tries, the engine started, Emerson grinned up at Watson as they both heard the engine purr. Emerson gave Watson thumbs up and started the runway roll.

As the craft gathered speed the chute filled with air. She slowly rose above the runway and Emerson banked the craft to his left in a tight circle to wave his appreciation to Watson, who stood on the ground with both hands on his hips and a big smile.

Watson looked at his watch so that he would know when to expect Emerson's return and headed back into his office as a vehicle pulled into the parking lot.

$\approx$ $\approx$ $\approx$

The ultralight responded well to his touch, and Emerson leveled the craft at a height of 500 feet. He flew northeasterly along the island's eastern shore and quickly found himself approaching Perry's Monument, which rose 350 feet from the ground, and his aunt's house nearby. He circled the monument and his aunt's house and returned the waves of tourists on the ground and on the observation level of the monument.

He headed over the harbor filled with powerboats and sailboats riding tranquilly at anchor. He returned waves from the swimsuited and bikini clad boaters.

What a fresh perspective of the island this gave him. He wished that he could have experienced this years ago as a teenager when he visited the island.

He took the craft down to 300 feet and circled Gibraltar Island in hopes of seeing Martine and Austin, but couldn't spot them there.

Enough for sightseeing, it's time to get down to business Emerson thought to himself and aimed the craft northwesterly toward Rattlesnake Island.

As he flew over the open water, he noticed a stronger crosswind from the west. He'd have to take that into consideration with his fuel usage.

He maintained his altitude at 300 feet as he approached Rattlesnake Island and commenced circling the island. As he had recalled from his explorations in his earlier years the shoreline of the island was rocky. He flew along the island's north side with its high promontory and its sheer cliff to the waters edge. He wasn't sure what he was looking for as it related to Lebec's death and the missing trunk, but he felt that once he saw it, it would make sense.

He flew over the area where LeBec's body had been discovered, but didn't discern anything striking.

Exasperated by his wild goose chase, Emerson pointed the craft towards the western side of South Bass Island and the L'Hoste Estate.

As he flew, he looked to his right and on the horizon. He could see smoke emitting from the twin cooling towers of the nuclear power plant which was located on the shore, just west of Port Clinton. Emerson never quite understood why they located such a potentially dangerous plant in western Lake Erie's recreational playground.

As he neared the L'Hoste estate, he took the craft down another 100 feet and flew low over the L'Hoste docks and saw the steel stairs from the dock climbing the cliff to the cliff top. He angled the craft into a climb and flew toward the state park on the island's southwest side where he turned the craft back for a flight over the L'Hoste Estate.

He throttled back on the engine speed so that he could take in a better look at the grounds of the L'Hoste Estate.

He flew dangerously slow over the compound. He saw the guards by the gate pointing at him and saw the helicopter on its landing pad. He saw a tennis court and swimmers in the large inground pool pausing in their activities to look up at him.

The grounds were immaculate with statuary located throughout. The bow of the ship was attached to the French chateau with a circular driveway leading to the front portico.

Must be nice to have money for all of this Emerson thought to himself.

A brilliant shining object caught Emerson's attention on the north side of the estate but it was now outside of his field of vision. He looked down and realized that he was now over the water again.

He decided to do one more flyover along the same flight path and headed back to the state park area to begin his run.

He dropped his attitude 50 feet lower so that he could take a closer look at the area on the north side of the house. As he approached the house, he saw people below. Some were shaking their fists at him in anger.

He swooped low over the north side and spotted the brilliant glare coming from a monument in what appeared to be a small landscaped garden. On the other side of the garden, was a small unkempt, fenced area with some sort of ruins.

Strange, he thought to himself as he banked the craft over the water and headed south in front of the L'Hoste Estate's ship's bow and toward the state park and their airport.

When he heard the first clang on the metal craft, he wondered what it was. It was followed rapidly by two more clangs.

It had to be rifle shots!

Emerson banked the craft away from the estate and in a more southerly direction.

One more shot rang out and connected with Emerson's engine. The engine died.

$$\approx \quad \approx \quad \approx$$

The figure standing in the shadows of the ship's bridge lowered the rifle and listened as the ultralight's engine went silent. He smirked as he watched the craft crash into the water and reentered the ship's study.

He handed the rifle to Jacques L'Hoste who said, "I thought you'd relish having this opportunity once we realized who was piloting the ultralight and invading our space."

"Yes, I did. He deserved it," the figure replied as he left the bridge area.

L'Hoste turned his back to the water and settled in a rich leather armchair. He picked up his wineglass for another swallow.

$$\approx \quad \approx \quad \approx$$

Emerson looked at the parachute and how low he was. He knew that he didn't have time to deploy the emergency chute. He remembered seeing the road by the state park where he might be able to land, but it was going to be too far away.

Emerson fought to control the craft as he lost altitude. Looks like he would get a chance to try out those floats for a water landing, although this one wouldn't be a controlled water landing. And it was a good thing that Watson had insisted on him wearing a life vest.

The ultralight hit the water hard. Emerson released his seat belt as the craft hit the water and his head was jerked to his right by the force of the landing. His head hit one of the craft's supports, knocking him unconscious.

As the ultralight began to sink in the water, Emerson's body began to float free. Then his foot became twisted in the ultralight's frame, and the ultralight began to drag Emerson down into a watery grave.

As the ultralight slowly sank 10 feet below the surface, the surface of the water was broken by a diver.

The diver swam rapidly to the ultralight and sensing that Emerson was tangled quickly ran his hands over Emerson to ascertain where the problem was. Finding his foot wedged in the frame, he pulled on it several times to free it. The diver then swam speedily to the surface with Emerson in tow.

As they broke the surface, Mr. Cassidy assisted the diver in pulling Emerson on board his boat.

"Here, help me turn him on his side," Mr. Cassidy directed the diver.

The diver knelt beside Emerson as he regained consciousness and coughed up water.

Emerson opened his eyes in shock when he heard the diver yell, "E, it's your main man to the rescue!"

Emerson looked aghast as he saw Sam standing over him.

"Sam, please tell me that you didn't give me mouth to mouth!"

"Somebody had too. You ever think about using Scope?"

"I'm going to be sick." Emerson started gagging at the thought of his friend giving him mouth to mouth.

"Not this time, buddy! I'm busting your chops. You missed out! You know how all the ladies feel about me giving mouth to mouth! They want more!"

Looking relieved and breathing more normally, Emerson demanded, "What in the world are you doing here?"

"You know I can't pass up an adventure, and it sounded like you were going to be working on something interesting based on the information that you wanted. So, I decided to surprise you. I went to your aunt's house since I had the address and she had Mr. Cassidy take me out to talk with the guy at Dairy Air. I love that name! He and I hit it right off. We could have talked for hours."

"Sam, you could talk with anyone for hours!"

"E, be nice! He even gave me a Dairy Air cap. See." Sam placed the black and white cap on his head at a jaunty angle. "You like?"

"This is too much!" Emerson feigned a despondent sigh.

"Dairy Air. Dairy Air. Dairy Air. I just love that name."

"Go figure. It's not the name of the planes that you're focused on," Emerson chided.

Sam responded with a deep laugh and continued.

"Well, he said that we just missed your take off and pointed to you flying an ultralight, so Mr. Cassidy suggested that he give me a tour of the island from his boat while we waited for you to return to your aunt's house. We saw you fly overhead by the state park and waved, but you ignored us."

"I was so focused on the L'Hoste Estate that I wasn't paying attention to anyone below."

"Well good thing for you that your Rapid Response team was in the area. Mr. Cassidy and I work well together," Sam retorted.

"That we do, son. That we do," Cassidy agreed as his tongue ran over his lips.

"Yes it was. Thank you both," Emerson stated appreciatively. He put his hand to his head and groaned for a moment. " I must have hit something on the ultralight."

"Let me see that bump on your noggin. I've done some doctoring of bumps and bruises in my life." Mr. Cassidy bent and examined the bump on Emerson's head. "No broken skin. But you've got one dandy of a bump there. Take two aspirin and call me in the morning. That'll be $40.00."

"But I'm in a PPO and I only have a $10.00 co-pay," Emerson responded with mock indignation.

Sam broke into a wide smile as he said, "My kind of guy, Mr. Cassidy. You and I will get along just fine."

Emerson began to shake his head, but groaned again when he did it.

"E, you better just rest easy."

Sam turned to Emerson, who was now sitting up, and in a serious tone inquired, "You do realize that someone was firing a high powered rifle at you? We heard the shots."

"Someone didn't want me around the estate."

"It will be difficult to prove that it was anyone at the L'Hoste Estate. They just seem to get away with anything they want on the island," sighed Mr. Cassidy warily.

"Mr. Cassidy, when I flew over the estate I saw a monument in the garden with something on top of it that shined. Do you know what that was?" Emerson asked.

"That would be the grave site of the first L'Hoste to settle here. Jacques' namesake. He was the one who started the L'Hoste fortune in shipping when he went to Cleveland," Mr. Cassidy replied.

"And the fenced in area just north of the monument? What is all that about?"

Cassidy thought for a moment and said, "That's probably the area where they had their inn. You may recall me telling you that they were run out of town and relocated their inn on the western side of the island. It burnt down a number years ago. For some reason, they seem to revere that site."

Mr. Cassidy started up the boat and they headed for the harbor and Emerson's aunt's house.

"Sam, thank you again. That was a little too close," Emerson said.

"No problema, E. I had to come. After doing all that research for you and seeing what an exciting place Put-in-Bay is, I had to come," Sam replied.

"And?"

"And?" Sam replied feigning ignorance.

"There's more to it."

"OK. OK. I saw that it was a resort town which means tourists which means lots of ladies. I had to come," Sam admitted.

"That roving eye of yours is going to get you in trouble, my friend."

"It usually does, but I enjoy it!" Sam grinned back and settled back to enjoy the ride into the harbor.

In a way Emerson was glad that his friend joined him. It might not be a bad idea to have someone watching his back.

∽ ∽ ∽

When they returned to his aunt's house, she made a big fuss over the bump on Emerson's head and thanked Mr. Cassidy and Sam for their rescue efforts.

Emerson placed a phone call to Watson at Dairy Air to

explain what had happened and to apologize for the loss of the aircraft. Watson indicated that it was no big issue, the ultralight was rarely used and it was covered by insurance. When Emerson suggested pursuing the issue with the legal authorities, Watson told him to just drop it.

After Sam was given a room next to Emerson's, they sat down for an early dinner together. Aunt Anne and Mr. Cassidy took immediately to Sam's winning ways as they exchanged stories about Sam, Emerson and Put-in-Bay.

As the jovial mood grew, Emerson's headache grew also. Emerson suggested one last story before he was going to excuse himself and make it an early night.

"Sam, why don't you tell them the story about you in your jogging shorts at the convenience store. Every time I hear him tell this story, I laugh so hard that I have tears in my eyes."

"You just had to bring that one up, didn't you?"

"Oh, go ahead. You're among friends," Emerson said as he already began to chuckle in anticipation.

"All right. It was a hot summer night and I was lounging around in my short jogging shorts and a tank top when I realized that I was out of milk and bread and needed to make a quick run over to the local convenience store. I drove over, parked my car and went into the store. No big deal.

"I picked up my bread and my milk and headed to the counter where I had to stand in an unusually long line. As I'm standing in line, the elastic in my underwear decides it's time to fail."

The laughter began around the table.

"So, I realize if I don't hold up my underwear which is white by the way, they will drop down the sides of my legs and below the bottom of my black jogging shorts. So, I shift my groceries to one hand and stick my free hand inside my pocket so that I can hold my underwear up. Everything's cool. No one suspects anything. Then it's my turn at the cash register."

"Oh my word," commented Aunt Anne. " I can just imagine."

"Well, I have to use both hands to set my groceries on the counter. As I take my hand out of my pocket, my underwear elastics goes into major failure and as I set my groceries down, my underwear drops down both sides of my legs. I hear tittering in the line behind me. I paid and left carrying my bag and dragging my underwear."

The laughter and guffaws echoed in the room as they all pictured him walking out of the store.

The hard laughter did not do much to help Emerson's headache as the throbbing reached a new level. Emerson excused himself to take two aspirin and headed to bed for some rest.

Mr. Cassidy offered to take Sam into town to show him the downtown bars and grab a beer.

~ ~ ~

During the night, Emerson tossed and turned with nightmares. They were nightmares of the crash and his experiences in caves.

At one point he thought he heard the sirens of a police car or fire engine. He just rolled over and went back to his fitful sleep.

$$\approx \ \approx \ \approx$$

The next morning, Emerson's head felt much better. He had an early breakfast with his aunt who told him that Sam woke her when he came into the house at 4:30 in the morning. Sam must have been out carousing and would probably sleep late.

Emerson borrowed his aunt's bicycle so he could bicycle out to the airport and retrieve the golf cart that he had parked at the airport the previous day.

Emerson enjoyed pedaling in the fresh morning air. There was a nice breeze and the dew was still on the ground.

As he neared the airport, he thought he smelled acrid fumes. Then as the airport came into view, he saw the smoking, charred remains of Dairy Air's hangar and the one plane that had been inside. It was the hangar that had housed the ultralight.

A fire truck was parked nearby and two firemen were searching through the still-smoking debris.

He parked the bike next to the golf cart and a Chevy Blazer with a decal on the side indicating it was the Put-in-Bay Police.

Emerson entered the building and saw Watson talking

to a police officer who was completing a report. Both of Watson's hands were bandaged.

"Denny, are you ok? What happened to your hands? What happened to the hangar?" the questions exploded out of Emerson.

"Not to worry. Everything will be ok." Turning to the police officer, Watson introduced them. "Emerson, this is Chet Wilkens, our Police Chief. Chet, meet Emerson Moore. He's Annie Gates' nephew."

Wilkens shook Emerson's extended hand as he greeted him. "Glad to meet you. Sorry about your uncle. He was a good man."

"Thanks, it seems like everyone here knew him."

"He was very well-liked," Wilkens responded as he turned back to his report. He looked up suddenly as if he recalled something and asked Emerson, "Would you be the nephew that was involved with the Duff's Cave incident some years back?"

"Yes, I was there."

"Sad situation. It never should have happened. Your aunt and uncle grieved for years about that one." He turned back to his report.

"Denny, what happened here?"

"Don't rightly know. I have a small apartment here in the back and I woke up about 2:00 a.m. and smelled smoke. When I looked out the window, I saw the hanger in flames. I called the fire department and rushed out to try to save the one plane that was housed there. Burnt my hands trying to save it. Couldn't get it out."

"Denny's a stubborn man. The firemen had to pull him back from the flames," the Chief added.

"Any ideas what caused it?" Emerson asked the Chief.

"May have been arson. But Denny can't think of anybody who would have any reason to come after him."

"Denny, did you tell him about the incident with the ultralight?"

"Nothing to tell, Emerson."

Emerson was perplexed by Watson's reluctance.

"What's this about an ultralight?" the Chief demanded.

Emerson explained about renting the ultralight but changed the story slightly to protect Watson. He indicated that he wanted to see the entire island from the air, had cruised out to Rattlesnake Island and back to South Bass Island. He then mentioned that he had seen this beautiful estate and decided to fly over it to see the ship's bow better when, for no apparent reason shots were fired at him, knocking out his engine and sending him crashing into the water where he was rescued.

"With all due respect, I doubt that there were any rifle shots fired at your aircraft – especially from the L'Hoste Estate. They are fine citizens here on the island and have done a lot for our community. I think your engine just failed."

"I don't think so. I have two witnesses who heard shots and rescued me when I splashed. I want to fil police report on this."

"I'll be glad to have you complete a report for insuranc purposes only. It would be difficult to prove where any so-called rifle shots came from," the Chief replied indignantly.

"Emerson, let's just let it drop. We don't need to make any big to do about this. The ultralight, the burned plane and hangar are all covered by insurance," Watson implored.

"There's more than one way to skin a cat, Chief. OK, we'll just complete the report for insurance purposes," Emerson stated indignantly.

The Chief completed taking the report from Denny and then from Emerson. Once Emerson's report was completed, the Chief left for town.

As Watson and Emerson watched the chief pull out of the parking lot, Watson commented, "He's a bit protective of the L'Hoste family. They treat him right. Real right! They buy the police department a new vehicle each year. It makes it hard on him to think badly against them. Other than that, he's really a good man."

"He may be a good man, but I think the L'Hoste influence is blinding him from doing his job to its full extent," Emerson said as he put his aunt's bike in the back of the golf cart and climbed into the driver's seat.

"Do you think that the L'Hostes had anything to do with the hangar fire, Denny? Would they know the ultralight came from you?"

"I don't want to talk about it. I'm just minding my own business," Watson stated.

"It seems more than a coincidence that after I'm shot down, your hangar goes up in flames." Emerson started the golf cart's engine and pulled out of the parking lot as he waved to Watson.

Watson returned the wave and entered his lobby area. He was concerned whether Emerson would stir things up a bit too much on South Bass Island. He wasn't the only one with that thought on his mind.

$$\approx \approx \approx$$

Chief Wilkens was troubled as he pulled out of the parking lot. What in the world did Emerson mean when he said that there was more than one way to skin a cat? Who did he know?

He recalled Emerson telling him that he was an investigative reporter for *The Washington Post* while they were completing the police report on his ultralight crash. So what was he going to do? Conduct his own investigation?

He'd have to keep an eye on Emerson to make sure he didn't cause trouble.

Life was good for the Chief. Other than dealing with a few rowdy and drunken tourists from time to time in the summer months, he had a good job.

And the L'Hostes – well they were a bit strange at times. Rich people in his eyes had the right to be a bit eccentric

from time to time. Sometimes he had to turn a blind eye to some of the shenanigans that their son got involved with in town when he'd had too much to drink. But it was more out of professional courtesy.

And he did like the new Blazer he was driving. He beeped his horn at four college girls as he passed them on the way to town.

~ ~ ~

When Emerson returned, he learned that Sam had left to go fishing with Mr. Cassidy. Emerson decided that the breeze from the morning had picked up in strength and it would be a good day for sailing.

He went to his aunt's dock and began to ready the 20-foot catboat for an afternoon sail since the neighbor didn't mind if he used it. As he was uncovering the boat, he was startled by a cheery hello from the direction of the shore.

He looked up and saw Martine with that 1,000-watt smile of hers. He returned the smile and shouted, "Hello stranger!"

Martine strode onto the dock. She was carrying a beach bag and wearing a Put-in-Bay cropped t-shirt and short shorts. She looked absolutely gorgeous Emerson thought to himself.

"You're the stranger. I haven't seen you around town in a while," she responded flashing him an even bigger smile.

"I've been real busy. Hey, how's the eye?"

Martine pulled her sunglasses off and he could see that it was almost healed.

"It's better, thanks."

"And where's my buddy, Austin?"

"Oh, he and his father took the Jet Express into Port Clinton to run some errands. I was on my way to the beach on the other side of Perry's Monument to catch some rays. Since I hadn't seen you, and your aunt's house is right here by the monument, I thought I'd stop by."

"I'm glad you did."

"And just who do we have here? Didn't we meet a few days ago after that scuffle on the Boardwalk?"

They had been so engrossed in their conversation, neither Martine nor Emerson heard his aunt emerge from the house and walk out on the dock.

"Yes we did. And you're Aunt Anne if I remember correctly. I'm Martine."

"Yes, yes, I remember, Martine."

"I just love the Victorian style of your home," Martine said enthusiastically.

"Would you like to take a tour? I have all sorts of antiques inside," Aunt Anne offered eagerly.

Martine looked at Emerson and asked, "Do you mind? I do love Victorian homes so much."

Emerson sensed the excitement between the two women. "No, go ahead. I'm just getting ready for a sail."

Martine dropped her beach bag and took Aunt Anne's arm. The two women went on their way to the house, chatting happily. Emerson grinned and went back to his work.

Emerson had lost all track of time when Martine's voice announced her return.

"Your aunt sent me out here with a sandwich for you. Her house is so special!" Martine said warmly.

Emerson could tell that they had a good visit together. He gratefully took the sandwich from her and sat on the dock to eat.

"Thanks. I'm just about ready to go for my sail." Then on a whim, he asked, "Would you like to go with me? I could sail over to Kelley's Island and show you the glacial grooves. You won't miss your swim because there's a great beach and swimming area at the state park right by there. What do you think?"

Martine thought for a moment. She was married and this good-looking guy wanted her to go sailing with him. Part of her wanted to say no, but part wanted to say yes. He seemed so much like a nice gentleman. She decided.

"Let's do it, but I need to be back by five."

Emerson was ecstatic. He just enjoyed being around her. She was so sweet!

"No problem. With this breeze, we should be back in plenty of time. Let's go."

She grabbed her beach bag and jumped on to the sailboat with Emerson. Emerson started the small outboard motor and untied the lines to the dock. He pointed the boat toward the harbor's entrance and open water.

Martine took off her t-shirt and shorts to reveal a brief bikini and opened her bag. She pulled out suntan lotion and began to apply it to herself.

"Like some lotion?" she asked Emerson as her green eyes peered provocatively over the top of her sunglasses. Emerson nodded and she threw him the plastic bottle so that he could apply it.

He watched as she moved up to the bow area and stretched out to catch some sun. He couldn't help but notice what a great figure she had. He sighed deeply.

As they cleared the harbor, Emerson raised the sail, and they headed east toward Kelley's Island.

It was a perfect day for sailing. Bright blue sky, some big white cumulus clouds, brisk breeze and a beautiful woman on his boat.

There was just one problem with this picture, Emerson thought to himself. She was married. She was a real heartbreaker!

Emerson removed his t-shirt and applied suntan lotion to his arms and chest.

It's a funny thing about life Emerson thought as the boat cut quickly through the water. Once in a great while you encounter people that you thoroughly enjoy being around. Like Martine or Sam. You just connect with them.

And when you connect, you respect the boundaries that any relationship has. Respecting his own self-imposed boundaries with women was going to be a challenge when it came to Martine. But he was determined not to violate his standards of conduct – as best as he could.

Martine enjoyed the solitude on the bow, the fresh breeze on her skin and the spray from time to time. She was a bit nervous about being alone with Emerson since she sensed that he found her attractive. She enjoyed being around him. He was so good-natured and caring! She would have to be on her guard to not let her emotions take over. She wanted a great relationship with Emerson – as very good friends.

Guys usually have a difficult time with that. She thought back to her single days and how they wanted to be more than just friends. It was a guy thing she decided.

She looked over her shoulder and saw him smiling at her. She smiled back and laid her head back down. She didn't intend to, but she fell asleep.

With the brisk wind at their back, it didn't take long for Emerson and Martine to sail to Kelley's Island. Martine had awakened from her nap and followed Emerson's instructions in anchoring the boat in the horseshoe-shaped bay on the north side of Kelley's Island at the State Park.

Martine slipped on her shorts and joined Emerson who had seated himself in the sailboat's small dinghy, which had been tethered to the stern. It took just a few minutes to row to the beach.

The beach was crowded due to the upcoming Fourth of July holiday and the nearby campgrounds were filled to capacity with a wide array of tents and camping vehicles.

Leading the way, Emerson guided Martine up a narrow path for the short walk to the glacial grooves. Martine was awed by the deep striations like giant footprints left in the limestone by the retreating glacier. As she bent closer she saw fossilized marine life embedded in the bedrock limestone.

They then headed back to the beach's far side where they doffed their shoes, shorts and t-shirts and dashed into the warm Lake Erie water. They cavorted and splashed each other playfully, like two children without a care in the world.

Suddenly Martine screamed as her arms came out of the water with a 3 1/2 foot, drab gray and brown snake entangled in her arms. Its mouth opened to show tiny sharp teeth which it then buried in Martine's arm.

"Emerson! Help!"

Emerson waded over to her as she dropped the writhing snake into the water. Free again, the snake swam away.

Trying to calm her as they walked to the shore, Emerson examined her arm, "It's no big deal. They scare you more than anything. They're Lake Erie water snakes and primarily inhabit the northeast point of the island. When I used to summer here, once in awhile, you would see one swimming with its head out of the water and holding a fish in its mouth."

"OOOhhhhh, I just don't like snakes," Martine shuddered as they sat on the beach.

"It'll take a while for the bleeding to stop. When they bite, they release an anticoagulant that will make the tiniest cut bleed like a vein was struck," he said soothingly.

"Are they on the other islands too?" she asked worriedly.

"There might be a few, but their primary habitation is on Kelley's Island. They're actually on the endangered species list as their numbers have been decreasing."

They stood and walked back to where they had dropped their clothes and a blanket that Emerson had been carrying – which they spread on the sand and sat on.

Emerson leaned back on his arms and looked at Martine. She smiled back as they both savored the carefree moment of being together.

Emerson thoroughly relished Martine's company. She caught him staring at her as she combed out her wet hair with the comb she had retrieved from her shorts' pocket. She asked, "And just what are you thinking, Mr. Moore?"

Caught drinking in her beauty! Emerson turned red as he struggled for a response.

"Just thinking."

"About?"

He paused for a second to weigh his response. He didn't want to say anything that would offend her or damage their special relationship.

"I was thinking about what a great time I've had today with you. You are a very special lady, Mrs. Tobin." He added the formality as a reminder to himself that she was very married.

Not grasping the intent of his formality, Martine responded, "Well, thank you Emerson. I have enjoyed today too! You're a lot of fun to be around."

"Shall we?" he asked as he pointed to the dinghy. She smiled as she nodded her head affirmatively.

Lost in their thoughts, they rowed in silence to the boat riding at anchor. They were both struggling with their own personal battles of self-control.

Once they boarded the boat, they started their conversations as they readied it to sail.

As they left the sheltered bay, Emerson became concerned. The water had stirred up with small waves and the wind was blowing stronger. He cast his eyes westward and saw dark clouds on the horizon. There was a storm brewing and they brewed very quickly on shallow Lake Erie.

Emerson cursed himself for not paying more attention to his surroundings. He had been totally enthralled by Martine

"Looks like we're in for a storm."

"Will it be bad?"

"Not sure yet. We may be able to outrun it and be back in Put-in-Bay before it hits. We'll tack northward."

The winds picked up strength and the clouds were almost overhead. Emerson felt that they could still make it back in time and didn't want to return to the Kelley's Island bay to wait out the storm.

The little boat surged through the waves which were growing higher. The clouds opened and a torrential rainfall began to pummel the boat's occupants.

Martine followed Emerson's instructions and found two slickers for them to don. The temperature began to drop.

As their tack took them off the northeast side of Middle Bass Island, Emerson brought the boat around and sailed to the lee side of Middle Bass, hoping to find better seas.

He was concerned. This was foolish of him not to have checked the weather. He had meant to take just a short sail, but that all changed when Martine had arrived unexpectedly. This was not like Emerson. He was usually very careful and a planner, and Martine was a distraction.

The lee side of Middle Bass afforded some protection, but they were not out of danger yet. They sailed between Middle Bass and Ballast Island and approached South Bass. There would be one more area of open water to sail through before they reached the relative safety of Put-in-Bay's harbor.

As the boat cleared the protection of Middle Bass and entered the open water, the storm's intensity increased. The little boat leaned dangerously to its side as the wind caught its sail and nearly swamped them.

Martine almost fell overboard as she lost her balance when the storm's fury hit. Only Emerson's quick reaction in grabbing her arm and pulling her to his side saved her from being swept overboard.

Emerson fought with the tiller to maintain control and continue the boat's progress to the harbor.

Finally, after what seemed like hours, they entered Put-in-Bay's harbor. And as they did, the storm subsided and the sun began to peek between the clouds. The harbor's waters began to settle.

Emerson lowered the sail and started the outboard. They began to motor to his aunt's dock. It was nearing 6:30 p.m.

As they neared the dock, they could see a number of people in slickers and with folded umbrellas on the dock. It looked like a welcoming party, but as they moved closer, Emerson was concerned as to how they would be greeted. He recognized Martine's husband standing on the dock with both hands on his hips.

Martine anxiously peered ahead at the dock and had a similar concern.

"Where in the Hell have you been, Martine? And who do you think you are taking my wife sailing? Just the two of you. How cozy!"

"Tim, you're jumping to conclusions," Martine said as she tried to calm him.

"Who's jumping to conclusions? I just put the facts together. You said you were going to the beach at Perry's Monument and you weren't there when we looked for you. We recognized the golf cart parked next to the house. So we came over here," yelled a very angry and obviously jealous Tim Tobin.

Interesting that you recognized my aunt's golf cart mused Emerson to himself.

"Mommy!" yelled Austin in relief at seeing his mother arrive safely.

"Hi Honey, did you have fun on the mainland with Daddy?" Martine asked him as she stepped onto the dock and Emerson secured the boat to the dock.

"Yes, Mommy. We had lunch and I ate a hamburger and drank a big milkshake."

"Martine, don't ignore me. I want an answer!" Tim barked.

"I'm not ignoring you. I'm taking one moment to respond to my son and now it's your turn. I was on my way to the beach by the monument and I stopped here to say hello and..."

"I took her on a tour of my house," proudly interjected Aunt Anne who was standing next to Martine's father on the dock.

"Yes she did. And Emerson was going for a quick sail and invited me to join him. We didn't expect a storm to materialize and make us late."

Emerson joined them on the dock and offered, "Tim, you're reading much too much into this. This was a spur of the moment thing. No harm intended."

"All I know is that Martine, a married woman, is out sailing with a single guy when my back is turned."

"Come along Austin. Let's you and me head over to our golf cart while they talk this over," Martine's father said as he sought to protect his grandson from the discussion. They walked toward the cart.

"I apologize if my actions have offended you. I assure you, Tim, that there is no reason for you to worry about Martine's behavior. She has the highest of ethics and so do I," Emerson offered.

"Tim, you're making a fool of yourself. Let it go," Martine warned.

"I will not let it go." Turning to Emerson, Tim cautioned, "Mister, stay away from my wife or you will bear the consequences."

Not wanting to cause any more of a scene than what had already transpired, Emerson chose to close the conversation for now.

"I fully understand."

Jerking Martine by the arm, Tim snapped, "Let's go bitch!"

Martine decided that things had gone far enough and she was embarrassed by Tim's crude behavior and actions. She felt that it was wiser to comply, so she permitted Tim to pull her along.

As he did, she cast a glance which pleaded for understanding to Emerson.

Emerson felt his anger boiling up within him. His fists clenched and unclenched.

"Emerson, she is a very beautiful woman. And a very married one, although, perhaps, not happily married. You need to think clearly now and not react. I can see how tense you are now. Please relax," his aunt said soothingly.

Emerson took a deep breath as he watched them climb into the golf cart. He had seen Tim strip the yellow slicker off Martine and cast it to the ground before pushing her into the cart.

If he saw her again with another black eye, there would be an accounting. One way or another, there would be an accounting. Married or not, Emerson thought as he followed his aunt into the house.

Without looking in either direction, Tim drove the golf cart across the sidewalk sending Sam Duncan diving to the ground to avoid being struck by Tim's careless driving.

As the cart careened down the road, Duncan stood up from the wet grass and began brushing the debris off. Calling to Emerson, Duncan asked, "So what's up with Dale Earnhardt?"

Emerson explained about Tim jumping to conclusions about Martine and him.

"So that's the lady that you have your eye on! I got a quick look at her as I was trying to dive into a rabbit's burrow. Quite a fox! She's a hottie!"

"Sam, I agree. She is extremely attractive – but let's get one thing straight. I don't have my eye on her. She's married."

"Yeah, yeah. I see the look in your eyes now as you talk about her." Looking at Aunt Anne, Duncan continued, "Aunt Anne, how do you call it? Is he interested in the girl or not?"

Smiling as she looked at Emerson, "Now that I think about it, he does seem to light up when he's around her."

"OK, you two! I think she's a wonderful person, someone that I just enjoy being around, and that's as far as it goes. She's very caring – almost as much as Julie was. Now, please, let's just drop it!" Emerson pleaded.

"Sounds like he has it bad," Duncan observed to Aunt Anne.

"Hey, a guy can have female friends!" Emerson countered.

"I'd like to have female friends that look like that!" Duncan rebutted mockingly.

"One of your struggles Sam, my man, is that you don't set boundaries with females and end up running them off. She's married and I have boundaries that I follow," he said with a tone of regret in his voice.

"She's just fun to be around." Emerson added wistfully, "If she wasn't married, I'd probably pursue her."

"I knew it. Now the truth comes out," Duncan exclaimed gleefully.

Aunt Anne began chuckling.

Playfully tossing his wet slicker at Duncan, Emerson bent down and swept up his Aunt Anne in his arms and began to run toward the house as he carried her.

"I've got my favorite girl right here," Emerson teased.

"Emerson, you put me down this second. You're going to hurt yourself and drop me," she shrieked.

Ignoring her pleas, Emerson carried her up the flight of steps to the porch and into the house with Duncan laughing as he pursued them.

≈ ≈ ≈

The number of customers crowding in at the Beer Barrel had grown since Emerson and Duncan had accepted Mr. Cassidy's offer to join him for a brewsky. They were seated in a far corner of the giant room, away from the band, where it was quieter so that they could talk.

Patrons were making their way to the dance floor.

As they were conversing, Emerson was surprised to see Martine making her way through the crowd toward them. He rose to greet her.

"What are you doing here?"

Martine greeted everyone at the table as she sat in the chair which Emerson offered her and replied, "I called your aunt's house to apologize for the way that Tim acted and she said you would be here. I'm not sure if you could tell that he had been drinking and when he does he can get grouchy like that."

Emerson quickly scanned her face for bruises and feeling relieved in not seeing any, responded, "No offense taken. I'm more concerned with his perception of the two of us together on our sail. I wouldn't want him to have any misconceptions."

"Tim can be understanding at times. But when he's drinking, watch out!" she said as she threw her hands in the air.

"And where is Doctor Jeckyll and Mr. Hyde tonight?" Duncan wanted to know.

"He went over to the L'Hoste Estate for a dinner meeting with Francois. I just wanted to make a quick trip out to see you and apologize. I really can't stay."

"I just don't want to create any difficulties between you and him," Emerson said with an air of concern.

"I'll deal with him and make sure he understands that we're just friends. I can say that can't I, Emerson?"

"I'd agree with that statement provided you qualify it as being very good friends."

"We're just friends, OK, Emerson?" Duncan teased as he mimicked their exchange. He and Mr. Cassidy snickered.

"OK, you two," Emerson warned as Martine's face reddened as she realized that they had overheard her. "Well, at least you can let me have a dance."

Martine paused before answering.

"OK, but just one," Martine replied as she stood to walk with Emerson to the dance floor. As they got there, the band announced that they were taking a break.

"Just our luck," Emerson groused.

Spying a jukebox in the corner, he suggested they make a selection from it so that she could get on her way. Dropping coins into the slot, Emerson stood back and let Martine choose the song.

"I like C7. What do you think?" she looked at Emerson demurely.

Emerson peered at C7 and saw that it was *"She's Not the Cheatin' Kind"* by Brooks and Dunn.

"Are you trying to tell me something?"

"Probably nothing that you haven't already figured out for yourself," she smiled. "Let's try this one!" And she selected Brooks and Dunn's *"She Used to Be Mine."*

As the music started, they headed for the dance floor and Emerson held her in his arms. She just snuggled in as they danced. A few other couples joined them on the floor.

Emerson wondered at how perfectly she seemed to fit in his arms. She danced well with him he thought.

As the song ended, Emerson spotted Duncan walking nearby and shouted to him to join them on the dance floor.

"One more dance before you go?" Emerson asked.

"I really shouldn't. I need to get back before Tim returns."

Thinking again, she said, "Oh, why not. One more won't hurt."

Turning to Duncan who was now standing next to him, Emerson gave him change and asked, "Sam, could you play that song again for us?"

"Yeah, yeah. Play it again, Sam so that Humphrey Bogart here can have one more dance," Duncan teased.

"Sam!"

"OK, OK, I'm on my way. Then I'm going to the john."

The music started up again and Emerson took her in his arms.

"As friends, er I should say as very good friends, I think it would be appropriate for me to be Vice President of your fan club," Emerson whispered in Martine's ear. "Tim can be President as he should be since he's your husband."

Martine stopped and stepped back.

"Emerson, I'm flattered. I'd love to have you as Vice President. How sweet!" And she stepped back into his embrace before he dipped her.

Emerson became overcome by the moment and continued, "Just let me know if his term expires or he doesn't run for reelection."

Martine just smiled to herself.

Just then Emerson felt a tap on his shoulder. Now what kind of tomfoolery was Duncan up to Emerson thought to himself as he turned to look at Duncan.

It wasn't Duncan he found himself facing. It was Francois L'Hoste!

Over L'Hoste's shoulder, Emerson saw what appeared to be one of Francois' burly bodyguards and Martine's husband. He was standing with his arms folded and smirking.

Detecting a movement out of the corner of his eye, Emerson ducked to his right, just missing a punch thrown by L'Hoste. Emerson pushed Martine to the side as he dodged another swing from L'Hoste.

"Tim, do something! Don't just let this happen!" Martine cried in despair.

Tim just ignored her. He was going to enjoy this. He was going to enjoy this very much.

Emerson connected with a right hook on L'Hoste's chin and was now circling L'Hoste. L'Hoste jabbed twice, then struck Emerson's right temple.

With his back now to the crowd, Emerson felt his arms grabbed from behind and pinned to his side. He had forgotten about the bodyguard.

"Thank you, Henri," L'Hoste smiled slyly as he approached the struggling Emerson.

The bodyguard held Emerson firmly as L'Hoste began to pummel Emerson with series of hard blows to the face and stomach. Emerson was weakening.

Tim's smile grew as he watched the punishment given to Emerson.

A guttural yell broke the silence in the crowd as Duncan returned to the room and saw Emerson's dilemma. He made his way through the crowd and quickly attacked the bodyguard from behind. The bodyguard dropped the beaten Emerson and turned to face his adversary.

The bodyguard swung at Duncan and missed the nimble fighter. Duncan turned away and as the bodyguard charged him, Duncan pirouetted with a powerful kick to the bodyguard's testicles.

The bodyguard dropped like a lead weight and writhed on the floor in pain.

Duncan approached L'Hoste who now had a look of fear

in his eyes. He hadn't been concerned with fighting Emerson, but this was a trained fighter facing him now.

L'Hoste swung and missed. Duncan was going to relish this confrontation. He stepped in and landed a judo blow on the side of the neck and retreated. He decided that he would give L'Hoste a surgical slice and dice.

The look of fear on L'Hoste's face widened.

Duncan positioned himself and swung his powerful leg toward L'Hoste's rib cage to snap a few ribs. His leg never connected.

It was grabbed in mid air by Chief Wilkens who had been summoned by the bartender when the fight broke out. The police department was a block away from the Beer Barrel.

Duncan felt the grip on his leg and prepared to face the new adversary. Then he saw the badge and the uniform.

"OK, boys, let's just calm down." Seeing L'Hoste, Wilkens stepped over to him and asked, "Are you okay Mr. L'Hoste?"

"Yes. These tourists got out of hand and started a fight with my friends and me."

Wilkens saw the bodyguard on the floor, still writhing in pain. He saw a beaten Emerson being helped to his feet by Martine and Duncan.

Looking at Emerson and Duncan, Wilkens asked suspiciously, "Causing trouble tonight Mr. Moore? You and your friend?"

"Not causing. I'd say we were bringing any trouble to a rightful conclusion," replied Duncan proudly.

"Rightful?" Wilkens questioned.

Emerson then explained what had transpired.

"Seems a little different from Mr. L'Hoste's explanation. I'd caution you two to behave yourself while you're visiting the island. Consider this a warning," Wilkens advised.

"You Deputy Dawg!" Duncan blurted without thinking. As anger welled up, Duncan started for Wilkens.

"Easy, Sam," Emerson cautioned as he laid his hand on Sam's to restrain him from going after the chief.

"Sir, it was as Mr. Moore explained," Martine offered.

"Let's not go any further with this. It's water over the dam. But do consider yourselves warned. Next time you're in trouble on the island, you'll have harder dealings with me," Wilkens cautioned as he turned to escort L'Hoste and his bodyguard from the bar.

"This is another fine mess you've gotten us into Stanley," Duncan said to Emerson as he mimicked Oliver Hardy from the Laurel and Hardy comedy team.

Emerson imitated Stanley Laurel's silly grin and said, "Let's go find Mr. Cassidy."

"Are you okay?" Martine looked carefully and concernedly into Emerson's eyes.

"Sure, I'm fine. I recover quickly." He didn't want her to

know how battered he really felt. "I should..."

"Martine!"

Tim's voice cut through the air like a knife. Martine turned to see her husband standing with another beer in his hand.

"It's time for you to head home. You shouldn't be here. And you," he said as he faced Emerson. "I've told you to stay away from my wife."

"We just bumped into each other here. It's merely a co-incidence," Emerson defended himself.

"Yeah, Yeah! Enough's enough. Consider this your final warning!"

It was Duncan's turn to put his hand on Emerson's to restrain him as Emerson started for Martine's husband. Emerson had a hot button when it came to people threatening him.

Emerson looked at Duncan and realized that he was on the verge of making a huge mistake. Emerson relaxed.

"Let's go."

Martine and her husband walked out together.

Trying to cheer up his good friend, Duncan said jovially, "Let's go find that rascal Mr. Cassidy. We haven't seen him in quite some time."

They made their way through the crowded bar and spied Mr. Cassidy still sitting at the corner table, but now with his arms around two beautiful tourists.

Breaking into a large smile, Duncan said, "Well, we can see who one of the smartest men in the world is."

Cassidy beamed a smile back.

"Hellooooo ladies," Duncan crooned as he pulled up a chair to join them.

Emerson sat resignedly in a chair and appeared distracted by his thoughts.

"I've been regaling these ladies with tales of the islands. Meet Doreen and Darlene," Mr. Cassidy offered.

"Well, hello double D's. I'm 'Slamming' Sammy Duncan and this quiet guy here is my faithful companion, Emerson Moore. And how are you two fine specimens of femininity tonight?"

The two ladies snickered at Duncan's flirtations.

"Did Mr. Cassidy tell you that I'm a former Seal? I can tell you a lot of tales about my adventures," Duncan told them eagerly.

"All tall tales, ladies. Be on guard with this one," warned Emerson.

"Oh, we know his type," the one called Doreen said.

"Ladies, you're breaking my heart," Duncan feigned.

"Folks, I'm going to excuse myself. I'm heading back to the house to soak in a hot bath. You guys have fun." Emerson

left to their disappointment and headed for the quieter surroundings of the house.

As he walked through the park, he realized that he needed
some time to think more about Martine and his feelings for
her. He cared, but she was in a relationship – and very early in
his dating period he had vowed as part of his own personal
values not to get involved with a married woman.

The loud rumblings of a boat engine starting interrupted
his thoughts. He looked out to the harbor and saw the L'Hoste
boat making its way through the moored sailboats and
powerboats as it headed out into open water.

Emerson's gut was uneasy. It was telling him that there
was something very wrong with the L'Hoste family. He
couldn't put his finger on it.

Emerson continued on his way to the house.

≈ ≈ ≈

Martine and her husband made the ride on the tender
to Gibraltar Island in silence. Upon docking, they climbed
the path to their house without speaking.

As they crested the hill, they could see the cottage was
darkened. It meant that her father and son had probably
gone to bed for the night.

Tim motioned for Martine to join him in the gazebo
which overlooked the water and Rattlesnake Island.

"I want to know exactly what is going on with you

and Moore," Tim demanded. His wife had never acted like this before.

"Nothing Tim. You're reading much too much into this."

"Then, why is it that every time I turn around, it appears that you are with him?"

"I'm not. Let me list them. I met him when he saved our son's life."

"Because you probably weren't watching Austin close enough," Tim sneered.

"No, we have gone through that. It was an accident. The second time was at the Boardwalk when your boss wanted to dance with me. You conveniently forgot that I had never met your boss, and I thought he was just another skirt chaser trying to bother me."

Tim had to agree that she had not met Francis L'Hoste before. He also knew and sometimes enjoyed the fact that other men found his wife attractive. This was really the first time that he felt a need to be protective and jealous.

Martine went on.

"He gave Austin and me a ride out to Perry's Cave and at Austin's invitation took the Cave tour and played putt putt with us. Other than tonight, the only other time I saw him was when we went for the sail – and that was a spur of the moment thing."

Tim remarked, "It just seems that you're spending a lot of time with him."

"That's not true." Martine rose from the bench where they had been seated together and stood against the rail of the gazebo. "And where are you spending your time? You're at the L'Hoste Estate or in Cleveland or in Columbus. I never see you anymore – especially since you started working for the L'Hostes."

"It's all business. We've got a big deal brewing that could make us set for life. I'm doing this for all of us."

He joined her at the rail.

Martine turned and looked into the eyes of the man she had deeply loved.

"Tim, where have we gone wrong? We're not as close anymore. You drink more and more. You get angrier and angrier. I can't live with you when you're like this. Does it all really go back to the accident?"

She saw his body tense as he responded with a rising voice.

"I don't want to talk about the accident! Just forget it. It's no use!"

He turned abruptly and strode angrily down the hill to the harbor side of the island.

Martine looked around quickly to see if his raised voice on the small island had caused any lights to go on in the other cottages or housing units. None were on as far as she could see.

She walked to her father's cottage and entered. As she was closing the door in the darkened cottage, she was startled by a voice.

"Tough night again?"

She looked and saw him sitting in a chair.

"Oh, Dad," she cried and she broke into tears as he stood to hold her in his arms and comfort her.

"Now, now. Everything will be fine," her dad said in a soothing tone.

He'd find a way to take care of Mr. Tim he thought to himself. These last several years had been tough on his daughter, and he saw how it was impacting his grandson.

It all traced back to the accident.

$$\approx \approx \approx$$

The sleek yellow boat picked up speed as it raced across the calm water on the starlit night.

The fresh air and the speed seemed to calm Francois L'Hoste as he turned the boat toward the dock at the L'Hoste Estate.

"Thank you for your help tonight, Henri," L'Hoste said sarcastically.

"Sorry, boss. I should have been aware of the other guy. I didn't see him."

"Don't let it happen again. I pay you to protect me. Tonight, you let me down. Do not let that happen again. Do you understand me?"

"Yes, boss!" Henri was well aware that he had been caught off guard by the unexpected appearance of Emerson's friend. He had to admit that he was a skilled combatant.

The boat eased up to the dock.

"Henri, secure the lines," L'Hoste commanded.

Henri moved quickly to secure the boat and followed L'Hoste up the stairwell on the cliffside to the house above.

~ ~ ~

Over the next three days, Emerson and Duncan spent time with additional research in the library, the historical society and on the internet for information concerning the L'Hoste shipping empire and the attempted raid to free the prisoners on Johnson's Island. They also took time for more sailing and to handle a few house maintenance jobs for Emerson's aunt. Their evenings were spent enjoying the sunset from the front porch and playing chess.

One evening, Duncan convinced Emerson to join him at the Roundhouse for a beer and a few dances with the tourists. That evening, Emerson's heart was just not into having fun, and he was eager to return to his aunt's home.

Duncan sensed that his good friend was becoming more melancholy.

~ ~ ~

About midmorning on the fourth day, Duncan was on the dock replacing the spark plug on the dinghy's motor. Emerson was in the garage stretched out underneath the 1929 Ford Model A truck as he changed the oil.

He was so engrossed in his work, he didn't hear them enter the garage,

Then it happened.

The truck's horn blasted loudly off the garage's walls.

Emerson was so surprised by it that he unconsciously raised his head abruptly and smacked it into the truck's undercarriage.

"Ohhhh," he groaned.

He heard a giggle in response to his groan.

He began to shimmy across the floor to get out from under the vehicle.

As he swung out from underneath the vehicle, his eyes rested on two long legs with Martine attached at the top. He grinned as he raised himself up to a sitting position.

Martine was having trouble trying to hide her smile.

"So, is this the way you greet friends?" Emerson asked.

Unexpectedly, the truck's door swung open quickly, catching Emerson off guard and hitting him in the back of the head.

"It was me!" cried out Austin in unrestrained exuberance.

Emerson let out another groan and began rubbing the back of his head.

"Austin, you shouldn't have done that. You need to be more careful," Martine scolded.

"Sorry," Austin responded as he bounded out of the vehicle and gave his buddy, Emerson, a big hug.

"You're forgiven," Emerson replied. "So, what brings you here today?"

"I baked banana bread early this morning and wanted to bring some to your aunt in appreciation for the house tour. Having engine trouble?" she asked as she looked at the antique truck.

Emerson explained as he stood up next to the vehicle, "No, just giving it an oil change. Duncan and I are going to clean it up so that we can drive it tomorrow in the parade through town."

"A parade! Mom, can we go watch? Can we ride with you?" Austin questioned eagerly.

"Well, I'm not sure Austin."

Emerson hesitated for a moment, then remarked, "Austin, you're more than welcome to join us."

Emerson then turned to Martine.

"And Martine, if you'd like to join us, I'd love to have your company."

As soon as he said it, he realized he said it with a little too much meaning.

Now it was Martine's turn to hesitate. Tim would not return from his business trip until late the next day. And, she did enjoy Emerson's company. I'll do this for Austin, she convinced herself.

"OK, where should we meet you?"

"We'll pick you at the Boardwalk at 11:30." Emerson turned and looked deeply into her eyes and remarked appreciatively, "I've missed seeing you."

"There's just something about you that energizes me, Mrs. Tobin," he added just to remind himself that she was married and to let her know that he remembered she was.

"Emerson, ...," she began.

Her response was interrupted by another blast on the truck's horn.

Unknown to them, Austin had climbed back into the truck and was now grinning impishly from over the steering wheel.

Emerson and Martine chuckled at his antics as he blew the horn two more times.

"Captain Hornblower, I am at your service sir," the loud voice at the front of the garage startled them. They looked up and saw Duncan standing in the doorway with a wrench and huge smile on his face.

"Oh, did I interrupt anything?" he asked mischievously.

"No, we were just leaving. Here's the banana bread for your aunt," she said as she handed the bread to Emerson.

"Let's go Austin." Martine and Austin began to leave the garage. "See you tomorrow then!"

"Bye, Mr. Moore – and I get to beep the horn in the parade!" Austin yelled.

"It's your job then, Austin. And thanks for the bread!" Emerson responded as he and Duncan waved.

"You sure have perked up. And now I think that I know why. It's that hottie, isn't it?" Duncan asked.

Emerson was silent.

"I think someone here has got it bad. And I've never seen that someone act this way before." Duncan looked at Emerson who was still silent.

"One word my friend," Duncan cautioned. "Dangerous. Married women are dangerous. Too many entanglements, too much baggage. You've got to count the cost."

Duncan stopped for a moment. "This is scary. Now I'm starting to sound like you, E."

"What's all the horn blowing out here? It looks like no one is paying any attention to my truck. Do I need to roll up my sleeves and wash and wax it myself?" Aunt Anne admonished the two.

Emerson broke out of his silence and said good-naturedly, "You go back into the house. We'll have it cleaned up shortly. And here's some banana bread that Martine dropped off for you."

His aunt rolled her eyes at her nephew as she took the bread and returned to the house.

Emerson turned and looked at what had been his uncle's pride and joy. His uncle had replaced its original 40 horse-power 4-cylinder engine with a 289 cubic inch V8 engine. He had also replaced the standard three-speed transmission and its standard "H" shifting pattern with an automatic transmission and a floor shifter.

Emerson and Duncan finished the oil change and spent the rest of the afternoon washing and waxing the truck's interior and exterior.

Emerson focused on putting a shine on the chrome – the front and rear bumpers, the bucket headlights, hubcaps, the trim around the radiator and windshield, and the gas cap which was mounted on the cowl in front of the windshield.

Emerson also cleaned up the vehicle's interior by polishing the chrome gauges and the dashboard and cleaning the rich brown leather bench seat and leather trim.

Duncan applied a fine hand polish to the truck's body and fenders which he followed with an application of carnauba wax to protect and enhance the vehicle's paint color. He worked painstakingly on the 19 louvers on each side of the engine hood to make sure they were cleaned and polished.

When they were finished, they stood back and admired the clean classic cream vehicle with the tan top and green fenders before heading for dinner.

"Well, boys, should we go out on the porch and wait for the sunset?" Mr. Cassidy asked as he pushed himself away from the dinner table and reached for his cane. "Annie, that fish just hit the spot."

"All of you, shoo, shoo. Out to the porch so I can clean up." She urged them on their way.

The three men settled into chairs on the big porch. The breeze across the harbor would make for a pleasant evening.

After a few minutes of small talk, Emerson moved the discussion to the L'Hostes.

"Sam and I have spent some time this week gathering additional information on the L'Hoste family and their wealth creation. The librarian said that she wouldn't be surprised to see the L'Hostes acquire more property on the island. Sounds like the rumor is getting around."

"Mary told you that? Doesn't surprise me. Mary knows more of what happens on this island – other than Kay over at the post office."

They all chuckled.

"As I told you, there's been talk that the L'Hostes want to acquire the land from their estate down to where the Hotel Victory stood and right up to the state park boundary."

"We read about the hotel and I can remember biking out to the ruins when I used to summer here," Emerson said.

"That hotel was a financial disaster. From the time she opened in 1892 to when she burned in 1919, whoever ran it couldn't make a go of it. She was a leading summer resort hotel for her time with 600 guest rooms parlors, writing rooms and a billiards room with ten tables."

"The research material said defective wiring caused the fire in 1919. Is that what really happened?" Duncan asked.

"That's the trouble with the world today, people just can't get the truth straight."

Mr. Cassidy was getting riled. "That's the official version of what happened. But we islanders think we know what really happened that night."

"And that was?" questioned Emerson.

"Francois' grandfather, who he is named after and who had the same hot temper, was involved in a high stakes poker card game the night of the fire. There were 5 players at the table and they all had been drinking a lot.

"Francois accused the other player of cheating after he won the biggest pot of the night. A fight broke out between Francois and the other man.

"The fight didn't last too long. The new manager of the hotel was notified about it and hurried down to break it up. That was his mistake."

"His mistake?" Emerson asked.

"I'm coming to that. He sided with the other player and had Francois escorted off the grounds by his staff. Francois was heard vowing revenge. One thing for sure, you don't want to cause any embarrassment to a L'Hoste."

Emerson raised his eyebrows.

"The fire broke out that night and burned the hotel to the ground. Funny thing about the new manager, though."

"And that was?" Emerson probed.

"He was one of the few who didn't escape the flames. They found his charred body in what used to be his office. He hadn't even tried to escape."

"Oh come on. Why wouldn't you try to escape from a fire?" Duncan queried incredulously.

"He couldn't. His body was bound by chains to his chair," Mr. Cassidy said knowingly.

"Was the other card player found in the same manner?" Emerson questioned.

"No, he made it out of the hotel and down the path to the ferry boat dock. That's where they found his body. His tongue had been cut out and a knife had been plunged through the ace of spades into his back. His valise and pockets had been emptied and his winnings were gone."

Cassidy paused for a moment to watch Emerson and Duncan shaking their heads in disbelief before he resumed his story.

"Remember what I told you about the first L'Hoste who came to the island? It was rumored that he had been a pirate earlier in his life. Cutting out tongues is something that pirates did so dead man could tell no tales. I wouldn't put that past Francois."

"Did the police go after Francois?" Duncan asked.

"Oh, they interviewed him all right. Had an alibi. He and four of his business associates – I like to call them gang members – were playing cards at the estate when they noticed the fire. They said that they watched the fire from the estate because they were fearful it would spread in their direction. The police didn't pursue it further. Didn't have the evidence to proceed."

"Who set the fire?" Duncan queried.

"Oh it was the L'Hostes and their gang. They've had a long history of getting away with murder," Mr. Cassidy replied.

Emerson shook his head in disbelief and asked as he recalled the librarian's comments, "Why would they be interested in acquiring the additional property today?"

"I'm not quite sure. Unless they see it as another money making venture for them. It's risky. That hotel was a financial disaster since it was only open during the short tourist season from May through September. The L'Hostes have a lot of business savvy. I can't believe that they'd let the hotel sit empty in the winter and not make any money from it."

"My curiosity is raised. Any ideas about who can give us any insight into what their plans might really be?" Emerson asked.

"They're pretty tight lipped over at the estate. They got guards and staff that they have brought in from the outside who actually live on the grounds. Maybe some of the folks who left would be open to talking to you. Over on Marblehead Peninsula near the lighthouse, there's the retired Russian groundskeeper who worked for Francois' father and grandfather. Then there's a chef who left the estate and works at the Mon Ami restaurant on Catawba Peninsula. They are about the only ones that I can recall that are still in the area."

"When could we go?" requested Emerson.

"We could go after the parade tomorrow."

Aunt Anne entered the room as Mr. Cassidy continued, "And Anne can join us. Anne, how about going over to the mainland tomorrow after the parade and we'll visit Marblehead Lighthouse and have dinner at Mon Ami?"

"Sounds like fun. You know how much I enjoy the Mon Ami. Let's do it."

With her joining them, the conversation was more subdued, and they relaxed to watch the sunset.

Emerson caught himself allowing his eyes to sweep across Gibraltar Island in hopes of catching a glimpse of Martine. He wondered how she was spending her evening.

The sun became a brilliant red on the western horizon as it began its final descent, signaling the end of another day on the island for Emerson.

≈ ≈ ≈

Traffic was relatively heavy as Emerson carefully drove the Model A along Bay View Avenue. Aunt Anne was seated next to him and Sam had climbed into the truck's bed.

The Model A glistened from the elbow grease that Sam and Emerson had used in cleaning and waxing it. The white-walls had been cleaned and the wooden spokes of the wheels had been waxed. Its engine purred.

Sam had produced several small flags which he pur-chased at the Island Market for the truck. They had mounted two flags on the front bumper and two at the far corners of the truck's little bed.

Tourists, bicyclists and golf carts jockeyed for space on the small harborfront road. It was the day before the Fourth of July and vacationers had swelled the island's already large summer population.

Emerson brought the proud little truck to a stop at the Boardwalk where Martine and Austin awaited them.

"Austin, why don't you hop up here in the seat between Aunt Anne and me so you can blow the horn when it's nec-essary," Emerson offered.

"Yessssss!" Austin shouted with glee. "Mr. Moore, I brought my recorder so we have music to listen to."

Emerson smiled as he helped Austin into the front seat. "Crank it up for us, Austin."

Austin turned on his favorite tape again from Disney's *The Littlest Mermaid* soundtrack.

Emerson turned to Martine and said, "I hope you don't

mind, but you'll have to ride in the back with Sam the Man."

"Oh, that will be just fine. Is there enough room for the two of us Sam?"

"If not, you can just sit on my lap," Sam offered with a large grin.

"Oh, I don't think that will be quite necessary Sam. I'm sure I can squeeze in right beside you," she laughed as she climbed into the back of the truck.

"Can't blame a guy for trying with a pretty girl," Sam replied.

"Sam, you're so bad," Martine teased. "What's with the candy?"

"It's an island tradition. As we drive through town, we toss candy to the parade watchers. We used to do this when I was here for my summer visits as a kid," Emerson said over his shoulder.

"Yeah. Sort of like Mardis Gras. Only I wish I had beads to toss," Sam said mischievously with a twinkle in his eye.

Martine shook her head.

"Mr. Sam Duncan, I will not have any of that type of talk in my vehicle. Is that clear, Mr. Duncan?" Aunt Anne admonished.

"Jeeesshh. Can't a guy have a little fun?" Sam's face feigned a hurt look.

"Not in my vehicle. Now zip it, buster," Aunt Anne said

sternly but with a tone of civility.

The Model A's horn blew and Austin cried out, "Let's go! It's parade time."

They drove to the outskirts of town and were positioned in the parade with the other vehicles. At noon, they followed each other along the parade route.

Austin honked the horn merrily while Sam and Martine threw candy to the parade watchers.

Sam borrowed a pen from Martine and wrote his name and his phone number at Aunt Anne's on several of the candy wrappers which he threw to some of the female parade watchers. Martine shook her head at his antics as she replaced the pen in her purse.

Following the parade's conclusion, they dropped Martine and Austin at the Boardwalk so they could return to Gibraltar Island.

$$\approx \quad \approx \quad \approx$$

"Sam, just secure the bow to the dock for me," Mr. Cassidy instructed Sam in the bow of his boat as they completed their short afternoon ride from Put-in-Bay to Catawba Peninsula. "We'll use this dockage and borrow one of the extra vehicles that the Miller Ferry folks let me use from time to time."

The Miller Ferry was located at Catawba Point, only 18 minutes away from the southeast side of Put-in-Bay's South Bass Island.

Mr. Cassidy climbed into the driver's seat of a well-worn, red Jeep Cherokee. Aunt Anne, Duncan and Emerson joined him in the vehicle.

After a couple of tries, the weathered engine started and they pulled onto Catawba Road. It was a brief, but scenic drive along the water's edge down the Catawba Peninsula and out North Shore Road to the Russian Orthodox Greek Catholic Church on East Main in Marblehead.

Mr. Cassidy parked the Jeep toward the rear of the building with its onion-shaped domes. As they stepped out of the vehicle, an older man appeared at the rear of the building.

"May I help you? Evening services don't start until 6:00," he offered.

"Vladimir Alexandrov, don't you recognize me," Mr. Cassidy said as he greeted the old caretaker.

"Cassidy, is that you? My eyes have got so bad."

"Yes, yes. It's been some time. Let me introduce my companions."

After introductions were made, Alexandrov escorted them to a picnic table located next to a small cottage at the rear of the church. He excused himself for a moment to get something from the cottage.

He returned slowly as he carried a tray complete with glasses and a bottle.

"Good Russian vodka for everyone."

"My kind of guy," Duncan beamed as he assisted in

pouring and distributing the drinks to the group.

Turning to Mr. Cassidy, Alexandrov asked, "And what brings Cassidy to visit me on this warm afternoon?"

"My friend, Emerson has some questions he'd like to ask you about your employment with the L'Hostes."

"Are you with the police?" a look of fear crossed Alexandrov's face as he asked.

"No, no," Emerson assured. "I'm a reporter with *The Washington Post* and I'm intrigued by the L'Hoste family and the magnitude of their business holdings. I have flown over their property and was just amazed by the grounds and the bow of the ship that they use as their home."

Alexandrov sat back with a look of relief.

Emerson continued, "I'd like to ask you some questions about the estate."

"Maybe I answer, maybe I don't. It's not good to talk about what you see there. They warned us."

"Why would they warn you?"

"This people, they are very private."

Mr. Cassidy leaned forward, "Alexandrov, Emerson will be careful how he uses the information, won't you. You'll be sure it can't be tied back to Alexandrov, won't you?"

Emerson nodded and asked, "When I flew over the grounds, I saw an area that was overgrown. It seemed strange when the rest of the grounds were so well kept."

"It is sacred ground to them," Alexandrov responded.

"Sacred?"

"It was where it all began for them. It's the remains of the inn that the great-grandfather started. They don't want it touched because it reminds them how far they have come."

"Because they were run out of town years ago?"

"Yes, they have not forgotten. The inn burned to the ground many years ago."

"I saw something mounted on a postlike structure in front of the unkempt area. It appeared to reflect sunlight. Do you know what that was?"

"Yes, yes. It is the granite monument to Jacques L'Hoste who built the inn and started their business. On top is a glass globe like a little lighthouse light. It reflects the light from the sun."

"I had no idea that they had that out there. That probably explains some of the reports about strange lights being seen out there from time to time over the years," Mr. Cassidy stated.

"Oh no, Cassidy. They rarely light it. The light you talk about came from the dock area."

"What are you talking about Mr. Alexandrov?" Emerson asked with curiosity.

"Some nights a large ship would be tied to the dock for several hours with its spotlights on. The cliff door would be opened...."

Emerson interrupted, "The cliff door?"

"Yes. It's a door in the cliff on the other side of the dock. It's hard to see. It's, it's...Oh, what's the word I want?"

"Camouflaged?" Duncan suggested.

"Yes, yes, that's it!"

"Why would they camouflage a door?" Emerson probed.

"I asked Mr. L'Hoste and he told me that it was none of my business. He was mad that I was there that night and saw it. I am not supposed to be there at night. He said that he would fire me if I asked questions about it. So, I need my job, so I don't ask questions."

"Did you see anything else that night?" Emerson probed.

"No, I don't ask anymore questions. And I think I answered more questions than I should have for you. It's time for you to go now."

Mr. Cassidy stood up as a signal to the others that they better go. They were wearing out their welcome. He sensed that Alexandrov was getting a bit nervous and restless.

"Cassidy, you come back by yourself and visit me some time, OK?"

Mr. Cassidy assured Alexandrov that he would and they bid him good-bye as they settled back into the Jeep. Rather than heading back down the drive, Mr. Cassidy headed the Jeep toward the Lake.

"Where to now?" Duncan asked from the back seat.

"We're so close. I'm going to show you the Marblehead Lighthouse. It's the oldest lighthouse on the Great Lakes."

Mr. Cassidy looked up in the rear view mirror and saw Duncan half turned in his seat looking at the church.

"Good architecture isn't it?" Mr. Cassidy asked.

"I just love those old Russian churches," Duncan answered.

"The Russians came to Marblehead and Kelley's Island in the late 1800's to work at the limestone quarries that the L'Hostes owned. It was back-breaking work, but they were used to it. They took a lot of pride in putting up that church to worship in."

"In the back of the church's altar are four icons that were gifts from Czar Nicholas II in the early 1900's," he added.

Emerson queried, "How did Alexandrov end up working as a caretaker for the L'Hostes?"

"His father was one of the supervisors at one of the quarries. One day there was a bad accident and his father was killed so the L'Hostes took him in and gave the young boy a job as a caretaker. There she is."

They had just rounded a bend in the drive and saw before them the white Marblehead Lighthouse perched on limestone outcroppings on the eastern most point of the Marblehead Peninsula.

Picnickers and visitors were walking throughout the bucolic 4-acre grounds and climbing on the scattered stacks of limestone outcroppings. Children could be seen sticking their feet in the water.

As they took a brief stroll, Emerson thought there was a certain ambiance to the area. It was so peaceful and relaxing with a light breeze blowing.

Seeing the couples on the grounds made him think briefly about Martine – but he quickly put her out of his mind.

Mr. Cassidy with his love for the area's history, offered as he pointed at the lighthouse, "They built the lighthouse back in 1821 on this rocky limestone headland to help guide ships into Sandusky Bay. Wave heights can get to 3 feet and pound the limestone."

Emerson and Duncan gazed up the 50-foot tower to the working light at its pinnacle. Its stark white sides contrasted brilliantly with the bright blue sky and the dark green foliage of the trees which seemed to stand as sentinels around it.

"Beautiful. That's all I can say," Duncan said in awe.

Everyone turned and looked at Duncan in surprise. For once, he seemed somewhat speechless.

Aunt Anne was the first to break the silence.

"Frank and I used to come here at least once a year. We'd just sit there on the rocks in the shade and have a picnic lunch. It's so tranquil here."

"Peaceful is the word that I'd use in describing this area," Emerson agreed.

"Anybody hungry?" Mr. Cassidy asked

To a chorus of affirmative responses, he said, "Well, then, let's be on our way."

"I'm ready for Mon Ami," chortled Aunt Anne.

≈ ≈ ≈

"Hey, that's Johnson's Island Prison Camp. Can we go there for a second?" Emerson asked as he spied the small sign announcing the site of the prison camp.

"We can make a quick tour. Not much to see there today. The buildings and the camp itself are gone. There's the cemetery and the monument to the dead prisoners," responded Mr. Cassidy.

Mr. Cassidy turned left onto the narrow road which led across a small bridge to the island.

The Jeep slowly approached the area where the cemetery was located and came to a stop in the nearby parking lot.

Everyone exited the Jeep and followed Emerson into the cemetery after stopping for a moment to read the inscription on the monument to the dead. The monument had been erected by the Daughters of the Confederacy.

They scanned the 206 marble headstones from Georgia which had replaced the wooden headboards that rotted. Each 1 x 3 headstone was two inches thick and listed the deceased's name, rank, regiment and state. Some headstones were marked "Unknown."

Emerson searched and found the two headstones he was most interested in. One listed the name of Colonel Harrington. The other listed the name of LeBec.

His research showed many positive comments about Harrington's leadership skills and achievements in battles.

Emerson's eyes rested on LeBec's headstone. Mr. Lebec, Emerson found himself pleading as if he would get an answer – where is the trunk that you escaped with and what was in it that was so secretive or valuable?

"Found LeBec's grave, did ya?" Mr. Cassidy asked.

"Yes, I was just wishing that he could communicate with us and tell us the secret of the missing trunk," Emerson lamented.

"Yup, a lot of people wish he could tell them." Mr. Cassidy glanced at his watch and urged, "We need to be moving if we are going to be on time for our reservations at Mon Ami."

"I'll race everyone to the car," Aunt Anne kidded.

"Last one there buys dinner," Duncan chimed in.

They all moved quickly to the vehicle and Mr. Cassidy drove them around the small island to show them where the actual prison had stood. Nothing remained from the original site, and vacation homes had been constructed where the prison had once stood.

As the Jeep began to move away from the prison site, Emerson took one last look around and toward the city of Sandusky across the bay. He tried to visualize what the prison looked like in the 1860's.

He settled back in his seat, deep in thought.

~ ~ ~

The red Jeep pulled off the main road and onto the narrow lane leading to the restaurant. They parked in the parking lot across from the Mon Ami Restaurant and Winery.

As they crossed the lane from the parking lot to enter the grounds, Emerson and Duncan took in the massive stone building which resembled a huge French chateau. The restaurant was flanked by an outdoor garden where jazz music softly filled the air and a wine and gift shop.

Aunt Anne pointed to a log cabin located adjacent to the restaurant and gift shop. "That cabin is the Betsy Mo-John cabin. The cabin has been moved around the peninsula about three times and finally made it back to its original site here. Would you like to hear about the Betsy Mo-John legend?"

Duncan eagerly responded, "Yes, tell us."

"Well," she said, "there was an Indian gal that used to live here and she did a lot of bartering and trading of goods. Folks around here gave her the name of Betsy. One day Betsy met a gentleman by the name of John whom she married. As she continued in the bartering business, she ended up adding wine trading. The only problem with her trading wine was that she got to liking it. And when she ran out of wine, she'd turn to her husband and ask for "mo' John." That's the local legend about Betsy Mo-John."

Mr. Cassidy, Duncan and Emerson groaned at the tale.

They all entered the restaurant and made their way to the chalet room. The cathedral ceiling interior of the chalet room was filled with hand-hewn walnut beams and supports as well as paneling and extensive stonework.

After looking over the wine list, the men deferred to Aunt Anne to make the appropriate selection for dinner when the waiter appeared.

Having placed the order for a white Catawba wine, Aunt Anne looked at the men seated with her and said sadly as she reminisced, "Frank would bring me here once a year for my birthday. The ambiance here was so special to us." They saw her eyes begin to fill with tears.

Emerson reached across the table and squeezed his aunt's hand.

In an effort to divert her attention from her memories, Emerson questioned Mr. Cassidy, "Why did so many vineyards spring up in this area?"

"That an easy one to answer. It's the limestone that's mixed into the soil and the moderate temperatures. The two combine to produce grapes of outstanding quality which, in turn, makes exceptional wine."

The waiter returned with the wine and took their orders.

Mr. Cassidy suggested, "While we're waiting for the food, you two boys might ask the hostess if you can see the wine cellar here and then try to meet the chef who had worked for the L'Hostes. I believe his name was Laraux."

"Good idea. Shall we Sam?"

"Sounds like a plan."

The hostess agreed to give them a brief tour of the cellar and led them down the stairs to the huge vaulted chamber, two stories underground. She explained that the winery and cellar dated back to 1872 and the cellar walls were 4 to 6 feet thick.

Emerson and Duncan gazed in amazement at the walls lined by giant, wooden casks which were used for aging and storing the wines.

The hostess explained that interlocking stone was used in constructing the wine cellar, and that a cooper had been brought on site during the construction to build the huge barrels.

They peered through an opening in the floor and could see to the first level where champagne was aging.

The hostess explained that the winery offered 26 varieties of wine from Catawba to Cabernet Sauvignon, but its specialty was its sparkling wines.

She glanced at her watch and indicated that the tour was complete. They climbed the steps to the main level where Emerson inquired as to whether they might meet the chef named Laraux. Emerson indicated he was a reporter writing an article about life on South Bass Island – and he would like to interview Laraux since he had spent time there.

The hostess excused herself to go into the kitchen and returned momentarily. Laraux, she indicated, was out the back door taking a cigarette break. She pointed them toward the door and returned to her duties.

Emerson and Duncan opened the heavy rear door and stepped out into the fresh warm air. They saw leaning against the building a rather tall, dark haired man in a white chef's hat and jacket. Dangling from his lips was a half smoked cigarette.

"Mr. Laraux?" Emerson inquired.

"Maybe and maybe not. Who's looking for him and why?" came the surly response.

Emerson and Duncan looked at each other. Both had the same thought – Mr. Tough Guy.

Emerson decided to take a soft approach to see if it would work.

"I'm Emerson Moore from *The Washington Post* and this is my assistant Sam Duncan. I'm writing a story about life on South Bass Island and heard that you had spent time there working at the L'Hoste Estate. I wondered if I might ask you some questions regarding your observations about life on the island at the L'Hoste Estate."

"I've got nothing to say. And another thing – I don't talk to reporters." Laraux angrily put out his cigarette and tried to walk around Emerson and Duncan.

Duncan placed a hand on Laraux's shoulder to slow him.

"Hang on one nanosecond, pal. Is there something scaring you not to talk to us?"

"Nothing scares me. Consider this interview over – in

fact, consider it as never having taken place."

Laraux knocked Duncan's hand off his shoulder and walked back into the kitchen.

"I guess that's that. He sure didn't want to talk to us," Emerson commented.

Duncan shrugged.

"Something's bothering that one all right. You could see it in his eyes."

Emerson nodded his head in agreement.

"We better return to our table," Emerson suggested.

Emerson and Duncan walked through the door and the kitchen to reenter the chalet dining area.

As they walked through the kitchen, they didn't notice Laraux watching them furtively. Once he saw them return to their table, he slipped out to the garden area and approached a table with two men in deep conversation.

Laraux squatted next to one of the men and whispered what had taken place with Moore and Duncan. The man leaned closer to Laraux and whispered instructions to him.

Laraux returned to the busy kitchen and pulled aside Emerson's waiter. He whispered in the waiter's ear and the waiter nodded his head in agreement.

Emerson and Duncan relayed their failed attempt to interview Laraux to their dinner companions.

"Aunt Anne, this was one of the best walleye dinners that I ever ate," Duncan said as he pushed back a bit from the table.

"You keep on eating like this and you'll fill out just fine," she teased.

They had requested the waiter to bring their check. The waiter notified Laraux and returned to present the check to Emerson. While Emerson was reviewing the check, Laraux slipped out of the kitchen and again approached the two men in the garden.

When the two men learned that the check had been presented, they quickly paid their bill and left to retrieve their car in the parking lot. Laraux returned to the busy kitchen.

Settling their bill, Emerson and his companions left the chalet dining area and made their way through the structure to the front entrance. They continued to marvel at the architecture of the stone building and the fine condition of the landscaping as they left the building and made their way to the narrow lane in front of the restaurant which they would cross to get to the parking lot.

Emerson was walking backwards so that he could enjoy one last look at the building. The others were half turned around so that they too could take in the building's beauty one last time.

The two men sat quietly in the car with its engine idling. They had moved the car to the end of the lane where it was partially hidden in the shade of several large oak trees.

The two men had put on caps and pulled them low on their brow. They were watching Emerson and his companions leave the restaurant.

Emerson was the first one to begin to walk into the lane.

The driver stepped on the accelerator hard and the sleek Jaguar responded with its powerful engine. It leaped down the lane quickly.

Emerson didn't see it coming until it was too late. He turned and froze as he tried to make out the driver's face.

Aunt Anne screamed when she realized that her nephew was going to be hit by the speeding car.

Emerson couldn't move.

The car was on the verge of hitting him when a force from the side drove Emerson out of the car's dangerous path and onto the pebbly side of the lane.

Emerson heard a groan come from the heavy weight which now rested on top of him. He looked up and rolled Duncan off of him.

"You OK, Sam?" Emerson questioned concernedly.

Duncan groaned, "Oh, I think my leg caught a glancing blow from that car."

Aunt Anne and Mr. Cassidy were now standing over the two of them. Eager hands reached down to help them up and assist them to a nearby park bench.

"Emerson, you need to pay attention to where you're walking," Aunt Anne admonished.

"I'm not sure it was so much me paying attention as it was someone trying to use me for target practice."

"Yeah, E. I thought for a second you were a goner. Why didn't you move?" Duncan inquired as he still worked at recapturing his breath.

"I guess, first of all, I was so surprised by what was happening that I just plain froze in my tracks. And second, I was trying to figure out who was behind the wheel."

"Did you recognize them?" Mr. Cassidy asked.

"No, they both had caps pulled down low on their faces. I thought I saw the passenger grab at the steering wheel and try to pull it to one side just before I was knocked down by my guardian angel, Saint Sammy," Emerson explained. "Any idea who owns a Jag around here, Mr. Cassidy?"

"Could be anyone. The Catawba Island Yacht Club is just around the corner from here and it could be one of their members. I seem to recall Francois L'Hoste driving some sort of foreign car about that color on the island. But I couldn't see who the driver was. Couldn't tell you if it was him driving. Things happened so fast," Mr. Cassidy replied.

Emerson and Duncan looked at each other with raised eyebrows.

"Looks like you're going to have a bruise on that leg." Aunt Anne was pointing at Duncan's leg which had already begun to swell.

"I'll be right back. I'll get some ice from the restaurant."

Emerson strode quickly to the restaurant where he encountered the hostess and asked for some ice for his friend. A few minutes later, he returned and stated as he handed the ice to Duncan, "It was Francois L'Hoste."

"How do you know, E?" Duncan asked.

"I told the hostess that I thought I had seen a friend of ours in the restaurant but he left before we had a chance to say hello. When I told her his name was Francois L'Hoste, she didn't even have to check the reservations. She quickly responded that he is a regular at the restaurant and left just before us."

"Mercy!" exclaimed Aunt Anne in surprise.

"This is not good," mused Mr. Cassidy.

"Let's get Mr. Hero here back to Put-in-Bay," Emerson suggested.

Not missing an opportunity, Duncan chimed in, "That's me, Mr. Hero. Yeah, they named a chain of restaurants after me." He chuckled at his own joke.

The others just shook their heads.

They carefully assisted Duncan to the vehicle and departed for their dockage at Catawba Point. The ride was made in silence as each one of them turned over in their minds the activities of the afternoon.

A plan was formulating in the back of Emerson's mind.

≋ ≋ ≋

"Goodness sakes Emerson. Look at this article in today's paper," Aunt Anne's concerned comment greeted Emerson the next morning as he entered her kitchen. He took the paper that his aunt was holding out for him.

The story's headline read *Mon Ami Chef Killed in Hit and Run*.

The brief article explained that the accident must have taken place after 2:00 a.m. following the restaurant's closing for the night. It appeared that Laraux was walking on the berm of the main road to his nearby apartment when a passing car struck him. The investigation was continuing and more details would be forthcoming.

Emerson looked up from the paper and at his aunt.

"I'm going to report our incident to the police and our suspicion that Francois L'Hoste was the driver in our incident. L'Hoste may have seen us talking to Laraux and gone after him."

"Emerson, we need to be careful about jumping to conclusions," his aunt cautioned.

"There's no jumping. All I'm going to do is to report our incident to the police," he replied.

Following breakfast, Emerson drove the golf cart into town and parked near the police department.

∿ ∿ ∿

"Could I see Chief Wilkens please?"

The police dispatcher gave a start as she was startled by the voice over her shoulder. She had been so engrossed in studying a chart of the local water depths that she had not heard anyone enter the station's reception area.

"Sir, I'll see if he's available. And your name is?"

"Emerson Moore. He may recall meeting me at the airport following the fire at Dairy Air," Emerson offered.

The receptionist smiled and hurried into the rear of the building. She returned and ushered Emerson into the chief's small, cluttered office.

"Mr. Moore, and how can I assist you today?" the chief asked as he stood with an extended hand.

Emerson grasped his hand in greeting and settled into one of the chairs. He then went on to explain what had transpired the night before.

"Did you get the license plate number?" Wilkens asked.

"No, everything happened so fast, no one saw it," Emerson responded.

"Why don't we take a few minutes then and complete a report on this incident. I'll relay it over to the Catawba authorities and we'll see what they dig up. Especially in light of the hit and run death of the chef," the chief suggested.

The chief assisted Emerson in completing the report. Once it was done, Emerson signed it and left.

Wilkens watched the door shut after Emerson left. He then picked up the completed report and read through it. Once he finished, he began to tear the report into narrow strips and threw it into the trash can.

Shaking his head, the chief thought to himself that Emerson and most of the tourists who filed reports with him had such wild imaginations. It appeared to the chief that Emerson had it in for L'Hoste, whatever the reason was.

The chief picked up the phone and dialed Jacques L'Hoste to make him aware of the "attempted report filing."

~ ~ ~

It didn't take more than ten minutes for Emerson to drive from the police department, down Portsmouth and out to Peach Point which was on the western side of the harbor.

He parked the cart and walked out to the end of Peach Point and turned slowly 360 degrees. Since visiting Johnson's Island, Emerson's mind had been teeming with thoughts about LeBec, his short-lived escape and the mysterious disappearance of the trunk.

Emerson was even more curious as to what was in the trunk.

He tried to place himself in LeBec's shoes. Emerson recalled his research about the attempted takeover of the *Philo Parsons* and LeBec's escape.

Having completed his turn, Emerson paused to stare at Rattlesnake Island on the horizon. In his mind that was a long way to row, especially in the rain that fell that day. But his research showed that the islanders – male and female– regularly rowed the distance.

He decided to visit Rattlesnake Island.

He climbed back into the golf cart and drove the two-minute drive to the Aquatic Visitors Center. The state owned center also provided logistical support, vehicles for getting around the island and dockage for the shuttle that ran between the center and Gibraltar Island.

He approached one of the uniformed employees who was manning the shuttle boat.

"Excuse me sir. I was trying to track down Professor Anderson. Do you know if he has already left for his cave work today?"

The worker removed his sweat-soaked cap and pulled out a handkerchief to wipe his sweaty brow. It looked like he may have found someone to complain to about his heavy workload. He was that type.

"Today, I brought him and his two assistants over around 9:00 a.m. I just wish he'd pick a time that's more convenient for everyone more often."

"How's that?"

"It's the night shuttles that I don't like. Some of these college professors with all of their high and mighty education think the world owes them. I don't owe anyone, period."

He's sure got a chip on his shoulder Emerson thought. "Night Shuttles?"

"Oh yeah. Mr. Big Britches gets it in his mind that he wants to go explore a cave at midnight. So he calls me to pick him up. Then, when he wants to return to the island at 5:00 in the morning, he's knocking at my door and I have to get up to take him back."

"You know it doesn't matter to him whether it's day or night, it looks the same when you're in a cave," Emerson chuckled as he commented.

"You're one of them professors aren't ya? I can just tell."

"No, I'm not. Do you know which cave he headed to today?"

"No, but there's a phone inside the door," he said as he pointed to one of the doors to one of the state support buildings. "Next to the phone is a list of numbers. Use it and call the Stone Building's Lab. They keep a sign out sheet. You gotta tell em which cave you're gonna work at. That's so they can try to find you if you don't return."

Emerson thanked him and went inside the building to call. The staff were very cooperative in not only telling Emerson which cave, but in also providing him directions for driving there.

Emerson walked up the hill to the parking lot and climbed into the golf cart. He started the cart and drove along the western side of the island on West Shore Drive. As he drove, he again turned over in his mind LeBec's ill-fated escape to Rattlesnake Island, which he could still see through the trees and on the horizon. Soon it was lost to his sight.

As he turned onto Trenton Ave, Emerson drove past the gated L'Hoste Estate with its prominent "No Trespassing" signage. He could see through the fence and the evergreens to catch glimpses of the stone French chateau structure, which he recalled from his flight, attached to the rear of the freighter's bow.

One day, he thought to himself, I'd like to see the inside of the building.

As he turned onto Catawba Avenue, he looked again at his directions and found that he was nearing the cave. He drove up a short, narrow drive and parked at the top.

He was surprised that there wasn't a vehicle parked close to the cave's entrance. He had been told that they were using one of the Ohio State pick up trucks, but he didn't see one nearby. He did see light coming from the cave's entrance and decided to investigate.

Emerson eased himself through the narrow opening and felt the cave's coolness provide a welcome relief from the day's heat. He also began to get a bit nervous as he had been when he had visited Perry's Cave with Martine and Austin.

He sat down for a moment on a rock protruding just inside the entrance. He took several deep breaths as he tried to calm himself. Visiting Perry's Cave was a first step in overcoming his fear. Today would be another step.

After resting for a few minutes, Emerson's breathing normalized and he stood up to make his way deeper into the cave where the light was brighter.

Soon he spied two college men with meters and other sorts of equipment.

"Excuse me gentlemen," he said.

The two men whipped their heads around quickly in the direction of the voice. Emerson had startled them.

"I was told I could find Professor Anderson here."

The closer of the two responded, "Oh, he's been gone for some time. He usually helps us set up our studies and tests and then goes out on his own to other caves to do other testing. He usually returns within 3 to 4 hours."

"Isn't that a bit dangerous with you not knowing where he is?"

"Oh, these caves are really quite safe," responded the other research assistant.

"Don't be too sure of that. I had a bad experience in one of these caves years ago," Emerson warned.

"We've been examining the caves all summer without one incident. Maybe a few bumps and bruises, but that's it. We're pretty careful and so is Professor Anderson," the research assistant added.

"Do you have any idea where the Professor went?"

"No, he's got the truck. It's got an Ohio State decal on the doors. If you find the truck, you'll find the Professor in a nearby cave."

"Thanks, I'll see if I can locate him," Emerson said as he began to leave. Emerson stopped and looked back at the two men. "Do you guys do a lot of research in the caves at night?"

"Not us, it's downtown party time at night or we're playing volleyball on Gibraltar Island," the one closest to Emerson responded. "Why?"

"Oh just curious, I guess. Thanks again."

Emerson made his way out of the cave and into the bright sunlight. He winced while his eyes adjusted to the sun's glare.

Emerson carefully turned the cart around and headed back to his aunt's. Shortly after he passed the Trenton Street intersection, a truck with an Ohio State decal on the doors pulled to a stop.

The road was relatively deserted other than a golf cart heading toward town. The truck eased onto Catawba and drove up to the cave site where the two research assistants were working.

Professor Anderson stepped out of the truck and joined his two assistants in completing their work for the day.

≈ ≈ ≈

He was looking intently through the binoculars at the bikini-clad girl on the cabin cruiser in the harbor when a voice piped over his shoulder.

"Anything interesting or are you just girl watching?"

Duncan jumped at his friend's voice and put down the binoculars.

"Both," he replied with a smile. "The girl was very interesting."

"Well you must be up to your old ornery self if you were able to come out here on the dock with the binoculars."

Duncan just winked at Emerson.

"Sam the man, since you're already out here on the dock, are you up to taking a ride with me over to Rattlesnake Island?"

"That LeBec still playing with your mind?"

Emerson nodded his head several times. "Yes, he is Sam. Other than crossing alligator reef in the channel between Put-in-Bay and Gibraltar Island, I'd like to try to duplicate LeBec's path to the Rattlesnake Island. I'd like to try to understand what he saw while he was rowing. Kind of putting ourselves in his shoes."

"Then, let's go E."

They both jumped into the dinghy with Duncan in the bow and Emerson at the stern. Emerson checked to make sure they had enough fuel and started the little outboard engine.

The engine caught and the little dinghy headed out of the harbor and around Gibraltar Island to Alligator Reef. Positioning themselves in the channel with Rattlesnake Island straight ahead, Emerson set the craft's course for Rattlesnake Island.

As they went through the relatively calm blue waters, they both scanned the horizon and tried to picture what it would have been like that rainy afternoon. They were unsure of the wind's direction during LeBec's journey so they couldn't estimate whether he was initially pushed farther west or east.

During one of their prior conversations, Mr. Cassidy had given them some rough directions to where it was believed that LeBec's body had been located. He said that some people rumored a group of millionaires had purchased the island and others rumored that Mafia members bought it. Regardless, the occupants did not like visitors and had security guards patrolling the island – so they would have to be vigilant.

Duncan had asked if rattlesnakes inhabited the island and was visibly relieved when Mr. Cassidy responded negatively.

The dinghy was closing the 2 miles to the island. Emerson found himself wishing that they had packed a cooler with ice water. The midafternoon sun beat down on them relentlessly in the open watercraft.

"Sam, any thoughts about what LeBec might have done? Anything that we've seen so far give you any ideas?"

"That's a negatory. The only idea that I had was that he

might have pushed the trunk overboard if the waves were getting too high."

"I don't think so Sam. The trunk weighed so much that it took several men to carry it on board the *Philo Parsons* in Windsor and there were reports that the winch on the *Philo Parsons* was used to lower the trunk into the skiff he used."

"Well, I don't know how he moved it then."

"Sam, what if he had accomplices waiting for him on Rattlesnake Island? They could have helped unload the trunk or placed it on a bigger ship? Then killed him and left him."

"You're forgetting two things, E."

"And they are?"

"One, I doubt that any sane accomplices would be just hanging out on Rattlesnake Island the way people said it was infested with rattlesnakes. Besides, there weren't any reports that we could find that listed any unusual shipping activity in the area."

"Good point. What's the second thing?" Sam was making some very good observations Emerson thought.

"The gunboat sailed around Rattlesnake Island after the storm broke and didn't find any evidence of recent landings. Even they were reluctant to go ashore and do a search on foot because of the rattlesnakes. They did search Green Island and found nothing. But the real point is that LeBec's body didn't show up until the next day. Where was he during all that time?"

"That we don't know. What we do know for certain is that he was on his way to the rainbow's end and that's what everyone called Rattlesnake Island."

Emerson continued, "Let's forget about the weight of the trunk for a second. If it was on the island, you'd think someone would have found it. They had extensive searches for the missing trunk on the island and no one found anything."

"Maybe the current owners found something and that's why they don't want anyone snooping around," Sam offered as he positioned himself to jump out of the dinghy onto the nearing shore.

Emerson cut the engine, and the dinghy continued its forward motion. Duncan jumped out and pulled the craft up on the rocky beach. He then turned around and scanned the ground.

When he looked up, he saw Emerson watching him and grinning.

"You know E, you just can't be too careful when it comes to rattlesnakes."

"There's one thing you may have missed," Emerson said as he pointed to a sign.

Duncan turned and looked at the sign.

Private Property – Absolutely No Trespassing

"Things like that have never stopped us before, E."

"Sam, earlier I suggested that LeBec may have had accomplices waiting for him here. On second thought, I don't think that's the case. We've got to remember that what happened that afternoon was not planned. It was the result of their plan's failure. And another thing – no one supposedly knew what was in the trunk. I know it still doesn't resolve the missing trunk issue, but I just don't believe there were any accomplices involved."

"Yeah, I forgot that what happened was kind of a spur of the moment thing," Duncan concurred.

"And another thing, I don't think LeBec rowed here first." Emerson continued as he looked back toward Put-in-Bay and Green Island, "I'd say the storm was too strong for him to row in and he put in a creek or small bay on the west side of the South Bass Island or on Green Island. Although I'm skeptical that he went to Green Island since it was searched after the storm broke."

They had been walking along the rocky shoreline in an area which did not appear to be inhabited. They didn't see anything that would lend credence to LeBec hiding the trunk here.

They also didn't see the security guard appear from behind a stand of trees.

"You boys lost?"

Emerson and Duncan looked up on the rocky ledge to where the uniformed guard held a shotgun loosely in his arms.

"Is this Cedar Point?" Duncan asked as he referred to the huge amusement park located on Sandusky Bay.

"No, but if you're looking for a thrill pal, you've come to

the right place." The guard responded in a menacing tone as he brought the shotgun up to bear on the two.

"Let me apologize for my friend, sir," Emerson said rapidly in hopes of not causing the situation to escalate. He could sense his friend tensing and didn't want him to do something rash.

Emerson tried to explain further by acting dumb. "We're tourists staying in Put-in-Bay and thought we'd take a ride out to this island so we could explore the beach."

Emerson wasn't sure whether the guard would buy the story or not. Then, he noticed that the guard seemed to relax a bit.

"You're on private property. The owners don't like trespassers so, if I was you two, I'd head right back to my boat and get out of here while the getting is good and I'm in a good mood. As a matter of fact, I'll escort you to your boat and give you a right fine bon voyage."

The guard motioned with his gun for them to turn around and head back in the direction from where they had come. He walked about 5 paces behind them.

Emerson looked sideways at Duncan and whispered, "Easy there Samurai Warrior. Let it drop."

Duncan relaxed for Emerson's sake. As happy-go-lucky as he appeared, Duncan still took his work seriously and didn't like the fact that he had allowed some one to catch him off guard. Duncan felt that he was slipping from his past training.

When they reached the dinghy, Emerson and Duncan pushed the boat out into the water. Emerson started the motor and they headed back to Put-in-Bay. They both looked anxiously over their shoulder at the guard who was watching them.

They were relieved when the guard turned and went back into the woods. He was apparently bluffing about a special bon voyage to make them nervous. It had worked. They both relaxed and enjoyed the ride back to Aunt Anne's dock.

$$\approx \ \approx \ \approx$$

The Marquis by Waterford ship's decanter was carefully placed on the tray. The decanter, which was today filled with a fine Bordeaux, was classically designed and bottom-heavy to ensure perfect balance on sea or land.

The cut crystal wineglass featured a formal distinction but with gentle, fine curves and soft lines.

Jacques L'Hoste gently swirled the wine in the glass before lifting it to his lips to savor the taste.

He had replayed in his mind the courtesy phone call that he had received that morning from Chief Wilkens. He had been perfunctory with the chief and had thanked him for calling with the information regarding Emerson Moore's complaint filing. He was pleased with the chief's actions in destroying the complaint.

Sometimes these types of matters would have a life of their own. Other times, he would find it necessary to forcibly intervene to finalize matters. That's the way it had always been for the L'Hoste family.

Jacques would speak to Francois to achieve a better comprehension of the matter. Once he had Francois' facts, he would devise the appropriate solution.

He sat down in the raised pilot's chair to watch what promised to be a spectacular sunset.

≈ ≈ ≈

The Fourth of July dawned with clear skies and calm waters. There was an air of festivity in Put-in-Bay as islanders and tourists alike looked forward to the day's celebration, which included another parade through town at noon, and a giant fireworks show that evening at 10:00 p.m.

There was additional excitement this year as the fireworks would be displayed for the first time behind Perry's Monument. It was anticipated that the monument would look absolutely magnificent with the exploding fireworks above and behind it.

Emerson and Duncan were trying to get an extra sheen of brightness on the Model A in preparation for the day's parade. Aunt Anne had purchased more candy to throw to the children lining the route. Duncan, the rascal, had purchased beads in case he saw any pretty ladies. He was careful to make sure that Aunt Anne did not see them hidden in the bottom of his candy bag.

The morning passed quickly and it was time for the

parade to start. Emerson had maneuvered the Model A into position. Aunt Anne sat next to him in the passenger side and Duncan sat in the truck's bed.

As the parade started, the Model A turned off Toledo Avenue and onto Delaware. Emerson spied Martine and Austin on the sidewalk as the Model A made the turn. They were waving at the folks and vehicles in the parade.

As they approached the two, Emerson gave the horn a loud toot and Austin's head quickly turned to look into Emerson's eyes. His face beamed upon recognizing his old buddy. So did Martine's when she saw Emerson.

Emerson slowed the vehicle and pulled in toward the curb.

"Austin, jump in fast, son. You can toot the horn for us."

Understanding that they couldn't lose a second, Martine helped Austin climb over Emerson and snuggle in between him and Aunt Anne. Austin started tooting the horn immediately.

"What about me, Emerson?" Martine asked as she walked rapidly along side the moving vehicle which Emerson began steering back into his position in the procession.

"Jump back here with me!" pleaded Duncan.

Martine took one look at Duncan's outstretched hands which were filled with beaded necklaces and asked again, "What about me, Emerson?"

Duncan gave her a mock frown.

"Jump up here on the running board next to me," shouted Emerson.

"But I might fall," she said nervously as she jumped.

Emerson reached out to steady her and swept his arm around her narrow waist. Smart move he grinned to himself.

She bent down to grab some candy that Aunt Anne handed her and threw candy to the children. Once the parade ended and Emerson stopped the vehicle, Martine, said, "OK, you can let go."

"Let go?" Emerson asked playing dumb.

"My waist, kind sir."

"Oh that, sure, I guess I could do that Mrs. Tobin," he responded.

They spent a few minutes chattering amongst the five of them. After Aunt Anne and Duncan had settled in the Model A, Austin spoke up to Emerson, "Mr. Moore, would you like to come with us tonight? We're going to watch the fireworks from the shuttle boat."

Emerson looked from Austin to his mother. There was nothing more that he would rather do this evening he thought to himself.

"That type of offer should be okayed by your mother, Austin," Emerson suggested.

"Mom. Mom, is it OK if he comes? Grandpa and Dad can't come tonight."

Martine mulled it over for a couple of seconds and decided. "Sure. If they want to run off and work tonight, that's their problem. They'll miss out on all the fun."

Turning to Emerson, she explained further, "Dad is in the middle of some sort of find and wants to work tonight. Tim has another one of those dinner meetings with some important visitors at the L'Hostes and will watch the fireworks with them."

It seemed strange to Emerson that they were not planning to spend the evening together as a family. He remembered how he, his wife and son drove into Washington DC together to watch Fourth of July fireworks on the mall.

Emerson recalled talk that this year's fireworks show was going to be even more spectacular than last year's due to a large contribution made by the L'Hostes to make it the best ever. L'Hoste must want to impress his visitors, Emerson thought to himself.

"Emerson, we'll pick you up at your aunt's dock at 9:45, OK?"

"That would be great," he said excitedly.

"Emerson, do you think your aunt and Sam would like to join us?"

"Oh Mom, why can't it just be Mr. Moore?" Austin begged. He didn't want anyone else stealing his hero's time or attention.

Trying to help, Emerson said, "I believe that they want to just sit out tonight on the dock and watch the fireworks from there. The fireworks are practically in her backyard."

"Fine, then. We will see you at 9:45. Let's go, Austin. We promised Daddy and Grandpa we would be back right after the parade was over."

"OK then, I'll see you both tonight," Emerson called as he settled in behind the steering wheel and started the Model A's engine.

The two of them waved as they headed the short distance to the dock and the shuttle to Gibraltar Island.

"That boy of hers sure has taken to you, Emerson," Aunt Anne commented.

"And so has that boy's mother," offered Duncan quickly from the pick up bed.

Emerson reached around and tried to playfully punch Sam, but Sam ducked just in time.

Emerson pulled onto Bay View and began the drive back to his aunt's house.

$$\approx \ \approx \ \approx$$

Promptly at 9:45, Martine nudged the shuttle against the dock where Emerson was waiting. Emerson, clad in a t-shirt, shorts and sandals, jumped aboard.

"You're right on time," he said as he greeted Martine. Austin charged across the boat into Emerson's arms and was swept up in the air. "And how's my little buddy?"

"Grrrreeeaaaaatttttt!" he beamed up at his idol. "Mom let me help drive the boat tonight." Turning to his mother, he asked, "Mom, can I show Mr. Moore that I know how to drive?"

"Sure, sweetie. Hop up here."

Austin hopped up on a bench which had been placed in front of the pilot wheel and began to help steer the boat as they sought an anchorage spot in the harbor for watching the fireworks.

"He's been so excited today about the fireworks and seeing you. I tried to get him to take his nap, but his energy level wouldn't subside," she smiled. "He's going to have a tough time staying up to watch all of the fireworks."

Emerson smiled back in understanding. He also took in her great smile. He felt a ripple of energy surge through his body as he looked at her smile. She just exuded a freshness and sense of optimism with that smile. And the sparkle in her eyes added to her alluring beauty.

Realizing that she had been talking to him and he hadn't heard a thing she said, Emerson commented, "I'm sorry. I wasn't paying attention. I was distracted for a moment."

"I said, would you mind dropping anchor. I think this is a good anchorage."

"Oh, sure." Emerson moved quickly to drop anchor at the edge of the main channel.

As he stepped away, Martine's eyes followed him and she thought to herself that Emerson's distraction may have been her. He seemed to have been staring at her. She had a feeling that he was attracted to her as much as she was becoming attracted to him.

She had always felt that even in married life one could become attracted to another person outside of the marriage. What was important was what you did to manage the attraction and not let it go beyond that stage. She had never strayed, but this ruggedly good-looking and kind man was going to make it difficult for her.

Emerson looked across the water and could see his aunt's house outlined in the shadows. He thought he saw three figures on his aunt's dock sitting in lawn chairs with their backs to the water.

Martine, Emerson and Austin moved to sit on a number of cushions which Martine placed on the deck.

$$\approx \ \approx \ \approx$$

The figure on the Boardwalk's outdoor deck on the second floor set down the beer bottle and stood up to leave.

From his vantage point on the second floor and with a panoramic view of the entire harbor, he had watched Martine and Austin board their borrowed boat and make their way to the green house's dock at the east end of the harbor. He then watched through the growing twilight as a figure boarded the boat and the boat made its way to its anchorage point.

He left a tip and made his way through the crowd to his golf cart which was parked in the nearby parking lot. He climbed in and began driving toward the L'Hoste Estate.

As they sat down, Martine produced a Catawba Chablis for Emerson and her – and poured grape juice in a cup for Austin. Austin with his ever-present mini-boom box/re-corder began playing his Disney soundtrack.

At 10:00, the first of the fireworks began to streak into the sky from behind Perry's Monument. Ooohs and aaahs could be heard across the water from the fireworks watchers as they built in magnificence and turned the black sky into a cornucopia of color.

It was as if the sky had become a canvas and an artist was scattering a wide array of colors from his palette to the accompaniment of the booming sound effects. Although each painting of color lasted but seconds, it was phenomenal.

Austin sat between Martine and Emerson and screamed with glee at the display. Like other children, he'd cover his ears from time to time to protect them from the deafening booms.

Once the 30-minute display was capped by the show-ending extravaganza, boat motors around them began to start up as the other watchers changed anchorage and headed for the downtown bars.

"Shall we wait until some of the boat traffic has died down?" Martine asked. She noticed that Austin had snuggled up against Emerson and seemed to have fallen asleep. She was not ready for the nice evening to end.

"Sure sounds like a great idea," Emerson agreed. "It's such a beautiful night. The air is fresh and the company sure is delightful."

Emerson looked at Martine and smiled at her. She had been looking down at Austin and just raised her eyes to look up at Emerson. The effect was devastating to him. She was so attractive he thought and he knew he better be careful or he'd begin spilling his guts to her. He promised himself that he wouldn't.

He broke that promise 10 seconds later.

"I really appreciate your friendship Martine. You just have a special something about you that energizes me and makes me realize that there is more to life than what I've been experiencing lately."

"Oh?" she asked curiously.

"I've been going through a desert time in my life and you are like an oasis that encourages me to go on."

"An oasis?"

"Yes, an oasis. An oasis is a place where one can go for nourishment and refreshment. And in some unexplainable way, you refresh and invigorate me."

Martine was now listening intently. It seemed that Emerson had some rough issues that he was hanging on to and not able to let go.

"Tell me about your travel in the desert," she said as she glanced down again at Austin.

Emerson explained about his marriage and the sudden death of his wife and son. He told her about how deeply he loved his wife and the acute despair that had overwhelmed him following her death.

"Emerson, I am so sorry. I had no idea," she said in a consoling tone.

He talked about his drinking and the leave of absence that the *Post* had given him. He recalled their first meeting and how he felt their friendship had grown.

"Emerson, I want you to know that I care about you. And I care about you deeply ... as a friend," Martine said. She wanted to say more but knew that they both were vulnerable emotionally.

"And I do care about you too," he added.

Just as he was going to say more a passing boat's wake rocked their boat and some sense in Emerson.

"Emerson. When we visited Perry's Cave, I noticed how uncomfortable you appeared as we began to enter the cave. You were shaking a few times and I saw beads of sweat on you even though it was cool down there. Does what you just explained have any bearing on that?"

Emerson took a deep breath. He had not discussed the accident with anyone since it happened. He had tried his best to blot it out of his mind.

Emerson began to tell her the story.

$\approx \approx \approx$

On one particularly hot July day, his cousin, Jack, and he had decided to cool off by exploring some of the caves. They had been warned not to go cave exploring on their own, but it was such a hot day – and they felt a quick exploration would hurt no one.

The boys grabbed rope, candles and flashlights and jumped on their bikes. They went along the harbor to Duff's Cave near Peach Point on the western side of the island.

Parking their bikes next to the limestone rock outcropping which marked the entrance to the cave the boys carefully made their way down the slippery slope to the cave's entrance. Not many of the island's residents ventured near the cave since it was full of water and offered little dry area to walk.

The boys were intrigued by the opportunity to cool off where the temperatures stayed at 55 degrees year round. They wanted to see the large stalactites, which hung from the ceiling and see if any bats were making the cave their home. They turned on their flashlights and entered the cave, enjoying the crisp coolness and relief from the heat.

Shining their lights upward, Jack and he admired the varied stalactite formations. They laughed as they assigned names like carrot top and fudgesicle to the different stalactites, depending on what they resembled.

Shining their lights downward, they could see the cave's floor quickly sloping away to reveal water and several stalagmites. The boys had heard that beneath the water's surface, stalagmites protruded like a deadly bed of razor sharp spikes from the cave's floor.

Being the more adventuresome of the two, Jack turned to Emerson and said, "There's a stalactite that may be thin enough to break off."

Looking to where Jack was pointing, Emerson saw that

it was about ten feet out of Jack's reach.

"There's no way that we can get to it from here. And we probably shouldn't break them off," Emerson replied.

"If I edge myself along this small shelf and hold onto the ledge above, I think I can get there." Jack began to slowly make his way along the edge.

"Jack, it's too dangerous. Just forget it. Let's just hang out," urged Emerson.

Jack's feet slipped off the ledge and he dangled above the water, holding on with both hands gripping the ledge above.

"Jaaacccckkkk," Emerson screamed at seeing his cousin out of his reach and hanging precariously.

Using his strength and nimbleness, Jack was able to swing his feet back onto the small edge. He turned to Emerson and smiling said, "Piece of cake."

Coming within arm's length of the small stalactite, Jack carefully let go of the ledge above with one hand and reached to grab the stalactite to shake it loose. As he let go of the slippery ledge, his other hand could not hold him.

Screaming, Jack tumbled backward into the water and impaled himself on two stalagmites jutting out of the water. They fatally pierced his lung and abdomen.

"Jaaacccckkkk," cried Emerson in anguish as he shone the light on Jack.

Jack moaned as blood seeped from his mouth and his

pierced body was filled with pain, "I don't want to die. Please, I'm too young to die."

"I'll get help," yelled Emerson and he stood to race from the cave when Jack's voice called him back.

"Emerson, please don't go. I don't want to die in here by myself. I don't want to be alone. Please don't leave me. I feel so weak." Jack's voice was barely audible.

"I won't leave you," Emerson replied with tears cascading from his eyes. He sat down and tried to console his cousin and himself by talking about all the fun that they had shared on the island over the years.

≈ ≈ ≈

When the boys missed dinner and it started to get dark, Uncle Frank and Aunt Anne with a few of their neighbors started searching the island for the boys. Knowing that the bikes were gone, they drove around trying to spot them.

One of the neighbors, who was an island fireman, spotted the two bikes outside the cave's entrance and feared the worst. He called in for support.

They found Emerson late that night in the cold cave shivering, but still talking to the lifeless body of his cousin. They placed blankets around Emerson to warm him and help him recover from the shock that he was in.

Carefully the rescuers retrieved Jack's body.

Emerson had refused to leave the cave until they laid

the recovered body next to where he was seated.

Emerson reached down and squeezed the hand of his cousin, "I didn't leave you."

The funeral took place on the island two days later. Jack was buried in the island's cemetery.

Emerson's parents, who had flown in for the funeral, took their son home.

Emerson would not return to the island again for a summer vacation.

~ ~ ~

"Emerson, I had no idea. I am so sorry about what you went through," Martine said as she placed her hand on Emerson's arm in a comforting manner.

"Thanks," he responded as he looked at her. "It's been tough. I relive that accident over and over."

"And now I understand your Aunt's reluctance."

"My Aunt's reluctance?"

"Yes. When she took me for a tour of the house and we went up to the second floor, she opened the door so that I could peek into Jack's room. She said she has kept it the way it was since the last time he used it. When I asked her about her son, she didn't want to discuss it. I think she wanted you to be the one to tell me. Your aunt is a wise woman."

"Maybe that's why," he agreed. "You know, she and my uncle used to send me notes over the years to let me know that I should not be so hard on myself and that they didn't hold me responsible. She's a great lady."

"Yes, she is Emerson."

They both were quiet for the next few minutes.

Emerson broke the silence.

"I just love being out here. It is so peaceful."

He turned toward Martine.

"And you make it even more special, Mrs. Tobin." He addressed her in this manner to again remind himself that she was a married woman.

"Why thank you very much Emerson."

The use of her married name was not lost on her. She realized that he was trying his best to respect boundaries.

"Where did your folks come up with the name Martine? It sounds just perfect for you."

"They honeymooned on the island of St. Martin and shortly after they returned mom realized she was pregnant. They both decided that they should name me after where I was conceived."

"Good thing they didn't honeymoon in a Winnebago," he teased.

"Stop it. You're bad," Martine responded good-naturedly.

"Would you like another glass of wine?"

"Sure."

Martine stood and began to make her way to the boat's cabin when a passing boat's unusually large wake rocked the boat and caused her to fall. As she fell, she brushed against Austin's mini boombox and inadvertently turned on the radio. The air was filled with strains of a romantic ballad.

Emerson laughed as he moved across the deck and reached down to assist her up. Martine took his outstretched hand and stood, finding herself very close to Emerson.

Emerson was caught up in the moment and asked, "Care to dance with a lonely sailor?"

"OK sailor. Let's dance."

Her eyes smiled invitingly at Emerson.

She felt herself surrounded by Emerson as he held her to dance to the song's slow, sensual beat.

The song's words filled the air with a story about two would be lovers who struggled to control their passions for one another and the man's desire to kiss the woman.

Their bodies began to mold together as the music played.

Emerson thought how perfectly she fit against him. She seemed meant for him.

They listened to the song's words intently as they danced slowly. The song ended, but they were oblivious to the announcer's ramblings. They stood together with their arms around each other. The moment was charged with electricity.

Martine looked deeply into Emerson's eyes and he dreamily returned her look. Their two heads began to move closer together. Emerson wetted his lips. Martine closed her eyes.

Just before their lips made contact, Martine felt Emerson pull away and saw him rush to the boat's edge and dive into the water. Martine rushed to the boat's side.

Emerson's head broke the water's surface.

"Emerson, what in the world are you doing?" she asked in astonishment and exasperation.

"Mrs. Tobin, you are a woman of honor and I need to respect it. It's time for me to go!"

"Don't be silly. I'll take you back to your aunt's. Come on. You can get back on board," she said as she looked at the distance to his aunt's house.

As he reached down and removed his sandals and secured them to his belt, he shouted, "No, no. I can use the exercise. See you sometime in the next few days. And Martine."

She leaned over the edge, "Yes?"

"Thanks for your company and tonight. I enjoyed it. In fact, I enjoyed it way too much." With that, he turned and began taking powerful strokes across the harbor to his aunt's dock.

Men Martine thought to herself. She knew in her heart

that Emerson was a man of character and, to her chagrin, she knew he did the right thing.

Martine checked to make sure that Austin was still sound asleep and walked into the pilothouse to start the shuttle's engine.

The shuttle moved slowly across the harbor to the docks at Gibraltar Island. Once docked, Martine picked up Austin and carried him to the cottage.

This certainly is an evening that I will not forget she thought.

$\sim$ $\sim$ $\sim$

The swim across the harbor was longer than Emerson thought it would be. When he reached the dock and pulled himself out of the water, he rested for a few minutes.

Wearily, he stood up and made his way to the house where he found the door to the enclosed porch unlocked for him. Not wanting to drip water from his wet clothes through the house, he stripped them off and spread them out to dry on the backs of the chairs on the porch.

He then made his way up the stairs and eased himself into his bed. Just before he fell asleep, he thought about Martine. What a good woman she was.

$\sim$ $\sim$ $\sim$

Tim stepped off the shuttle onto the dock at Gibraltar Island. It had been a long night entertaining business guests.

They had the guests in for the dinner at the L'Hoste's. Mr. L'Hoste had excused himself as planned from attending the fireworks display but had encouraged the guests to go with Francois and Tim.

The group carefully descended the iron stairway from the house to the dock below where the *Mon Ami* awaited. The group boarded the sleek craft and Francois started its powerful engine.

Shortly after he eased it away from the dock, he opened the throttle suddenly causing their guests to catch them selves from falling as the boat surged forward, virtually leaping out of the water. Francois' face had a sly grin.

Once they had recovered, they laughed nervously at each other. They were concerned that Francois would run the boat at full speed in the early darkness of the evening. Francois' recklessness and seeming lack of caution concerned the guests.

It always concerned Tim, but Francois was his boss and he needed the job. Sometimes, it was just easier to do and say nothing.

Francois eased off the throttle as the boat began to enter the waters between Gibraltar Island and Middle Bass Island. The boat anchored closer to Middle Bass Island and they settled back to enjoy the fireworks which had already started behind Perry's Monument.

~ ~ ~

From the windows of the pilothouse, Jacques L'Hoste watched as the boat sped away from the dock with Francois at the helm.

Jacques slowly eased himself into the large raised chair behind the ship's wheel in the pilothouse. He sighed deeply.

Foolish boy, foolish boy he thought. When will he or better yet, will he ever be able to become what Jacques had become – a ruthless, successful businessman? Jacques doubted it. He was too hotheaded, he couldn't focus on business issues and make sound decisions. As far as interpersonal skills, they were virtually nonexistent.

The psychologists and neurologists felt that he had the same mental disorder as Jacques' wife, a condition which caused Jacques to divorce her. Due to her continued mental deterioration, she was now housed in a full-time care facility, and he was paying her housing costs.

The lack of interpersonal skills was one of the reasons Francois couldn't find a decent wife. There were women interested. Of course, they were interested. They wanted to tap into the L'Hoste wealth. But Jacques had taken care of them. He ran some off with threats. Others he bought off. When the paternity suit was filed by one of the woman, Jacques had been shocked when he learned that the tests showed not only was Francois not the father, but Francois could never be a father.

Jacques had arranged for a series of exams by a number of leading doctors and for batteries of testing on Francois. All had come back with the same result – Francois would never be able to father a child.

That would mean that it would be the end of the line for the L'Hoste family. Jacques had a concern with Francois' long-term mental capacity and his ability to effectively manage projects or a business. For that matter, Francois couldn't even manage himself well. Jacques would have to be the one to fulfill his namesake's vow for revenge against the islanders for driving the L'Hostes from town.

This vow had been passed from father to son with each son unquestionably committed to taking revenge when the timing was appropriate to uphold the family's honor.

Jacques felt the necessity to fulfill the vow was on his shoulders. He had set the wheels in motion several years ago as he became more and more aware of Francois' shortcomings.

≈ ≈ ≈

The shade on the light tilted as Professor Anderson adjusted it to better see the map he was studying in the new cave that he had discovered.

He knew that he should have spent the evening with his daughter and grandson, but he was running out of time. He would only be staying on the island for another four weeks before needing to return to Ohio State to continue research in the lab and prepare for his fall classes.

His studies were showing that South Bass Island and probably the other area islands were made up of an erosional resistant limestone base. Erosion of the less resistant limestone created the island's many caves – especially the ones with underwater channels.

The cave that he was in now also had an underwater channel, and he had observed that the water seemed to rise and fall with the water level of Lake Erie. He was convinced that many of the underwater channels were interconnected.

To prove that he would have to employ a scuba diver to assist in his research. But his research was too sensitive, and he couldn't afford to have word leak as to what his findings were. It was even too delicate for his two research assistants to be made aware of.

The professor glanced at his watch and was surprised at how late it was. It was almost 5:00 a.m. He finished his notes for the evening and placed everything in his portable desk before closing and locking it.

He grabbed his flashlight and turned off the portable desk light.

Leaving the cave, he climbed into the truck's cab. As he started the truck, he realized how tired he was. Too many late nights he thought to himself as he headed to the State Fish Hatchery's parking lot and the shuttle boat to Gibraltar Island.

≈ ≈ ≈

"Sir, security indicates that a vehicle just parked across from the main gate. It appears to be an old truck."

William had interrupted Jacques L'Hoste's review of his company's quarterly financial results which showed a net profit increase of 16%.

Jacques looked up from his desk.

"Why are you interrupting me about this intrusion? Vehicles stop occasionally to view the estate. People want to peer at the ship's superstructure as close as possible. You don't need to interrupt me with inconsequential matters. You know better than that!"

As much as he liked having the ship's bow as part of the residence, it did have one downfall. It attracted quite a few sightseers.

William was nervous. He was well aware that Mr. L'Hoste did not like interruptions when he was concentrating on financial reports.

He cleared his throat and began nervously.

"Henri is on duty in the security center. He observed on the closed circuit monitor that one of the vehicle's occupants is the man with whom Francois fought in town a few nights ago. Henri had accompanied Francois into town and recognized him."

Jacques leaned back in his chair and thought. This must be the person about whom Chief Wilkens had phoned. The chief had told him about Francois' alleged involvement in a hit and run near the Mon Ami Restaurant and the man who had filed the report was an investigative reporter with *The Washington Post*.

Jacques recalled that the chief had called previously about the fire at the Island Airport and indicated that this reporter was the one who flew over the estate and crashed into the lake. A police report had been filed at that time also.

Jacques did not need an investigative reporter trying to use his investigative methods to learn more about the L'Hostes or nosing around the estate at this time. It was time to take a direct and a controlling approach with this matter.

"Sir, what would you like me to do?"

Jacques turned back from staring out the window at the lake and said, "I'd like you to tell them that we noticed them admiring the estate and we would like to welcome them in for a guided tour. I'd like you to escort them here to my study to meet me."

"Yes, sir." William turned and made his way through the huge residence and toward the main gate.

Jacques closed his financial report file. It was now time to meet his son's adversary. He would make him very comfortable as he brought him into his lair for a discussion.

The old man thought about others who tried to take advantage of him or wouldn't honor his requests. They paid a stiff price.

～ ～ ～

Emerson and Duncan had driven the old truck to the far side of Put-in-Bay's harbor to Peach Point, the narrow point of land extending like a finger and pointing to Rattlesnake Island. It had been a warm morning and a fresh breeze helped to moderate the temperature on what promised to be a very warm July day.

They had made their way south along the western edge of the island and pulled over across from the L'Hoste Estate's main gate.

They exited the vehicle and leaned against it as they stared at what they could see of the estate through the gate's iron grillwork. The entire estate as far as they could tell was surrounded by an eight-foot high iron fence with barbed wire on top to discourage intruders. To further provide privacy, rows of evergreen trees effectively prevented outsiders from seeing the grounds.

Looking through the gate, they could see the driveway making its way through a well-manicured lawn with statuary and flowerbeds. The drive led to the three storied building through a covered entryway and back to the main gate.

They could see part of the bow section of the huge freighter, *SAUVIGNON*. "Bet you can see some great sunsets from that bow section," Duncan commented as he imagined himself sitting there at day's end.

"They would be magnificent," concurred Emerson.

"And that's not the only thing that the occupants can see," Duncan said with an air of mystery.

Emerson looked at Duncan and saw Duncan's eyes motioning to a security camera atop the gate. Emerson allowed his eyes to follow the top of the estate's fence and noticed several security cameras mounted.

"Hey, we're on Candid camera. I'm going to moon them." Duncan began to turn around and unbuckle his shorts when Emerson spoke softly.

"We've got company."

Emerson nodded toward the main gate.

Since their attention had been diverted from the chateau to the camera, they did not see the figure approaching them.

The huge gate swung open magically without any action by the approaching figure.

"Good morning gentlemen," William stated stiffly.

Emerson and Duncan returned his greeting.

"Mr. L'Hoste, the owner of our estate, was made aware that you appeared to be admiring our beautiful grounds and has decided to extend to you an invitation to take a brief tour of the property and to meet with him for coffee. Would you like to follow me?"

"Well, that's real nice. Just real nice," Duncan said sarcastically.

Emerson put his hand on Duncan's arm to stop him from going further.

"Thank you. We would love to take a tour and meet Mr. L'Hoste."

They jumped into the Model A, started it and followed William up the drive.

"He probably wants to size us up to see how much of a threat we are. I'm sure that he's heard a lot about us from his son and I'll bet the police chief has kept him informed of anything he knows about us."

"Come into my web said the spider to the fly," Duncan said ominously.

"This will be interesting," Emerson responded.

The Model A stopped under the portico and Emerson and Duncan stepped out of the vehicle onto the gleaming white cement.

"Excuse me, gentlemen. Does your vehicle leak oil or any fluids which may stain the cement?" William asked.

Emerson and Duncan looked at each other.

"It does leak a bit. Would you like us to move it?" Emerson asked.

"Please do, sir."

"Picky, picky," Duncan muttered under his breath as he moved the vehicle to the white limestone area on the other side of the portico.

William led them through the massive double oak-doored entryway into the center hall with its three-storied open area. The entryway would have been darker save for the installation of huge skylights in the roof. The skylights were hidden so that they could not be seen from the road.

Duncan nodded his head toward a complete suit of armor with chain mail.

"Hey, looky here. They've got me here already. I'm the

knight in shining armor."

Emerson just smiled at his friend's comments.

The helmeted suit of armor stood at attention and was holding a shield and sharp pointed halberd. The shield and breastplate had what Emerson assumed to be a family crest on it. It was a lion's head imposed on a cross.

William motioned for them to follow him up the curving, dark stained oak stairway.

As they ascended the stairs to the second floor, Emerson and Duncan noticed the numerous paintings on the walls.

"You ever get the impression that somebody who lives here has got a lot of money?" Duncan asked.

"Yep. And they want to make a point of it to anyone who visits. I thinks it's part of a strategy to be intimidating. We shall see," Emerson replied.

William paused outside a door on the second floor and knocked.

~ ~ ~

The knock interrupted Jacques' review of a background file on Emerson Moore. Henri had assembled it for Jacques a few days earlier after Jacques had received the phone calls from Chief Wilkens. Henri was very good at his job as the head of security for the L'Hoste Groupe. His ability to dig up information on people prior to Jacques' meeting with them had worked to his advantage many times.

Sometimes, it was necessary to expose some hidden sin in an adversary's past in order to gain the upper hand in a negotiation or partnership. Without hesitation, Jacques would resort to threats of public disclosure in order to close a deal. And, it usually worked. After all, business was business.

And if the threats didn't work, there were other consequences that Henri could arrange such as mysterious accidents.

Jacques had studied the file extensively and had wanted to briefly refamiliarize himself with some of the more salient facts about Mr. Emerson Moore. Jacques was disappointed that the file did not contain any material that would give Jacques a true edge if he needed one.

His review did reveal that this investigative reporter was particularly skilled at research and writing blockbuster stories.

Jacques placed the file in the desk drawer, slowly stood up and bade them to enter.

≈ ≈ ≈

The door to Jacques' study was opened by William; Emerson and Duncan stepped into the opulent room with their mouths open in surprise.

Emerson thought that Jacques had accomplished his goal if it was to create a sense of awe and power to visitors when they stepped into the room.

Their eyes swept the study with its black walnut paneling, leather furniture, marble fireplace, oil paintings, tapestries, fine assorted tables and massive desk and chair.

Along one wall stood a table with a cover over it. Based on what he had seen in major development projects, Emerson wondered if this was the rumored layout of the new hotel on the former site of the Victory Hotel.

Three walls were filled with windows and offered unparalleled views of the island and Lake Erie's waters. Each of the three walls had a door which opened to a railed walkway outside of the study.

The exterior walkway appeared to also have been expanded to allow for the placement of a number of chairs and tables so that entertaining could take place outside.

Absolutely impressive Emerson thought. He glanced at Duncan and saw Duncan also awed by the surroundings.

Catching himself, he turned to face Jacques L'Hoste who seemed pleased by the stunned reaction of his guests.

"Gentlemen, I am Jacques L'Hoste," he said simply but with an air of arrogance.

The hairs on the back on Emerson's neck stood up. Emerson sensed that he had more than met his match in the man standing across the room from them.

Emerson put his thoughts aside and walked across the room, extending his hand.

"I'm Emerson Moore," and pointing to Duncan, "This is my associate, Sam Duncan."

They all shook hands and settled into the chairs as Jacques motioned to them.

"Gentlemen. It is my pleasure to welcome you to the L'Hoste Estate. When William mentioned that we had visitors admiring the estate from the gate, I suggested we invite you in for a brief tour. We do this from time to time. But alas, we cannot do this for everyone who stops in front to look at our beautiful grounds."

"Thank you. This was an unexpected surprise for us and very timely, I might add."

Emerson decided to drop the bait and see what he could land.

William had moved the coffee cart close to Emerson and Duncan and began to pour them fresh brewed coffee.

Jacques leaned forward.

"Very timely? How so?" he asked curiously as he waved off the cup of coffee that William offered him.

"Well, I'm a newspaper reporter writing a series of stories about life in the islands, and I planned on writing a story about this beautiful home of yours. Sam is my research associate, and we've completed some work on the basics, but actually needed a visit to your home in order to really describe it properly to our readers."

Emerson had thought quickly that this might be the best type of response without saying how much of an investigation he really wanted to conduct.

Jacques nodded and thought it a preposterous response

from Emerson. He was suspicious as to what the true story would be about, but he was a risk taker and would play their silly little game for a while. There were ways to kill stories. He had done it in the past.

And research associate? Jacques recalled a one-page summary in Emerson's file that highlighted the accomplishments and skills of an ex-SEAL named Sam Duncan.

"Your visit today then is indeed fortuitous. I would love to assist you in preparing your story about our home. Why don't I give you a brief tour of the bow and William can complete your visit with a tour of the grounds?"

Seeing Emerson nod his head in agreement, Duncan also nodded.

"Then, let's begin with this room which was the foyer and observation lounge of our fleet's flagship, the *SAUVIGNON*. I trust your research has turned up background information on our fleet and our process of moving the bow section to the top of this cliff."

Emerson responded, "Yes, we have completed our research in that area."

"Good, good. Well the *SAUVIGNON* was my fleet's flagship for many years. She was 620 feet long with a beam of 62 feet and a draft of 32 feet when fully loaded. Her gross tonnage is 8,666 tons with a total cargo capacity of 15,000 tons. She operated with a crew of anywhere from 29 to 37.

"In her day, she was the Queen of the Lakes and carried a wide variety of material from iron ore, coal, grain, limestone to distinguished visitors including President Roosevelt, Clark Gable and Amelia Earhart.

"You can see that I've had this area enlarged. I had the wall between the original observation lounge and adjoining dunnage room removed in order to expand the amount of space that I required for my study.

"The deck area outside the study has been enlarged to, what I call, my party deck. Sitting out there and looking westerly, you can view some spectacular sunsets"

"I knew it!" Duncan exclaimed knowingly.

They stepped out onto the party deck and took in the breathtaking views.

"And that must be the pilothouse up there," Duncan stated as he leaned against the rail across from the study's doorway and looked above the study. Duncan was startled as the rail moved and appeared to be loose.

"I am sorry. I should have cautioned you that it was loose. It's scheduled for repair next week."

Duncan and Emerson looked over the rail and down to the ground about two stories below. They both moved away from the edge.

"Now, allow me to take you to the pilothouse. Please follow me," Jacques offered.

They made their way back into the study and approached a paneled wall. Jacques reached out and pushed a hidden button and the panel retracted, displaying a hidden elevator.

"We had this installed to give us access to the pilothouse and also to my private wine cellar which I'll show you momentarily."

They crowded into the small elevator and took the short ride to the pilothouse. The doors opened to an impressive windowed room of brass navigational gear. The metal ceiling was painted a gloss white, the walls were oak trimmed and the floor was a white tile.

In the center of the room and on a raised deck stood the ship's wheel, binnacle and the gyro compass repeater. The entire raised area was framed by a brass rail with brass supports. Behind the ship's wheel and with a view of the water was mounted a raised armchair with a side tray that could be swung into position to become a desktop.

Pointing to the armchair, Jacques explained, "I had the chair installed to use as a place to sit and brainstorm. I spend time here and in my study planning our business expansion."

Jacques went on to proudly point out the various instruments and controls across the front of the pilothouse and in front of the windows. He pointed out the radar, bow thruster controls, the engine room telegraph, the light and whistle control panel and the radio directional finder.

In the aft section of the pilothouse stood the original chart table and aft windows which provided a view toward the main gate. Through a partially closed door, they saw a flight of stairs to the second floor.

Emerson noted that the entire pilothouse contained but the one chair. It appeared that this room was not meant for socializing.

Jacques opened one of the pilothouse's two exterior doors which were located on each side and motioned for

Emerson and Duncan to follow him out onto the deck.

Duncan and Emerson grinned at each other as they took in the panoramic view.

"Breathtaking. Absolutely breathtaking," Emerson stated appreciatively.

"Thank you. I promised you a look at my wine cellar, so gentlemen shall we go back in and board the elevator for a ride into the depths of my chateau?"

Following Jacques, Emerson and Duncan reentered the pilothouse and entered the elevator.

They watched with particular interest as Jacques withdrew a key and inserted it next to one of the buttons on the elevator control panel. When he turned the key, the button lit and Jacques depressed it. They started their descent.

As they were descending, Emerson studied the control panel as closely as he could without drawing attention to himself. He noticed that there were three floors listed and two floors below the first floor with limited access. It appeared that both floors required a key in order for the elevator to access them.

One was obviously for the wine cellar and he must have a large collection of valuable wines. The other, Emerson guessed, may be for access to the dock at the base of the cliff so that one did not always have to take the stairwell which clung to the cliff – the stairwell which Emerson had seen on his flyover and his ferryboat ride over to the island. But he didn't recall seeing the doorway which Alexandrov had said was concealed.

The elevator lurched to a stop and the door opened to a wine cellar carved out of the limestone rock. Jacques reached to the right of the elevator's door and flipped a light switch. Light from the overhead fixture provided a warm glow to the twenty by forty-foot room.

They stepped out of the elevator and onto a raised wooden floor.

"Sometimes, the floor would get wet from water seepage, so I had this raised wooden floor installed," Jacques offered as an explanation when he noticed the two looking down at the floor.

"Since we are about ten feet below ground level, the temperature remains a constant 55 degrees throughout the year." Jacques flourished as his arm swept around showing his huge collection of bottles at rest in their racks on three walls.

"Outstanding," Emerson stated as he moved to the far end. He felt a bit nauseous at being in a cave again. He reached into his pocket for his handkerchief and wiped his brow. As he went to place it back in his pocket, he accidentally dropped it on the wooden floor in front of the far wall's rack. He bent down, retrieved it, and then carefully placed the handkerchief back in his pocket.

"I bet you wouldn't find any Ripple or Mad Dog on these shelves," Duncan chortled.

"I can assure you, my dear sir, that there is nothing but the finest in island wines and vintage French wines in my cellar," Jacques said with disdain. "Shall we return to my study where I'm sure that William will be available to conclude your tour?"

"Whatever you say. You're the guide," Duncan replied.

"That I am," Jacques said. He was tiring of this game of cat and mouse.

When they boarded the elevator, Emerson questioned, "I assume that the next level below would take one to your boat dock. Is that a safe assumption?"

"No. The only access to the boat dock is the stairwell on the cliff. The lowest level here is a storage area and I don't give tours of it." The tone in Jacques' voice clearly indicated that he did not want to discuss the lower level.

The elevator rose slowly to the study level and the door opened.

Emerson and Duncan took a step back in surprise when the open doorway was filled with the presence of Francois, Henri and William.

"I was sure that you would make an appearance to greet our two guests when you heard that they were in our home," Jacques stated as he exited the elevator. Turning to Emerson and Duncan who were following him, Jacques commented cunningly, " I believe you know my son, Francois, and our security chief, Henri."

Duncan quick-wittedly asserted, "I believe you ran into us the other night." He looked closely at Francois for a reaction and saw a thin smile break on his face.

"It seems quite possible. I run into people all over this island."

So the charade was up, Emerson thought. They would

have to be careful since they were in the lion's den.

Emerson decided to go a step beyond where he had planned to go when they first entered the house. "I plan to also write about the first L'Hoste to settle here. I believe some of the research rumored that he had been a pirate at one time and he was run out the downtown area by the islanders. Can you give me any insight into the family history?"

Jacques L'Hoste had been facing the windows during the exchange between Duncan and Francois. As Emerson finished his question, he saw the fury in Jacques' face as he turned to face them. Emerson had apparently stepped on a landmine.

"He was a business man and the other islanders were jealous of his prowess. What they did to him and his family was an unforgivable sin."

His voice was beginning to rise like a fiery evangelist preaching salvation. He began to flick his ear with his finger.

"A sin committed by the islanders. That sin has been retold to every member of my family each generation. And I'm sure the islanders have their version which has been embellished over the years."

His face was red with rage. His finger was pointed directly at Emerson as he continued his verbal rampage.

Francois stared at his father. He had seen him angry about business deals, but his father's anger was always very controlled. He had never seen his father become unraveled like this. Perhaps, it was triggered by the potential damage to their family reputation if a newspaper story was printed about them.

"I will tell you two things and let me make this absolutely, crystal clear to you Mr. Emerson Moore. First, one day the islanders will pay for their sin against my family and they will pay in a very big way. Second, I am warning you not to write anything about any of the L'Hostes – past or present – which would cast any aspersions to our family name. You go against my warning and you have made a clear-cut choice that you desire to bear the consequences. Do I make myself perfectly clear to you, sir?"

Emerson pushed the edge. "I seemed to have upset you. I certainly did not intend to threaten your emotional well-being Mr. L'Hoste."

"I take umbrage at that comment," Jacques barked as he started toward Emerson.

Henri stepped in and restrained Jacques as he softly said, "Sir, not here. Not now. There are ways as you know."

Jacques composed himself as he settled into his red leather chair.

"William, I believe our guests have overstayed their welcome. I would like you to escort them off the estate."

William quickly opened the door from the study and urged the two visitors into the hallway.

As they walked to the staircase, Duncan asked, "Is this typical behavior for your boss, William?"

"No, I assure you it is not. Mr. L'Hoste has many things on his mind these days. He has been very stressed."

"Well, you really lit him up Emerson. You have a death

wish? Throwing more gasoline on a raging inferno?" Duncan questioned.

"Sam, you know me well enough. I have a problem with anyone who's so arrogant. He thinks all of his money makes him better than anyone and, at the click of his finger, people crumble. Well, this cookie does not crumble. I had to throw the last jab on his emotional well-being. You, of all people, know that I do not take kindly to threats."

"You newspaper guys sure know how to play with words."

"And you don't. Come on. Give me a break Sam. Who was wordplaying with his buddy Francois about him running into us the other night? Hmmm?"

"Well, that's different. Even a blind squirrel finds an acorn once in awhile."

They reached the bottom of the stairs, walked through the large foyer and out the front door.

"Gentlemen, if you would kindly leave at this time," William said as graciously as he could.

"Just a second here. I recall Mr. L'Hoste saying that we were to have a tour of the grounds before we left," Duncan pushed.

"Under the circumstances, I believe that Mr. L'Hoste would prefer to cancel that portion of your tour," William stated nervously.

"I believe that he is the type of individual who stands by his word. We want the rest of the tour. If you're in doubt, why don't you just call him and see what he would like you to do?" Emerson suggested. He didn't think that William would want to call his enraged boss – and it worked.

William made a decision – the wrong decision.

"I will give you a very brief tour of the grounds, but it must be very brief."

William walked them quickly through the area with the swimming pool, tennis court and the helicopter landing pad on one side of the house. As they walked by the various statuary, Emerson had to request to sit on the ground for a few seconds as he indicated that he was becoming dizzy.

The delays made William even more nervous and he urged them to complete the brief tour.

On the other side of the house, he showed them the over-grown area surrounded by a low fence where the ruins of the L'Hoste's inn were located. In front of the ruins was located a small cemetery containing the graves of Jacques, Jules, Francois and Jean L'Hoste and their respective families.

It happened as they were leaving the cemetery.

"I told you to leave my estate," Jacques L'Hoste's voice boomed from the party patio outside of his study. Cradled in his arm was a rifle.

"Sir, they were just leaving," William started to explain.

"I do not want explanations. I want them gone and now."

"Yes sir, we are leaving right now," Emerson called up.

It made absolutely no sense to argue with someone holding what appeared to be a loaded weapon and especially when he felt you were trespassing. You might be right, but then again, you could be dead right.

Emerson and Duncan quickened their pace to the Model A. They jumped in, started it and sped down the drive. They were apparently being watched on the closed circuit monitor because the gate began to swing open as they neared it.

The little truck sped through the open gate and ground to a sudden halt.

"What are you doing now?" Emerson asked Duncan who had been driving.

"Here, you scoot over here and drive when I get back in the truck. I've got to do something for the Candid Camera crew."

"Sam, don't!"

"Nah, you'll like it. This will really agitate them."

Duncan slipped out of the truck and walked up to the intercom on the gate and pushed the button.

"Who's there?" came the voice from the security center.

"Ben."

"Ben, who?" the voice asked.

"Ben Dover," Sam replied with glee.

"Ben Dover?" the voice asked not totally comprehending the joke.

With the question, Duncan bent over and dropped his shorts and underwear to wiggle his bare butt at the camera. Laughing at his own antics, Duncan pulled his shorts and underwear up and raced to the idling Model A.

"Serves them right for messing with us today," Duncan said as they rounded the first curve.

"There could be consequences, my friend," Emerson cautioned.

"No big deal. I'm a big boy. Say, what was that with you getting dizzy and needing to sit down by those lawn statues? It looked to me like you were putting something in your pockets both times."

"Very observant, Doctor Watson," Emerson teased. "Think back to when we entered the wine cellar. Do you remember me dropping my handkerchief?"

"Yes."

"I noticed on the floor what appeared to be a yellow dust that seemed to disappear the farther away from the wall that you went."

"So, there's limestone dust dropping down from the ceiling. What's the big deal?"

"No, If you recall the room was a bit damp and the floor was wet. That's why they had to install the wooden floor. The dust didn't come from the ceiling."

"Okay smart guy, where did it come from?"

"Behind the wine racks. I believe there's a hidden passageway behind the racks and when you leave the area you leave a trail of limestone out onto the wooden flooring."

"So that's where the old guy keeps the really good stuff," Duncan suggested.

"I don't think so. I dropped my handkerchief so that I could pick up some samples of the dust. When we were by the statues, I noticed yellow dust on the ground around them and on them. I also grabbed a handful before I got up both times and put one in each pocket of my shorts."

"Yeah, I thought you were up to something."

"Did you notice anything unusual about the statues?"

"No, Sherlock. What did you notice?"

"When we were on the party deck, I thought that each of the statues had openings at the top as if they were the part of a ventilation system."

"Like for underground bunkers?"

"Somewhat. I'm not sure what we may be stumbling on."

They both fell quiet for the remainder of the drive to Aunt Anne's house.

～ ～ ～

"Yes, I'm trying to reach Professor Anderson."

"One moment please and I'll connect you."

"Hello!"

The warmth in her voice was evident over the phone. Emerson smiled as he recognized Martine's voice.

"Well. Hello there stranger! It's your knight in shining armor."

"Are you a bit rusty from your sudden urge to take a swim the other night?" she asked good-naturedly.

"I'm squeaky clean," he joked back. "Actually I was calling to speak to your father. Is he available?"

"He's down at the stone lab building going over his research findings."

"Oh, good. Duncan and I might take a run over then. I have something I'd like to show him and get his opinion."

"He'll be around there most of the night if you'd like to stop by. I'll keep an eye out for the two of you and maybe stop by to say hello."

"Great. See you soon."

Emerson placed the receiver down and went out on the front porch from where he could hear voices rising in anger. As he crossed the front porch, he saw the flashing lights from the police car and Duncan being handcuffed by two police officers who were overseen by Chief Wilkens.

Emerson could hear his Aunt's voice lecturing the policemen.

"This is absolutely ridiculous!" she said sternly. "You

should be spending more time on the drunks and rowdiness in town rather than picking on this man," she continued indignantly.

"You deputy dawgs just don't get it," Duncan seethed.

"Easy Sam," Emerson cautioned. "Chief, can you tell me what's going on here?"

The Chief flashed a document at Emerson and stated with an air of confidence, "We've had a formal complaint of public indecency filed by one of our islanders. It appears that Mr. Duncan dropped his shorts in front of several employees at the L'Hoste Estate today."

"Balderdash!" Emerson said angrily. "All he did was moon the camera at their gate when we left. I would hardly call that public indecency when we have seen more than a guy's butt flashed at your bars in town."

"The law is what it is – and we've had a complaint filed. So, we're taking action." The chief turned to his officers, "Put him in the car and we'll take him to the station."

"You're more than welcome to follow us to the station and post bond," he called over his head as they led a now somewhat subdued Duncan to the Blazer.

"This is ridiculous," Aunt Anne muttered in complete disgust.

"He does anything that Mr. L'Hoste tells him to do. Yes, Mr. L'Hoste. Can I help you, Mr. L'Hoste?" she mocked.

"I'll take the golf cart and get Sam released." Emerson could tell that his aunt was upset by the way one of her guests had been treated. She was real particular about her hospitality and would take this as a serious affront.

"Well, I've never," she started.

Emerson put an arm around his aunt and gently guided her up the steps and into the covered porch.

"I'm heading over to the police department, and then Sam and I are going over to Gibraltar Island to see Professor Anderson."

An all-knowing smile crossed his aunt's face.

"Might you be stopping in to see that Martine girl?"

"Actually, we are really going to see the Professor to ask him some questions about caves. I'd bet that we might say hello to her if we see her. But, remember, she's married Aunt Anne."

"Oh, I remember. Just make sure that you do." His aunt walked into the house and thought about the potential danger that Emerson faced with his feelings for Martine.

She sensed in watching them when they were together or the manner in which Emerson lit up when mentioning her name that he had more than a casual interest in her. She felt that his ethical standards would guide him, but she was concerned that he would walk away with a broken heart.

≈ ≈ ≈

Duncan and Emerson walked down the short flight of

steps from the police station and headed towards the Board-walk to catch the shuttle boat to Gibraltar Island.

"E, I'm sorry for the mess," Duncan said as he rubbed his wrist.

"No problem, Sam. I think it was really meant as a means of sending a message to us," Emerson responded.

"Message?"

"More or less. Probably more of a warning. I think we riled up Mr. L'Hoste as we were leaving and your antics were fuel on the fire. We need to be careful."

"So are you going to do a story?"

"Yes, I am. And with a twist that the L'Hoste family won't like. We're going to expose them for what they really are."

"And that is?"

"I don't have that completely answered yet. But I think we're getting close."

They arrived at the shuttle and boarded it for the short ride across the harbor to the main dock on Gibraltar Island.

As they stepped off the shuttle, a security guard greeted them on the dock and allowed them to pass since they were meeting with Professor Anderson. The guard sat back in his chair in his small security hut on the dock's edge. The University had placed security on the island primarily to keep trespassers off, especially unruly partygoers from the boats anchored in the harbor.

Emerson and Duncan approached the three-storied Stone Laboratory Building which was just a few dozen footsteps away from the dock.

They saw lights coming from a room on the second floor and headed for the stairs.

The door to the office was partially open. Emerson knocked and inquired, "Professor Anderson?"

"Yes, yes. What is it?"

"Emerson Moore and Sam Duncan, sir," Emerson replied.

Emerson and Duncan walked into the cluttered office and saw the white-haired professor standing at a worktable with a number of maps and charts piled on it. The professor hurriedly turned over a map that he had been studying.

"Yes boys. Don't mind me in turning this map over," he offered as an explanation. "I'm very secretive about my work."

"No explanation necessary, Professor. We understand. When I'm working on a story, I do my best to limit the number of people in the know. You've got to protect your work," Emerson said with a knowing smile.

"What can I do for you boys? Seems strange that you'd track me down in my lab."

"I'm the guilty one, Dad."

Everyone turned at the sound of the voice in the doorway and saw a radiant Martine.

"Emerson called the cottage looking for you, Dad, and I told him that he could find you here since I knew that you had planned on spending the afternoon and early evening here. And with today's heat, I thought everyone would enjoy some fresh iced tea."

She set the pitcher and glasses on a nearby counter and began pouring tea for everyone. As she poured Emerson's and handed it to him, they exchanged warm smiles.

"That's my girl. She's always thinking about Dad," Professor Anderson commented. "So what brings you boys to see me?"

Emerson began pulling the three samples, which he had transferred into three plastic bags, from his pocket.

"Professor, we found this yellow dust where we were hiking earlier today and thought it was strange."

As Emerson went to hand the bags to the professor, he dropped one and picked it up from the floor.

"Hmm. And where on the island did you find the dust?"

"At the L'Hoste Estate," Duncan blurted.

Emerson threw Duncan a glance to silence him. Emerson did not want to show all of his cards yet.

"It was actually near their estate. Any ideas? I've never seen this color of dust on the island before – even back to my days as a kid here exploring."

"This is strange. Were you near any work sites where dust and debris could have come from a construction project?" the professor asked.

"No, we just found it on the ground in a couple of places and it aroused our curiosity," Emerson explained.

"Curious, curious," the professor commented as he held the bags up to the light. "Why don't you leave these with me and I'll have them analyzed. It could take a day or two."

Emerson moved to the worktable and next to the professor to also look at the dust particles in the light.

"Sure, that would be fine. We appreciate your help, sir."

They excused themselves and headed back to the dock with Martine as their escort.

"I'll keep you two company while you wait for the shuttle to pick you up," she volunteered. "I wouldn't want you to get lost here on the island."

"Yeah, it's a long and dangerous walk from the building down to the dock," Duncan joked. "We might need a female's protection."

More seriously, Emerson asked Martine, "Do you know the scope of your father's research on the island?"

"Oh, Dad is so secretive. He thinks that someone is going to steal his research notes on the caves and the island's geology. He even locks up his research in the old safe in his office."

"That's strange. Why the secrecy?"

"Dad's a little paranoid. He had a big research project

on caves in Kentucky and he thought one of his research assistants stole his notes. The assistant published an article on Kentucky caves and received national recognition for it. Dad swears to this day that the assistant stole his notes but he can't prove it."

"I would take it that the assistant no longer works for him," Duncan stated.

"That would be correct. He actually ended up with a good position in the University of Kentucky's geology department. So, if you think Dad acts a little protective, you'll understand."

"Thanks for sharing that with us. Say, how's my man, Austin, doing?" Emerson asked with interest.

"Well, he's doing well. One of the other professors has children on the island and he's been spending time playing with them. I'll tell him hello for you."

"I'd like that. He's quite a young man!" Emerson commented as he thought briefly about his son.

"E, here's the shuttle."

Duncan and Emerson bid goodbye to Martine and boarded the shuttle for the short ride back to the Boardwalk's dock.

Martine stood on the dock and watched the shuttle as it crossed the harbor before she turned and headed up the path past the Gibraltar House and the gazebo to the cottage.

She didn't see the figure in the shadow of the dining hall, which had been observing the three of them on the dock. The figure withdrew from the corner of the dining hall and kept out of sight by staying below the hill and along the island's north shore as it made its way to the cottage.

∽ ∽ ∽

"Sam, are you curious as to what the professor is working on?" Emerson asked as they stepped off the shuttle onto the dock at the Boardwalk.

"Yes. He sure does seem secretive about whatever it is," Sam responded as he scratched his thick curly hair. "What do you think he's up to?"

Emerson seemed pensive.

"I'm not quite sure, but my gut tells me that something's screwy. Besides, I'm suspicious of something I saw in his lab."

"And that is?"

"Sam, I'd prefer to keep that to myself for awhile. It may be nothing."

Turning to him, Emerson asked, "How would you like to make a little visit to the lab tonight? I seem to recall that you've had some training in opening safes. Think you could crack that one?"

"Something that old should be no problem. Let's do it. I suppose we'd use your aunt's dinghy for most of the way and then paddle in."

"I think that's the right approach. But we need to figure where to beach it." Seeing the stairs to the Boardwalk's second level deck which overlooked Gibraltar Island across the harbor, Emerson added, "Let's take a look from the upper deck."

They climbed the stairs and were able to secure a table overlooking the harbor. The bar and restaurant were crowded and the band was playing.

Emerson and Sam sat down and placed their drink order with the waitress who seemed to appear from nowhere. After she left, Emerson produced a brochure from his pocket.

"I picked this up as we were leaving the lab."

The brochure was entitled "Stone Laboratory" and showed the complete layout of Gibraltar Island and its seven main buildings.

Looking at the map and across the harbor at the dock and south side of the island, Duncan said, "There's no way that we can consider the south side. Too much visibility from the lighted dock and the boats that anchor off the island."

"I agree. The best place to come in might be the swimming hole area on the northeast corner of the island. It's the farthest point from the island's residences. We can pull the dinghy ashore there, make our way to the lab and take a quick look at the papers in the safe."

They finished their drinks which the waitress had provided, paid their bill and returned to Aunt Anne's house.

~ ~ ~

The dinghy bumped against the rocky shore of Gibraltar Island's swimming hole at approximately 2:00 a.m., and Sam, who had been seated in the bow, jumped out of the boat to pull it up on the stone covered beach.

All had gone according to plan so far. They had cut the boat's motor as they crossed the main channel and paddled around the island's northeast point to the swimming hole. They hadn't encountered any other watercraft under the clouded sky which had blocked out the moon's light.

They had both dressed in black swim trunks and dark tee shirts for their evening's adventure. Their tennis shoes were wet from stepping in the water as they pulled the dinghy further up the shore and under a rocky ledge where it would not be obvious to a security guard on his nightly patrol or to passing boaters.

Duncan and Emerson paused to listen to the night sounds to make sure that they couldn't hear anything out of the ordinary. They then made their way to the staircase from the swimming hole to the top of the cliff overlooking the swimming area.

Again, they paused to listen to the night sounds before moving toward the south side of the island. The north side of the island had steep cliffs and a number of cottages.

They skirted Cooke's Castle and approached the south corner of Harborview House, a residence hall for research assistants and grad students working on projects for the summer. As they neared the building, they heard music and saw light coming from an open window on the corner.

They moved furtively past the window and crept along the bushes and trees on the south side of the island. As they neared the Bat House, the old boathouse which was now a covey for bats according to the brochure, Emerson dropped to the ground. Duncan followed suit.

A bright light from a flashlight was sweeping the grounds. It appeared that the security guard was patrolling along the south path and would be rounding the Gibraltar House in a matter of minutes.

Emerson quickly looked for cover and motioned to Duncan to follow him over the small cliff and down to the Bat House. They dropped over the edge just as the security guard's light swept across the area they had just vacated.

As quietly as they could, they scrambled to the Bat House and tried the door. To their relief it was unlocked. They opened it and entered as Duncan muttered, "The things you get me into E!"

They entered the darkened room and dropped to the floor behind the door.

"Be glad it's night. Bats go out at night to hunt for food so there won't be anyone in here but us."

Duncan ducked his head as a bat suddenly swept out of the darkness, buzzing his head as it continued out of the Bat House.

"OK, Batman, someone forgot to tell that one that he should be out hunting for food. He thinks I'm lunch."

"Well you always tell me that you're so sweet," Emerson retorted good-naturedly.

Thinking he saw movement near the top of the cliff overlooking the Bat House, the security guard stepped off the path and made his way to the cliff's edge. He shone his flashlight onto the Bat House and the area around it. He also shone the light on the firepit area which was nearby and at the water's edge. Not seeing anything, the security guard continued on his patrol of the island.

Emerson and Duncan saw the bright beam from the guard's flashlight through the cracks in the Bat House's walls. They waited to see if they would hear someone approach the Bat House and breathed a deep sigh of relief when nothing happened after a few minutes.

Emerson cautiously opened the Bat House's door and peered around it. He sensed that no one was around and motioned for Duncan to follow up him back up the side of the cliff.

As they made their way through the undergrowth, Duncan muttered loud enough for Emerson to hear.

"You do recall that I'm allergic to poison ivy, don't you. I just bet the side of this cliff is covered with it!"

"Shhhhh," Emerson admonished.

They reached the top of the cliff and looked around the grounds. To the northeast, they could see the guard's flashlight sweeping as he patrolled.

"This is good. At least we know that he's not sitting on the dock and that should make our entrance easier," Emerson commented.

"And what about our exit when he's back at his post on

the dock?" Duncan questioned.

"We'll handle it," Emerson stated encouragingly.

They climbed over the edge and crept past Gibraltar House, keeping close to the bushes and trees at the cliff's edge.

Now they faced the most dangerous part of their trek. The last 100 feet to the Stone Lab was virtually without cover. There were a few large trees but no shrubs or bushes to conceal their passage.

Emerson said in a low voice, "Sam, with the guard gone, I think our best bet is to just step out in the open and walk the path to the lab as if we belong here on the island."

"Yeah. If anyone is up and saw us sneaking around, it'd just draw attention to us. Let's go."

They stepped onto the path and boldly walked to the lab's side entrance without encountering anyone. Once inside, they went up the flight of stairs to the second floor and walked down the darkened hallway to Professor Anderson's office door.

Emerson grasped the handle and turned it. It was locked.

"Here, let me at it." Duncan stepped in front of Emerson and withdrew what looked like a stainless steel pocketknife from his pocket.

He held it up to Emerson and said, "I've got a master key that usually works on these old doors."

"A pocketknife?"

"No, it's actually a jack knife style pick set. It's got a blade and 5 picks. Watch."

Duncan bent over and examined the lock quickly. Choosing one of the picks, he carefully inserted it into the keyway and began to manipulate the pins so that the lock could be opened.

After hearing a noticeable click, Duncan stood.

"May I show you to your room, sir?" he said jokingly as he pushed the door open.

They entered and relocked the door as they closed it. They quickly pulled the window blinds and Duncan approached the safe. He pulled out a pocket flashlight which Emerson held for him as he examined the safe.

"The dial is connected to a cam, or metal wheel, on the other side of the door. Between the dial and the cam is the wheel pack. When you have the right combination, the notches on the wheel and cam align to form a groove into which the lever drops. Then you open the door," Duncan lectured.

"Okay Houdini, just get on with it, would you?" Emerson smiled to himself in the darkened office. He remembered his friend's training as a SEAL and experience as a CIA operative. A part of Duncan's past responsibilities included missions in which he was sent in to secure or photograph secret documents in various foreign government offices. Hopefully, this safe would be child's play for Duncan.

Duncan pressed his ear to the safe and began turning the dials. He could hear the tumblers clicking as he carefully searched for the right combination.

In a few minutes, Duncan swung open the old safe's door.

"Old safe's are no problem for me. It's the new ones that cause a problem. But again nothing that some plastique can't handle," Duncan said proudly.

Pulling out his own pocket flashlight and returning Duncan's, Emerson looked in the safe.

"Sam, here. You review these charts and maps and I'll look through his notes to see what I can glean."

After 5 minutes, Duncan said as he pointed to one chart, "This looks interesting."

"What is it?" Emerson asked as he crept next to Duncan and looked where his light was pinpointing an area on the island.

"This appears to be a map showing the location of the island's caves. I had no idea that there were so many here. And it looks like he's noted a number of new caves. Looks like he's been busy. Did you find anything in the papers that you were looking through?"

"No. Some which were pretty basic in talking about the geography of the caves. The other was way too complex for a layman like me. I don't understand all the terms that he was using."

Loud laughter interrupted their conversation. They extinguished their penlights and raced to the window overlooking the dock. Carefully raising the blinds, they peered out.

On the dock and laughing together were the security

guard and Professor Anderson. Emerson froze as he recalled Martine's comments that her father worked unusual hours.

Emerson stood back from the window and said, "He may be heading up here. We've got to put everything back and get out of here quickly."

They hurriedly picked up the charts, maps and research notes and returned them to the safe. As Emerson was placing the research papers in the safe, he heard a noise and groan behind him. He turned as he shoved the papers on to the top shelf. He didn't see one sheet of paper fall to the floor and under the front of the safe.

"What's wrong?" he queried Duncan.

"I just walked into the edge of the worktable and banged my thigh pretty hard. I'm OK though."

Emerson turned back to the safe and swung the door shut.

"Do I just spin the dial?"

"Yes."

Emerson spun the dial a few turns and tried the safe's door to make sure that it was locked.

They stepped out into the hallway and made sure that the door locked behind them. They heard footsteps coming up the stairs.

Emerson pointed to the red glowing exit sign at the far end of the hall and they ran as quietly as they could down the hall. They had just turned the corner when Professor Anderson stepped out of the stairwell.

He paused momentarily as he thought he had seen movement at the end of the hall. No, you're just imagining things he said to himself as he inserted the key in his office door.

He unlocked the door and entered his office, turning on the overhead lights as he walked by the switch.

Strange he thought. He didn't recall pulling down his window shades. In fact, he never pulled the shades down. As he turned away from the windows, he spied the paper on the floor under the safe.

He walked over to the safe and bent down to pick it up. There was no doubt in his mind that he had placed all of his notes inside the safe. He reached for the phone and called the guard on the dock.

"Ralph, this is Professor Anderson. Could you please come up to my office right away?"

He replaced the receiver and checked the safe to see if it was locked. Seeing that it was, he dialed the safe's combination to see if anything was missing. He opened the door and noticed that the papers appeared to have been rifled.

≈ ≈ ≈

Emerson and Duncan were looking out the exit door at the northwest corner of the lab building. With the guard on the dock, it would be too dangerous to walk across the open space the way they had when they entered the building.

Emerson could see the Dining Hall just north of the lab building. He said in a hushed voice, "Since we can't leave the way we came in, we'll need to make a run across the lawn to the far corner of the dining hall and make our way along the top of the cliff on the north side of the island back to where they dinghy is."

"Sure can't go back the way we came in with the guard back. I'm good to go," Duncan replied.

They eased open the door and began to sprint across the lawn to the dining hall. The lab building served to block them from the guard's view on the dock and from Professor's Anderson's view since his office windows overlooked the dock.

They had almost reached the far side of the dining hall when the door of the lab building which Emerson and Duncan had exited suddenly opened and the guard and Professor Anderson walked out. The guard swung his flashlight from left to right – just missing Emerson and Duncan who just ducked around the dining hall's far corner.

"I know that I saw someone run down the hall just as I stepped out from the stairway. He or she has got to be out here somewhere. And I'm certain that it wouldn't be one of the grad or research assistants. They wouldn't know how to open my safe," the professor worried.

"Let's take a quick walk down to the glacial grooves and see if they are there. There's brush to hide in and if they had a boat, it could be anchored there. We know that whoever it was, they didn't come in from the harborside. Too much light and visibility from the harbor – and besides, I was on duty there," the guard stated. He was proud of how quickly he used his logic to determine where the most likely landing point would be. It had been a quiet summer and this was an opportunity for him to get recognition for his skills.

"Agreed. Let's check and then we can make our way around the rest of the island."

As he put his hand reassuredly on his holstered pistol, the guard led the professor to the island's western end. They looked around and began to work their way along the north side of the island as they looked for the intruder.

≈ ≈ ≈

From the shadow of the dining hall, Emerson and Duncan watched as the guard and the professor moved westward.

"That should buy us some time. Let's head back to the dinghy," Emerson urged as they quickened their pace along the island's north side. They skirted the rear of the Stone Cottage and walked along the side of the Barney Cottage where the Professor resided with Martine and her family.

Passing the Lakeview shelter, they moved rapidly as the ground began to slope toward the swimming hole. It took them less than ten minutes to reach the stairs down to the area where they had left the dinghy.

Reaching the bottom of the stairs first, Duncan stopped abruptly. "Holy cow, Batman. The Batboat is missing."

Ignoring his reference to their unplanned visit to the Bat House, Emerson asked, "What do you mean it's missing?"

"Look for yourself, it's gone," Duncan responded.

Emerson couldn't believe it. They had pulled the boat

up on the rocks and hidden it from view under a ledge. There was no way that it could have drifted out to the lake.

"Looks like we're in for a long swim. Follow me," Emerson said as he began to climb back up the stairs to head for the eastern end of the island.

As they reached the top of the stairs they both dove into the shadows as the beam from two flashlights swept the swimming hole area and they heard voices coming from Perry's Lookout, an area with benches which overlooked the swimming hole.

They crawled forward to where the brush was thicker and then broke into a trot. They reached the eastern edge of the island in three minutes and looked across the harbor toward Aunt Anne's house.

"It's now or never. Let's hit it," Emerson said as he began wading out into the water until it was deep enough to swim. Duncan followed closely as they began swimming with powerful strokes toward Aunt Anne's dock.

$$\approx \ \approx \ \approx$$

"You surprised us hiding in the shadows, Tim," Professor Anderson said as he and the guard walked onto Perry's Lookout.

"I wasn't hiding, Professor," Tim said as he stepped out. He took another swig from his can of beer.

"See anyone run by here in the last few minutes? Someone broke into my office and we're trying to track down the intruder," the professor stated. He thought to himself that Tim seemed to have a smug look on his face tonight.

"No, I didn't, and I've been out here for a couple of hours contemplating," Tim answered. Tim wondered what Emerson and Duncan had been doing in the professor's office?

More like drinking the professor deduced from the number of empty beer cans littering the lookout.

Tim had decided not to divulge what he had seen. He had observed Emerson and Duncan landing and hiding their dinghy.

He wondered what they were up to as he had pulled the dinghy from its concealment and pushed it out in the lake. With two of them landing, he was confident that they weren't there to see Martine. He had chuckled to himself as he imagined the look on their faces when they returned to find their dinghy gone.

"Did the intruders get anything from your office?" Tim asked with feigned interest.

"No. At least not from what I can tell," the professor replied. Then realizing what Tim had just said, the professor queried, "Tim, you said intruders. Why do you think there was more than one person? Are you sure that you're not holding back on us?"

Realizing that he slipped and knowing that they had seen his empty beer cans, Tim replied, "Nah, I'm just feeling a little woozy from my contemplating."

With a look of disgust on his face, Professor Anderson

turned to the guard and urged, "Let's continue our search. We're losing time."

"Right you are. Follow me."

They left Tim and proceeded past the swimming hole area to the eastern end of the island where they paused to beam their lights out toward the channel and the harbor.

~ ~ ~

"Dive!" Duncan urgently instructed Emerson as the lights' beam made their way out to the channel.

Gulping large amounts of air, Emerson and Duncan dove under the water's surface. They remained under water for about thirty seconds before resurfacing. They rolled over and looked toward Gibraltar Island where they could see the flashlight beams moving now along the south shore of the island.

They were in the clear.

"Too close for comfort, E," Duncan advised.

"Yeah, a little too close," Emerson agreed as he began swimming again.

It seemed like it took forever to reach Aunt Anne's dock, but they finally made it. The last 100 yards were difficult for Emerson. He wasn't sure that he was going to make it. If it had been a night with waves, it would have been virtually impossible.

They pulled themselves onto the dock and lay on their backs, looking at the stars as they rested.

"What are you going to tell her, E?"

"Tell who?"

"Your aunt about the missing dinghy?"

"First, she doesn't know that we were out tonight and that we took it. We'll just let it turn up missing in the morning. Ready to call it a night?"

"Best idea I've heard in a long time."

Emerson and Duncan slowly stood up and walked to the house and up to their rooms. It didn't take long for either of them to fall asleep.

$$\sim \sim \sim$$

The phone was ringing on the other end. The professor waited anxiously for it to be answered. He didn't want to make the call, but he felt that it would be better if he did.

"Yes," the sleepy voice at the other end answered.

"It's me. Someone broke into my office tonight and my safe."

"Did they get anything?" The voice sounded more alert now.

"No, all my critical research findings including my breakthrough findings are at my other office."

"Good then. Any ideas as to who it was?"

"No. And the security guard has not finished checking out the rest of the building to see if anything was stolen from any other office. It may have been some petty thief."

"Keep me advised."

The phone clicked dead as it was hung up. Professor Anderson placed the receiver in the cradle and sat back.

Beads of sweat were evident on his forehead. He was nervous because he had not told the complete truth. He had not mentioned that the chart which showed new caves had been in his safe. He vowed to return the chart to his other office in the morning.

Professor Anderson stood up from his desk and walked out of his office, locking the door behind him. He wearily took the path up the hill to his cottage.

$$\approx \approx \approx$$

The ringing phone awoke Emerson from his deep sleep. He let it ring so that his aunt could answer it.

He rolled over to look at the clock on his nightstand and saw that it was 9:00 a.m. He had slept late that morning. He arose, shaved, showered and descended the stairs to greet Aunt Anne.

He could smell the coffee coming from the kitchen.

"Morning Aunt Anne," he cried cheerily as he walked in

and saw her and Duncan sipping coffee at the kitchen table.

"Good morning to you sleepy head," she responded.

"Hi Rip Van Winkle," Duncan joked.

"Joke, joke joke. That's all you do."

"Hey, I'm a morning person. I'm wound up and ready to go first thing. Besides, I enjoy spreading my charm to people. It brightens their day, E."

"OK, OK!"

"Emerson, I just had a call from the Hablers who live out farther, close to Buckeye Point on the northeastern end of the island."

"Hmmm," Emerson muttered as he poured his first cup for the day.

"They said my dinghy washed ashore by their dock."

"Must have gotten loose from your dock last night," Emerson commented as he looked briefly at Duncan, who averted his gaze.

"It just doesn't make sense, Emerson. The winds here are from the west. If it broke loose from my dock, it would have washed ashore here. I just don't understand how it would have ended up down their way," she said perplexed.

Trying to help, Duncan offered, "Maybe the positive energy from a vortex caused it to move in that direction. Or you've got a bit of the Bermuda Triangle happening around here."

"That's enough boys! Emerson, I need you to go down to the Hablers and retrieve the dinghy this morning."

"Be glad to Aunt Anne. Sam, you can give me a ride to their house and then I can just motor it back to Aunt Anne's dock."

"You just let me know when you're ready and we'll do it."

≈ ≈ ≈

Later that afternoon after retrieving the dinghy, Emerson and Duncan were taking a sail in the sailboat on the east side of the island.

"Sam, I'd like to make another visit to the L'Hoste Estate."

"Based on the way we were escorted out of there and my mooning them, I don't expect that we'll find an invitation in the mailbox when we return to your aunt's house."

"I'm talking about a visit late at night. Interested?"

"Yes. How are we going to get in with the surveillance cameras they have on the fence?"

"That my friend, we have to determine. Tonight, we'll reconnoiter the outside wall."

"You're on."

The breeze stiffened and they turned their attention to running with the wind. As they rounded the southeastern tip of the island, they spotted the Miller Ferryboat returning to the island's southern point from the Catawba Peninsula.

"Let's sail over by the ferry and wave at the pretty tourists," Duncan suggested mischievously.

It didn't take long for them to catch up to the ferry. As they sailed by the ferry and waved at the passengers, Emerson noticed that Martine and Austin were onboard and waving exuberantly at them. Emerson pointed them out to Duncan and said, "Let's come about and catch them at the dock."

They brought the boat around and headed to the dock. It took awhile for them to arrive and Emerson was concerned that they had missed Martine and Austin. As they sailed closer, they could see that the passengers and vehicles had disembarked and the ferry was boarding vehicles and passengers for the return to the mainland.

Emerson was just about to point the boat toward the island's eastern side when Duncan shouted, "There they are."

Emerson then saw Martine and Austin standing on the edge of one of the docks and waving. He continued the craft on its course and within a matter of minutes, they were tying up at the dock.

Emerson had barely finished when two small arms encircled his neck in a big hug.

"Hi Mr. Moore!"

"Hello Austin – and where has my little buddy been today?"

"I had to take Mom on the ferry to see the dentist. She had a toothache."

Emerson looked up at Martine and noticed that her lips were a bit crooked. Must still be numb, but nevertheless looked inviting Emerson thought.

Martine teased, "I won't be able to drink anything for awhile without dribbling until the numbness wears off."

Duncan muttered under his breath to Emerson, "She can dribble on me anytime."

Emerson playfully hit his friend in the arm for making the comment.

"I hate going to dentists. Say, need a ride back to Gibraltar Island? You're welcome to join us and avoid the hot bus ride back to Put-in-Bay and the shuttle over to Gibraltar."

"Can we Mom, can we?" Austin was now jumping up and down on the boat's deck in anticipation of the sailboat ride with his friend.

"As long as we go straight there. I need to make sure that Dad is okay," Martine said as she stepped aboard.

Duncan and Emerson untied the boat, unfurled the sails and pointed the boat toward the eastern end of the island.

Duncan joined the three of them in the cockpit where Emerson was guiding Austin at the tiller.

"Is something wrong with your father?" Emerson inquired.

"Yes and no. He worked virtually all night, but joined us for breakfast before we left. As we were leaving, he was going to bed. I could just tell that he was upset about something, but he didn't want to talk about it when I asked him what was wrong. He was muttering about the island's security and that's all I could get."

Emerson looked at Duncan with raised eyebrows. Duncan shrugged his shoulders in response.

"He has seemed especially tense about this project of his. He's overly concerned that someone is going to steal his work and reveal it before he's ready."

"I can tell that he's the kind of guy who takes a lot of pride in what he does," Emerson offered.

"Yes, he does. Sometimes too much pride."

"Hey, look at the tree growing out of the water," Austin squealed with delight.

"That's Starve Island, Austin. It's just a very small reef with the one small tree and a lot of sea gulls. At night, some boaters forget it's there and sometimes run aground on it."

The rest of the sail around the island and the final motoring to Gibraltar's dock was focused on teaching Austin how to operate the boat's tiller, sails and outboard motor. Once they deposited Austin and Martine, they motored over to Emerson's aunt's dock.

$$\approx \approx \approx$$

Emerson and Duncan parked the golf cart at midnight in the rear of a vacant cottage on Trenton Street and began walking toward the L'Hoste Estate.

Under the clear moonlight night, they neared the entrance to the estate. They decided to move to the shadows offered by the underbrush and shrubs on the side of the road opposite the estate for concealment.

They had carefully crawled to various vantage points to observe the positions of the security cameras and light fixtures. They noticed a couple of vehicles leaving the estate and one arriving. The security cameras had been strategically positioned to make it very difficult for any intruders to crash the gate or vault over the gate in some fashion without being observed.

Emerson stated softly, "Looks nearly impossible, doesn't it, Sam?"

"Oh, I don't know about that. See that line?"

Emerson looked up and saw the electrical line that Duncan was pointing to.

"I bet that provides electrical service to the estate. If I could interrupt service for awhile, it would buy us time to penetrate their perimeter."

"Sam, don't you suppose that with all of their money, they'd have a back up generator?"

"Yep. But we just need to have the lights and cameras down for a few minutes."

"Once, we have them off, where do you suggest we enter the grounds? I'm sure the gate will remain locked – and you certainly will not have time to pick that lock."

"Don't have that piece figured out yet."

They crept back toward the area where they had first entered the underbrush. As they emerged onto Trenton Avenue at about 4:00 a.m. for the short walk back to the golf cart, they had still not resolved the entry issue.

Duncan stopped in his tracks.

"What's that dog chasing?"

Emerson looked down the road and saw that a dog was chasing something toward them. Duncan motioned for Emerson to step into a stand of trees and they watched as the chase grew near to them.

It appeared that the dog was chasing a mechanical object.

As it grew closer, Emerson and Duncan realized what it was and said in unison, "It's a robot!"

"What in the world is a robot doing out here?" Emerson asked.

The dog was so intense on following the robot that it didn't see Emerson and Duncan following both of them through the trees and underbrush.

As the robot approached the corner of the L'Hoste Estate, it stopped along the side of the road. A whirling noise could be heard and they saw what appeared to be a camera eye turn toward the dog.

Following another whirling sound, they saw a small tubular structure extend itself from the robot. The dog commenced sniffing the robot.

Suddenly, a flash of light emitted from the robot and struck the dog resulting in a sharp howl from the dog. The dog turned on its heels and streaked down the road.

"Probably a laser blast at the poor pooch," Duncan reasoned.

They heard the whirling sounds again and observed the laser retracting and the camera repositioning itself. As the robot started on its way again, Duncan softly said, "Stay here. I'll be right back."

Duncan ran across the road and looked the robot over as it slowly traveled closer to the L'Hoste Estate. He thought he saw something stamped on the back of the robot's turtle shaped shell and turned on a flashlight to read it.

When he did, the robot stopped.

Duncan thought to himself that the robot must have light sensors mounted on its shell.

The whirling sounds started again. The camera began to swing around and the laser extended. The camera completed a 360-degree sweep without encountering any source for the light sensor activation. The whirling sounds started again and the camera returned to its normal position and the laser retracted.

The robot continued on the roadside for another ten feet and came within range of the L'Hoste Estate's cameras. It turned abruptly to its left and disappeared into the estate's fence.

Everything had happened so quickly that Emerson couldn't determine where the robot had disappeared.

Within a few minutes, Duncan reappeared at Emerson's side – and with a huge smile.

"Where have you been and what was that all about?" Emerson seemed irked by his friend's apparent impulsiveness.

"Elementary, my dear Doctor Watson," Duncan replied with a hint of mystery. "That robot is the property of Columbia University."

"How do you know that?"

"I read it on the back of the robot."

"So that's why you turned your flashlight on?"

"Yep. But I didn't realize it had a light sensor. But that does make sense, if it's being used for covert purposes, you need to know when you'll be in the light or if a car is approaching so you can take evasive action."

"I assume you took evasive action. Where did you disappear to?"

"When I heard the whirling, I knew the camera would be looking for me and I didn't want to get hit by the laser. With my luck, it would have been set to aim low and would have hit my privates. So, I jumped into the ditch next to the road and stayed still."

Emerson just shook his head. "One of these days my friend, it's all going to catch up to you."

Emerson and Duncan started back to the vacant cottage to retrieve the golf cart and call it quits for the night.

Smugly, Duncan leaned closer to Emerson and in an all-knowing manner stated, "And I've got the key to entering the L'Hoste Estate."

"Just like that, you have the key? What gives here?"

"The robot is the key."

"The robot disappeared."

"And so shall we."

"Huh?"

"While I was laying in the ditch, I saw the robot approach the fence and saw the bottom on the fence open. It's on hinges and gives you about three feet of clearance when it opens. Plenty of room for us to crawl through."

"And they're just going to open up the hidden gate for us when we stand in front of it in view of the cameras?" Emerson asked incredulously.

"It's easy. I take out the electrical service. That cuts off the cameras and the lights. We head to the hidden gate and jimmy the hinges open. The gate can't be that strong. Since it's hidden, they wouldn't expect anyone to try to penetrate the grounds through it. We'd have two to three minutes once I take out the electrical service before their generator would turn the lights and camera back on."

"Aren't you concerned that the cameras would sweep the grounds for intruders?"

"Normally, I would be. They have a flaw in their security system. Based on our observations tonight, it appears that the cameras are fixed. They can't rotate. I'll bet they just didn't get around to upgrading the system. But I would be concerned that their internal security team would do a quick sweep of the grounds. So we would need to find somewhere to hide while they are patrolling."

"I knew there was a reason for inviting you to join me on this island."

"E, I invited myself or did you forget about your little flying mishap?"

"Just kidding, just kidding! When can you be ready to go with blowing the electric?"

"Midnight will be perfect."

"Let's do it at midnight. Tomorrow, though, I want to do an internet search for some information on our Columbia University robot. I'd like to understand what they are using a robot for."

"E, just one question."

"Yes?"

"How do we get out when we're ready to leave?"

Emerson thought for a moment and answered, "We can go out the same way we went in. The cameras will be on then, but we could slip a mask or bandana over our faces and run straight across the road, then down to where we leave our vehicle parked. By the time they react and race out from the house, we will be gone. As an alternative, we can slip down the stairs along the cliff and swim to one of the small beaches along West Shore Boulevard."

"Sounds like a plan, E."

They reached the golf cart and drove to the house just as dawn was breaking. They were too tired to notice the red sky and heed the sailor's warning.

Red sky at night, sailor's delight.
Red sky at morning, sailors take warning!

≈ ≈ ≈

After Duncan returned from the island hardware store the next afternoon, Emerson had Duncan join him in his room.

"Look what I've discovered with my internet search today regarding our little friendly robot. It's from a *New York Times* story," Emerson said excitedly.

Duncan leaned over the computer screen as Emerson retrieved his saved research notes.

"Using a $2 million grant from the National Science Foundation, Columbia University's computer science and archaeology departments developed a robot with remote sensing equipment, primarily for non-invasive archaeological discoveries in the western desert of Egypt."

"The robot creates 3-D images of what lies deep below the layers of sand and identifies the most likely spots for excavation. It's equipped with a global positioning system, data transmission software, a camera and a laser."

"That last part sounds like what we saw last night," Duncan commented.

Emerson continued.

"It uses sensors like ground penetrating radar to create images of what's below the ground's surface. It actually creates a geophysical map much in the same manner that a doctor uses ultrasound to make an image of a baby in its mother's womb. Here's a picture of their robot."

Emerson clicked and opened the file which showed the 24-inch tall robot and its turtle like shell with the camera, laser and transmission antenna.

"That's it. That's what we saw last night. I wonder what the L'Hoste's are doing with one and why at night," Duncan contemplated out loud.

"Maybe they're mapping out their plans for the development and are doing it at night so as not to attract attention. Who knows? Maybe we will get additional insight tonight. Did you get what you needed from the hardware store?"

"Yes. It's not exactly what I would use on an operation where I would be properly outfitted – but it will suffice."

"I'm looking forward to tonight's tour," Emerson stated.

∾ ∾ ∾

"I don't know what you boys are up to and I don't want to know. But, I'll just tell you one thing."

Emerson and Duncan looked at Mr. Cassidy expectantly as they picked up their gear from the back of his truck.

"Be damn careful."

"That we will, sir. We'll tell you more tomorrow," Emerson said with an air of mystery.

"Thanks for the lift," Duncan added as Mr. Cassidy pulled away.

When Mr. Cassidy stopped by unexpectedly to visit Aunt Anne earlier in the evening, Emerson decided to ask him to give the two of them a ride out to the intersection of Catawba Ave and Trenton Avenue at 11:30 p.m. Not knowing the outcome of their plans, Emerson did not want to risk parking the golf cart nearby since it could be identified as belonging to Aunt Anne.

Mr. Cassidy's curiosity was stirred, but he sensed that it had something to do with the L'Hostes since he would be dropping them off just down the road from the estate. He agreed, and he also promised not to tell anyone.

Emerson and Duncan, dressed in black t-shirts and dark supple slacks, walked ten minutes along the roadside to an area near the corner of the L'Hoste Estate, but outside of camera range.

Duncan's eyes followed the electrical service line from the estate out to the utility pole. He reached into his duffel bag and extracted a 24-inch wire cutter with center cut blades and aluminum handles with rubber grips.

"This baby produces 4,000 pounds of cutting pressure when I place only 50 pounds of hand pressure on the handles," he explained to Emerson who was looking concerned.

"You're sure that you know what you're doing with cutting the electrical service wire?"

"Sure. No problema." Duncan pulled out a pair of rubber gloves which he tucked in the waistband of his slacks. "And these gloves will give me added protection. There are three strands which provide service. As long as I don't let the strands touch each other or grab hold of two to create a circuit, I should be fine."

"If I connect them accidentally, you'll be treated to a light show. Just tell my ma that I loved her," Duncan teased.

Emerson was relieved that he wouldn't be the one climbing the pole and cutting the line.

Duncan walked across the road and strapped on the extra large carpenter's belt that he had been carrying. One end he swung around the pole before snapping it. He also tied one end of a rope around his waist. The other end was tied to the wire cutters which were lying on the ground.

He then began to climb the pole using the belt to leverage himself up. He would move up a few feet and stop. He'd grip the pole's sides with the soles of his tennis shoes and lean against the pole to take the pressure off the belt, then swing the belt upward and inch his way up. He repeated the maneuver several times until he was within reach of the service wire.

He then pulled the rubber gloves from his waist and placed them on his hands. He looked over to Emerson, giving him a nod that he was ready.

Emerson crawled along the ditch to the edge of the estate to position himself to dash to the robot's hidden entrance gate. He had a number of small hand tools with him so that he could pry open the gate.

Emerson waited.

Duncan pulled up the rope with the wire cutter and carefully positioned the blade near the first strand. He said a brief prayer and cut the first strand. The lights flickered and he quickly cut the second and the third strands.

The service line dropped away to the road below as the estate lights went out. Duncan reversed his technique for climbing the pole and worked his way quickly down the pole. He removed his utility belt and threw it, the wirecutters and gloves far into the underbrush.

He ran across the road in the darkness to join Emerson at the small gate.

When the lights went out, Emerson ran to the small gate and tried to open it. It gave a little but would not open. Seeing that a number of shrubs offered some cover from a direct view of the house, he flashed his penknife momentarily at the mechanism on the other side of the gate and saw that he could reach the hinges which were in a locked position.

He reached through the fence with his screwdriver and began unscrewing the three screws on the first hinge. He had just started working on the second hinge when Duncan dropped to the ground next to him.

"How's it going? We're running out of time. We don't want to be caught here when the lights and camera come back on."

"How long do you think it's been?" Emerson grimaced as he fought with the last screw.

"A little over a minute. We gotta move it."

Emerson finally unscrewed it and grabbed the gate with both hands. He was able to pull the gate downward far enough that it was able to clear the locked hinges. He swung it in and up as he crawled through the opening.

Duncan quickly followed him. As they were placing the gate back into its position, the lights came back on.

"That was close," Duncan said softly.

"Too close!" Emerson replaced a screw in each hinge in the event that the robot would be using the gate that evening. Emerson placed the tools in their small dark duffel bag and stashed the bag under the bushes. "Let's go."

They concealed themselves from the house's view by stepping between the high evergreens and the fence. Carefully, they made their way toward the drive.

As they reached the drive, they looked up at the top of the gate to confirm that the cameras were pointed out the gate. Seeing that they were, they dashed across the drive and to the evergreens on the other side.

As they began to work themselves along the fenceline, a number of floodlights were turned on at the main house. Emerson and Duncan looked at each other.

"We missed those," Emerson said dejectedly.

They heard voices and saw three security guards with flashlights and armed with Kalishnikov machine guns begin to sweep the grounds on the far side of the house.

"We better find good cover and quick!" Duncan's eyes scoured the grounds and saw the cemetery and the overgrown area with the ruins of the original inn. "Probably good cover there. Let's go."

Duncan led the way between the evergreens and the fence until they neared the rear of the cemetery. They darted across a narrow open lawn area, jumped over the low fence and dove into the ruins.

They were crawling up to one of the partially standing walls when Emerson groaned in pain.

"What is it?"

"I think I just took a nail into my knee from this piece of wood." Emerson pulled the wood away from his knee and saw some blood oozing out of the puncture wound caused by the nail. "Just figures, but no big deal."

Emerson's curiosity was aroused by the wood's shape. It appeared to be some sort of sign. "Anyone nearby?"

Duncan peered over the top of the wall. "No."

Emerson carefully turned on his penlight and gasped at what he saw on the sign.

"Sam, look at this! I can't believe it! Look what we just found. It's the key."

"Key? What are you talking about?" Sam turned his head and looked at the lighted sign.

It's faded lettering read Rainbow's Inn.

"I don't get it," Sam said with consternation.

"Think back to the conversations and research that we were doing on the missing trunk. Everyone was looking for it on Rattlesnake Island because it was where rainbow's end. And that was all based on what the girl thought she heard LeBec yell in the boat and where they found LeBec's body. I bet the Rainbow's Inn was where he was heading.

"And don't forget that LeBec had accomplices on Lake Erie working with him. Someone provided the Confederate agent in Sandusky with explosives. I bet the island's first L'Hoste was involved. This has all got to tie together some-how."

"I'd be putting that light out or the only thing getting tied together will be us because they're going to find us," Duncan warned.

Emerson turned the penlight off. His heart was racing with the excitement of finding the sign. He had overlooked asking for the name of the inn in all of his conversations!

"E, we need to move out to where the overgrown area is thicker. Follow me."

They crept out from behind the inn's ruins and made their way to a thicker patch of undergrowth.

"Let's crawl in here until they stop sweeping the grounds."

Duncan crawled into the area which was depressed from the surrounding area. Emerson quickly followed. As they settled in, Emerson remembered Professor Anderson's earlier warning about caves and depressed areas. Before he could mention it to Duncan, it happened.

The ground below them gave way and they dropped down about ten feet and landed with a resounding thud.

They both moaned as they recovered from the wind being knocked out of them.

Emerson was the first to recover and speak.

"I was just going to remind you that Professor Anderson said to be careful of any depressed areas. They were probably indications that a cave was underneath and that there were previous cave-ins. Looks like this was one of them."

"Well, this is another fine mess you've gotten us into Stanley," Duncan chided.

They both looked up and could see stars through the opening high above their heads. It would be virtually impossible for them to reach ground level.

"Sam, let's take a look around here and see if there's another way out."

They turned on their penlights and began to examine the cave into which they had fallen.

Emerson's body shuddered as he realized that he was once again in a cave. He struggled to overcome the nausea which was beginning to well up within him.

∽ ∽ ∽

William knocked before entering the study.

"Sir, I've brought you a fluorescent lantern to provide you light until they restore power."

Jacques L'Hoste had been perusing a summary of his stock investments when the lights went out. He had stood and walked to the window to gaze out and noticed that the lights were only out on the estate. The rest of the island from what he could tell had electrical service. Very suspicious he thought to himself.

"Thank you, William." He picked up the phone and dialed the security center.

"Henri, I'd like you to have a sweep of the property made."

"Yes sir, we have already initiated it."

"Good. Henri, one more thing."

"Sir?"

"Dispatch someone to check the electrical service line from the house to the street and inform me once it is completed."

"Yes, sir."

Henri hung up and dispatched one of the guards. He wondered what L'Hoste thought caused the electrical outage.

Checking all possibilities had kept Jacques ahead of his competition in the business world. It carried over to his other practices also. He had a feeling that something was amiss.

As the emergency generator powered up, the lights in the house were restored. Jacques sat down at his desk and thought about what may have triggered the power outage and why.

~ ~ ~

"Hey, look at these old wooden stairs going up to ground level." Emerson's light pointed to the stairs along one wall of the small cavern and followed them upward. The lights showed the stairs somewhat charred near the top.

"I bet they lead up to the inn," Emerson said as he slowly started up the stairs. He tested the stairs strength and found them somewhat rotted from the moisture in the cave over the years.

"If I keep close to the edge, I think the steps are less rotted than in the middle."

He tested each step before putting his full weight on it. He continued working his way up. In a couple of places, stairs had completely rotted through, leaving just the riser for him to step on.

When he finally reached the top, he found an old latch on the trap door. He pulled it free and pushed, but the door would only move up an inch or two.

"There's something heavy on top of it. Probably some of the debris from the inn's ruins," he yelled down to Duncan.

"Come on down. That looks way too dangerous. We'll finish looking around for a passageway down here," Duncan called.

Emerson slowly made his way down the precarious stairs and was relieved to stand on firm ground. "This must have been a hidden stairway for L'Hoste's rogues."

As they looked around the room, they found a rotted table and the remains of a couple of chairs and a wine barrel.

Duncan had been following one of the walls when it disappeared and he was left with open space. As he moved into it, he found that it sloped downward.

"E, this looks like a passageway!"

Emerson joined Duncan and they moved down the passageway. Their penlights revealed the passageway to be about five feet wide. They had walked down the sloping path about 50 yards when it opened into a larger cave and they sensed more moisture in the room.

The light from the lowered penlights showed water in the bottom of the cave, and the water seemed to be moving as if driven by some underground current.

"I wonder if this is one of those underground lakes that Professor Anderson said could be linked through an underground passage to Lake Erie. Let's each of us walk around this lake in each direction and see if the land reconnects," Emerson suggested.

Duncan agreed and they started their exploration.

They couldn't complete circling the lake as it appeared that there had been a cave-in. Huge slabs of limestone impeded their progress.

"I bet this was the entrance from Lake Erie to the cave

and L'Hoste used it during their early years. Now, it's caved in," Duncan offered as an explanation.

"Sam, come over here!"

Duncan looked across the underground lake and saw Emerson moving quickly to a large object in the corner. As he moved closer to Emerson, he saw that it was an old, large trunk. The trunk had two keyholes.

"Sam, I wonder if this could be the missing trunk. What if LeBec rowed here to the cave first? That would explain why the crew of the *Michigan* couldn't find anyone the first couple of days after the incident."

Emerson continued as his thought process became more aroused, "Then, maybe there was a disagreement with L'Hoste and L'Hoste put the bullet in LeBec's head and had the body taken to Rattlesnake Island to throw everyone off the scent. He had to know that there was an attempt to commandeer the *Philo Parsons* and they were looking for LeBec at the rainbow's end."

"Fascinating," Duncan commented as he saw the excitement building in his friend. "Absolutely fascinating!"

Emerson lit the inside of the trunk and saw that it was empty.

"Now, I think we know where the L'Hoste wealth came from. Do you remember that L'Hoste left the island shortly after the incident and returned a few years later as a wealthy businessman?"

Duncan nodded as Emerson continued, "He probably used whatever money was in the chest to start his business ventures."

Emerson peered into the trunk again and thought that he saw something through the rotting trunk floor. He reached in and parted the rotting boards to reveal a folded oilskin and withdrew it from the trunk.

"Look at this, Sam!" Emerson said excitedly.

Emerson began unrolling the oilskin and withdrew a document that had been fairly well preserved while wrapped up.

"Sam, shine your penlight on this while I try to read it!"

Duncan moved next to him and held both Emerson's and his penlight on the document.

Emerson completed reading the document and turned to Duncan. "This is a critical part of the Civil War's Northwest Conspiracy. It's an agreement for peace between England, France, Spain, the Confederacy and Lincoln's cabinet members for an end to the war and recognition of the Confederacy as a separate nation. Each of the cabinet members signed below. And there's no line for Lincoln to sign. The only signature missing is Jefferson Davis' for the Confederacy.

"This constitutes a palace revolt. Lincoln's cabinet was going to assume powers that they didn't have by entering into this agreement. I recall from our research that Lincoln had considered replacing them all. I wonder if he had an inkling as to what they were up to?"

"With all the spies on all sides, it makes you wonder," Duncan noted.

"I bet that the raiders were going to take this trunk with

them as they freed the prisoners and raided south so they could present it and whatever money was inside to Jefferson Davis. The failed piracy foiled their plans. And it ended up in this cave where no one would look for it!" Emerson stated.

He continued, "I'm going to hide it over here until we can come back for it. If we're captured, I don't want this on us."

Emerson moved to the cave-in as he wrapped the document up in the oilskin. He pulled some of the smaller pieces aside and inserted the oilskin in the space. Then, he rearranged the rock to cover the small opening.

Duncan had been walking along the cave's walls in hopes of finding another passage but to no avail. He did find another lake and noticed that the water was moving there too. Must be another underground tunnel he thought.

"E," he said as he returned to the first lake and the cave in, "I've got stronger lungs and better training in underwater swimming. I'm going to see if there is a tunnel under here that we may be able to follow out to Lake Erie."

"You're sure about this?"

Duncan pulled off his shirt, socks and shoes and began walking into the water.

"No problem. Glad its summertime. I'd hate to do this in the winter." Duncan walked near to the caved in area and submerged himself.

Emerson aimed his penlight at his watch and timed Duncan. It wasn't long before his wet head emerged from the water.

"No way out here. There's a channel all right, but there are too many rocks blocking our passage and we can't work our way through them. It's not safe enough. Let me check the other one."

Duncan walked across the cave's floor and into the water on the other side. Once he reached the far side, he submerged again and Emerson began timing him on his watch.

After one minute, Emerson was very nervous. At a minute and a half, Emerson began to remove his own shirt, shoes and socks. At two minutes, he was beginning to enter the water to find his friend.

The water in front of him swirled as Duncan reemerged and took a huge breath. Emerson held off questioning him until he was breathing normally.

"I take it you're okay. You had me worried, my friend."

"There's an underwater tunnel leading to another cave. It's a long swim, but I found a small air pocket about half-way just as I felt my lungs ready to burst. Give me a few minutes and we can give it a go."

"Okay, I'm game."

After a few minutes, they tied their shoes and t-shirts together and reentered the water.

"Take a few deep breaths to expand your lung capacity," Duncan coached as they stood in the water next to the cave's wall.

"I'm ready."

"Let's rock and roll then. Stay close to me." Duncan led Emerson underwater and into the tunnel.

Emerson was no match for Duncan and knew that he was slowing down Duncan. He could sense Duncan next to him as they swam through the rock-lined tunnel.

It seemed that they had been underwater for ten minutes the way that Emerson's lungs began to burn. He tried to convince himself that he could make it. It had to be farther since Duncan had said that even his lungs were burning when he reached the air pocket.

Emerson was losing control. He began to open his mouth and take in water. His lungs screamed in pain. Emerson actually stopped swimming and felt more like sinking.

Duncan's hand reached down and pulled a coughing and sputtering Emerson up to the air pocket.

"Close, huh?" he said as he gasped for his breath.

"Uh huh!" was Emerson's sole response until he refilled his lungs with air.

"I hope our next swim is not that long."

"Good news, it's shorter. Ready?"

"As ready as I'll ever be."

They took deep breaths and resubmerged. Before Emerson knew it, his kicking legs touched bottom and he sensed that Duncan had stopped to stand up. Emerson did the same and emerged from the water in another cave. They waited a few minutes to again catch their breath and slipped their t-shirts and shoes on.

It would be more difficult to find their way around as they left their penlights which were not waterproof in the other cave.

"Sam, do you hear that hum?"

Duncan cocked his head to one side and heard a hum in the distance. It sounded like a power generator.

"Do you think we're under the L'Hoste's residence?"

"Maybe. Let's follow the noise."

Emerson led them carefully toward the far end of the cave. As they reached the far wall, the noise was louder and they could see light at the end of a passageway.

"Shall we?" Emerson asked.

"Since we have no alternative, why not?"

They moved down the passageway and stopped where it opened into a larger lighted cavern. They could see the elevator shaft which ran up to the L'Hoste residence and a large, lighted passageway off to the right which probably led to the dock on Lake Erie.

To the left of the elevator shaft was a small wooden building. To the left of the building, they could see another lighted passageway.

Completing their survey, they looked to see what was along the wall to the left of where they were standing. They saw a tow motor and a smaller trailer parked.

"Let's take a peek down the passageway next to the building," Emerson suggested.

They looked before stepping out into the open to make sure that no one was around. Walking briskly, they made their way along the other passageway.

"Look at your shoes," Emerson commented.

Sam looked down and saw that he had yellow dust on his shoes.

"This is just like the dust that we found the other day."

"Right you are. And it looks like it's all over the place."

They walked through a large tunnel into another larger cavern.

"E, what do you think those casks are for?"

Emerson looked and saw a dozen metal casks on two sides of the cavern. One set had tags on them and the others did not.

They approached the tagged casks.

"Oh, oh, I don't think I like this, E."

Emerson saw it too. The labels read "RADIOACTIVE".

Emerson was puzzled. He couldn't understand what Department of Energy radioactive casks were doing in a cave on South Bass Island and below the L'Hoste Estate.

"Let's go back to that building in the first cave Sam and see what we can find in there."

Emerson and Duncan walked to the building and when Emerson tried the door, it was locked.

"Looks like one for you to open," he said as he looked at his friend confidently.

Duncan bent down to examine the lock.

"This one's a bit more difficult," he said scratching his head as he stood and pulled out his pocket lock pick set.

After a few minutes, the door's lock clicked and Duncan stood up with a smile, "There you go."

Emerson turned the handle and the door opened allowing both of them to enter the small windowless room. Emerson found the light switch and turned it on to see that they were entering a small office. Duncan locked the door as he closed it behind them.

The office contained a computer, several pieces of lab equipment, two file cabinets, a desk and two chairs. A Mr. Coffee coffeemaker was in a corner on a small cabinet.

"Let's see what we have here," Emerson said as he looked at papers strewn on a desk in the corner. "Why don't you check the filing cabinet?"

Duncan walked over the cabinet and pulled on the top drawer.

"Locked. Should I try to pick the lock?"

"Not yet. Come here, Sam. Look at this. These papers

were issued by the Atomic Energy Commission. They are titled 'The Dangers of Inappropiate Storage of Nuclear Waste.'"

They began reading through several of the papers.

Emerson held up a paper for Duncan to see.

"This photo looks like our casks in the other cave."

Duncan moved next to him and they both began to read the article which discussed the safe transportation of spent nuclear material from nuclear power plants. It described each cask as holding nine spent nuclear rods and comprised of a stainless steel inner and outer shell. Between the two shells was a layer of lead or depleted uranium to provide gamma shielding.

The ends of the cask had an internal closure and external closure which had an impact limitor to provide additional protection to the ends in the event of damage during shipping.

"Kind of reminds me of hand weights or even a dog bone," Duncan joked.

Before they could converse further, they heard a key being inserted in the lock. Looking around quickly, they saw there was no placc to hide.

"Turn out the lights and stand on the other side of the door where you'll be hidden behind the door. I'll take this side. When the door opens, I'll turn the lights on and we'll use the element of surprise."

They moved quickly to their positions.

The door opened and a lone figure appeared in the doorway.

Emerson switched on the light.

Standing in front of him with a look of surprise was Professor Anderson!

"What is the meaning of this? What are you doing here in my office?" he shouted angrily as he recovered from his initial surprise.

"I should ask you the same, Professor," Emerson responded. The professor didn't notice Duncan standing behind the door.

Emerson continued.

"What are these papers on your desk? What in the world are you involved in?"

Ignoring his questions, the professor said, "Now I know who caused all the commotion tonight. You were the one who cut the electricity to the house. You know they are sweeping the grounds? It's only a matter of time before they find you."

"I'm not worried. What's going on here professor?"

The professor sighed and sat wearily in a chair.

"You know they will never let you leave here alive now that you've been in this cavern. I don't need another death on my conscience!"

"Another death? What do you mean?"

Ignoring his question, the professor asked.

"Why did you have to come to the island? First, you flirt with my daughter and now you come here."

The professor bowed his head and shook it from side to side in despair.

"Sir, your daughter and I are just very good friends. There's nothing more to it than that. She's so gorgeous, she'd make a blind man take a second look. If she wasn't married, it might be a different story."

"I saw the two of you talking on the dock together the first time that you came to take a tour of Gibraltar Island. I was in the shadows on the hill overlooking the dock and I could see where things were heading. I didn't want her to become like her mother."

"Her mother?"

"I don't want to discuss her mother." The professor reached into his pocket and produced a knife.

Emerson saw Duncan start around the door and Emerson gave him a barely imperceptible look not to advance.

"Remember the day that you found your tires slashed on your golf cart and when your ultralight crashed into the lake?"

Emerson nodded.

"I did that to warn you to stay away, but you wouldn't take the hint. I've been observing the two of you for some time from the shadows," the professor shrugged.

"She was beginning to take an interest in you. I could tell. She needs to focus on salvaging her marriage with Tim so they can raise Austin in a good home." The professor added, "Tim is better than he gives himself credit for."

"Sir, are you then working for the L'Hostes?"

"I shouldn't tell you, but it won't make any difference because they will rid themselves of one nosy reporter when they find you. Especially, now that you have stumbled across this. There's no way out for you. It'll just be a matter of time before they find you tonight."

Emerson knew that he should be leaving, but he was intrigued and wanted to hear more.

The professor settled back in his chair and began to explain.

"The L'Hostes have a long relationship with Ohio State University. It goes back many years to one of the sons attending and graduating from Ohio State in the 1870's. They have been very generous with donations to the school. So when they approached me in January with a lucrative research grant to study the caves in South Bass Island for the summer, how could I resist?"

"Did your research have anything to do with the yellow dust that I gave you? It smelled like sulfur," Emerson inquired.

"A bit at first although it was not their primary focus. We had been trying to develop a method to extract sulfur from the gypsum deposits in the caves. If you recall from your Chemistry 101 classes, sulfur is the king of chemicals because it has so many industrial uses – but it's so expensive to mine. Unfortunately, our experiment didn't work.

The device we were using exploded. No one was hurt, but sulfur dust was blown over everything and out through the ventilation portals in the cavern's roof."

Emerson observed, "When we dropped the dust off at your lab, I noticed that you had similar dust on your shoes."

"Very observant – and yet you did not inquire?" the professor asked.

"I had my suspicions but didn't want to comment at the time. I noticed too that you never did anything with the dust once you locked it in your safe."

The professor's eyes widened by this new revelation.

"You broke into my safe, didn't you? I knew that someone had been in my office that night. You amaze me, Mr. Moore," the professor uttered.

"Actually, it was my associate, Mr. Duncan," Emerson explained.

"Amazing!" the professor commented.

"You said that the sulfur research wasn't their primary focus. What was, then?"

"The caves. We held a series of planning meetings from January through May in the L'Hoste residence. At first, we spent time going over charts and maps of known caves on the island, then, we began to talk about caves under the area where he proposed building his resort. He spared no expense. To help me with my research, he provided me with a state of the art robot from Columbia University which can..."

Emerson cut him off.

"We've met. I did some research on the robot and understand it's capable of creating geophysical maps. One question though, why was the robot used at night?"

The professor was visibly surprised by Emerson's revelation.

"Mr. Moore, you impress me by your knowledge and initiative. I assume these skills assist you well in your investigative reporting."

He continued, "L'Hoste said he didn't want to bring any undue attention to his plans to build the resort. So it would be better to use the robot at night. Beside myself, a couple of his security men were trained on how to use it. It transmitted data to the computer in the corner here and we created more accurate maps of the caves and actually found several more."

"So why does he have all of this interest in caves?"

"At first, I thought that he wanted to make sure that there would be no problems with potential cave-ins once he purchased the property and constructed the resort hotel over some of the caves. A few weeks ago, he asked me about connecting the caves together. He wanted to know if a laser beam could cut through the limestone quietly and connect the caves."

"Why did he want to connect he caves?" Emerson asked.

"I didn't realize it at first, but over the last two weeks, there have been shipments of nuclear waste delivered here at night from one of his small freighters. They unloaded them in containers onto his dock and brought them in here with his tow motor."

Emerson commented, "I saw them down the passageway. What's he planning to do with them and what does that have to do with connecting the caves?"

"I shouldn't say any more," the professor said as his shoulders drooped.

"That's right big mouth!"

Startled, Emerson and the professor looked toward the door and saw Francois standing just inside the doorway with a .45 automatic aimed at them.

"Spilled your guts, didn't you Professor?" he taunted as he pointed the .45 automatic first at the professor, then at Emerson.

"You've been nothing more than a thorn in my side, Mr. Moore," he sneered. "And now that you've discovered our little project, you have given me the perfect opportunity to pay you back for all of the embarrassment you have caused me. I'll just tell my father that I found you and you resisted."

Francois smiled sardonically as his finger began to tighten on the trigger.

Duncan chose that moment to throw his weight against the door, knocking Francois out of the doorway while pinning his arm between the door and the door's frame.

Francois screamed at the same time that Emerson charged the pistol and switched off the light, throwing the office into darkness.

A gunshot echoed in the small building as Francois pulled the trigger, then dropped the .45. A moan was heard in the darkened office and Duncan released his pressure on the door.

Francois pulled his arm away and ran down the passageway.

Emerson reached for the light switch, turned the light on, and looked around the bright office.

The professor was slumped to the floor with blood oozing out of his body. Emerson looked at Duncan who was examining the wound.

"It's mortal," Duncan whispered.

"Oh you don't need to whisper. I know my time is running out." The professor stopped for a moment to take a breath. "It's been running out for years. It goes back to my wife's death."

"Sir, I know about her death."

"So Martine told you?"

He was finding it more difficult to breathe.

"Tell her that it wasn't Tim's fault. We all had too much to drink that night. I was mad at Martine's mother for flirting with the men at the party."

He took another deep breath.

"She was as beautiful as Martine. I was driving and we were arguing in the front seat. Tim and Martine were too drunk and fell asleep in the back seat. I crashed a red light and a truck hit my wife's side of the car. Tim, Martine and the driver of the truck were knocked unconscious. I did a despicable thing and I've been ashamed of it for years."

His next breath was painful and he seemed to be weakening from the loss of blood.

"I pulled Tim out of the back seat and put him in the driver's seat. I then got in the back seat. I didn't want any bad press to tarnish my reputation as one of the country's leading authorities on geology. If you see Martine and Tim, please tell them and ask them to forgive me."

He took one last painful breath and died.

"Wow. Some story. E, we've got to go before your buddy, Francois, returns."

Emerson stood up and followed Duncan to the door. At the doorway, Emerson paused and took one last look at the professor.

"Which way, chief?" Duncan asked as he picked up the .45 that Francois had dropped.

Emerson looked around and said, "We've got two choices. One's the elevator but it looks like it's already descending."

Duncan whirled around and saw the lights on the wall panel flickering, indicating the elevator was descending. He also heard the whir of its electrical motor.

"And I'll bet someone's in it and probably armed. What's the other choice?"

Emerson had noticed a ledge with a narrow path on it leading upward into another, but higher passage way.

"Could be a dead end, but it may be our best chance," he said as he began climbing up on the ledge to follow the path. Duncan quickly followed.

In just a few feet, they entered a darkened passageway which dead ended after ten feet in a wooden wall.

"E, looks like the dead end."

"I don't think so. Bear with me a second. Let's run our hands over the wall and along the edges."

"What are we looking for?"

"A handle or knob of some sort and hinges."

"I found a hinge."

"Good, that means that we're on the right track. The knob has got to be on my side then."

Emerson hands touched cold metal.

"I found it!"

They heard voices shouting from the cavern that they had just exited.

Emerson slowly turned the knob and began to swing the wall back, revealing the L'Hoste wine cellar.

"I thought so," he said as they stepped into the dimly lit room and swung the hidden door shut.

"How did you know?" Duncan asked incredulously.

"It was the yellow dust. We saw it in the cave and you can see it here on the floor. They must have used this as some sort of back up entrance or perhaps it was the main entrance to the cave at one time, before the elevator was built."

They moved to the elevator doors and began to pry them apart with their hands.

"Easier than I expected," Duncan said as the doors opened.

They looked below and saw the elevator below them. They turned their attention to the shaft above them.

"Shall we climb?" Duncan asked as if it was something he did every day. He tucked Francois' .45 in the waist of his trousers.

"Why not? With the rough limestone walls and the steel supports, this will be a lot easier than climbing an elevator shaft in an office building."

They started to climb.

The rough limestone outcroppings provided hand and toe holds as they carefully made their way to the floor above them which Emerson recalled would open to the study.

Several minutes later, Emerson and Duncan were at the study's floor level.

"I hope this door is as easy to pry open as the one below," Duncan said as he reached for the doors.

The doors opened as did the study's hidden door.

"Opening one must trigger opening the other," Emerson commented as they pulled themselves up and onto the study's floor. Emerson stood and pushed the button to close the elevator door and the wood paneling.

They quickly scanned the room and saw that it was unoccupied.

"Now, we'll have to find a way out of here," Duncan said as he looked out of one of the study's windows. Emerson walked over to join him and saw movement in the window's reflection.

"Oh, I'll make sure that you get out of here."

The high back chair which had been facing away from them swiveled around to reveal Jacques L'Hoste sitting in it and pointing a .45 automatic at them.

He was dressed in a maroon smoking jacket and his hair appeared to be a bit tousled.

"And, I'll make sure that you never come back, mon amis. Please remove the weapon from your waist and place it on my desk, Mr. Duncan."

Duncan measured the distance from where they were standing to Jacques. It was too far for him to try to take the gun away from Jacques.

"I know what you are thinking Mr. Ex-SEAL Duncan and warn you that I am an expert marksman. I wouldn't take the chance."

"You certainly seem to know a lot about us," Emerson said in hopes of distracting Jacques so that Duncan could move closer to him.

"Stay where you are Mr. Duncan. It is my business to know about people and their weaknesses. It's the key to my success," he replied arrogantly.

The door to the elevator opened and into the study entered Francois with a sly grin, Henri the security chief and Tim. Francois and Henri were carrying .45's.

"What's he doing here?" Jacques asked his son angrily as he looked at Tim.

"When I ran out to the dock, he had just tied up one of the boats from the university. He had planned on taking the steps but saw me run out through the cave's concealed door onto the dock. I was trying to find the dock's guard so that we could reenter the cave and track down Moore and his friend."

"So you had no choice once he saw the cave's door open?"

"I didn't know what to do, so I brought him here to you."

"We will deal with him also. Did you fire the shot in the cave?"

Francois quickly filled in his father with what had happened when he encountered the intruders and the professor.

"And, where is the professor now?"

Henri responded, "Dead sir. From Francois' pistol shot."

Tim was visibly shaken by the news of his father-in-law's death.

"My, my. But this evening is getting quite messy." With the others training their guns on Emerson and Duncan, Jacques placed his pistol on his desk. He continued, "What we have tonight, gentlemen, is a conundrum."

Looking at Emerson, Duncan whispered, "A con what?"

"No need to whisper my dear Monsieur Duncan. I should have anticipated that you would have a very limited vocabulary. Not one that would come close to rivaling that of your investigative reporter friend whose business is words. Isn't that your business Mr. Moore?" Jacques asked in a condescending tone.

Emerson nodded as Jacques continued.

"A conundrum is a riddle. It's a dilemma that must be solved. But, I have a surprise for you, Monsieur Duncan."

Duncan raised his eyebrows.

"I have solved the riddle. And shortly, you will also learn the answer." He turned to Francois as he picked up the .45 from his desk.

Tim Tobin appeared crestfallen as he realized that his timing that evening was off. He should have never left Gibraltar Island.

"Francois, why don't you have the dock security guard assist you in putting the proper gear aboard the *Mon Ami*? Then, you two can take our three friends here for a friendly boat ride," Jacques said ominously.

Francois took the elevator down to the cave's floor.

"I think we all know where this is headed. Can you answer one question for me?" Emerson asked.

"Perhaps."

"What were you going to do with the nuclear waste?"

"I am going to make this island uninhabitable for years," Jacques bragged confidently. "Our plan was to create a diversion with this nonsense of building a resort hotel where the Victory Hotel stood many years ago. While this diversion is taking place, we planned to link the caves together, using the hotel construction to cover what we were doing underground."

Tim's eyes widened as he began to comprehend the extent to which he had been misled.

"Where are you getting the nuclear waste?" Emerson queried.

"There are two nuclear power plants on Lake Erie, the plant which you can see on the western horizon and the plant on the other side of Cleveland. It was a long process, but I was able to secure a contract for my ships to transport the waste to Lake Superior where it would be offloaded and taken to a nuclear waste dump. There were severe requirements that had to be met about transporting via water, but we were able to meet them."

"That doesn't explain how they ended up in your cave or what happens when the shipments don't arrive on Lake Superior," Emerson stated.

"My dear boy. It is so simple that I am somewhat aston-ished that you didn't reach the answer yourself. Once the ship picks up its cargo, it changes its schedule slightly. Re-member this is one of my ships! It makes a night stop at my dock here. The nuclear waste containers are offloaded and the ship continues to Lake Superior."

"And no one says anything about the missing containers? It's that simple?"

"Rest assured that we have thought through the entire process, Mr. Moore. We have duplicate containers stored here and transfer them into the ship's hold after offloading the real containers. My nephew, who has undergone ex-tensive nuclear training and serves aboard the ship, takes care of any necessary paperwork and duplicating tags that must be supplied. No one is the wiser," he said smugly.

"Once we fill the connected caves with the containers, one of the last things we will do is to uncap them, allowing the island to become contaminated for years!" Jacques re-vealed proudly.

"But why do this? This island was the start of your family's success." Emerson added as an afterthought, "We found the open chest below the Rainbow Inn's ruins."

"Oh, you found that? How fortuitous of you!"

Jacques had seemed very surprised that they had been in the cave below the inn!

"Let me tell you why I am doing this. In 1855, my great grandfather built an inn in Put-in-Bay. It was a very suc-cessful inn and many of the islanders were jealous of his success. There were rumors of robberies and counterfeit money which may or may have not been true. But, he was run out of town and forced to rebuild his business here on the western side of the island. He vowed that one day he or one of his family members would repay the islanders for the embarrassment he incurred. He never forgave them and the vow has been passed down from father to son ever since. I will have the distinction of fulfilling the vow.

"The year that he searched for a new location for his inn the water level of the lake was low and he discovered a cave entrance at water level. When he realized that he could row into the cave, he explored it to see how large it was. He decided to build the inn above it. Once he completed the inn, he built the stairs which you probably saw remnants of and which led from the inn's floor down to the cave's floor. He thought that this would serve some of his more nefarious dealings. He also concealed the cave's entrance."

"Did he work for the Confederacy during the Civil War?" Emerson asked as he became more intrigued about the family history despite his unstable circumstances.

"Ah, you're looking for the tie in with the chest. I see no harm in telling you. He assisted a Confederate agent in Sandusky in providing him with some explosives and gathered information from time to time for various Confederate spies. The incident you're probably most interested in is the chest and Monsieur LeBec."

Emerson nodded his head in agreement.

"I'm sure that your research has given you insight as to what happened with the attempted takeover of the ferry boat in Put-in-Bay in 1864. LeBec never rowed anywhere but here. He and my great grandfather had worked together on several occasions, so he was very comfortable in rowing here. He knew where the concealed entrance was and entered the cave.

"He quickly found my great grandfather and mistakenly showed him the wealth contained in the trunk. He offered to share a good portion of it with him if he would provide passage for him from the island. My great grandfather said why share, pulled a pistol from his belt and shot LeBec in the forehead as he laughed at LeBec's foolishness.

"When he learned that the runaway slave girl mistakenly told everyone that LeBec had shouted that he was going to the rainbow's end which everyone around here knew was Rattlesnake Island, he decided to take LeBec's body and boat to Rattlesnake Island to keep everyone from snooping around Rainbow's Inn. No one made the connection until you found the chest."

"Why wasn't the chest destroyed?" Emerson asked.

"Why? No particular reason. No one was going to come onto our grounds without our being aware of it. Then there was a landslide due to the ground weakening from the erosion caused by the lake's waves and the entrance was sealed."

"Do you know how much money was in the chest?" Duncan asked.

"Of course. You would be the one interested in the money and not the history," Jacques scoffed at Duncan. "Let's just say there was a small fortune. My great grandfather took it to Cleveland and established himself as a very proper businessman before returning to the small log cabin."

"But it was money which was meant for the Confederacy's Treasury," Emerson concluded.

"Yes, but they didn't need it. They lost the war," Jacques concluded smugly.

Emerson thought to himself that no one must have realized what had been in the false bottom of the chest. The document would have changed the outcome of the war and world events. Lincoln may never have been assassinated.

A knock at the door interrupted them.

"Yes?" Jacques asked.

The door opened to reveal William.

"Excuse me for interrupting sir. Chief Wilkens is at the gate and is inquiring whether everything is all right or not. A utility crew is working on restoring power and he's aware that the line was cut."

"Henri, why don't you go down to see our local police and put them at ease?"

"Sir, are you sure you want to be left alone with the three of them?"

"Henri, you disappoint me. You've witnessed my prowess with a pistol."

"Excuse me, sir."

Henri and William left the study.

"Why are you so financially supportive of the islanders? You even buy the police a new vehicle each year," Emerson questioned.

"It's part of the game. It's to convince your opponent that he can let his guard down. None of them truly suspect what I am up to."

"But why now? Why not let Francois or his heirs fulfill your family's vow of revenge?" Emerson persisted with his questioning, trying to buy time.

"Francois can never have children. He has been tested. He will be the last of the L'Hoste's. And you've seen him enough to know that he is not capable of implementing a plan of the magnitude of mine. I will fulfill the L'Hoste vow!"

Emerson looked at Duncan who was also awed by Jacques' pervading feeling of his destiny.

Emerson looked at Tim and commented, "Tim, you never knew about any of this did you?"

"No," he responded rapidly.

Beads of sweat were gathering on Tim's brow. He was very anxious about his immediate future. "I was only involved with marketing plans to fill the resort hotel. I wasn't a part of any of this other crap."

"Tim, when your father-in-law died, do you know what he wanted to me to tell you and Martine?"

"No, what?"

Jacques looked somewhat amused by the exchange.

"He said that the night the car crashed in Columbus, he was driving the car."

Tim looked incredulously and his face became ashen.

"You all had too much to drink. When the accident occurred, you and Martine were knocked unconscious. He pulled you out of the backseat and put you in the driver's seat. Then, he took your place. He did it all to protect his reputation. He died asking me to tell you and Martine and hoping you both would forgive him."

Tim took a deep breath and seemed to recover. It seemed like a great weight had been lifted from his shoulders.

"You mean that I have been carrying this albatross for all of these years and I didn't have to?"

"Enough of this melodrama," Jacques said as he wearied of the chitchat.

"I've got to tell Martine. You've got to let me go." Without thinking Tim started towards Jacques who swung the pistol around to aim at Tim.

It was the moment that Duncan had been waiting for. As Jacques' attention was diverted, Duncan dived at Jacques.

Jacques was just pulling the trigger when he noticed motion out of the corner of his eye. His concentration was interrupted causing him to misaim as he fired and hit Tim in the chest.

Emerson ran to Tim's side to try to stop the flow of blood.

Duncan hit Jacques hard and the two wrestled for control of the .45 as Duncan's momentum carried them through the study's side door and out onto the deck area. They fell heavily against the railing.

The weight of the two men against it caused the already weakened bolts to give. The railing twisted and fell to dangle over the side as Duncan and L'Hoste plunged over the edge. Duncan and L'Hoste separated as they fell down the side of the ship's bow.

Emerson heard L'Hoste scream and ran out the study to the open space where the railing had been secured. Just as he approached it, Duncan's head with a huge smile appeared at floor level.

"E,I,E,I,O. I'm back!"

Emerson looked in disbelief.

"How did you survive?" Emerson asked as he helped Duncan to his feet and looked to the ground below where he saw Jacques L'Hoste's crumpled form on the ground. It had been a two-story fall.

"As we went over, I grabbed the rail, hoping that part of it would hold and it did. I think I about used up my nine lives," he grinned.

"We've got to get out of here!"

"What about Martine's husband?" Duncan asked.

"The bleeding has stopped, but he can't be moved. We need to get out of here and get him some help."

They saw Henri stoop by Jacques' body and look up at them. He said something into his radio.

"Looks like time is running out. Let's go around to the other side. We certainly can't escape through the front door,"

Duncan quickly suggested as he ran into the study and picked up the .45 from the desk.

Reaching the other side of the ship's bow, they looked down the side of the hull and around the deck. Grabbing a coil of rope and securing one end, Duncan dropped it over the side and it almost reached the ground.

"Let's rappel down!"

Not waiting for a reply from Emerson, Duncan went over the side. Emerson ran inside to Tim and said, "You're doing okay. Hang in there. We're going for help."

Tim nodded his head and moaned from the pain.

As Emerson went over the side, he heard the elevator returning to the study. It was probably Francois he thought. He quickly rappelled to the ground and joined Duncan in the shadow of some evergreens.

They made their way to the edge of the cliff to check the stairs to the dock before starting down. That's when they saw the armed guard stationed halfway up the stairs looking toward the top.

"There's no way we can take him out. Good positioning on his part. Where now?" Duncan asked.

"On the other side of the pool, near the cliff's edge is the gardener's building. Let's try it."

They sprinted across the grounds keeping in the shadows as well as they could to the gardener's building. They found the door unlocked and went inside.

Emerson raced across the room and opened the windows at the rear. "We're in luck. We're overlooking the sides of the cliff. If we can find a rope, we can rappel down the cliff and get to the boat on the dock. By the time the guard hears the engine start and looks down at us, it'll be too late for him to take action."

Duncan produced several ropes from a workbench which they quickly unraveled and tied together. They climbed out of the widow onto a narrow ledge and secured one end of the rope to one of the building's supports. They threw the other end over the cliff's edge and watched as it dropped down to the dock below.

"Shall we?" Duncan asked.

Emerson grabbed the rope to begin letting himself down. Duncan tucked the .45 in his waistband and quickly followed.

As they were a quarter of the way down, they heard the whine of the helicopter's engines start.

With Henri at the controls the helicopter began to rise above the ground. Gaining height, it swept to the far end of the estate and Henri switched on its searchlight.

Emerson and Duncan were near the halfway mark in their descent when they heard the helicopter coming along the island's western shore and saw it plying its searchlight as it tried to locate the escaped intruders.

"When the light hits us, we'll be sitting ducks," Emerson called to Duncan above him.

"You better move faster!" Duncan yelled back.

When the light first hit them, Emerson and Duncan were blinded by its brightness. When it swept past them, they thought for a moment that they were missed. Then they saw it begin to sweep ominously back to them.

Before the light reached them, they saw two figures seated at the controls in the copter's dim interior light. Henri was at the controls. Seated next to him and staring vehemently at them was Jacques L'Hoste!

Dried blood matted his hair and he appeared battered by his fall. Emerson was stunned by Jacques' resiliency. They must have carried him to the copter so that he could direct the hunt.

"Tough guy, isn't he?" Duncan asked.

"I'm sorry about getting you into this," Emerson yelled up to his friend as the copter's whirling blades began to come closer.

Emerson realized that Henri was trying to maneuver the copter so that blades would hit him. He could see Jacques gesturing animatedly at Henri and Emerson.

He felt the wind from the blades as the copter edged closer to him. It was a matter of just a few feet.

Jacques was bruised by his fall, but his drive for revenge had helped him overcome the pain. Henri had helped him to the copter to begin the search. They couldn't let those two escape and reveal their secrets.

Jacques ordered Henri to move the chopper closer to Emerson. Jacques' face broke into a victorious smile as he watched Henri skillfully maneuver the chopper within killing range.

It was just a matter of feet and Mr. Emerson Moore would be mincemeat. With an evil grin on his face, Jacques settled back in his seat to take in Emerson's growing fear and demise.

A crack interrupted his thoughts as he saw a hole appear in the windshield and Henri slump in his seat. Blood began to pump from a wound in his neck, and Henri looked at Jacques with a look of panic in his eyes.

Jacques reached for the cyclic as he tried to take control of the copter.

Two more shots crashed through the windshield, one hitting Jacques in the lower stomach. As he recoiled to his right, he inadvertently pulled on the cyclic, sending the copter to the right. He pushed in the other direction and overcompensated, driving the copter toward the cliff wall on the other side of the iron stairwell.

Jacques' eyes widened as he saw the onrushing wall.

The copter burst in a ball of fire and the guard on the stairs crouched to avoid the debris sailing through the air around him.

"Nice shooting, Sam!"

"Just plain dumb luck," Sam retorted as they both hurriedly made their way to the cliff's base and onto the dock.

The guard was still looking at the fire as Emerson and Duncan moved quickly to the far end of the dock to the *Mon Ami.*

"No keys," Emerson yelled as he looked at its ignition.

The sound of several shots averted their attention to the stairs on the side of the cliff. They saw that Francois had joined the guard and they both were firing on Duncan and Emerson as they descended the stairs.

"The jet skis!" Duncan shouted as he pointed to two jet skis tied to the dock.

"We've got keys!" Duncan exclaimed satisfactorily.

They jumped aboard and started the jet skis. Emerson's started first and he raced out from the dock and stopped to wait for his friend.

Duncan was having trouble with his. He finally got it started and began to pull away from the dock when the engine died.

Duncan shrugged his shoulders helplessly at his predicament, but waved for Emerson to go on without him. Emerson saw the guard and Francois board the *Mon Ami*. He throttled the engine and raced back to pick up Duncan.

"Now what did you do that for? I'll slow you down."

"We came together and we leave together."

They both hunched over as the jet ski picked up speed.

Emerson and Duncan looked over their shoulder as they raced close to the western shore toward Peach Point. They saw the yellow cigarette boat move away from its dock and pick up speed.

The little jet ski would be no match with the yellow boat's speed and power. The only advantage they had was in maneuverability and ability to move in shallower water.

The cigarette boat sped by them just after Duncan warned Emerson that it was bearing down on them. Emerson had aimed it closer to shore where it was shallower. They could hear gunshots and had hunched lower.

After it passed them the boat continued to Peach Point and waited. Francois had correctly anticipated that Emerson would head for Peach Point and down its narrow channel between Peach Point and Gibraltar Island to Alligator Reef.

The jet ski might just clear the reef and the pointed rocks hidden just below the water's surface.

Francois' plan was to block that avenue of escape and force them out into the open water. He waited and waited, but did not sight the jet ski.

Carefully, he edged the *Mon Ami* out around Peach Point and it was then that he saw the jet ski moving at a brisk clip across the open water toward Rattlesnake Island.

Francois swore and pushed the throttle forward causing the *Mon Ami* to leap out of the water as he sought to catch Emerson and Duncan who he now held responsible for his father's death. He would make them pay dearly.

When they didn't see the *Mon Ami* turn and come back at them, Emerson guessed that Francois might have anticipated his plan to cross Alligator Reef where the *Mon Ami* could not follow. Emerson decided to head for Rattlesnake Island.

Duncan nudged Emerson in the side and Emerson looked

over his shoulder at the yellow cigarette boat as it bore down on them. He pointed the jet ski toward the northeast corner of the island where the owners of the island maintained a small dock and he recalled seeing armed guards.

Might as well seek protection where there are other armed individuals Emerson thought to himself.

Francois' lips broke into a thin smile as he realized that they would overtake the jet ski before it reached Rattle-snake Island. He kept a firm grip on the wheel as his guard hung on to one of the side rails. With the way they were moving, it would be difficult hitting them on the jet skis with a shot. The guard had holstered his .45.

"Nudge me just before they get to us, then hang on tight!" Emerson shouted back to Duncan.

The *Mon Ami* was just feet away and Francois was relishing his final victory.

Duncan nudged Emerson and Emerson whipped the jet ski sharply to the right and away from the island, a move that Francois might not have anticipated. The jet ski screamed as it turned and the two leaned into the turn.

The *Mon Ami* missed the jet ski by inches.

Francois swore as he tried to bring the fast boat around in a tight turn to resume his attack.

Duncan yelled in Emerson's ear, "That was so close. I think they just shaved off the hair on my butt."

Emerson shouted, "Let me know when they get that close again."

Emerson had the jet ski pointed back toward the northeast corner of the island again as the jet ski recovered speed after completing its turn.

Emerson's actions caused Francois to make virtually a 360-degree turn in order to position himself to make another run at them and, at the same time, block any attempt that Emerson had to turn toward Rattlesnake Island and its relative safety.

Francois recovered ground quickly and began to move in for the kill. Just as he was nearing the jet ski, Duncan yelled in Emerson's ear, "My extra weight's slowing you down. I'm out of here. Kick butt!"

Before Emerson could speak, Duncan pushed himself off the side of the jet ski and bobbed momentarily in the water.

Francois watched as Duncan went into the water and spied him bobbing. Francois licked his lips as he turned away from the jet ski and sped toward Duncan.

The twin propellers were rotating at maximum thrust.

Duncan waited until the last second and dove beneath the water.

Francois laughed sinisterly as he felt a thump under the bottom of the boat. He looked behind the boat but didn't see Duncan's body surface.

"One down, one to go!" he chortled wickedly to the guard next to him. He looked ahead of him and saw Emerson. Even without the extra weight, Emerson couldn't outrun the powerful cigarette boat.

Francois moved in for the kill.

Emerson turned abruptly to the right and away from the island.

This was a surprise to Francois. He had expected Emerson to turn and head toward Rattlesnake Island.

Francois looked over his shoulder at the jet ski as he began to put the *Mon Ami* into a long turn. The boat's momentum carried it out past the high promontory on the northeast point of Rattlesnake Island into the shipping channel.

Francois heard the guard scream and looked around to see the bow of the *Aragon* bearing down on them at top speed. It appeared without warning and had been hidden, until the last few seconds, by the high promontory on the island's northeast point.

 The speeding cigarette boat exploded as it hit the *Aragon* which shuddered as it cut threw the debris.

$\approx \approx \approx$

Alarm bells were sounding on the *Aragon* as the first mate and the crew tried to bring the freighter to a stop.

Captain Neuhouser awoke from his sleep in his cabin when he felt the ship shudder and heard the explosion and alarms. Their departure had been delayed in Duluth for six hours, and he had given orders to put on all speed possible and to take any calculated risks to get as close to being on schedule as possible – including the use of the narrow channel on the north side of Rattlesnake Island at full speed in the middle of the night. It was highly unlikely that the Coast Guard would be out patrolling that late at night, and fisherman usually stayed out of the channel.

Dressing quickly, the captain headed to the pilothouse and looked astern at the remains of a boat still burning. The captain gave a long sigh. This would call for some serious explanations to Mr. L'Hoste he feared.

He didn't realize that both L'Hostes were dead.

~ ~ ~

Emerson watched the flames momentarily and then headed back to the area where Duncan had jumped off the jet ski.

He switched off the jet ski's engine and began to call for his friend. He was concerned, very concerned. He had seen Francois turn from chasing Emerson to running down Duncan.

A log with a streak of yellow paint floated by as Emerson peered anxiously in the water.

"E,I,E,I,O," came the cry from the beach.

Emerson looked toward the beach and could make out two figures standing there. One was holding a flashlight with a strong beam. He started the jet ski and headed to the beach.

Standing there were Duncan and the same security guard that they had encountered on their previous visit to Rattlesnake Island.

"Still trying to find Cedar Point boys?" the guard asked

with a grin.

"I think we've had enough excitement for one night, don't you think, Emerson?" Duncan sighed as he ignored the guard.

"How did you end up here, Sam?"

"When that boat bore down on me, I took my bearings and a veeerrrryyy deep breath – and dove like I never dove before. He missed me and I kept swimming underwater toward the beach. By the time I came up for air, I was more than half way here. I finished swimming in and sat here with our good buddy to watch you finish him off."

"I don't know where that freighter came from, but timing is everything."

"That freighter would be the *Aragon*, the pride of the L'Hoste fleet," the guard spoke up.

"How fitting then," Emerson calmly stated.

"Before you boys cause trouble for me, I need you to head out of here."

"No problem," Duncan said as he climbed onto the back of the jet ski.

As they started toward Put-in-Bay, they heard the sirens of the Put-in-Bay rescue squad and saw the Coast Guard helicopter from the Marblehead station hovering with its searchlight over the now diminishing fire on the scattered remains of the *Mon Ami*.

$$\approx \ \approx \ \approx$$

It had been three days since their adventure ended. There were meetings with the authorities including the Atomic Energy Commission representatives. They had completed report after report and were ready to head home.

Aunt Anne had hugged Emerson and Duncan as they boarded the Jet Express for their trip to Port Clinton. They both promised to return next summer for a very brief and hopefully quiet visit.

Mr. Cassidy had wished them well and thanked them for finally ridding the island of the L'Hoste family and solving the mystery of the missing chest. He would now have more stories to share with islanders and visitors.

Emerson hadn't told him about the oilskin wrapped document which now lay in the bottom of his duffel bag. He would eventually after he had completed writing his story about their island adventure.

When Emerson and Duncan were showing the investigators the grounds of the L'Hoste Estate, Emerson had been able to disappear briefly and, using a length of rope which he secured to the ruins' wall, lower himself into the cave where he and Duncan had first fallen. He retrieved the oilskin, hid it under his garments and climbed up the rope.

Chief Wilkens had changed. He realized the real truth about the L'Hostes when he heard the gunshot followed by the copter explosion and returned to the Estate to discover Tim lying in a pool of blood. Tim was coherent enough to provide him with details before he was lifeflighted out to

Magruder Hospital in Port Clinton.

The chief and his men rounded up the remaining guards and William for questioning.

The chief had even stopped by the house earlier and wished Emerson and Duncan well.

The engines on the Jet Express started and the boat eased out of Put-in-Bay's harbor. Emerson looked at his aunt's house as they pulled away. He was looking forward to returning next year and, this time, keeping a lower profile.

The Jet Express moved out of the harbor and began to gain speed as it passed Gibraltar Island. Memories, Emerson thought as they cruised past the picturesque island.

Duncan was staring at him and thought he saw a tear in Emerson's eye.

The Jet Express rounded Peach Point and moved down the western side of the island. Behind them and getting smaller was Rattlesnake Island – and the remains of Francois in its waters, Emerson thought to himself since Francois' body had not been recovered.

As they drew abreast of the L'Hoste Estate, they could see the blackened sides of the cliff from where the copter had crashed into it. A large Coast Guard cutter was tied up at the dock and the hidden doors to the cave's entrance were wide open. Figures were seen moving in and out of the cave and the estate.

Emerson looked westward and saw clouds on the horizon. Looked like they might be in for some rain, he thought.

Emerson and Duncan walked down the ramp to the Jet Express' dock once it docked and picked up the rental car that they had reserved for the hour-long drive to Cleveland Hopkins Airport.

Duncan drove the car onto Perry Street as the first drops of rain began to fall. As he switched on the windshield wipers, Emerson saw the sign and stared.

"Do you want to stop?" Duncan asked when he noticed his friend's gaze.

"Would you mind? I'd just be a second," Emerson responded eagerly.

Following the signs, Duncan drove the car and parked it in front of Magruder Hospital.

Emerson ran through the rain into the building to the front desk and following the directions they provided, he walked to one of the rooms.

"May I come in?" he inquired somewhat awkwardly from the doorway.

"Mr. Moore!"

Austin ran to Emerson and Emerson swept him up as he gave him a big bear hug.

"You didn't think I'd leave without saying bye to you did you?"

"No way. My dad's got a big booboo. You want to see how big of a Band-Aid they put on him? He's getting better."

"Sure, why not?"

Austin grabbed Emerson's left hand and towed him to his father's side.

"Hello Tim, how do you feel?"

"A lot better. I want to thank you for telling me what my father-in-law said. I'd been carrying that guilt for years and it was turning me into someone that I didn't like. Quite frankly, into someone that few people liked including my wife. Isn't that so, Honey?"

Emerson turned to where Tim was looking. Standing in the doorway with fresh flowers and looking as radiant as ever was Martine. She blushed briefly at seeing Emerson.

She remembered when he had shown up at her cottage that morning looking quite disheveled from the night before. He had broken the news to her about her father's death and given her the message about who had been driving the car as her father wished. She had collapsed on the floor sobbing and he had placed his arm around her to comfort her.

They had stayed liked that for a few minutes when he took her face in his hands and looked at her. "I have something else to tell you," he had said. And then told her about Tim being wounded and how his brave actions resulted in them being able to overpower L'Hoste.

He helped her get Austin ready and walked the two of them down to the waiting police boat for the ride to the hospital. They had not seen each other since that morning.

"Well, I just stopped in to wish you folks well. Sam's in the rental car waiting for me and we have a plane to catch."

Emerson gave Austin another hug.

"Thank you again for your role in waking me up. I could have lost a lot," Tim said as he looked at Martine and Austin.

Emerson started cautiously, "Tim, I hope there's no ill will between us."

"Not really. You actually were a big help to me! I was too internally focused and lost on my problems. Again, I feel like a big weight has been lifted from my shoulders. I feel like a new person!" Tim beamed as he responded.

Emerson recognized a change in Tim. "Well I need to catch a flight. Good luck!"

Emerson gave Austin a hug and shook the hand that Tim extended to him.

Tim looked at his wife standing silently next to the doorway.

"Honey, why don't you walk Emerson to his car. It's time for you to say good bye to him."

She looked at him quizzically as she tried to understand what he was really telling her to do.

"Go ahead now. It's okay." Tim urged as he turned his attention to Austin.

Emerson and Martine walked down the hallway in silence.

As they turned the corner and started walking toward the front door, Emerson said wistfully, "You're a very special woman, Martine. I really care about you!"

He looked into her green eyes which she averted downward.

"I know Emerson. I've always known."

She paused and said with a tone of sorrow, "Emerson, I care about you too!"

Here he was, with one of the most beautiful, caring women that he had ever met, and he was about to walk through those doors and leave her. This was one of the toughest things that he would ever have to do in his life.

"You're the only woman who has ever made me want to violate my personal code of ethics."

"But you didn't, did you?"

"Would you have wanted me to?" Emerson asked entranced.

"On the boat after we finished dancing, I felt very vulnerable," she responded coyly. "And you had to jump into the water!"

They both chuckled.

"That was probably one of the smartest things that I have ever done."

"Or one of the dumbest," she replied.

Sitting in the car with the motor running, Duncan saw them standing on the other side of the door and glanced at his watch. They had to get going to catch their flight. He beeped the horn.

Martine waved at Duncan, and he waved back.

"Someone's anxious to go," she said.

"And someone else is not. Martine, thank you. I'll always cherish you as a dear friend and what could have been."

Emerson touched a finger to her lips and she kissed his finger.

Emerson turned and walked briskly through the rain to the car and jumped in next to Duncan. He turned and looked back at Martine who was silhouetted in the doorway.

Duncan began to put the car in gear.

"Oh, hold on a second!"

Emerson opened the door and began to walk back through the rain to the hospital. Martine stepped out and ran into his arms. They stood with their arms wrapped around each other in the rain and kissed.

It was a long, deep kiss of pent up feelings for each other.

"You know this can never go anywhere. You're married. Another time, another place who knows?" Emerson whispered in her ear as they embraced.

"I know my dear. You will always have a special place in my heart. When I need encouragement, I will meet you in that special place." She choked with tears streaking her already rain streaked face.

The car's horn honked again.

They broke apart and Emerson started for the car, stopped and turned back one more time to run up to her. She hadn't moved. They embraced again and kissed one last time.

The car's window rolled down and Duncan yelled, "Hey kids, I hate to break up anything but we're going to miss our flight."

"I'll miss you," Emerson yelled as he ran to the car and entered it.

"You're in my heart," she answered and turned to go back into the hospital to her son and husband. She appreciated her husband giving her the time to say a final goodbye and to bring to an end this chapter in her life. Her husband was a wise man she thought to herself.

"I didn't think you two were coming up for air. What was that all about?" Duncan was going to continue his banter until he saw the tears rolling down his friend's cheek. It would be better to ride in silence, he thought.

As they crossed the Edison Memorial Bridge across Sandusky Bay, Duncan spoke, "The rain's stopped and we've got a rainbow out toward Lake Erie."

Emerson looked out Duncan's side of the car and saw it. With a sense of melancholy, Emerson said, "And I know where rainbows end."

≈ ≈ ≈

Ten months passed since Emerson had left Put-in-Bay.

During that period, Emerson wrote a glaring recount of his adventure on the island and revealed his investigative findings on the L'Hostes and their plans for radioactively contaminating the island. He also recounted his unearthing of the oilskin wrapped document which caused many revisions to Civil War history books.

After appearing on a number of talk shows to discuss the document with Civil War history experts, Emerson donated the document to the Smithsonian for public display.

John Sedler, his managing editor at the *Post*, placed his hand on Emerson's shoulder.

"This was just delivered for you," and handed Emerson an envelope from a courier service. Emerson opened the envelope and found a smaller one inside.

He smiled as he opened and read it.

The note was simple. It read:

Congratulations!
I wish I could be there today!
See you in my heart!
Martine

They were calling his name now. Emerson dropped the note in his pocket and adjusted his tie as he walked to the podium at Low Library on the Columbia University campus in New York City.

The master of ceremonies continued, "Winner of this Year's prestigious Pulitzer Prize for Investigative Reporting...."

Emerson nodded his head in acknowledgment to the

applause as he walked across the room to receive his award and check.

He smiled again. The note in his pocket meant more to him than the award.

≈ ≈ ≈